M000166723

THE CRAWLING CHAOS
AND OTHERS

THE CRAWLING CHAOS AND OTHERS

THE ANNOTATED REVISIONS AND COLLABORATIONS OF H. P. LOVECRAFT
VOLUME I

Edited, with an Introduction and Notes

By

S. T. Joshi

2012

The Crawling Chaos and Others © 2012 Arcane Wisdom
Introduction © 2012 by S.T. Joshi
Appendix and Notes © 2012 by S.T. Joshi

Cover Art and Signature Sheet © 2012 Zach McCain
Copyediting by Leigh Haig

This edition © 2012 by Arcane Wisdom an imprint of
Bloodletting Press

Arcane Wisdom
P. O. Box 130
Welches, OR 97067

www.miskatonicbooks.com
arcanewisdom@me.com

Book Design & Typesetting by Larry L. Roberts

All rights reserved. No part of this book may be used or
reproduced in any manner whatsoever without the written
permission of the author and publisher.

First Paperback Edition

5

Introduction

It is difficult to find, in the entire realm of world literature, a parallel for H. P. Lovecraft's chosen profession as a "literary revisionist"—one who would revise, edit, or sometimes ghostwrite entire works, ranging from short stories to poems to essays to textbooks, for a fee. To be sure, writers have occasionally engaged in the informal (and usually non-remunerative) revision of other writers' works; Samuel Johnson is credited with having revised Oliver Goldsmith's celebrated poems *The Traveller* (1764) and *The Deserted Village* (1770), apparently writing some of their most celebrated lines; and Ezra Pound's numerous suggestions to and partial rewrites of a draft of T. S. Eliot's *The Waste Land* (1922) can be seen in the facsimile publication of that draft. But few authors engaged in the task of "revisionist" while at the same time attempting to maintain their status as writers of original work.

For Lovecraft (1890–1937), the job of revisionist ultimately became a matter of economic survival. Having, to his later regret, failed to receive a high school diploma, let alone a college degree, and having also failed to be trained in even the humblest of white-collar jobs that could bring in an income and allow him to write in his spare time, Lovecraft found that the only employment he could secure was by his pen—whether by selling his own fiction or poetry (something he rarely accomplished before 1923) or by revising the work of others. This occupation appears to have evolved in the course of his work in the amateur journalism movement. He had joined the United Amateur Press Association in the spring of 1914, and not long thereafter he became chairman of the Department of Public Criticism, an office that allowed him to write critiques of all the amateur papers published during a given period; these critiques, published in the "Department of Public Criticism" column of the *United Amateur,* at times betray Lovecraft's hand in fixing up some members' contributions, especially in his own journal, the *Conservative* (1915–23). By late 1916 Lovecraft was announcing that he was part of something called the Symphony Literary Service, which appears to have been a revisory service operated by Anne Tillery Renshaw (editor of an amateur paper called the *Symphony*) and others.[1] At this point Lovecraft stated that he was revising verse, but no doubt he was revising other kinds of writing as well.

We do not hear much about this service beyond the single mention in a letter of 1916, and there is little evidence that Lovecraft was actually earning much of an income by this work during this period. Indeed, the first "revisions" of stories—especially weird stories—were clearly non-remunerative, emerging in the course of his dealings with various amateur colleagues. Short fiction was not extensively cultivated in amateur journals, chiefly because the journals were so short that they rarely provided space for anything more than vignettes or prose-poems; moreover, their primary models were newspapers, so that they were largely filled with news reports, autobiographical reflections, editorials, and other such matter. Weird fiction was a particular rarity, since it appears that few amateurs had much of an inclination to read this kind of work, let alone write it. Lovecraft's recommencement of his own original fiction-writing career in 1917 (he had written no fiction after 1908, when he destroyed many of the stories he had written up to that date) was indeed largely triggered by the enthusiasm of W. Paul Cook, a leading amateur writer and publisher; but Cook did not write much fiction, and what he wrote was not generally weird. He was a reader and appreciator of the weird, and he had an extensive library of weird fiction that he would make available to Lovecraft over the whole of the latter's career; but that was enough for Lovecraft. Thrilled to learn of Cook's approbation of the early tale "The Alchemist" (published in the *United Amateur* for November 1916), Lovecraft promptly wrote "The Tomb" and "Dagon" in the summer of 1917.

One of the colleagues with whom he worked extensively during this period was Winifred Virginia Jackson, an amateur writer who, in spite of being fourteen years older than Lovecraft, was rumored to have romantic feelings for Lovecraft—feelings that Lovecraft himself, although one of the most asexual of beings, apparently did not entirely discourage. Their correspondence exists only in fragments, but Lovecraft's numerous remarks about her in letters of the 1918–21 period bespeak more than merely a literary collegiality. So when Jackson sent Lovecraft an account of a weird dream in 1918 or 1919, he took it upon himself to write it up as a more or less coherent narrative. The result, "The Green Meadow," may still be more of a vignette than an actual story, but its brooding prose-poetry is not entirely ineffective. Somewhat later, Lovecraft wrote up another Jackson dream-account into "The Crawling Chaos." A few months before writing that story, he collaborated with Anna Helen Crofts on the odd Grecian fantasy "Poetry and the Gods." Crofts is a mystery woman in Lovecraft's life; we have no idea how he came in touch with her, as no correspondence between the two survives and he never mentions her or the story in any extant letters. Crofts may have been a member of Winifred Jackson's literary circle, even though Jackson lived in the Boston area and Crofts in the far northwestern corner of Massachusetts. At any rate, the story allowed Lovecraft to express both his love of classical Greece and his persistent notion that poetry is the highest expression of the human imagination.

The distinction between "revisions" and "collaborations" in the Lovecraft corpus may ultimately be slight, insofar as the degree of his actual contribution to the work in question is concerned, but it is nonetheless significant in reflecting Lovecraft's own attitude toward the work. There are in fact only a few actual collaborations, or works where Lovecraft explicitly allowed his byline (whether his own name or a pseudonym) to appear next to that of his collaborator: the two stories with Winifred Jackson, "Poetry and the Gods" with Crofts, "Through the Gates of the Silver Key" with E. Hoffmann Price (not included in this edition), the round-robin story "The Challenge from Beyond," and "In the Walls of Eryx" with Kenneth Sterling. It is likely that Lovecraft would have allowed several of the six collaborations with R. H. Barlow to appear with his byline; but only three were published in his lifetime, and of these, "The Battle That Ended the Century" was sent out anonymously precisely so that its authorship could be concealed. Of the other two, "'Till A' the Seas'" is probably more than half Lovecraft's, but he no doubt wished to encourage its young author by allowing it to appear under Barlow's name only; while "The Night Ocean" is probably 90% Barlow's, so a collaborative byline would have been inappropriate.

Another story to which Lovecraft might have chosen to affix his byline is "The Horror at Martin's Beach," written in 1922 by Sonia H. Greene, who in 1924 would become Mrs. H. P. Lovecraft. But again, it becomes apparent that Lovecraft was striving to encourage Greene's literary work by allowing the story to appear solely under her own name. Quite frankly, it seems unlikely that Sonia would ever have become a practicing writer, especially a fiction writer, for her memoir of Lovecraft at times verges on illiteracy; but Lovecraft, like Poe, was chivalrously charitable to his female colleagues, so he no doubt declined a collaborative byline when the story was accepted for an early issue of *Weird Tales*. Late in life Sonia sent to August Derleth another story, previously unpublished, on which she claimed that Lovecraft had worked, "Four O'Clock"; Derleth published it in the first edition of *The Horror in the Museum and Other Revisions* (1970). Much earlier, however, Sonia had told the early Lovecraft scholar Winfield Townley Scott that Lovecraft only suggested changes in the prose, so on that basis I excluded it from the revised edition of *The Horror in the Museum* (1989); but in fact, the prose seems quite Lovecraftian in spots, so I suspect Lovecraft had more of a hand in the story than Sonia suggested to Scott; I have therefore included it here in an appendix. He mentions the story in no correspondence that I have seen.

Lovecraft came closer to his occupation as "revisionist" in the tales he revised for C. M. Eddy, Jr., in 1923–24.[2] By this time Lovecraft was fully engaged as a professional revisionist, doing considerable work for the pop psychologist David Van Bush, beginning no later than 1920. For the most part, however, he was revising Bush's psychology manuals and (regrettably) his unspeakably bad poetry, and he no doubt welcomed the task of tackling some revisory work more suited to his interests. Eddy was a friend and colleague in Lovecraft's hometown of Providence, R.I. If the various memoirs by Eddy's wife, Muriel E. Eddy, can be trusted (and it is not entirely certain that they can be), Lovecraft would come over frequently to the Eddys' house in East Providence, both to read his own stories and to work on Eddy's tales, for which he no doubt declined to accept any payment. "Ashes" and "The Ghost-Eater" had already been rejected by Edwin Baird, the first editor of *Weird Tales,* but after Lovecraft fixed them up they were accepted, "Ashes" constituting Eddy's first appearance in the magazine. If Lovecraft had not said so, it would be impossible for anyone to deduce that he had anything to do with this story, which must rank as the single worst of his revisions. The other Eddy stories are substantially better, although even they are not exactly stellar. "The Ghost-Eater" is a relatively conventional ghost story of the sort that Lovecraft himself never wrote; "The Loved Dead" is a cheerfully morbid tale of necrophilia with no supernatural elements; and "Deaf, Dumb, and Blind" is, conceptually, the most interesting of the Eddy tales, as a deaf, dumb, and blind man senses weird presences in his isolated cottage. "The Loved Dead" caused a controversy by being briefly banned in the state of Indiana; that contretemps passed quickly, but its effects on *Weird Tales'* new editor, Farnsworth Wright, lingered for many years, for he became almost pathologically afraid of accepting any tales of explicit horror from Lovecraft's pen, so that several of his later tales were rejected on that basis alone.

In his own lifetime, Lovecraft's most celebrated excursion into ghostwriting came when he was assigned by Edwin Baird to write a story in conjunction with the famous escape artist Harry Houdini. The importance that Baird attached to the endeavor is signaled by his paying Lovecraf $100 in advance for the tale. The work was actually designed to be a collaboration, and would have appeared as "By Houdini and H. P. Lovecraft";[3] but Baird was taken aback when Lovecraft wrote the story in the first person, as if it is being told by Houdini. Baird couldn't wrap his mind around the fact that a collaborative account could be written in the first person singular, so the story appeared under Houdini's byline alone. Baird also changed the title from "Under the Pyramids" to "Imprisoned with the Pharaohs." An argument could be made that Baird's title is actually the more effective, but the documentary evidence is clear that "Under the Pyramids" is Lovecraft's chosen title.

Weird Tales was the chosen venue for most of Lovecraft's subsequent revisions—that is, those works that he worked on for a fee. Although the next story in chronological sequence, "Two Black Bottles" (1926), was again an instance of Lovecraft helping a friend—the young Wilfred Blanch Talman, who went on to publish a few other stories in *Weird Tales* that do not bear any traces of Lovecraft's revisory hand—he became a professional fiction revisionist in earnest when, through the intercession of his friend Samuel Loveman, he came into contact with Adolphe de Castro. De Castro, formerly Gustav Adolphe Danziger, was attempting to capitalize on his friendship with Ambrose Bierce; he ultimately published a weak and at times unintentionally comical memoir, *Portrait of Ambrose Bierce* (1929), and sought Lovecraft's help in revising several stories out of his early and dreadful story collection, *In the Confessional and the Following* (1893), self-published in

San Francisco. Between 1927 and 1929, Lovecraft worked over two stories, "A Sacrifice to Science" and "The Automatic Executioner," retitling them "The Last Test" and "The Electric Executioner." He later stated that "I did accidentally land . . . three tales of Old Dolph's,"[4] but I believe this is a slip of the pen on Lovecraft's part. His use of the term "land" would mean that he actually *sold* the story; but no work by de Castro aside from the two mentioned above have been found in any periodical during this period, and in his extant correspondence Lovecraft never mentions revising any but these two.

The de Castro revisions highlight an important distinction between Lovecraft's original fiction and his revisions. It is clear that he himself would never have written stories along the lines of "The Last Test" or "The Electric Executioner" if he were not being paid to do so; the plots, topography, characterization, and other features of these tales are antipodal to the tales that Lovecraft wrote under his own name. Indeed, because he was obliged to retain at least the skeleton of the plots of the stories in question, Lovecraft was forced to engage in story construction of a sort that did not suit his strengths as a writer; hence, these tales are full of dialogue, attempts at detailed character portrayal, and "action" scenes that Lovecraft was clearly incapable of handling with any great competence. The fact that he was significantly more competent than his bumbling revision clients means little. As a result, these stories, if judged as independent aesthetic entities on their own merits, would undoubtedly be classified as failures and be promptly forgotten; but Lovecraft's involvement in them has given them a kind of zombie life that allows their mediocrities to be exposed to all.

Another revision client during this period, Zealia

Brown Reed Bishop, was, by a series of accidents, the trigger for some highly meritorious works from Lovecraft's pen. Bishop was a journalism student who came into contact with Lovecraft no later than the spring of 1927; amusingly enough, she actually wished to write stories fit for *Woman's Home Companion* and other such magazines, but there is mercifully no evidence that she actually published any such stories or that Lovecraft had any involvement with them. What she did do was to come up with synopses for three stories of a weird nature. As my notes to the stories indicate, the synopses themselves, so far as we can gauge them, are quite weak and conventional; and Lovecraft has done an admirable job in expanding and elaborating upon them to make them genuine weird tales in their own right. Of all his revisions, the first two of the Bishop tales, "The Curse of Yig" and "The Mound," are closest in texture and quality to Lovecraft's original stories; and the fact that they are based in the Southwest lends a distinctive air of novelty to them, expanding upon the settings of Lovedraft's own tales, dominated as they are by locales in New England, New York, and England. "The Curse of Yig" is as compact and effective a weird tale as he ever wrote. "The Mound," conversely, is a richly textured novella fully as long as "The Whisperer in Darkness" (1930) and as aesthetically substantial as *At the Mountains of Madness* (1931), anticipating that novel's use of alien species as metaphors for the future political, economic, and cultural development of the human race. The third of the Bishop revisions, "Medusa's Coil," is considerably less successful; it will be discussed in the introduction to the next volume.

Lovecraft's job as a "literary revisionist" was, in point of fact, the very worst occupation he could have chosen for himself. Not only did he charge a criminally low fee even for full-fledged ghostwriting; he also worked so assiduously on revision that he was left with little time or mental energy to work on his own fiction. During the last decade of his creative life (1927–36), he wrote scarcely more than one original story a year; but during this same period he worked on more than twenty revisions and collaborations of various sorts, whether it be with promising novices such as R. H. Barlow and Duane W. Rimel or established veterans such as Henry S. Whitehead; his chief paying revision client during this period was Hazel Heald, for whom he wrote five substantial stories. Interesting as these revisions sometimes are, we would no doubt have been much better off if we had seen more compeers of "The Shadow over Innsmouth" or "The Shadow out of Time."

Late in life Lovecraft gave an interesting assessment of his general motives in revising the work of his friends and colleagues:

> First—I help all genuine *beginners* who need a start. I tell them at the outset that I shan't keep it up for long, but that I'm willing to help them get an idea of some of the methods needed. If they have real stuff in them, they soon outgrow the need for such help. In either event, no one of them has my assistance for more than a year or so. Second—I help certain *old or handicapped people* who are pathetically in need of some cheering influence—these, even when I recognise them as incapable of improvement. In my opinion, the good accomplished by giving these poor souls a little more to live for, vastly overbalances any harm which could be wrought through their popular overestimation. Old Bill Lumley &

old Doc Kuntz[5] are typical cases of this sort. The good old fellows need a few rays of light in their last years, & anybody would be a damned prig not to let 'em have such if possible—irrespective of hyper-ethical minutiae.[6]

If any passage in Lovecraft's letters speaks more poignantly of his generosity, kindness, and consideration, I am not aware of it. It is actions like this that caused Lovecraft to be revered by all who had come into contact with him, and who were the recipients of his knowledge, his aesthetic sensibility, and his literary gifts. His revisions and collaborations may not, in every instance, be testimonials of his literary greatness, but they are without question tokens of his humanity.

S. T. JOSHI

A Note on the Text

The stories in these volumes are presented in chronological order by date of writing, so far as that can be ascertained. Since, in most cases, manuscripts do not exist, the texts are based upon existing printed editions, usually in magazines. The editorial procedures used in the stories vary depending on the nature of Lovecraft's involvement with them. In those cases where Lovecraft appears to have written a story from beginning to end, based only on a synopsis or outline, the texts have been edited in accordance with his usual spelling and punctuational preferences. These include the stories "Under the Pyramids," "The Last Test," "The Curse of Yig," "The Electric Executioner," and "The Mound" in Volume 1; and "Medusa's Coil," "The Man of Stone," "Winged Death," "The Horror in the Museum," "Out of the Aeons," "The Horror in the Burying-Ground," and "The Diary of Alonzo Typer" in Volume 2. In the other stories, in which Lovecraft appears to have made revisions on a pre-existing draft, the texts have followed the most reliable appearance, whether it be a manuscript or a published version.

The original versions of "The Last Test" ("A Sacrifice

to Science"), "The Electric Executioner" ("The Automatic Executioner"), and "The Diary of Alonzo Typer" are extant and are presented in the appendix to the volume in which the revised versions appear. "Four O'Clock" and "The Sorcery of Aphlar," stories in which it is unclear whether Lovecraft's involvement is significant enough to classify the story as a revision, are also included in the appendix.

In my commentary at the end of the book, I provide introductory notes on each of the stories, outlining the details of their writing and the possible degree of Lovecraft's contribution to them. I then list the "texts" used to prepare the text of the story; these texts are not meant to be an exhaustive list of the publications of the story, but only an indication of those texts that are relevant to the textual history of the tale. I then list critical articles on the story; some stories have not been the subject of any specific discussion by critics. My explanatory notes seek to elucidate historical, literary, and other references in the stories that are not commonly known, and also to indicate relations with Lovecraft's life and other work.

I am grateful to David E. Schultz for his assistance in preparing the text.

—S. T. J.

The Green Meadow

Translated by Elizabeth Neville Berkeley and Lewis Theobald, Jun.

INTRODUCTORY NOTE: The following very singular narrative or record of impressions was discovered under circumstances so extraordinary that they deserve careful description. On the evening of Wednesday, August 27,
1913, at about 8:30 o'clock, the population of the small
seaside village of Potowonket, Maine, U.S.A.,[1] was aroused
by a thunderous report accompanied by a blinding flash;
and persons near the shore beheld a mammoth ball of fire
dart from the heavens into the sea but a short distance
out, sending up a prodigious column of water. The following Sunday a fishing party composed of John Richmond,
Peter B. Carr, and Simon Canfield caught in their trawl
and dragged ashore a mass of metallic rock, weighing 360
pounds, and looking (as Mr. Canfield said) like a piece of
slag. Most of the inhabitants agreed that this heavy body
was none other than the fireball which had fallen from the
sky four days before; and Dr. Richmond M. Jones, the local scientific authority, allowed that it must be an aerolite
or meteoric stone. In chipping off specimens to send to an
expert Boston analyst, Dr. Jones discovered imbedded in
the semi-metallic mass the strange book containing the en-

suing tale, which is still in his possession.

In form the discovery resembles an ordinary notebook, about 5 × 3 inches in size, and containing thirty leaves. In material, however, it presents marked peculiarities. The covers are apparently of some dark stony substance unknown to geologists, and unbreakable by any mechanical means. No chemical reagent seems to act upon them. The leaves are much the same, save that they are lighter in colour, and so infinitely thin as to be quite flexible. The whole is bound by some process not very clear to those who have observed it; a process involving the adhesion of the leaf substance to the cover substance. These substances cannot now be separated, nor can the leaves be torn by any amount of force. The writing is *Greek* of the purest classical quality, and several students of palaeography declare that the characters are in a cursive hand used about the second century B. C.[2] There is little in the text to determine the date. The mechanical mode of writing cannot be deduced beyond the fact that it must have resembled that of the modern slate and slate-pencil. During the course of analytical efforts made by the late Prof. Chambers of Harvard, several pages, mostly at the conclusion of the narrative, were blurred to the point of utter effacement before being read; a circumstance forming a well-nigh irreparable loss. What remains of the contents was done into modern Greek letters by the palaeographer Rutherford and in this form submitted to the translators.

Prof. Mayfield of the Massachusetts Institute of Technology, who examined samples of the strange stone, declares it a true meteorite; an opinion in which Dr. von Winterfeldt of Heidelberg (interned in 1918 as a dangerous enemy alien) does not concur. Prof. Bradley of Columbia College adopts a less dogmatic ground; pointing out that certain utterly unknown ingredients are present in large quantities, and warning that no classification is as yet possible.

The presence, nature, and message of the strange book form so momentous a problem, that no explanation can even be attempted. The text, as far as preserved, is here rendered as literally as our language permits, in the hope that some reader may eventually hit upon an interpretation and solve one of the greatest scientific mysteries of recent years.

—E.N.B.—L.T., Jun.

It was a narrow place, and I was alone. On one side, beyond a margin of vivid waving green, was the sea; blue, bright, and billowy, and sending up vaporous exhalations which intoxicated me. So profuse, indeed, were these exhalations, that they gave me an odd impression of a coalescence of sea and sky; for the heavens were likewise bright and blue. On the other side was the forest, ancient almost as the sea itself, and stretching infinitely inland. It was very dark, for the trees were grotesquely huge and luxuriant, and incredibly numerous. Their giant trunks were of a horrible green which blended weirdly with the narrow green tract whereon I stood. At some distance away, on either side of me, the strange forest extended down to the water's edge; obliterating the shore line and completely hemming in the narrow tract. Some of the trees, I observed, stood in the water itself; as though impatient of any barrier to their progress.

I saw no living thing, nor sign that any living thing save myself had ever existed. The sea and the sky and the wood encircled me, and reached off into regions beyond my imagination. Nor was there any sound save of the wind-tossed wood and of the sea.

As I stood in this silent place, I suddenly commenced to tremble; for though I knew not how I came there, and could scarce remember what my name and rank had been, I felt that I should go mad if I could understand what lurked about me. I recalled things I had learned, things I had dreamed, things I had imagined and yearned for in some other distant life. I thought of long nights when I had gazed up at the stars of heaven and cursed the gods that my free soul could not traverse the vast abysses which were inaccessible to my body. I conjured up ancient blasphemies, and terrible delvings into the papyri of Democritus;[3] but as memories appeared, I shuddered in deeper fear, for I knew that I was alone—horribly alone. Alone, yet close to sentient impulses of vast, vague kind; which I prayed never to comprehend nor encounter. In the voice of the swaying green branches I fancied I could detect a kind of malignant hatred and daemoniac triumph. Sometimes they struck me as being in horrible colloquy with ghastly and unthinkable things which the scaly green bodies of the trees half hid; hid from sight but not from consciousness. The most oppressive of my sensations was a sinister feeling of alienage. Though I saw about me objects which I could name—trees, grass, sea, and sky; I felt that their relation to me was not the same as that of the trees, grass, sea, and sky I knew in another and dimly remembered life. The nature of the difference I could not tell, yet I shook in stark fright as it impressed itself upon me.

And then, in a spot where I had before discerned nothing but the misty sea, I beheld the Green Meadow; separated from me by a vast expanse of blue rippling water with sun-tipped wavelets, yet strangely near. Often I would peep fearfully over my right shoulder at the trees, but I preferred to look at the Green Meadow, which affected me oddly.

It was while my eyes were fixed upon this singular tract, that I first felt the ground in motion beneath me. Beginning with a kind of throbbing agitation which held a fiendish suggestion of conscious action, the bit of bank on which I stood detached itself from the grassy shore and commenced to float away; borne slowly onward as if by some current of resistless force. I did not move, astonished and startled as I was by the unprecedented phenomenon; but stood rigidly still until a wide lane of water yawned betwixt me and the land of trees. Then I sat down in a sort of daze, and again looked at the sun-tipped water and the Green Meadow.

Behind me the trees and the things they may have been hiding seemed to radiate infinite menace. This I knew without turning to view them, for as I grew more used to the scene I became less and less dependent upon the five senses that once had been my sole reliance. I knew the green scaly forest hated me, yet now I was safe from it, for my bit of bank had drifted far from the shore.

But though one peril was past, another loomed up before me. Pieces of earth were constantly crumbling from the floating isle which held me, so that death could not be far distant in any event. Yet even then I seemed to sense that death would be death to me no more, for I turned again to watch the Green Meadow, imbued with a curious feeling of security in strange contrast to my general horror.

Then it was that I heard, at a distance immeasurable, the sound of falling water. Not that of any trivial cascade such as I had known, but that which might be heard in the far Scythian lands[4] if all the Mediterranean were poured down an unfathomable abyss. It was toward this sound that my shrinking island was drifting, yet I was content.

Far in the rear were happening weird and terrible things; things which I turned to view, yet shivered to behold. For in the sky dark vaporous forms hovered fantastically, brooding over trees and seeming to answer the challenge of the waving green branches. Then a thick mist arose from the sea to join the sky-forms, and the shore was erased from my sight. Though the sun—what sun I knew not— shone brightly on the water around me, the land I had left seemed involved in a daemoniac tempest where clashed the will of the hellish trees and what they hid, with that of the sky and the sea. And when the mist vanished, I saw only the blue sky and the blue sea, for the land and the trees were no more.

It was at this point that my attention was arrested by the *singing* in the Green Meadow. Hitherto, as I have said, I had encountered no sign of human life; but now there arose to my ears a dull chant whose origin and nature were apparently unmistakable. While the words were utterly undistinguishable, the chant awaked in me a peculiar train of associations; and I was reminded of some vaguely disquieting lines I had once translated out of an Egyptian book, which in turn were taken from a papyrus of ancient Meroë.[5] Through my brain ran lines that I fear to repeat; lines telling of very antique things and forms of life in the days when our earth was exceeding young. Of things which thought and moved and were alive, yet which gods and men would not consider alive. It was a strange book.

As I listened, I became gradually conscious of a circumstance which had before puzzled me only subconsciously. At no time had my sight distinguished any definite objects in the Green Meadow, an impression of vivid homogeneous verdure being the sum total of my perception. Now, however, I saw that the current would cause my island to pass the shore at but a little distance; so that I might learn more of the land and of the singing thereon. My curiosity to behold the singers had mounted high, though it was mingled with apprehension.

Bits of sod continued to break away from the tiny tract which carried me, but I heeded not their loss; for I felt that I was not to die with the body (or appearance of a body) which I seemed to possess. That everything about me, even life and death, was illusory; that I had overleaped the bounds of mortality and corporeal entity, becoming a free, detached thing; impressed me as almost certain. Of my location I knew nothing, save that I felt I could not be on the earth-planet once so familiar to me. My sensations, apart from a kind of haunting terror, were those of a traveller just embarked upon an unending voyage of discovery. For a moment I thought of the lands and persons I had left behind; and of strange ways whereby I might some day tell them of my adventurings, even though I might never return.

I had now floated very near the Green Meadow, so that the voices were clear and distinct; but though I knew many languages I could not quite interpret the words of the chanting. Familiar they indeed were, as I had subtly felt when at a greater distance, but beyond a sensation of vague and awesome remembrance I could make nothing of them. A most extraordinary *quality* in the voices—a quality which I cannot describe—at once frightened and fascinated me. My eyes could now discern several things amidst the omnipresent verdure—rocks, covered with bright green moss, shrubs of considerable height, and less definable shapes of great magnitude which seemed to move or vibrate amidst the shrubbery in a peculiar way. The chanting, whose authors I was so anxious to glimpse, seemed loudest at points where these shapes were most numerous and most vigorously in motion.

And then, as my island drifted closer and the sound of the distant waterfall grew louder, I saw clearly the *source* of the chanting, and in one horrible instant remembered everything. Of such things I cannot, dare not tell, for therein was revealed the hideous solution of all which had puzzled me; and that solution would drive you mad, even as it almost drove me. . . . I knew now the change through which I had passed, and through which certain others who once were men had passed! and I knew the endless cycle of the future which none like me may escape. . . . I shall live forever, be conscious forever, though my soul cries out to the gods for the boon of death and oblivion. . . . All is before me: beyond the deafening torrent lies the land of Stethelos, where young men are infinitely old. . . . The Green Meadow . . . I will send a message across the horrible immeasurable abyss. . . .[6]

[*At this point the text becomes illegible.*]

Poetry and the Gods

By Anna Helen Crofts and Henry Paget-Lowe

A damp, gloomy evening in April it was, just after the close of the Great War, when Marcia found herself alone with strange thoughts and wishes; unheard-of yearnings which floated out of the spacious twentieth-century drawing-room, up the misty deeps of the air, and eastward to far olive-groves in Arcady[1] which she had seen only in her dreams. She had entered the room in abstraction, turned off the glaring chandeliers, and now reclined on a soft divan by a solitary lamp which shed over the reading table a green glow as soothing and delicious as moonlight through the foliage about an antique shrine. Attired simply, in a low-cut evening dress of black, she appeared outwardly a typical product of modern civilisation; but tonight she felt the immeasurable gulf that separated her soul from all her prosaic surroundings. Was it because of the strange home in which she lived; that abode of coldness where relations were always strained and the inmates scarcely more than strangers? Was it that, or was it some greater and less explicable misplacement in Time and Space, whereby she had been born too late, too early, or too far away from the haunts of her spirit ever to harmonise with the unbeautiful things of contemporary reality? To dispel the mood which was engulfing her more deeply each moment, she took a magazine from the table and searched for some healing bit of poetry. Poetry had always relieved her troubled mind better than anything else, though many things in the poetry she had seen detracted from the influence. Over parts of even the sublimest verses hung a chill vapour of sterile ugliness and restraint, like dust on a window-pane through which one views a magnificent sunset.

Listlessly turning the magazine's pages, as if searching for an elusive treasure, she suddenly came upon something which dispelled her languor. An observer could have read her thoughts and told that she had discovered some image or dream which brought her nearer to her unattained goal than any image or dream she had seen before. It was only a bit of *vers libre,* that pitiful compromise of the poet who overleaps prose yet falls short of the divine melody of numbers;[2] but it had in it all the unstudied music of a bard who lives and feels, and who gropes ecstatically for unveiled beauty. Devoid of regularity, it yet had the wild harmony of winged, spontaneous words; a harmony missing from the formal, convention-bound verse she had known. As she read on, her surroundings gradually faded, and soon there lay about her only the mists of dream; the purple, star-strown mists beyond Time, where only gods and dreamers walk.

"Moon over Japan,
White butterfly moon!
Where the heavy-lidded Buddhas dream
To the sound of the cuckoo's call. . . .
The white wings of moon-butterflies

Flicker down the streets of the city,
Blushing into silence the useless wicks of round
  laterns in the hands of girls.

Moon over the tropics,
A white-curved bud
Opening its petals slowly in the warmth of heaven....
The air is full of odours
And languorous warm sounds....
A flute drones its insect music to the night
Below the curving moon-petal of the heavens.

Moon over China,
Weary moon on the river of the sky,
The stir of light in the willows is like the flashing of a
  thousand silver minnows
Through dark shoals;
The tiles on graves and rotting temples flash like rip-
  ples,
The sky is flecked with clouds like the scales of a drag-
  on."

Amid the mists of dream the reader cried to the rhyth-
mical stars, of her delight at the coming of a new age of
song, a rebirth of Pan. Half closing her eyes, she repeated
words whose melody lay hid like crystals at the bottom of
a stream before the dawn; hidden but to gleam effulgently
at the birth of day.

"Moon over Japan,
White butterfly moon!

Moon over the tropics,

A white-curved bud
Opening its petals slowly in the warmth of heaven.
The air is full of odours
And languorous warm sounds . . . languorous warm
    sounds.

Moon over China,
Weary moon on the river of the sky . . . weary moon!"

               * * * * *

Out of the mists gleamed godlike the form of a youth
in winged helmet and sandals, caduceus-bearing, and of
a beauty like to nothing on earth. Before the face of the
sleeper he thrice waved the rod which Apollo had given
him in trade for the nine-corded shell of melody, and upon
her brow he placed a wreath of myrtle and roses. Then,
adoring, Hermes spoke:[3]

"O Nymph more fair than the golden-haired sisters of
Cyane or the sky-inhabiting Atlantides,[4] beloved of Aphrodite and blessed of Pallas,[5] thou hast indeed discovered
the secret of the Gods, which lieth in beauty and song. O
Prophetess more lovely than the Sybil of Cumae[6] when
Apollo first knew her, thou hast truly spoken of the new
age, for even now on Maenalus, Pan sighs and stretches in
his sleep, wishful to awake and behold about him the little
rose-crowned Fauns and the antique Satyrs.[7] In thy yearn-
ing hast thou divined what no mortal else, saving only a few
whom the world rejects, remembereth; *that the Gods were
never dead,* but only sleeping the sleep and dreaming the
dreams of Gods in lotos-filled Hesperian[8] gardens beyond
the golden sunset. And now draweth nigh the time of their
awaking, when coldness and ugliness shall perish, and Zeus

sit once more on Olympus. Already the sea about Paphos[9] trembleth into a foam which only ancient skies have looked on before, and at night on Helicon[10] the shepherds hear strange murmurings and half-remembered notes. Woods and fields are tremulous at twilight with the shimmering of white saltant forms, and immemorial Ocean yields up curious sights beneath thin moons. The Gods are patient, and have slept long, but neither man nor giant shall defy the Gods forever. In Tartarus the Titans writhe,[11] and beneath the fiery Aetna groan the children of Uranus and Gaea.[12] The day now dawns when man must answer for centuries of denial, but in sleeping the Gods have grown kind, and will not hurl him to the gulf made for deniers of Gods. Instead will their vengeance smite the darkness, fallacy, and ugliness which have turned the mind of man; and under the sway of bearded Saturnus[13] shall mortals, once more sacrificing unto him, dwell in beauty and delight. This night shalt thou know the favour of the Gods, and behold on Parnassus[14] those dreams which the Gods have through ages sent to earth to shew that they are not dead. For poets are the dreams of the Gods, and in each age someone hath sung unknowing the message and the promise from the lotos-gardens beyond the sunset."

Then in his arms Hermes bore the dreaming maiden through the skies. Gentle breezes from the tower of Aiolos[15] wafted them high above warm, scented seas, till suddenly they came upon Zeus holding court on the double-headed Parnassus; his golden throne flanked by Apollo and the Muses on the right hand, and by ivy-wreathed Dionysus and pleasure-flushed Bacchae on the left hand.[16] So much of splendour Marcia had never seen before, either awake or in dreams, but its radiance did her no injury, as would have the radiance of lofty Olympus; for in this lesser court the Father of Gods had tempered his glories for the sight of mortals. Before the laurel-draped mouth of the Corycian cave[17] sat in a row six noble forms with the aspect of mortals, but the countenances of Gods. These the dreamer recognised from images of them which she had beheld, and she knew that they were none else than the divine Maeonides, the Avernian Dante, the more than mortal Shakespeare, the chaos-exploring Milton, the cosmic Goethe, and the Musaean Keats.[18] These were those messengers whom the Gods had sent to tell men that Pan had passed not away, but only slept; for it is in poetry that Gods speak to men. Then spake the Thunderer:[19]

"O Daughter—for, being one of my endless line, thou art indeed my daughter—behold upon ivory thrones of honour the august messengers that Gods have sent down, that in the words and writings of men there may be still some trace of divine beauty. Other bards have men justly crowned with enduring laurels, but these hath Apollo crowned, and these have I set in places apart, as mortals who have spoken the language of the Gods. Long have we dreamed in lotos-gardens beyond the West, and spoken only through our dreams; but the time approaches when our voices shall not be silent. It is a time of awaking and of change. Once more hath Phaeton ridden low, searing the fields and drying the streams.[20] In Gaul lone nymphs with disordered hair weep beside fountains that are no more, and pine over rivers turned red with the blood of mortals.[21] Ares[22] and his train have gone forth with the madness of Gods, and have returned, Deimos and Phobos[23] glutted with unnatural delight. Tellus[24] moans with grief, and the faces of men are as the faces of the Erinyes,[25] even as when Astraea fled to the skies,[26] and the waves of our bidding encompassed all the land saving this high peak alone. Amidst this chaos, prepared to herald his coming yet to conceal his arrival, even now toileth our latest-born messenger, in whose dreams are all the images which other messengers have dreamed before him. He it is that we have chosen to blend into one glorious whole all the beauty that the world hath known before, and to write words wherein shall echo all the wisdom and the loveliness of the past. He it is who shall proclaim our return, and sing of the days to come when Fauns and Dryads shall haunt their accustomed groves in beauty. Guided was our choice by those who now sit before the Corycian grotto on thrones of ivory, and in whose songs thou shalt hear notes of sublimity by which years hence thou shalt know the greater messenger when he cometh. Attend their voices as one by one they sing to thee here. Each note shalt thou hear again in the poetry which is to come; the poetry which shall bring peace and pleasure to thy soul, though search for it through bleak years thou must. Attend with diligence, for each chord that vibrates away into hiding shall appear again to thee after thou hast returned to earth, as Alpheus, sinking his waters into the soul of Hellas, appears as the crystal Arethusa in remote Sicilia."[27]

Then arose Homeros, the ancient among bards, who took his lyre and chaunted his hymn to Aphrodite.[28] No word of Greek did Marcia know, yet did the message not fall vainly upon her ears; for in the cryptic rhythm was that which spake to all mortals and Gods, and needed no interpreter.

So too the songs of Dante and Goethe, whose unknown words clave the ether with melodies easy to read and to adore. But at last remembered accents resounded before the listener. It was the Swan of Avon, once a God among men, and still a God among Gods:

"Write, write, that from the bloody course of war,
My dearest master, your dear son, may hie;
Bless him at home in peace, whilst I from far,
His name with zealous fervour sanctify."[29]

Accents still more familiar arose as Milton, blind no
more, declaimed immortal harmony:

"Or let thy lamp at midnight hour
Be seen in some high lonely tower,
Where I might oft outwatch the Bear
With thrice-great Hermes, or unsphere
The spirit of Plato, to unfold
What worlds or what vast regions hold
Th' immortal mind, that hath forsook
Her mansion in this fleshly nook.

* * * *

Sometime let gorgeous Tragedy
In sceptred pall come sweeping by,
Presenting Thebes, or Pelops' line,
Or the tale of Troy divine."[30]

Last of all came the young voice of Keats, closest of all
the messengers to the beauteous faun-folk:

"Heard melodies are sweet, but those unheard
Are sweeter; therefore, ye soft pipes, play on....
When old age shall this generation waste,
Thou shalt remain, in midst of other woe
Than ours, a friend to man, to whom thou say'st,

'Beauty is truth—truth beauty'—that is all
Ye know on earth, and all ye need to know."[31]

As the singer ceased, there came a sound in the wind blowing from far Egypt, where at night Aurora mourns by the Nile for her slain son Memnon.[32] To the feet of the Thunderer flew the rosy-fingered Goddess, and kneeling, cried, "Master, it is time I unlocked the gates of the East." And Phoebus,[33] handing his lyre to Calliope, his bride among the Muses, prepared to depart for the jewelled and column-raised Palace of the Sun, where fretted the steeds already harnessed to the golden car of day. So Zeus descended from his carven throne and placed his hand upon the head of Marcia, saying:

"Daughter, the dawn is nigh, and it is well that thou shouldst return before the awaking of mortals to thy home. Weep not at the bleakness of thy life, for the shadow of false faiths will soon be gone, and the Gods shall once more walk among men. Search thou unceasingly for our messenger, for in him wilt thou find peace and comfort. By his word shall thy steps be guided to happiness, and in his dreams of beauty shall thy spirit find all that it craveth." As Zeus ceased, the young Hermes gently seized the maiden and bore her up toward the fading stars; up, and westward over unseen seas.

* * * *

Many years have passed since Marcia dreamt of the Gods and of their Parnassian conclave. Tonight she sits in the same spacious drawing-room, but she is not alone. Gone is the old spirit of unrest, for beside her is one whose name is luminous with celebrity; the young poet of poets

at whose feet sits all the world. He is reading from a manuscript words which none has ever heard before, but which
when heard will bring to men the dreams and fancies they
lost so many centuries ago, when Pan lay down to doze in
Arcady, and the greater Gods withdrew to sleep in lotos-
gardens beyond the lands of the Hesperides. In the subtle
cadences and hidden melodies of the bard the spirit of the
maiden has found rest at last, for there echo the divinest
notes of Thracian Orpheus;[34] notes that moved the very
rocks and trees by Hebrus' banks. The singer ceases, and
with eagerness asks a verdict, yet what can Marcia say but
that the strain is "fit for the Gods"?

And as she speaks there comes again a vision of Parnassus and the far-off sound of a mighty voice saying, "By
his word shall thy steps be guided to happiness, and in his
dreams of beauty shall thy spirit find all that it craveth."

The Crawling Chaos

By Elizabeth Berkeley and Lewis Theobald, Jun.

f the pleasures and pains of opium much has been written. The ecstasies and horrors of De Quincey and the *paradis artificiels* of Baudelaire[1] are preserved and interpreted with an art which makes them immortal, and the world knows well the beauty, the terror, and the mystery of those obscure realms into which the inspired dreamer is transported. But much as has been told, no man has yet dared intimate the *nature* of the phantasms thus unfolded to the mind, or hint at the *direction* of the unheard-of roads along whose ornate and exotic course the partaker of the drug is so irresistibly borne. De Quincey was drawn back into Asia, that teeming land of nebulous shadows whose hideous antiquity is so impressive that "the vast age of the race and name overpowers the sense of youth in the individual",[2] but farther than that he dared not go. Those who *have* gone farther seldom returned; and even when they have, they have been either silent or quite mad. I took opium but once—in the year of the plague, when doctors sought to deaden the agonies they could not cure. There was an overdose—my physician was worn out with horror and exertion—and I travelled very far indeed. In the end I returned and lived, but my nights are filled with strange memories, nor have I ever permitted a doctor to give me opium again.

The pain and pounding in my head had been quite unendurable when the drug was administered. Of the future I had no heed; to escape, whether by cure, unconsciousness, or death, was all that concerned me. I was partly delirious, so that it is hard to place the exact moment of transition, but I think the effect must have begun shortly before the pounding ceased to be painful. As I have said, there was an overdose; so my reactions were probably far from normal. The sensation of falling, curiously dissociated from the idea of gravity or direction, was paramount; though there was a subsidiary impression of unseen throngs in incalculable profusion, throngs of infinitely diverse nature, but all more or less related to me. Sometimes it seemed less as though I were falling, than as though the universe or the ages were falling past me. Suddenly my pain ceased, and I began to associate the pounding with an external rather than internal force. The falling had ceased also, giving place to a sensation of uneasy, temporary rest; and when I listened closely, I fancied the pounding was that of the vast, inscrutable sea as its sinister, colossal breakers lacerated some desolate shore after a storm of titanic magnitude. Then I opened my eyes.

For a moment my surroundings seemed confused, like a projected image hopelessly out of focus, but gradually I realised my solitary presence in a strange and beautiful room lighted by many windows. Of the exact nature of the apartment I could form no idea, for my thoughts were still far from settled; but I noticed vari-coloured rugs and draperies, elaborately fashioned tables, chairs, ottomans, and divans, and delicate vases and ornaments which conveyed a suggestion of the exotic without being actually alien. These things I noticed, yet they were not long uppermost in my mind. Slowly but inexorably crawling upon my consciousness, and rising above every other impression, came a dizzying fear of the unknown; a fear all the greater because I could not analyse it, and seeming to concern a stealthily approaching menace—not death, but some nameless, unheard-of thing inexpressibly more ghastly and abhorrent.

Presently I realised that the direct symbol and excitant of my fear was the hideous pounding whose incessant reverberations throbbed maddeningly against my exhausted brain. It seemed to come from a point outside and below the edifice in which I stood, and to associate itself with the most terrifying mental images. I felt that some horrible scene or object lurked beyond the silk-hung walls, and shrank from glancing through the arched, latticed windows that opened so bewilderingly on every hand. Perceiving shutters attached to these windows, I closed them all, averting my eyes from the exterior as I did so. Then, employing a flint and steel which I found on one of the small tables, I lit the many candles reposing about the walls in Arabesque sconces. The added sense of security brought by closed shutters and artificial light calmed my nerves to some degree, but I could not shut out the monotonous pounding. Now that I was calmer, the sound became as fascinating as it was fearful, and I felt a contradictory desire to seek out its source despite my still powerful shrinking. Opening a portiere at the side of the room nearest the pounding, I beheld a small and richly draped corridor ending in a carven door and large oriel window. To this window I was irresistibly drawn, though my ill-defined apprehensions seemed almost equally bent on holding me back. As I approached it I could see a chaotic whirl of waters in the distance. Then, as I attained it and glanced out on all sides, the stupendous picture of my surroundings burst upon me with full and devastating force.

I beheld such a sight as I had never beheld before, and which no living person can have seen save in the delirium of fever or the inferno of opium. The building stood on a narrow point of land—or what was *now* a narrow point of land—fully 300 feet above what must lately have been a seething vortex of mad waters. On either side of the house there fell a newly washed-out precipice of red earth, whilst ahead of me the hideous waves were still rolling in frightfully, eating away the land with ghastly monotony and deliberation. Out a mile or more there rose and fell menacing breakers at least fifty feet in height, and on the far horizon ghoulish black clouds of grotesque contour were resting and brooding like unwholesome vultures. The waves were dark and purplish, almost black, and clutched at the yielding red mud of the bank as if with uncouth, greedy hands. I could not but feel that some noxious marine mind had declared a war of extermination upon all the solid ground, perhaps abetted by the angry sky.

Recovering at length from the stupor into which this unnatural spectacle had thrown me, I realised that my actual physical danger was acute. Even whilst I gazed the bank had lost many feet, and it could not be long before the house would fall undermined into the awful pit of lashing waves. Accordingly I hastened to the opposite side of the edifice, and finding a door, emerged at once, locking it after me with a curious key which had hung inside. I now beheld more of the strange region about me, and marked a singular division which seemed to exist in the hostile ocean and firmament. On each side of the jutting promontory different conditions held sway. At my left as I faced inland was a gently heaving sea with great green waves rolling peacefully in under a brightly shining sun. Something about that sun's nature and position made me shudder, but I could not then tell, and cannot tell now, what it was. At my right also was the sea, but it was blue, calm, and only gently undulating, while the sky above it was darker and the washed-out bank more nearly white than reddish.

I now turned my attention to the land, and found occasion for fresh surprise; for the vegetation resembled nothing I had ever seen or read about. It was apparently tropical or at least sub-tropical—a conclusion borne out by the intense heat of the air. Sometimes I thought I could trace strange analogies with the flora of my native land, fancying that the well-known plants and shrubs might assume such forms under a radical change of climate; but the gigantic and omnipresent palm trees were plainly foreign. The house I had just left was very small—hardly more than a cottage—but its material was evidently marble, and its architecture was weird and composite, involving a quaint fusion of Western and Eastern forms. At the corners were Corinthian columns,[3] but the red tile roof was like that of a Chinese pagoda. From the door inland there stretched a path of singularly white sand, about four feet wide, and lined on either side with stately palms and unidentifiable flowering shrubs and plants. It lay toward the side of the promontory where the sea was blue and the bank rather whitish. Down this path I felt impelled to flee, as if pursued by some malignant spirit from the pounding ocean. At first it was slightly uphill, then I reached a gentle crest. Behind me I saw the scene I had left; the entire point with the cottage and the black water, with the green sea on one side and the blue sea on the other, and a curse unnamed and unnamable lowering over all. I never saw it again, and often wonder. . . . After this last look I strode ahead and surveyed the inland panorama before me.

The path, as I have intimated, ran along the right-hand shore as one went inland. Ahead and to the left I now viewed a magnificent valley comprising thousands of acres, and covered with a swaying growth of tropical grass higher than my head. Almost at the limit of vision was a colossal palm tree which seemed to fascinate and beckon me. By this time wonder and escape from the imperilled peninsula had largely dissipated my fear, but as I paused and sank fatigued to the path, idly digging with my hands into the warm, whitish-golden sand, a new and acute sense of danger seized me. Some terror in the swishing tall grass seemed added to that of the diabolically pounding sea, and I started up crying aloud and disjointedly, "Tiger? Tiger? Is it Tiger? Beast? Beast? Is it a Beast that I am afraid of?" My mind wandered back to an ancient and classical story of tigers which I had read; I strove to recall the author, but had difficulty. Then in the midst of my fear I remembered that the tale was by Rudyard Kipling;[4] nor did the grotesqueness of deeming him an ancient author occur to me. I wished for the volume containing this story, and had almost started back toward the doomed cottage to procure it when my better sense and the lure of the palm prevented me.

Whether or not I could have resisted the backward beckoning without the counter-fascination of the vast palm tree, I do not know. This attraction was now dominant, and I left the path and crawled on hands and knees down the valley's slope despite my fear of the grass and of the serpents it might contain. I resolved to fight for life and reason as long as possible against all menaces of sea or land, though I sometimes feared defeat as the maddening swish of the uncanny grasses joined the still audible and irritating pounding of the distant breakers. I would frequently pause and put my hands to my ears for relief, but could never quite shut out the detestable sound. It was, as it seemed to me, only after ages that I finally dragged myself to the beckoning palm tree and lay quiet beneath its protecting shade.

There now ensued a series of incidents which transported me to the opposite extremes of ecstasy and horror; incidents which I tremble to recall and dare not seek to interpret. No sooner had I crawled beneath the overhanging foliage of the palm, than there dropped from its branches a young child of such beauty as I never beheld before. Though ragged and dusty, this being bore the features of a faun or demigod, and seemed almost to diffuse a radiance in the dense shadow of the tree. It smiled and extended its hand, but before I could arise and speak I heard in the upper air the exquisite melody of singing; notes high and low blent with a sublime and ethereal harmoniousness. The sun had by this time sunk below the horizon, and in the twilight I saw that an aureola of lambent light encircled the child's head. Then in a tone of silver it addressed me: "It is the end. They have come down through the gloaming from the stars. Now all is over, and beyond the Arinurian streams we shall dwell blissfully in Teloe."[5] As the child spoke, I beheld a soft radiance through the leaves of the palm tree, and rising greeted a pair whom I knew to be the chief singers among those I had heard. A god and goddess they must have been, for such beauty is not mortal; and they took my hands, saying, "Come, child, you have heard the voices, and all is well. In Teloe beyond the Milky Way and the Arinurian streams are cities all of amber and chalcedony. And upon their domes of many facets glisten the images of strange and beautiful stars. Under the ivory bridges of Teloe flow rivers of liquid gold bearing pleasure-barges bound for blossomy Cytharion[6] of the Seven Suns.

And in Teloe and Cytharion abide only youth, beauty, and pleasure, nor are any sounds heard, save of laughter, song, and the lute. Only the gods dwell in Teloe of the golden rivers, but among them shalt thou dwell."

As I listened, enchanted, I suddenly became aware of a change in my surroundings. The palm tree, so lately overshadowing my exhausted form, was now some distance to my left and considerably below me. I was obviously floating in the atmosphere; companioned not only by the strange child and the radiant pair, but by a constantly increasing throng of half-luminous, vine-crowned youths and maidens with wind-blown hair and joyful countenance. We slowly ascended together, as if borne on a fragrant breeze which blew not from the earth but from the golden nebulae, and the child whispered in my ear that I must look always upward to the pathways of light, and never backward to the sphere I had just left. The youths and maidens now chaunted mellifluous choriambics[7] to the accompaniment of lutes, and I felt enveloped in a peace and happiness more profound than any I had in life imagined, when the intrusion of a single sound altered my destiny and shattered my soul. Through the ravishing strains of the singers and the lutanists, as if in mocking, daemoniac concord, throbbed from gulfs below the damnable, the detestable pounding of that hideous ocean. And as those black breakers beat their message into my ears I forgot the words of the child and looked back, down upon the doomed scene from which I thought I had escaped.

Down through the aether I saw the accursed earth turning, ever turning, with angry and tempestuous seas gnawing at wild desolate shores and dashing foam against the tottering towers of deserted cities. And under a ghastly moon there gleamed sights I can never describe, sights I can never forget; deserts of corpse-like clay and jungles of ruin and decadence where once stretched the populous plains and villages of my native land, and maelstroms of frothing ocean where once rose the mighty temples of my forefathers. Around the northern pole steamed a morass of noisome growths and miasmal vapours, hissing before the onslaught of the ever-mounting waves that curled and fretted from the shuddering deep. Then a rending report clave the night, and athwart the desert of deserts appeared a smoking rift. Still the black ocean foamed and gnawed, eating away the desert on either side as the rift in the centre widened and widened.

There was now no land left but the desert, and still the fuming ocean ate and ate. All at once I thought even the pounding sea seemed afraid of something, afraid of dark gods of the inner earth that are greater than the evil god of waters, but even if it was it could not turn back; and the desert had suffered too much from those nightmare waves to help them now. So the ocean ate the last of the land and poured into the smoking gulf, thereby giving up all it had ever conquered. From the new-flooded lands it flowed again, uncovering death and decay; and from its ancient and immemorial bed it trickled loathsomely, uncovering nighted secrets of the years when Time was young and the gods unborn. Above the waves rose weedy, remembered spires. The moon laid pale lilies of light on dead London, and Paris stood up from its damp grave to be sanctified with star-dust. Then rose spires and monoliths that were weedy but not remembered; terrible spires and monoliths of lands that men never knew were lands.

There was not any pounding now, but only the unearthly roaring and hissing of waters tumbling into the rift. The smoke of that rift had changed to steam, and almost hid the world as it grew denser and denser. It seared my face and hands, and when I looked to see how it affected my companions I found they had all disappeared. Then very suddenly it ended, and I knew no more till I awaked upon a bed of convalescence. As the cloud of steam from the Plutonic gulf finally concealed the entire surface from my sight, all the firmament shrieked at a sudden agony of mad reverberations which shook the trembling aether. In one delirious flash and burst it happened; one blinding, deafening holocaust of fire, smoke, and thunder that dissolved the wan moon as it sped outward to the void.

And when the smoke cleared away, and I sought to look upon the earth, I beheld against the background of cold, humorous stars only the dying sun and the pale mournful planets searching for their sister.

The Horror at Martin's Beach

With Sonia H. Greene

I have never heard an even approximately adequate explanation of the horror at Martin's Beach. Despite the large number of witnesses, no two accounts agree; and the testimony taken by local authorities contains the most amazing discrepancies.

Perhaps this haziness is natural in view of the unheard-of character of the horror itself, the almost paralytic terror of all who saw it, and the efforts made by the fashionable Wavecrest Inn to hush it up after the publicity created by Prof. Alton's article "Are Hypnotic Powers Confined to Recognized Humanity?"

Against all these obstacles I am striving to present a coherent version; for I beheld the hideous occurrence, and believe it should be known in view of the appalling possibilities it suggests. Martin's Beach is once more popular as a watering-place, but I shudder when I think of it. Indeed, I cannot look at the ocean at all now without shuddering.

Fate is not always without a sense of drama and climax, hence the terrible happening of August 8, 1922, swiftly followed a period of minor and agreeably wonder-fraught excitement at Martin's Beach. On May 17 the crew of the fishing smack *Alma* of Gloucester, under Capt. James P. Orne,[1] killed, after a battle of nearly forty hours, a marine monster whose size and aspect produced the greatest possible stir in scientific circles and caused certain Boston naturalists to take every precaution for its taxidermic preservation.

The object was some fifty feet in length, of roughly cylindrical shape, and about ten feet in diameter. It was unmistakably a gilled fish in its major affiliations; but with certain curious modifications, such as rudimentary forelegs and six-toed feet in place of pectoral fins, which prompted the widest speculation. Its extraordinary mouth, its thick and scaly hide, and its single, deep-set eye were wonders scarcely less remarkable than its colossal dimensions; and when the naturalists pronounced it an infant organism, which could not have been hatched more than a few days, public interest mounted to extraordinary heights.

Capt. Orne, with typical Yankee shrewdness, obtained a vessel large enough to hold the object in its hull, and arranged for the exhibition of his prize. With judicious carpentry he prepared what amounted to an excellent marine museum, and, sailing south to the wealthy resort district of Martin's Beach, anchored at the hotel wharf and reaped a harvest of admission fees.

The intrinsic marvelousness of the object, and the importance which it clearly bore in the minds of many scientific visitors from near and far, combined to make it the season's sensation. That it was absolutely unique—unique to a scientifically revolutionary degree—was well understood. The naturalists had shown plainly that it radically differed from the similarly immense fish caught off the Florida coast; that, while it was obviously an inhabitant of almost incredible depths, perhaps thousands of feet, its brain and principal organs indicated a development startlingly vast, and out of all proportion to anything hitherto associated with the fish tribe.

On the morning of July 20 the sensation was increased by the loss of the vessel and its strange treasure. In the storm of the preceding night it had broken from its moorings and vanished forever from the sight of man, carrying with it the guard who had slept aboard despite the threatening weather. Capt. Orne, backed by extensive scientific interests and aided by large numbers of fishing boats from Gloucester, made a thorough and exhaustive searching cruise, but with no result other than the prompting of interest and conversation. By August 7 hope was abandoned, and Capt. Orne had returned to the Wavecrest Inn to wind up his business affairs at Martin's Beach and confer with certain of the scientific men who remained there. The horror came on August 8.

It was in the twilight, when grey sea-birds hovered low near the shore and a rising moon began to make a glittering path across the waters. The scene is important to remember, for every impression counts. On the beach were several strollers and a few late bathers; stragglers from the distant cottage colony that rose modestly on a green hill to the north, or from the adjacent cliff-perched Inn whose imposing towers proclaimed its allegiance to wealth and grandeur.

Well within viewing distance was another set of spectators, the loungers on the Inn's high-ceiled and lantern-lighted veranda, who appeared to be enjoying the dance music from the sumptuous ballroom inside. These spectators, who included Capt. Orne and his group of scientific confreres, joined the beach group before the horror progressed far; as did many more from the Inn. Certainly there was no lack of witnesses, confused though their stories be with fear and doubt of what they saw.

There is no exact record of the time the thing began, although a majority say that the fairly round moon was "about a foot" above the low-lying vapors of the horizon. They mention the moon because what they saw seemed subtly connected with it—a sort of stealthy, deliberate, menacing ripple which rolled in from the far skyline along the shimmering lane of reflected moonbeams, yet which seemed to subside before it reached the shore.

Many did not notice this ripple until reminded by later events; but it seems to have been very marked, differing in height and motion from the normal waves around it. Some called it *cunning* and *calculating*. And as it died away craftily by the black reefs afar out, there suddenly came belching up out of the glitter-streaked brine a cry of death; a scream of anguish and despair that moved pity even while it mocked it.

First to respond to the cry were the two life guards then on duty; sturdy fellows in white bathing attire, with their calling proclaimed in large red letters across their chests. Accustomed as they were to rescue work, and to the screams of the drowning, they could find nothing familiar in the unearthly ululation; yet with a trained sense of duty they ignored the strangeness and proceeded to follow their usual course.

Hastily seizing an air-cushion, which with its attached coil of rope lay always at hand, one of them ran swiftly along the shore to the scene of the gathering crowd; whence, after whirling it about to gain momentum, he flung the hollow disc far out in the direction from which the sound had come. As the cushion disappeared in the waves, the crowd curiously awaited a sight of the hapless being whose distress had been so great; eager to see the rescue made by the massive rope.

But that rescue was soon acknowledged to be no swift and easy matter; for, pull as they might on the rope, the two muscular guards could not move the object at the other end. Instead, they found that object pulling with equal or even greater force in the very opposite direction, till in a few seconds they were dragged off their feet and into the water by the strange power which had seized on the proffered life-preserver.

One of them, recovering himself, called immediately for help from the crowd on the shore, to whom he flung the remaining coil of rope; and in a moment the guards were seconded by all the hardier men, among whom Capt. Orne was foremost. More than a dozen strong hands were now tugging desperately at the stout line, yet wholly without avail.

Hard as they tugged, the strange force at the other end tugged harder; and since neither side relaxed for an instant, the rope became rigid as steel with the enormous strain. The struggling participants, as well as the spectators, were by this time consumed with curiosity as to the nature of the force in the sea. The idea of a drowning man had long been dismissed; and hints of whales, submarines, monsters, and demons now passed freely around. Where humanity had first led the rescuers, wonder kept them at their task; and they hauled with a grim determination to uncover the mystery.

It being decided at last that a whale must have swallowed the air-cushion, Capt. Orne, as a natural leader, shouted to those on shore that a boat must be obtained in order to approach, harpoon, and land the unseen leviathan.

Several men at once prepared to scatter in quest of a suitable craft, while others came to supplant the captain at the straining rope, since his place was logically with whatever boat party might be formed. His own idea of the situation was very broad, and by no means limited to whales, since he had to do with a monster so much stranger. He wondered what might be the acts and manifestations of an adult of the species of which the fifty-foot creature had been the merest infant.

And now there developed with appalling suddenness the crucial fact which changed the entire scene from one of wonder to one of horror, and dazed with fright the assembled band of toilers and onlookers. Capt. Orne, turning to leave his post at the rope, found his hands held in their place with unaccountable strength; and in a moment he realized that he was unable to let go of the rope. His plight was instantly divined, and as each companion tested his own situation the same condition was encountered. The fact could not be denied—every struggler was irresistibly held in some mysterious bondage to the hempen line which was slowly, hideously, and relentlessly pulling them out to sea.

Speechless horror ensued; a horror in which the spectators were petrified to utter inaction and mental chaos. Their complete demoralization is reflected in the conflicting accounts they give, and the sheepish excuses they offer for their seemingly callous inertia. I was one of them, and know.

Even the strugglers, after a few frantic screams and futile groans, succumbed to the paralyzing influence and kept silent and fatalistic in the face of unknown powers. There they stood in the pallid moonlight, blindly pulling against a spectral doom and swaying monotonously backward and forward as the water rose first to their knees, then to their hips. The moon went partly under a cloud, and in the half-light the line of swaying men resembled some sinister and gigantic centipede, writhing in the clutch of a terrible creeping death.

Harder and harder grew the rope, as the tug in both directions increased, and the strands swelled with the undisturbed soaking of the rising waves. Slowly the tide advanced, till the sands so lately peopled by laughing children and whispering lovers were now swallowed by the inexorable flow. The herd of panic-stricken watchers surged blindly backward as the water crept above their feet, while the frightful line of strugglers swayed hideously on, half submerged, and now at a substantial distance from their audience. Silence was complete.

The crowd, having gained a huddling-place beyond reach of the tide, stared in mute fascination; without offering a word of advice or encouragement, or attempting any kind of assistance. There was in the air a nightmare fear of impending evils such as the world had never before known.

Minutes seemed lengthened into hours, and still that human snake of swaying torsos was seen above the fast rising tide. Rhythmically it undulated; slowly, horribly, with the seal of doom upon it. Thicker clouds now passed over the ascending moon, and the glittering path on the waters faded nearly out.

Very dimly writhed the serpentine line of nodding heads, with now and then the livid face of a backward-glancing victim gleaming pale in the darkness. Faster and faster gathered the clouds, till at length their angry rifts shot down sharp tongues of febrile flame. Thunders rolled, softly at first, yet soon increasing to a deafening, maddening intensity. Then came a culminating crash—a shock whose reverberations seemed to shake land and sea alike—and on its heels a cloudburst whose drenching violence overpowered the darkened world as if the heavens themselves had opened to pour forth a vindictive torrent.

The spectators, instinctively acting despite the absence of conscious and coherent thought, now retreated up the cliff steps to the hotel veranda. Rumors had reached the guests inside, so that the refugees found a state of terror nearly equal to their own. I think a few frightened words were uttered, but cannot be sure.

Some, who were staying at the Inn, retired in terror to their rooms; while others remained to watch the fast sinking victims as the line of bobbing heads showed above the mounting waves in the fitful lightning flashes. I recall thinking of those heads, and the bulging eyes they must contain; eyes that might well reflect all the fright, panic, and delirium of a malignant universe—all the sorrow, sin, and misery, blasted hopes and unfulfilled desires, fear, loathing and anguish of the ages since time's beginning; eyes alight with all the soul-racking pain of eternally blazing infernos.

And as I gazed out beyond the heads, my fancy conjured up still another eye; a single eye, equally alight, yet with a purpose so revolting to my brain that the vision soon passed. Held in the clutches of an unknown vise, the line of the damned dragged on; their silent screams and unuttered prayers known only to the demons of the black waves and the night-wind.

There now burst from the infuriate sky such a mad cataclysm of satanic sound that even the former crash seemed dwarfed. Amidst a blinding glare of descending fire the voice of heaven resounded with the blasphemies of hell, and the mingled agony of all the lost reverberated in one apocalyptic, planet-rending peal of Cyclopean[2] din. It was the end of the storm, for with uncanny suddenness the rain ceased and the moon once more cast her pallid beams on a strangely quieted sea.

There was no line of bobbing heads now. The waters were calm and deserted, and broken only by the fading ripples of what seemed to be a whirlpool far out in the path of the moonlight whence the strange cry had first come. But as I looked along that treacherous lane of silvery sheen, with fancy fevered and senses overwrought, there trickled upon my ears from some abysmal sunken waste the faint and sinister echoes of a laugh.

Under the Pyramids

With Harry Houdini

ystery attracts mystery. Ever since the wide appearance of my name as a performer of unexplained feats,[1] I have encountered strange narratives and events which my calling has led people to link with my interests and activities. Some of these have been trivial and irrelevant, some deeply dramatic and absorbing, some productive of weird and perilous experiences, and some involving me in extensive scientific and historical research. Many of these matters I have told and shall continue to tell freely;[2] but there is one of which I speak with great reluctance, and which I am now relating only after a session of grilling persuasion from the publishers of this magazine, who had heard vague rumours of it from other members of my family.

The hitherto guarded subject pertains to my nonprofessional visit to Egypt fourteen years ago, and has been avoided by me for several reasons. For one thing, I am averse to exploiting certain unmistakably actual facts and conditions obviously unknown to the myriad tourists who throng about the pyramids and apparently secreted with much diligence by the authorities at Cairo, who cannot be wholly ignorant of them. For another thing, I dislike to recount an incident in which my own fantastic imagination must have played so great a part. What I saw—or thought I saw—certainly did not take place; but is rather to be viewed as a result of my then recent readings in Egyptology, and of the speculations anent this theme which my environment naturally prompted. These imaginative stimuli, magnified by the excitement of an actual event terrible enough in itself, undoubtedly gave rise to the culminating horror of that grotesque night so long past.

In January, 1910, I had finished a professional engagement in England and signed a contract for a tour of Australian theatres.[3] A liberal time being allowed for the trip, I determined to make the most of it in the sort of travel which chiefly interests me; so accompanied by my wife[4] I drifted pleasantly down the Continent and embarked at Marseilles on the P. & O. Steamer *Malwa,* bound for Port Said. From that point I proposed to visit the principal historical localities of lower Egypt before leaving finally for Australia.

The voyage was an agreeable one, and enlivened by many of the amusing incidents which befall a magical performer apart from his work. I had intended, for the sake of quiet travel, to keep my name a secret; but was goaded into betraying myself by a fellow-magician whose anxiety to astound the passengers with ordinary tricks tempted me to duplicate and exceed his feats in a manner quite destructive of my incognito. I mention this because of its ultimate effect—an effect I should have foreseen before unmasking to a shipload of tourists about to scatter throughout the Nile Valley. What it did was to herald my identity wherever

I subsequently went, and deprive my wife and me of all the placid inconspicuousness we had sought. Travelling to seek curiosities, I was often forced to stand inspection as a sort of curiosity myself!

We had come to Egypt in search of the picturesque and the mystically impressive, but found little enough when the ship edged up to Port Said and discharged its passengers in small boats. Low dunes of sand, bobbing buoys in shallow water, and a drearily European small town with nothing of interest save the great De Lesseps statue,[5] made us anxious to get on to something more worth our while. After some discussion we decided to proceed at once to Cairo and the Pyramids, later going to Alexandria for the Australian boat and for whatever Graeco-Roman sights that ancient metropolis might present.[6]

The railway journey was tolerable enough, and consumed only four hours and a half. We saw much of the Suez Canal, whose route we followed as far as Ismailiya, and later had a taste of Old Egypt in our glimpse of the restored fresh-water canal of the Middle Empire. Then at last we saw Cairo glimmering through the growing dusk; a twinkling constellation which became a blaze as we halted at the great Gare Centrale.

But once more disappointment awaited us, for all that we beheld was European save the costumes and the crowds. A prosaic subway led to a square teeming with carriages, taxicabs, and trolley-cars, and gorgeous with electric lights shining on tall buildings; whilst the very theatre where I was vainly requested to play, and which I later attended as a spectator, had recently been renamed the "American Cosmograph". We stopped at Shepherd's Hotel,[7] reached in a taxi that sped along broad, smartly built-up streets; and amidst the perfect service of its restaurant, elevators, and generally Anglo-American luxuries the mysterious East and immemorial past seemed very far away.

The next day, however, precipitated us delightfully into the heart of the Arabian Nights atmosphere; and in the winding ways and exotic skyline of Cairo, the Bagdad of Haroun-al-Raschid seemed to live again.[8] Guided by our Baedeker,[9] we had struck east past the Ezbekiyeh Gardens along the Mouski[10] in quest of the native quarter, and were soon in the hands of a clamorous cicerone who—notwithstanding later developments—was assuredly a master at his trade. Not until afterward did I see that I should have applied at the hotel for a licenced guide. This man, a shaven, peculiarly hollow-voiced, and relatively cleanly fellow who looked like a Pharaoh[11] and called himself "Abdul Reis el Drogman", appeared to have much power over others of his kind; though subsequently the police professed not to know him, and to suggest that *reis* is merely a name for any person in authority, whilst "Drogman" is obviously no more than a clumsy modification of the word for a leader of tourist parties—*dragoman.*

Abdul led us among such wonders as we had before only read and dreamed of. Old Cairo is itself a story-book and a dream—labyrinths of narrow alleys redolent of aromatic secrets; Arabesque balconies and oriels nearly meeting above the cobbled streets; maelstroms of Oriental traffic with strange cries, cracking whips, rattling carts, jingling money, and braying donkeys; kaleidoscopes of polychrome robes, veils, turbans, and tarbushes; water-carriers and dervishes, dogs and cats, soothsayers and barbers; and over all the whining of blind beggars crouched in alcoves, and the sonorous chanting of muezzins from minarets limned delicately against a sky of deep, unchanging blue.

The roofed, quieter bazaars were hardly less alluring.

Spice, perfume, incense, beads, rugs, silks, and brass—old Mahmoud Suleiman squats cross-legged amidst his gummy bottles while chattering youths pulverise mustard in the hollowed-out capital of an ancient classic column—a Roman Corinthian, perhaps from neighbouring Heliopolis, where Augustus stationed one of his three Egyptian legions.[12] Antiquity begins to mingle with exoticism. And then the mosques and the museum[13]—we saw them all, and tried not to let our Arabian revel succumb to the darker charm of Pharaonic Egypt which the museum's priceless treasures offered. That was to be our climax, and for the present we concentrated on the mediaeval Saracenic glories of the Caliphs whose magnificent tomb-mosques form a glittering faery necropolis on the edge of the Arabian Desert.

At length Abdul took us along the Sharia Mohammed Ali to the ancient mosque of Sultan Hassan, and the tower-flanked Bab-el-Azab, beyond which climbs the steep-walled pass to the mighty citadel that Saladin himself built with the stones of forgotten pyramids.[14] It was sunset when we scaled that cliff, circled the modern mosque of Mohammed Ali, and looked down from the dizzying parapet over mystic Cairo—mystic Cairo all golden with its carven domes, its ethereal minarets, and its flaming gardens. Far over the city towered the great Roman dome of the new museum; and beyond it—across the cryptic yellow Nile that is the mother of aeons and dynasties—lurked the menacing sands of the Libyan Desert, undulant and iridescent and evil with older arcana. The red sun sank low, bringing the relentless chill of Egyptian dusk; and as it stood poised on the world's rim like that ancient god of Heliopolis—Re-Harakhte, the Horizon-Sun[15]—we saw silhouetted against its vermeil holocaust the black outlines of the Pyramids of Gizeh—the palaeogean tombs there were hoary with a

thousand years when Tut-Ankh-Amen mounted his gold-
en throne in distant Thebes.[16] Then we knew that we were
done with Saracen Cairo, and that we must taste the deeper mysteries of primal Egypt—the black Khem of Re and
Amen, Isis and Osiris.[17]

The next morning we visited the pyramids, riding out
in a Victoria across the great Nile bridge with its bronze
lions, the island of Ghizereh with its massive lebbakh trees,
and the smaller English bridge to the western shore. Down
the shore road we drove, between great rows of lebbakhs
and past the vast Zoölogical Gardens to the suburb of
Gizeh, where a new bridge to Cairo proper has since been
built. Then, turning inland along the Sharia-el-Haram, we
crossed a region of glassy canals and shabby native villages
till before us loomed the objects of our quest, cleaving the
mists of dawn and forming inverted replicas in the roadside
pools. Forty centuries, as Napoleon had told his campaign-
ers there,[18] indeed looked down upon us.

The road now rose abruptly, till we finally reached our
place of transfer between the trolley station and the Mena
House Hotel. Abdul Reis, who capably purchased our pyramid tickets, seemed to have an understanding with the
crowding, yelling, and offensive Bedouins[19] who inhabited
a squalid mud village some distance away and pestiferously
assailed every traveller; for he kept them very decently at
bay and secured an excellent pair of camels for us, himself
mounting a donkey and assigning the leadership of our animals to a group of men and boys more expensive than use-
ful. The area to be traversed was so small that camels were
hardly needed, but we did not regret adding to our experience this troublesome form of desert navigation.

The pyramids stand on a high rock plateau, this group
forming next to the northernmost of the series of regal and

aristocratic cemeteries built in the neighbourhood of the extinct capital Memphis, which lay on the same side of the Nile, somewhat south of Gizeh, and which flourished between 3400 and 2000 B. C. The greatest pyramid, which lies nearest the modern road, was built by King Cheops or Khufu about 2800 B. C.,[20] and stands more than 450 feet in perpendicular height. In a line southwest from this are successively the Second Pyramid, built a generation later by King Khephren,[21] and though slightly smaller, looking even larger because set on higher ground, and the radically smaller Third Pyramid of King Mycerinus, built about 2700 B. C.[22] Near the edge of the plateau and due east of the Second Pyramid, with a face probably altered to form a colossal portrait of Khephren, its royal restorer, stands the monstrous Sphinx—mute, sardonic, and wise beyond mankind and memory.[23]

Minor pyramids and the traces of ruined minor pyramids are found in several places, and the whole plateau is pitted with the tombs of dignitaries of less than royal rank. These latter were originally marked by *mastabas,* or stone bench-like structures about the deep burial shafts, as found in other Memphian cemeteries and exemplified by Perneb's Tomb in the Metropolitan Museum of New York.[24] At Gizeh, however, all such visible things have been swept away by time and pillage; and only the rock-hewn shafts, either sand-filled or cleared out by archaeologists, remain to attest their former existence. Connected with each tomb was a chapel in which priests and relatives offered food and prayer to the hovering *ka* or vital principle of the deceased. The small tombs have their chapels contained in their stone *mastabas* or superstructures, but the mortuary chapels of the pyramids, where regal Pharaohs lay, were separate temples, each to the east of its corresponding pyramid, and connected by a causeway to a massive gate-chapel or propylon at the edge of the rock plateau.

The gate-chapel leading to the Second Pyramid, nearly buried in the drifting sands, yawns subterraneously southeast of the Sphinx. Persistent tradition dubs it the "Temple of the Sphinx";[25] and it may perhaps be rightly called such if the Sphinx indeed represents the Second Pyramid's builder Khephren. There are unpleasant tales of the Sphinx before Khephren—but whatever its elder features were, the monarch replaced them with his own that men might look at the colossus without fear. It was in the great gateway-temple that the life-size diorite statue of Khephren now in the Cairo Museum was found; a statue before which I stood in awe when I beheld it.[26] Whether the whole edifice is now excavated I am not certain, but in 1910 most of it was below ground, with the entrance heavily barred at night. Germans were in charge of the work, and the war or other things may have stopped them. I would give much, in view of my experience and of certain Bedouin whisperings discredited or unknown in Cairo, to know what has developed in connexion with a certain well in a transverse gallery where statues of the Pharaoh were found in curious juxtaposition to the statues of baboons.

The road, as we traversed it on our camels that morning, curved sharply past the wooden police quarters, post-office, drug-store, and shops on the left, and plunged south and east in a complete bend that scaled the rock plateau and brought us face to face with the desert under the lee of the Great Pyramid. Past Cyclopean[27] masonry we rode, rounding the eastern face and looking down ahead into a valley of minor pyramids beyond which the eternal Nile glistened to the east, and the eternal desert shimmered to the west. Very close loomed the three major pyramids, the greatest devoid of outer casing and shewing its bulk of great stones, but the others retaining here and there the neatly fitted covering which had made them smooth and finished in their day.

Presently we descended toward the Sphinx, and sat silent beneath the spell of those terrible unseeing eyes. On the vast stone breast we faintly discerned the emblem of Re-Harakhte, for whose image the Sphinx was mistaken in a late dynasty; and though sand covered the tablet between the great paws, we recalled what Thutmosis IV inscribed thereon, and the dream he had when a prince.[28] It was then that the smile of the Sphinx vaguely displeased us, and made us wonder about the legends of subterranean passages beneath the monstrous creature, leading down, down, to depths none might dare hint at—depths connected with mysteries older than the dynastic Egypt we excavate, and having a sinister relation to the persistence of abnormal, animal-headed gods in the ancient Nilotic pantheon. Then, too, it was I asked myself an idle question whose hideous significance was not to appear for many an hour.

Other tourists now began to overtake us, and we moved on to the sand-choked Temple of the Sphinx, fifty yards to the southeast, which I have previously mentioned as the great gate of the causeway to the Second Pyramid's mortuary chapel on the plateau. Most of it was still underground, and although we dismounted and descended through a modern passageway to its alabaster corridor and pillared hall, I felt that Abdul and the local German attendant had not shewn us all there was to see. After this we made the conventional circuit of the pyramid plateau, examining the Second Pyramid and the peculiar ruins of its mortuary chapel to the east, the Third Pyramid and its miniature southern satellites and ruined eastern chapel, the rock tombs and the honeycombings of the Fourth and Fifth Dynasties, and the famous Campbell's Tomb[29] whose shadowy shaft sinks precipitously for 53 feet to a sinister sarcophagus which one of our camel-drivers divested of the cumbering sand after a vertiginous descent by rope.

Cries now assailed us from the Great Pyramid, where Bedouins were besieging a party of tourists with offers of guidance to the top, or of displays of speed in the performance of solitary trips up and down. Seven minutes is said to be the record for such an ascent and descent, but many lusty sheiks and sons of sheiks assured us they could cut it to five if given the requisite impetus of liberal *baksheesh*. They did not get this impetus, though we did let Abdul take us up, thus obtaining a view of unprecedented magnificence which included not only remote and glittering Cairo with its crowned citadel and background of gold-violet hills, but all the pyramids of the Memphian district as well, from Abu Roash on the north to the Dashur on the south. The Sakkara step-pyramid, which marks the evolution of the low *mastaba* into the true pyramid, shewed clearly and alluringly in the sandy distance.[30] It is close to this transition-monument that the famed Tomb of Perneb was found—more than 400 miles north of the Theban rock valley where Tut-Ankh-Amen sleeps. Again I was forced to silence through sheer awe. The prospect of such antiquity, and the secrets each hoary monument seemed to hold and brood over, filled me with a reverence and sense of immensity nothing else ever gave me.

Fatigued by our climb, and disgusted with the importunate Bedouins whose actions seemed to defy every rule of taste, we omitted the arduous detail of entering the cramped interior passages of any of the pyramids, though we saw several of the hardiest tourists preparing for the suffocating crawl through Cheops' mightiest memorial. As we dismissed and overpaid our local bodyguard and drove back to Cairo with Abdul Reis under the afternoon sun, we half regretted the omission we had made. Such fascinating things were whispered about lower pyramid passages not in the guide-books; passages whose entrances had been hastily blocked up and concealed by certain uncommunicative archaeologists who had found and begun to explore them. Of course, this whispering was largely baseless on the face of it; but it was curious to reflect how persistently visitors were forbidden to enter the pyramids at night, or to visit the lowest burrows and crypt of the Great Pyramid. Perhaps in the latter case it was the psychological effect which was feared—the effect on the visitor of feeling himself huddled down beneath a gigantic world of solid masonry; joined to the life he has known by the merest tube, in which he may only crawl, and which any accident or evil design might block. The whole subject seemed so weird and alluring that we resolved to pay the pyramid plateau another visit at the earliest possible opportunity. For me this opportunity came much earlier than I expected.

That evening, the members of our party feeling somewhat tired after the strenuous programme of the day, I went alone with Abdul Reis for a walk through the picturesque Arab quarter. Though I had seen it by day, I wished to study the alleys and bazaars in the dusk, when rich shadows and mellow gleams of light would add to their glamour and fantastic illusion. The native crowds were thinning, but were still very noisy and numerous when we came upon a knot of revelling Bedouins in the Suken-Nahhasin, or bazaar of the coppersmiths. Their apparent leader, an insolent youth with heavy features and saucily cocked tarbush, took some notice of us; and evidently recognised with no great friendliness my competent but admittedly supercilious and sneeringly disposed guide. Perhaps, I thought, he resented that odd reproduction of the Sphinx's half-smile which I had often remarked with amused irritation; or perhaps he did not like the hollow and sepulchral resonance of Abdul's voice. At any rate, the exchange of ancestrally opprobrious language became very brisk; and before long Ali Ziz, as I heard the stranger called when called by no worse name, began to pull violently at Abdul's robe, an action quickly reciprocated, and leading to a spirited scuffle in which both combatants lost their sacredly cherished headgear and would have reached an even direr condition had I not intervened and separated them by main force.

My interference, at first seemingly unwelcome on both sides, succeeded at last in effecting a truce. Sullenly each belligerent composed his wrath and his attire; and with an assumption of dignity as profound as it was sudden, the two formed a curious pact of honour which I soon learned is a custom of great antiquity in Cairo—a pact for the settlement of their difference by means of a nocturnal fist fight atop the Great Pyramid, long after the departure of the last moonlight sightseer. Each duellist was to assemble a party of seconds, and the affair was to begin at midnight, proceeding by rounds in the most civilised possible fashion. In all this planning there was much which excited my interest. The fight itself promised to be unique and spectacular, while the thought of the scene on that hoary pile overlooking the antediluvian plateau of Gizeh under the wan moon of the pallid small hours appealed to every fibre of imagination in me. A request found Abdul exceedingly willing to admit me to his party of seconds; so that all the rest of the early evening I accompanied him to various dens in the most lawless regions of the town—mostly northeast of the Ezbekiyeh—where he gathered one by one a select and formidable band of congenial cutthroats as his pugilistic background.

Shortly after nine our party, mounted on donkeys bearing such royal or tourist-reminiscent names as "Rameses", "Mark Twain", "J. P. Morgan", and "Minnehaha",[31] edged through street labyrinths both Oriental and Occidental, crossed the muddy and mast-forested Nile by the bridge of the bronze lions, and cantered philosophically between the lebbakhs on the road to Gizeh. Slightly over two hours were consumed by the trip, toward the end of which we passed the last of the returning tourists, saluted the last in-bound trolley-car, and were alone with the night and the past and the spectral moon.

Then we saw the vast pyramids at the end of the avenue, ghoulish with a dim atavistical menace which I had not seemed to notice in the daytime. Even the smallest of them held a hint of the ghastly—for was it not in this that they had buried Queen Nitokris alive in the Sixth Dynasty; subtle Queen Nitokris, who once invited all her enemies to a feast in a temple below the Nile, and drowned them by opening the water-gates?[32] I recalled that the Arabs whisper things about Nitokris, and shun the Third Pyramid at certain phases of the moon. It must have been over her that Thomas Moore was brooding when he wrote a thing muttered about by Memphian boatmen—

"The subterranean nymph that dwells
'Mid sunless gems and glories hid—
The lady of the Pyramid!"[33]

Early as we were, Ali Ziz and his party were ahead of us; for we saw their donkeys outlined against the desert plateau at Kafr-el-Haram; toward which squalid Arab settlement, close to the Sphinx, we had diverged instead of following the regular road to the Mena House, where some of the sleepy, inefficient police might have observed and halted us. Here, where filthy Bedouins stabled camels and donkeys in the rock tombs of Khephren's courtiers, we were led up the rocks and over the sand to the Great Pyramid, up whose time-worn sides the Arabs swarmed eagerly, Abdul Reis offering me the assistance I did not need.

As most travellers know, the actual apex of this structure has long been worn away, leaving a reasonably flat platform twelve yards square. On this eerie pinnacle a squared circle was formed, and in a few moments the sardonic desert moon leered down upon a battle which, but for the quality of the ringside cries, might well have occurred at some minor athletic club in America. As I watched it, I felt that some of our less desirable institutions were not lacking; for every blow, feint, and defence bespoke "stalling" to my not inexperienced eye. It was quickly over, and despite my misgivings as to methods I felt a sort of proprietary pride when Abdul Reis was adjudged the winner.

Reconciliation was phenomenally rapid, and amidst the singing, fraternising, and drinking which followed, I found it difficult to realise that a quarrel had ever occurred. Oddly enough, I myself seemed to be more of a centre of notice than the antagonists; and from my smattering of Arabic I judged that they were discussing my professional performances and escapes from every sort of manacle and confinement, in a manner which indicated not only a surprising knowledge of me, but a distinct hostility and scepticism concerning my feats of escape. It gradually dawned on me that the elder magic of Egypt did not depart without leaving traces, and that fragments of a strange secret lore and priestly cult-practices have survived surreptitiously amongst the fellaheen to such an extent that the prowess of a strange "hahwi" or magician is resented and disputed. I thought of how much my hollow-voiced guide Abdul Reis looked like an old Egyptian priest or Pharaoh or smiling Sphinx . . . and wondered.

Suddenly something happened which in a flash proved the correctness of my reflections and made me curse the denseness whereby I had accepted this night's events as other than the empty and malicious "frameup" they now shewed themselves to be. Without warning, and doubtless in answer to some subtle sign from Abdul, the entire band of Bedouins precipitated itself upon me; and having produced heavy ropes, soon had me bound as securely as I was ever bound in the course of my life, either on the stage or off. I struggled at first, but soon saw that one man could make no headway against a band of over twenty sinewy barbarians. My hands were tied behind my back, my knees bent to their fullest extent, and my wrists and ankles stoutly linked together with unyielding cords. A stifling gag was forced into my mouth, and a blindfold fastened tightly over my eyes. Then, as the Arabs bore me aloft on their shoulders and began a jouncing descent of the pyramid, I heard the taunts of my late guide Abdul, who mocked and jeered delightedly in his hollow voice, and assured me that I was soon to have my "magic powers" put to a supreme test which would quickly remove any egotism I might have gained through triumphing over all the tests offered by America and Europe. Egypt, he reminded me, is very old; and full of inner mysteries and antique powers not even conceivable to the experts of today, whose devices had so uniformly failed to entrap me.

How far or in what direction I was carried, I cannot

tell; for the circumstances were all against the formation of any accurate judgment. I know, however, that it could not have been a great distance; since my bearers at no point hastened beyond a walk, yet kept me aloft a surprisingly short time. It is this perplexing brevity which makes me feel almost like shuddering whenever I think of Gizeh and its plateau—for one is oppressed by hints of the closeness to every-day tourist routes of what existed then and must exist still.

The evil abnormality I speak of did not become manifest at first. Setting me down on a surface which I recognised as sand rather than rock, my captors passed a rope around my chest and dragged me a few feet to a ragged opening in the ground, into which they presently lowered me with much rough handling. For apparent aeons I bumped against the stony irregular sides of a narrow hewn well which I took to be one of the numerous burial shafts of the plateau until the prodigious, almost incredible depth of it robbed me of all bases of conjecture.

The horror of the experience deepened with every dragging second. That any descent through the sheer solid rock could be so vast without reaching the core of the planet itself, or that any rope made by man could be so long as to dangle me in these unholy and seemingly fathomless profundities of nether earth, were beliefs of such grotesqueness that it was easier to doubt my agitated senses than to accept them. Even now I am uncertain, for I know how deceitful the sense of time becomes when one or more of the usual perceptions or conditions of life is removed or distorted. But I am quite sure that I preserved a logical consciousness that far; that at least I did not add any full-grown phantoms of imagination to a picture hideous enough in its reality, and explicable by a type of cerebral illusion vastly short of actual hallucination.

All this was not the cause of my first bit of fainting. The shocking ordeal was cumulative, and the beginning of the later terrors was a very perceptible increase in my rate of descent. They were paying out that infinitely long rope very swiftly now, and I scraped cruelly against the rough and constricted sides of the shaft as I shot madly downward. My clothing was in tatters, and I felt the trickle of blood all over, even above the mounting and excruciating pain. My nostrils, too, were assailed by a scarcely definable menace; a creeping odour of damp and staleness curiously unlike anything I had ever smelt before, and having faint overtones of spice and incense that lent an element of mockery.

Then the mental cataclysm came. It was horrible— hideous beyond all articulate description because it was all of the soul, with nothing of detail to describe. It was the ecstasy of nightmare and the summation of the fiendish. The suddenness of it was apocalyptic and daemoniac—one moment I was plunging agonisingly down that narrow well of million-toothed torture, yet the next moment I was soaring on bat-wings in the gulfs of hell; swinging free and swoopingly through illimitable miles of boundless, musty space; rising dizzily to measureless pinnacles of chilling ether, then diving gaspingly to sucking nadirs of ravenous, nauseous lower vacua. . . . Thank God for the mercy that shut out in oblivion those clawing Furies of consciousness which half unhinged my faculties, and tore Harpy-like at my spirit! That one respite, short as it was, gave me the strength and sanity to endure those still greater sublimations of cosmic panic that lurked and gibbered on the road ahead.

II.

It was very gradually that I regained my senses after

that eldritch flight through Stygian space. The process was infinitely painful, and coloured by fantastic dreams in which my bound and gagged condition found singular embodiment. The precise nature of these dreams was very clear while I was experiencing them, but became blurred in my recollection almost immediately afterward, and was soon reduced to the merest outline by the terrible events— real or imaginary—which followed. I dreamed that I was in the grasp of a great and horrible paw; a yellow, hairy, five-clawed paw which had reached out of the earth to crush and engulf me. And when I stopped to reflect what the paw was, it seemed to me that it was Egypt. In the dream I looked back at the events of the preceding weeks, and saw myself lured and enmeshed little by little, subtly and insidiously, by some hellish ghoul-spirit of the elder Nile sorcery; some spirit that was in Egypt before ever man was, and that will be when man is no more.

I saw the horror and unwholesome antiquity of Egypt, and the grisly alliance it has always had with the tombs and temples of the dead. I saw phantom processions of priests with the heads of bulls, falcons, cats, and ibises; phantom processions marching interminably through subterraneous labyrinths and avenues of titanic propylaea beside which a man is as a fly, and offering unnamable sacrifices to indescribable gods. Stone colossi marched in endless night and drove herds of grinning androsphinxes down to the shores of illimitable stagnant rivers of pitch. And behind it all I saw the ineffable malignity of primordial necromancy, black and amorphous, and fumbling greedily after me in the darkness to choke out the spirit that had dared to mock it by emulation. In my sleeping brain there took shape a melodrama of sinister hatred and pursuit, and I saw the black soul of Egypt singling me out and calling me in inaudible whispers; calling and luring me, leading me on with the glitter and glamour of a Saracenic surface, but ever pulling me down to the age-mad catacombs and horrors of its dead and abysmal pharaonic heart.

Then the dream-faces took on human resemblances, and I saw my guide Abdul Reis in the robes of a king, with the sneer of the Sphinx on his features. And I knew that those features were the features of Khephren the Great, who raised the Second Pyramid, carved over the Sphinx's face in the likeness of his own, and built that titanic gateway temple whose myriad corridors the archaeologists think they have dug out of the cryptical sand and the uninformative rock. And I looked at the long, lean, rigid hand of Khephren; the long, lean, rigid hand as I had seen it on the diorite statue in the Cairo Museum—the statue they had found in the terrible gateway temple—and wondered that I had not shrieked when I saw it on Abdul Reis. . . . That hand! It was hideously cold, and it was crushing me; it was the cold and cramping of the sarcophagus . . . the chill and constriction of unrememberable Egypt. . . . It was nighted, necropolitan Egypt itself . . . that yellow paw . . . and they whisper such things of Khephren. . . .

But at this juncture I began to awake—or at least, to assume a condition less completely that of sleep than the one just preceding. I recalled the fight atop the pyramid, the treacherous Bedouins and their attack, my frightful descent by rope through endless rock depths, and my mad swinging and plunging in a chill void redolent of aromatic putrescence. I perceived that I now lay on a damp rock floor, and that my bonds were still biting into me with unloosened force. It was very cold, and I seemed to detect a faint current of noisome air sweeping across me. The cuts and bruises I had received from the jagged sides of the rock shaft were paining me woefully, their soreness enhanced to a stinging or burning acuteness by some pungent quality in the faint draught, and the mere act of rolling over was enough to set my whole frame throbbing with untold agony. As I turned I felt a tug from above, and concluded that the rope whereby I was lowered still reached to the surface. Whether or not the Arabs still held it, I had no idea; nor had I any idea how far within the earth I was. I knew that the darkness around me was wholly or nearly total, since no ray of moonlight penetrated my blindfold; but I did not trust my senses enough to accept as evidence of extreme depth the sensation of vast duration which had characterised my descent.

Knowing at least that I was in a space of considerable extent reached from the surface directly above by an opening in the rock, I doubtfully conjectured that my prison was perhaps the buried gateway chapel of old Khephren—the Temple of the Sphinx—perhaps some inner corridor which the guides had not shewn me during my morning visit, and from which I might easily escape if I could find my way to the barred entrance. It would be a labyrinthine wandering, but no worse than others out of which I had in the past found my way. The first step was to get free of my bonds, gag, and blindfold; and this I knew would be no great task, since subtler experts than these Arabs had tried every known species of fetter upon me during my long and varied career as an exponent of escape, yet had never succeeded in defeating my methods.

Then it occurred to me that the Arabs might be ready to meet and attack me at the entrance upon any evidence of my probable escape from the binding cords, as would be furnished by any decided agitation of the rope which they probably held. This, of course, was taking for granted that my place of confinement was indeed Khephren's Temple of the Sphinx. The direct opening in the roof, wherever it might lurk, could not be beyond easy reach of the ordinary modern entrance near the Sphinx; if in truth it were any great distance at all on the surface, since the total area known to visitors is not at all enormous. I had not noticed any such opening during my daytime pilgrimage, but knew that these things are easily overlooked amidst the drifting sands. Thinking these matters over as I lay bent and bound on the rock floor, I nearly forgot the horrors of the abysmal descent and cavernous swinging which had so lately reduced me to a coma. My present thought was only to outwit the Arabs, and I accordingly determined to work myself free as quickly as possible, avoiding any tug on the descending line which might betray an effective or even problematical attempt at freedom.

This, however, was more easily determined than effected. A few preliminary trials made it clear that little could be accomplished without considerable motion; and it did not surprise me when, after one especially energetic struggle, I began to feel the coils of falling rope as they piled up about me and upon me. Obviously, I thought, the Bedouins had felt my movements and released their end of the rope; hastening no doubt to the temple's true entrance to lie murderously in wait for me. The prospect was not pleasing—but I had faced worse in my time without flinching, and would not flinch now. At present I must first of all free myself of bonds, then trust to ingenuity to escape from the temple unharmed. It is curious how implicitly I had come to believe myself in the old temple of Khephren beside the Sphinx, only a short distance below the ground.

That belief was shattered, and every pristine apprehension of preternatural depth and daemoniac mystery re-

vived, by a circumstance which grew in horror and significance even as I formulated my philosophical plan. I have
said that the falling rope was piling up about and upon me.
Now I saw that it was *continuing to pile,* as no rope of normal length could possibly do. It gained in momentum and
became an avalanche of hemp, accumulating mountainous-
ly on the floor, and half burying me beneath its swiftly multiplying coils. Soon I was completely engulfed and gasping
for breath as the increasing convolutions submerged and stifled me. My senses tottered again, and I vainly tried to fight
off a menace desperate and ineluctable. It was not merely
that I was tortured beyond human endurance—not merely that life and breath seemed to be crushed slowly out of
me—it was the knowledge of *what those unnatural lengths
of rope implied,* and the consciousness of what unknown
and incalculable gulfs of inner earth must at this moment
be surrounding me. My endless descent and swinging flight
through goblin space, then, must have been real; and even
now I must be lying helpless in some nameless cavern world
toward the core of the planet. Such a sudden confirmation
of ultimate horror was insupportable, and a second time I
lapsed into merciful oblivion.

When I say oblivion, I do not imply that I was free
from dreams. On the contrary, my absence from the conscious world was marked by visions of the most unutterable
hideousness. God!... If only I had not read so much Egyptology before coming to this land which is the fountain of
all darkness and terror! This second spell of fainting filled
my sleeping mind anew with shivering realisation of the
country and its archaic secrets, and through some damnable chance my dreams turned to the ancient notions of the
dead and their sojournings in soul *and body* beyond those
mysterious tombs which were more houses than graves. I

recalled, in dream-shapes which it is well that I do not re-member, the peculiar and elaborate construction of Egyp-tian sepulchres; and the exceedingly singular and terrific doctrines which determined this construction.

All these people thought of was death and the dead. They conceived of a literal resurrection of the body which made them mummify it with desperate care, and preserve all the vital organs in canopic jars near the corpse; whilst besides the body they believed in two other elements, the soul, which after its weighing and approval by Osiris dwelt in the land of the blest, and the obscure and portentous *ka* or life-principle which wandered about the upper and lower worlds in a horrible way, demanding occasional ac-cess to the preserved body, consuming the food offerings brought by priests and pious relatives to the mortuary cha-pel, and sometimes—as men whispered—taking its body or the wooden double always buried beside it and stalking noxiously abroad on errands peculiarly repellent.

For thousands of years those bodies rested gorgeously encased and staring glassily upward when not visited by the *ka,* awaiting the day when Osiris should restore both *ka* and soul, and lead forth the stiff legions of the dead from the sunken houses of sleep. It was to have been a glorious re-birth—but not all souls were approved, nor were all tombs inviolate, so that certain grotesque *mistakes* and fiendish *abnormalities* were to be looked for. Even today the Arabs murmur of unsanctified convocations and unwholesome worship in forgotten nether abysses, which only winged invisible *kas* and soulless mummies may visit and return unscathed.

Perhaps the most leeringly blood-congealing legends are those which relate to certain perverse products of deca-dent priestcraft—*composite mummies* made by the artificial union of human trunks and limbs with the heads of animals in imitation of the elder gods.[34] At all stages of history the sacred animals were mummified, so that consecrated bulls, cats, ibises, crocodiles, and the like might return some day to greater glory. But only in the decadence did they mix the human and animal in the same mummy—only in the decadence, when they did not understand the rights and prerogatives of the *ka* and the soul. What happened to those composite mummies is not told of—at least publicly—and it is certain that no Egyptologist ever found one. The whispers of Arabs are very wild, and cannot be relied upon. They even hint that old Khephren—he of the Sphinx, the Second Pyramid, and the yawning gateway temple—lives far underground wedded to the ghoul-queen Nitokris and ruling over the mummies that are neither of man nor of beast.

It was of these—of Khephren and his consort and his strange armies of the hybrid dead—that I dreamed, and that is why I am glad the exact dream-shapes have faded from my memory. My most horrible vision was connected with an idle question I had asked myself the day before when looking at the great carven riddle of the desert and wondering with what unknown depths the temple so close to it might be secretly connected. That question, so innocent and whimsical then, assumed in my dream a meaning of frenetic and hysterical madness . . . *what huge and loathsome abnormality was the Sphinx originally carven to represent?*

My second awakening—if awakening it was—is a memory of stark hideousness which nothing else in my life—save one thing which came after—can parallel; and that life has been full and adventurous beyond most men's. Remember that I had lost consciousness whilst buried beneath a cascade of falling rope whose immensity revealed the cataclysmic depth of my present position. Now, as perception returned, I felt the entire weight gone; and realised upon rolling over that although I was still tied, gagged, and blindfolded, *some agency had removed completely the suffocating hempen landslide which had overwhelmed me.* The significance of this condition, of course, came to me only gradually; but even so I think it would have brought unconsciousness again had I not by this time reached such a state of emotional exhaustion that no new horror could make much difference. I was alone . . . with *what?*

Before I could torture myself with any new reflection, or make any fresh effort to escape from my bonds, an additional circumstance became manifest. Pains not formerly felt were racking my arms and legs, and I seemed coated with a profusion of dried blood beyond anything my former cuts and abrasions could furnish. My chest, too, seemed pierced by a hundred wounds, as though some malign, titanic ibis had been pecking at it. Assuredly the agency which had removed the rope was a hostile one, and had begun to wreak terrible injuries upon me when somehow impelled to desist. Yet at the time my sensations were distinctly the reverse of what one might expect. Instead of sinking into a bottomless pit of despair, I was stirred to a new courage and action; for now I felt that the evil forces were physical things which a fearless man might encounter on an even basis.

On the strength of this thought I tugged again at my bonds, and used all the art of a lifetime to free myself as I had so often done amidst the glare of lights and the applause of vast crowds. The familiar details of my escaping process commenced to engross me, and now that the long rope was gone I half regained my belief that the supreme horrors were hallucinations after all, and that there had never been any terrible shaft, measureless abyss, or interminable rope. Was I after all in the gateway temple of Khephren beside the Sphinx, and had the sneaking Arabs stolen in to torture me as I lay helpless there? At any rate, I must be free. Let me stand up unbound, ungagged, and with eyes open to catch any glimmer of light which might come trickling from any source, and I could actually delight in the combat against evil and treacherous foes!

How long I took in shaking off my encumbrances I cannot tell. It must have been longer than in my exhibition performances, because I was wounded, exhausted, and enervated by the experiences I had passed through. When I was finally free, and taking deep breaths of a chill, damp, evilly spiced air all the more horrible when encountered without the screen of gag and blindfold edges, I found that I was too cramped and fatigued to move at once. There I lay, trying to stretch a frame bent and mangled, for an indefinite period, and straining my eyes to catch a glimpse of some ray of light which would give a hint as to my position.

By degrees my strength and flexibility returned, but my eyes beheld nothing. As I staggered to my feet I peered diligently in every direction, yet met only an ebony blackness as great as that I had known when blindfolded. I tried my legs, blood-encrusted beneath my shredded trousers, and found that I could walk; yet could not decide in what direction to go. Obviously I ought not to walk at random, and perhaps retreat directly from the entrance I sought; so I paused to note the direction of the cold, foetid, natron-scented air-current which I had never ceased to feel. Accepting the point of its source as the possible entrance to the abyss, I strove to keep track of this landmark and to walk consistently toward it.

I had had a match box with me, and even a small electric flashlight; but of course the pockets of my tossed and tattered clothing were long since emptied of all heavy articles. As I walked cautiously in the blackness, the draught grew stronger and more offensive, till at length I could regard it as nothing less than a tangible stream of detestable vapour pouring out of some aperture like the smoke of the genie from the fisherman's jar in the Eastern tale. The East. .. Egypt... truly, this dark cradle of civilisation was ever the well-spring of horrors and marvels unspeakable! The more I reflected on the nature of this cavern wind, the greater my sense of disquiet became; for although despite its odour I had sought its source as at least an indirect clue to the outer world, I now saw plainly that this foul emanation could have no admixture or connexion whatsoever with the clean air of the Libyan Desert, but must be essentially a thing vomited from sinister gulfs still lower down. I had, then, been walking in the wrong direction!

After a moment's reflection I decided not to retrace my steps. Away from the draught I would have no landmarks, for the roughly level rock floor was devoid of distinctive configurations. If, however, I followed up the strange current, I would undoubtedly arrive at an aperture of some sort, from whose gate I could perhaps work round the walls to the opposite side of this Cyclopean and otherwise unnavigable hall. That I might fail, I well realised. I saw that this was no part of Khephren's gateway temple which tourists know, and it struck me that this particular hall might be unknown even to archaeologists, and merely stumbled upon by the inquisitive and malignant Arabs who had imprisoned me. If so, was there any present gate of escape to the known parts or to the outer air?

What evidence, indeed, did I now possess that this

was the gateway temple at all? For a moment all my wildest speculations rushed back upon me, and I thought of that vivid mélange of impressions—descent, suspension in space, the rope, my wounds, and the dreams that were frankly dreams. Was this the end of life for me? Or indeed, would it be merciful if this moment *were* the end? I could answer none of my own questions, but merely kept on till Fate for a third time reduced me to oblivion. This time there were no dreams, for the suddenness of the incident shocked me out of all thought either conscious or subconscious. Tripping on an unexpected descending step at a point where the offensive draught became strong enough to offer an actual physical resistance, I was precipitated headlong down a black flight of huge stone stairs into a gulf of hideousness unrelieved.

That I ever breathed again is a tribute to the inherent vitality of the healthy human organism. Often I look back to that night and feel a touch of actual *humour* in those repeated lapses of consciousness; lapses whose succession reminded me at the time of nothing more than the crude cinema melodramas of that period. Of course, it is possible that the repeated lapses never occurred; and that all the features of that underground nightmare were merely the dreams of one long coma which began with the shock of my descent into that abyss and ended with the healing balm of the outer air and of the rising sun which found me stretched on the sands of Gizeh before the sardonic and dawn-flushed face of the Great Sphinx.

I prefer to believe this latter explanation as much as I can, hence was glad when the police told me that the barrier to Khephren's gateway temple had been found unfastened, and that a sizeable rift to the surface did actually exist in one corner of the still buried part. I was glad, too, when the doctors pronounced my wounds only those to be expected from my seizure, blindfolding, lowering, struggling with bonds, falling some distance—perhaps into a depression in the temple's inner gallery—dragging myself to the outer barrier and escaping from it, and experiences like that . . . a very soothing diagnosis. And yet I know that there must be more than appears on the surface. That extreme descent is too vivid a memory to be dismissed—and it is odd that no one has ever been able to find a man answering the description of my guide Abdul Reis el Drogman—the tomb-throated guide who looked and smiled like King Khephren.

I have digressed from my connected narrative—perhaps in the vain hope of evading the telling of that final incident; that incident which of all is most certainly an hallucination. But I promised to relate it, and do not break promises. When I recovered—or seemed to recover—my senses after that fall down the black stone stairs, I was quite as alone and in darkness as before. The windy stench, bad enough before, was now fiendish; yet I had acquired enough familiarity by this time to bear it stoically. Dazedly I began to crawl away from the place whence the putrid wind came, and with my bleeding hands felt the colossal blocks of a mighty pavement. Once my head struck against a hard object, and when I felt of it I learned that it was the base of a column—a column of unbelievable immensity—whose surface was covered with gigantic chiselled hieroglyphics very perceptible to my touch. Crawling on, I encountered other titan columns at incomprehensible distances apart; when suddenly my attention was captured by the realisation of something which must have been impinging on my subconscious hearing long before the conscious sense was aware of it.

From some still lower chasm in earth's bowels were proceeding certain *sounds,* measured and definite, and like nothing I had ever heard before. That they were very ancient and distinctly ceremonial, I felt almost intuitively; and much reading in Egyptology led me to associate them with the flute, the sambuke, the sistrum, and the tympanum.[36] In their rhythmic piping, droning, rattling, and beating I felt an element of terror beyond all the known terrors of earth—a terror peculiarly dissociated from personal fear, and taking the form of a sort of objective pity for our planet, that it should hold within its depths such horrors as must lie beyond these aegipanic[37] cacophonies. The sounds increased in volume, and I felt that they were approaching. Then—and may all the gods of all pantheons unite to keep the like from my ears again—I began to hear, faintly and afar off, *the morbid and millennial tramping of the marching things.*

It was hideous that footfalls so *dissimilar* should move in such perfect rhythm. The training of unhallowed thousands of years must lie behind that march of earth's inmost monstrosities . . . padding, clicking, walking, stalking, rumbling, lumbering, crawling . . . and all to the abhorrent discords of those mocking instruments. And then . . . God keep the memory of those Arab legends out of my head! The mummies without souls . . . the meeting-place of the wandering *kas* . . . the hordes of the devil-cursed pharaonic dead of forty centuries . . . the *composite mummies* led through the uttermost onyx voids by King Khephren and his ghoul-queen Nitokris. . . .

The tramping drew nearer—heaven save me from the sound of those feet and paws and hooves and pads and talons as it commenced to acquire detail! Down limitless reaches of sunless pavement a spark of light flickered in the malodorous wind, and I drew behind the enormous circumference of a Cyclopic column that I might escape for a while the horror that was stalking million-footed toward me through gigantic hypostyles of inhuman dread and phobic antiquity. The flickers increased, and the tramping and dissonant rhythm grew sickeningly loud. In the quivering orange light there stood faintly forth a scene of such stony awe that I gasped from a sheer wonder that conquered even fear and repulsion. Bases of columns whose middles were higher than human sight . . . mere bases of things that must each dwarf the Eiffel Tower to insignificance . . . hieroglyphics carved by unthinkable hands in caverns where daylight can be only a remote legend. . . .

I *would not* look at the marching things. That I desperately resolved as I heard their creaking joints and nitrous wheezing above the dead music and the dead tramping. It was merciful that they did not speak . . . but God! *their crazy torches began to cast shadows on the surface of those stupendous columns.* Heaven take it away! *Hippopotami should not have human hands and carry torches . . . men should not have the heads of crocodiles. . . .*

I tried to turn away, but the shadows and the sounds and the stench were everywhere. Then I remembered something I used to do in half-conscious nightmares as a boy, and began to repeat to myself, "This is a dream! This is a dream!" But it was of no use, and I could only shut my eyes and pray . . . at least, that is what I think I did, for one is never sure in visions—and I know this can have been nothing more. I wondered whether I should ever reach the world again, and at times would furtively open my eyes to see if I could discern any feature of the place other than the wind of spiced putrefaction, the topless columns, and the thaumatropically[38] grotesque shadows of abnormal horror.

The sputtering glare of multiplying torches now shone, and unless this hellish place were wholly without walls, I could not fail to see some boundary or fixed landmark soon. But I had to shut my eyes again when I realised *how many* of the things were assembling—and when I glimpsed a certain object walking solemnly and steadily *without any body above the waist.*

A fiendish and ululant corpse-gurgle or death-rattle now split the very atmosphere—the charnel atmosphere poisonous with naphtha and bitumen blasts—in one concerted chorus from the ghoulish legion of hybrid blasphemies. My eyes, perversely shaken open, gazed for an instant upon a sight which no human creature could even imagine without panic fear and physical exhaustion. The things had filed ceremonially in one direction, the direction of the noisome wind, where the light of their torches shewed their bended heads . . . or the bended heads of such as had heads. . . . They were worshipping before a great black foetor-belching aperture which reached up almost out of sight, and which I could see was flanked at right angles by two giant staircases whose ends were far away in shadow. One of these was indubitably the staircase I had fallen down.

The dimensions of the hole were fully in proportion with those of the columns—an ordinary house would have been lost in it, and any average public building could easily have been moved in and out. It was so vast a surface that only by moving the eye could one trace its boundaries . . . so vast, so hideously black, and so aromatically stinking. . . . Directly in front of this yawning Polyphemus-door[39] the things were throwing objects—evidently sacrifices or religious offerings, to judge by their gestures. Khephren was their leader; sneering King Khephren *or the guide Abdul Reis,* crowned with a golden pshent and intoning endless formulae with the hollow voice of the dead. By his side knelt beautiful Queen Nitokris, whom I saw in profile for a moment, noting that the right half of her face was eaten away by rats or other ghouls. And I shut my eyes again when I saw *what* objects were being thrown as offerings to the foetid aperture or its possible local deity.

It occurred to me that judging from the elaborateness of this worship, the concealed deity must be one of considerable importance. Was it Osiris or Isis, Horus or Anubis,[40] or some vast unknown God of the Dead still more central and supreme? There is a legend that terrible altars and colossi were reared to an Unknown One before ever the known gods were worshipped. . . .

And now, as I steeled myself to watch the rapt and sepulchral adorations of those nameless things, a thought of escape flashed upon me. The hall was dim, and the columns heavy with shadow. With every creature of that nightmare throng absorbed in shocking raptures, it might be barely possible for me to creep past to the faraway end of one of the staircases and ascend unseen; trusting to Fate and skill to deliver me from the upper reaches. Where I was, I neither knew nor seriously reflected upon—and for a moment it struck me as amusing to plan a serious escape from that which I knew to be a dream. Was I in some hidden and unsuspected lower realm of Khephren's gateway temple— that temple which generations have persistently called the Temple of the Sphinx? I could not conjecture, but I resolved to ascend to life and consciousness if wit and muscle could carry me.

Wriggling flat on my stomach, I began the anxious journey toward the foot of the left-hand staircase, which seemed the more accessible of the two. I cannot describe the incidents and sensations of that crawl, but they may be guessed when one reflects on *what I had to watch steadily in that malign, wind-blown torchlight* in order to avoid detection. The bottom of the staircase was, as I have said, far away in shadow; as it had to be to rise without a bend to the dizzy parapeted landing above the titanic aperture. This placed the last stages of my crawl at some distance from the noisome herd, though the spectacle chilled me even when quite remote at my right.

At length I succeeded in reaching the steps and began to climb; keeping close to the wall, on which I observed decorations of the most hideous sort, and relying for safety on the absorbed, ecstatic interest with which the monstrosities watched the foul-breezed aperture and the impious objects of nourishment they had flung on the pavement before it. Though the staircase was huge and steep, fashioned of vast porphyry blocks as if for the feet of a giant, the ascent seemed virtually interminable. Dread of discovery and the pain which renewed exercise had brought to my wounds combined to make that upward crawl a thing of agonising memory. I had intended, on reaching the landing, to climb immediately onward along whatever upper staircase might mount from there; stopping for no last look at the carrion abominations that pawed and genuflected some seventy or eighty feet below—yet a sudden repetition of that thunderous corpse-gurgle and death-rattle chorus, coming as I had nearly gained the top of the flight and shewing by its ceremonial rhythm that it was not an alarm of my discovery, caused me to pause and peer cautiously over the parapet.

The monstrosities were hailing something which had poked itself out of the nauseous aperture to seize the hellish fare proffered it. It was something quite ponderous, even as seen from my height; something yellowish and hairy, and endowed with a sort of nervous motion. It was as large, perhaps, as a good-sized hippopotamus, but very curiously shaped. It seemed to have no neck, but five separate shaggy heads springing in a row from a roughly cylindrical trunk; the first very small, the second good-sized, the third and fourth equal and largest of all, and the fifth rather small, though not so small as the first. Out of these heads darted curious rigid tentacles which seized ravenously on the *excessively great* quantities of unmentionable food placed before the aperture. Once in a while the thing would leap up, and occasionally it would retreat into its den in a very odd manner. Its locomotion was so inexplicable that I stared in fascination, wishing it would emerge further from the cavernous lair beneath me.

Then it *did* emerge . . . it *did* emerge, and at the sight I turned and fled into the darkness up the higher staircase that rose behind me; fled unknowingly up incredible steps and ladders and inclined planes to which no human sight or logic guided me, and which I must ever relegate to the world of dreams for want of any confirmation. It must have been dream, or the dawn would never have found me breathing on the sands of Gizeh before the sardonic dawn-flushed face of the Great Sphinx.

The Great Sphinx! God!—that *idle question* I asked myself on that sun-blest morning before . . . *what huge and loathsome abnormality was the Sphinx originally carven to represent?* Accursed is the sight, be it in dream or not, that revealed to me the supreme horror—the Unknown God of the Dead, which licks its colossal chops in the unsuspected abyss, fed hideous morsels by soulless absurdities that should not exist. The five-headed monster that emerged . . . that five-headed monster as large as a hippopotamus . . . the five-headed monster—*and that of which it is the merest fore paw.* . . .[41]

But I survived, and I know it was only a dream.[42]

Two Black Bottles

With Wilfred Blanch Talman

ot all of the few remaining inhabitants of Daalbergen, that dismal little village in the Ramapo Mountains,[1] believe that my uncle, old Dominie[2] Vanderhoof, is really dead. Some of them believe he is suspended somewhere between heaven and hell because of the old sexton's curse. If it had not been for that old magician, he might still be preaching in the little damp church across the moor.

After what has happened to me in Daalbergen, I can almost share the opinion of the villagers. I am not sure that my uncle is dead, but I am very sure that he is not alive upon this earth. There is no doubt that the old sexton buried him once, but he is not in that grave now. I can almost feel him behind me as I write, impelling me to tell the truth about those strange happenings in Daalbergen so many years ago.

It was the fourth day of October when I arrived at Daalbergen in answer to a summons. The letter was from a former member of my uncle's congregation, who wrote that the old man had passed away and that there should be some small estate which I, as his only living relative, might inherit. Having reached the secluded little hamlet by a wearying series of changes on branch railways, I found my way to the grocery store of Mark Haines, writer of the letter, and he, leading me into a stuffy back room, told me a peculiar tale concerning Dominie Vanderhoof's death.

"Y' should be careful, Hoffman," Haines told me, "when y' meet that old sexton, Abel Foster. He's in league with the devil, sure's you're alive. 'Twa'n't two weeks ago Sam Pryor, when he passed the old graveyard, heared him mumblin' t' the dead there. 'Twa'n't right he should talk that way—an' Sam does vow that there was a voice answered him—a kind o' half-voice, hollow and muffled-like, as though it come out o' th' ground. There's others, too, as could tell y' about seein' him standin' afore old Dominie Slott's grave—that one right agin' the church wall—a-wringin' his hands an' a-talkin' t' th' moss on th' tombstone as though it was the old Dominie himself."

Old Foster, Haines said, had come to Daalbergen about ten years before, and had been immediately engaged by Vanderhoof to take care of the damp stone church at which most of the villagers worshipped. No one but Vanderhoof seemed to like him, for his presence brought a suggestion almost of the uncanny. He would sometimes stand by the door when the people came to church, and the men would coldly return his servile bow while the women brushed past in haste, holding their skirts aside to avoid touching him. He could be seen on week days cutting the grass in the cemetery and tending the flowers around the graves, now and then crooning and muttering to himself. And few failed to notice the particular attention he paid to the grave of the Reverend Guilliam Slott, first pastor of the church in 1701.

It was not long after Foster's establishment as a village fixture that disaster began to lower. First came the failure of the mountain mine where most of the men worked. The vein of iron had given out, and many of the people moved away to better localities, while those who had large holdings of land in the vicinity took to farming and managed to wrest a meager living from the rocky hillsides. Then came the disturbances in the church. It was whispered about that the Reverend Johannes Vanderhoof had made a compact with the devil, and was preaching his word in the house of God. His sermons had become weird and grotesque— redolent with sinister things which the ignorant people of Daalbergen did not understand. He transported them back over ages of fear and superstition to regions of hideous, unseen spirits, and peopled their fancy with night-haunting ghouls. One by one the congregation dwindled, while the elders and deacons vainly pleaded with Vanderhoof to change the subject of his sermons. Though the old man continually promised to comply, he seemed to be enthralled by some higher power which forced him to do its will.

A giant in stature, Johannes Vanderhoof was known to be weak and timid at heart, yet even when threatened with expulsion he continued his eerie sermons, until scarcely a handful of people remained to listen to him on Sunday morning. Because of weak finances, it was found impossible to call a new pastor, and before long not one of the villagers dared venture near the church or the parsonage which adjoined it. Everywhere there was fear of those spectral wraiths with whom Vanderhoof was apparently in league.

My uncle, Mark Haines told me, had continued to live

in the parsonage because there was no one with sufficient courage to tell him to move out of it. No one ever saw him again, but lights were visible in the parsonage at night, and were even glimpsed in the church from time to time. It was whispered about the town that Vanderhoof preached regularly in the church every Sunday morning, unaware that his congregation was no longer there to listen. He had only the old sexton, who lived in the basement of the church, to take care of him, and Foster made a weekly visit to what remained of the business section of the village to buy provisions. He no longer bowed servilely to everyone he met, but instead seemed to harbor a demoniac and ill-concealed hatred. He spoke to no one except as was necessary to make his purchases, and glanced from left to right out of evil-filled eyes as he walked the street with his cane tapping the uneven pavements. Bent and shriveled with extreme age, his presence could actually be felt by anyone near him, so powerful was that personality which, said the townspeople, had made Vanderhoof accept the devil as his master. No person in Daalbergen doubted that Abel Foster was at the bottom of all the town's ill luck, but not a one dared lift a finger against him, or could even approach him without a tremor of fear. His name, as well as Vanderhoof's, was never mentioned aloud. Whenever the matter of the church across the moor was discussed, it was in whispers; and if the conversation chanced to be nocturnal, the whisperers would keep glancing over their shoulders to make sure that nothing shapeless or sinister crept out of the darkness to bear witness to their words.

The churchyard continued to be kept just as green and beautiful as when the church was in use, and the flowers near the graves in the cemetery were tended just as carefully as in times gone by. The old sexton could occasionally be seen working there, as if still being paid for his services, and those who dared venture near said that he maintained a continual conversation with the devil and with those spirits which lurked within the graveyard walls.

One morning, Haines went on to say, Foster was seen digging a grave where the steeple of the church throws its shadow in the afternoon, before the sun goes down behind the mountain and puts the entire village in semi-twilight. Later, the church bell, silent for months, tolled solemnly for a half-hour. And at sundown those who were watching from a distance saw Foster bring a coffin from the parsonage on a wheelbarrow, dump it into the grave with slender ceremony, and replace the earth in the hole.

The sexton came to the village the next morning, ahead of his usual weekly schedule, and in much better spirits than was customary. He seemed willing to talk, remarking that Vanderhoof had died the day before, and that he had buried his body beside that of Dominie Slott near the church wall. He smiled from time to time, and rubbed his hands in an untimely and unaccountable glee. It was apparent that he took a perverse and diabolic delight in Vanderhoof's death. The villagers were conscious of an added uncanniness in his presence, and avoided him as much as they could. With Vanderhoof gone they felt more insecure than ever, for the old sexton was now free to cast his worst spells over the town from the church across the moor. Muttering something in a tongue which no one understood, Foster made his way back along the road over the swamp.

It was then, it seems, that Mark Haines remembered having heard Dominie Vanderhoof speak of me as his nephew. Haines accordingly sent for me, in the hope that I might know something which would clear up the mystery of my uncle's last years. I assured my summoner, however, that I knew nothing about my uncle or his past, except that my mother had mentioned him as a man of gigantic physique but with little courage or power of will.

Having heard all that Haines had to tell me, I lowered the front legs of my chair to the floor and looked at my watch. It was late afternoon.

"How far is it out to the church?" I inquired. "Think I can make it before sunset?"

"Sure, lad, y' ain't goin' out there t'night! Not t' that place!" The old man trembled noticeably in every limb and half rose from his chair, stretching out a lean, detaining hand. "Why, it's plumb foolishness!" he exclaimed.

I laughed aside his fears and informed him that, come what may, I was determined to see the old sexton that evening and get the whole matter over as soon as possible. I did not intend to accept the superstitions of ignorant country folk as truth, for I was convinced that all I had just heard was merely a chain of events which the over-imaginative people of Daalbergen had happened to link with their ill-luck. I felt no sense of fear or horror whatever.

Seeing that I was determined to reach my uncle's house before nightfall, Haines ushered me out of his office and reluctantly gave me the few required directions, pleading from time to time that I change my mind. He shook my hand when I left, as though he never expected to see me again.

"Take keer that old devil, Foster, don't git ye!" he warned, again and again. "I wouldn't go near him after dark fer love n'r money. No siree!" He re-entered his store, solemnly shaking his head, while I set out along a road leading to the outskirts of the town.

I had walked barely two minutes before I sighted the moor of which Haines had spoken. The road, flanked by a whitewashed fence, passed over the great swamp, which was overgrown with clumps of underbrush dipping down into the dank, slimy ooze. An odor of deadness and decay filled the air, and even in the sunlit afternoon little wisps of vapor could be seen rising from the unhealthful spot.

On the opposite side of the moor I turned sharply to the left, as I had been directed, branching from the main road. There were several houses in the vicinity, I noticed; houses which were scarcely more than huts, reflecting the extreme poverty of their owners. The road here passed under the drooping branches of enormous willows which almost completely shut out the rays of the sun. The miasmal odor of the swamp was still in my nostrils, and the air was damp and chilly. I hurried my pace to get out of that dismal tunnel as soon as possible.

Presently I found myself in the light again. The sun, now hanging like a red ball upon the crest of the mountain, was beginning to dip low, and there, some distance ahead of me, bathed in its bloody iridescence, stood the lonely church. I began to sense that uncanniness which Haines had mentioned; that feeling of dread which made all Daalbergen shun the place. The squat, stone hulk of the church itself, with its blunt steeple, seemed like an idol to which the tombstones that surrounded it bowed down and worshipped, each with an arched top like the shoulders of a kneeling person, while over the whole assemblage the dingy, gray parsonage hovered like a wraith.

I had slowed my pace a trifle as I took in the scene. The sun was disappearing behind the mountain very rapidly now, and the damp air chilled me. Turning my coat collar up about my neck, I plodded on. Something caught my eye as I glanced up again. In the shadow of the church wall was something white—a thing which seemed to have no definite shape. Straining my eyes as I came nearer, I saw that it was a cross of new timber, surmounting a mound of freshly turned earth. The discovery sent a new chill through me. I realized that this must be my uncle's grave, but something told me that it was not like the other graves near it. It did not seem like a *dead* grave. In some intangible way it appeared to be *living,* if a grave can be said to live. Very close to it, I saw as I came nearer, was another grave; an old mound with a crumbling stone about it. Dominie Slott's tomb, I thought, remembering Haines's story.

There was no sign of life anywhere about the place. In the semi-twilight I climbed the low knoll upon which the parsonage stood, and hammered upon the door. There was no answer. I skirted the house and peered into the windows. The whole place seemed deserted.

The lowering mountains had made night fall with disarming suddenness the minute the sun was fully hidden. I realized that I could see scarcely more than a few feet ahead of me. Feeling my way carefully, I rounded a corner of the house and paused, wondering what to do next.

Everything was quiet. There was not a breath of wind, nor were there even the usual noises made by animals in their nocturnal ramblings. All dread had been forgotten for a time, but in the presence of that sepulchral calm my apprehensions returned. I imagined the air peopled with ghastly spirits that pressed around me, making the air almost unbreathable. I wondered, for the hundredth time, where the old sexton might be.

As I stood there, half expecting some sinister demon to creep from the shadows, I noticed two lighted windows glaring from the belfry of the church. I then remembered what Haines had told me about Foster's living in the basement of the building. Advancing cautiously through the blackness, I found a side door of the church ajar.

The interior had a musty and mildewed odor. Everything I touched was covered with a cold, clammy moisture. I struck a match and began to explore, to discover, if I could, how to get into the belfry. Suddenly I stopped in my tracks.

A snatch of song, loud and obscene, sung in a voice that was guttural and thick with drink, came from above me. The match burned my fingers, and I dropped it. Two pin-points of light pierced the darkness of the farther wall of the church, and below them, to one side, I could see a door outlined where light filtered through its cracks. The song stopped as abruptly as it had commenced, and there was absolute silence again. My heart was thumping and blood racing through my temples. Had I not been petrified with fear, I should have fled immediately.

Not caring to light another match, I felt my way among the pews until I stood in front of the door. So deep was the feeling of depression which had come over me that I felt as though I were acting in a dream. My actions were almost involuntary.

The door was locked, as I found when I turned the knob. I hammered upon it for some time, but there was no answer. The silence was as complete as before. Feeling around the edge of the door, I found the hinges, removed the pins from them, and allowed the door to fall toward me. Dim light flooded down a steep flight of steps. There was a sickening odor of whisky. I could now hear someone stirring in the belfry room above. Venturing a low halloo, I thought I heard a groan in reply, and cautiously climbed the stairs.

My first glance into that unhallowed place was indeed startling. Strewn about the little room were old and dusty books and manuscripts—strange things that bespoke almost unbelievable age. On rows of shelves which reached to the ceiling were horrible things in glass jars and bottles—snakes and lizards and bats. Dust and mold and cobwebs encrusted everything. In the center, behind a table upon which was a lighted candle, a nearly empty bottle of whisky, and a glass, was a motionless figure with a thin, scrawny, wrinkled face and wild eyes that stared blankly through me. I recognized Abel Foster, the old sexton, in an instant. He did not move or speak as I came slowly and fearfully toward him.

"Mr. Foster?" I asked, trembling with unaccountable fear when I heard my voice echo within the close confines of the room. There was no reply, and no movement from the figure behind the table. I wondered if he had not drunk himself to insensibility, and went behind the table to shake him.

At the mere touch of my arm upon his shoulder, the strange old man started from his chair as though terrified. His eyes, still having in them that same blank stare, were fixed upon me. Swinging his arms like flails, he backed away.

"Don't!" he screamed. "Don't touch me! Go back—go back!"

I saw that he was both drunk and struck with some kind of a nameless terror. Using a soothing tone, I told him who I was and why I had come. He seemed to understand vaguely and sank back into his chair, sitting limp and motionless.

"I thought ye was him," he mumbled. "I thought ye was him come back fer it. He's been a-tryin' t' get out—a-tryin' t' get out sence I put him in there." His voice again rose to a scream and he clutched his chair. "Maybe he's got out now! Maybe he's out!"

I looked about, half expecting to see some spectral

shape coming up the stairs.

"Maybe who's out?" I inquired.

"Vanderhoof!" he shrieked. "Th' cross over his grave keeps fallin' down in th' night! Every morning the earth is loose, and gets harder t' pat down. He'll come out an' I won't be able t' do nothin.'"

Forcing him back into the chair, I seated myself on a box near him. He was trembling in mortal terror, with the saliva dripping from the corners of his mouth. From time to time I felt that sense of horror which Haines had described when he told me of the old sexton. Truly, there was something uncanny about the man. His head had now sunk forward upon his breast, and he seemed calmer, mumbling to himself.

I quietly arose and opened a window to let out the fumes of whisky and the musty odor of dead things. Light from a dim moon, just risen, made objects below barely visible. I could just see Dominie Vanderhoof's grave from my position in the belfry, and blinked my eyes as I gazed at it. That cross *was* tilted! I remembered that it had been vertical an hour ago. Fear took possession of me again. I turned quickly. Foster sat in his chair watching me. His glance was saner than before.

"So ye're Vanderhoof's nephew," he mumbled in a nasal tone. "Waal, ye might's well know it all. He'll be back arter me afore long, he will—jus' as soon as he can get out o' that there grave. Ye might's well know all about it now."

His terror appeared to have left him. He seemed resigned to some horrible fate which he expected any minute. His head dropped down upon his chest again, and he went on muttering in that nasal monotone.

"Ye see all them there books and papers? Waal, they was once Dominie Slott's—Dominie Slott, who was here years ago. All them things is got t' do with magic—black magic that th' old Dominie knew afore he come t' this country. They used t' burn 'em an' boil 'em in oil fer knowin' that over there, they did. But old Slott knew, and he didn't go fer t' tell nobody. No sir, old Slott used to preach here generations ago, an' he used to come up here an' study them books, an' use all them dead things in jars, an' pronounce magic curses an' things, but he didn't let nobody know it. No, nobody knowed it but Dominie Slott an' me."

"You?" I ejaculated, leaning across the table toward him.

"That is, me after I learned it." His face showed lines of trickery as he answered me. "I found all this stuff here when I come t' be church sexton, an' I used t' read it when I wa'n't at work. An' I soon got t' know all about it."

The old man droned on, while I listened, spellbound. He told about learning the difficult formulae of demonology, so that, by means of incantations, he could cast spells over human beings. He had performed horrible occult rites of his hellish creed, calling down anathema upon the town and its inhabitants. Crazed by his desires, he tried to bring the church under his spell, but the power of God was too strong. Finding Johannes Vanderhoof very weak-willed, he bewitched him so that he preached strange and mystic sermons which struck fear into the simple hearts of the country folk. From his position in the belfry room, he said, behind a painting of the temptation of Christ which adorned the rear wall of the church, he would glare at Vanderhoof while he was preaching, through holes which were the eyes of the Devil in the picture. Terrified by the uncanny things which were happening in their midst, the congregation left one by one, and Foster was able to do what he pleased with the church and with Vanderhoof.

"But what did you do with him?" I asked in a hollow voice as the old sexton paused in his confession. He burst into a cackle of laughter, throwing back his head in drunken glee.

"I took his soul!" he howled in a tone that set me trembling. "I took his soul and put it in a bottle—in a little black bottle! And I buried him! But he ain't got his soul, an' he cain't go neither t' heaven n'r hell! But he's a-comin' back after it. He's a-tryin' t' get out o' his grave now. I can hear him pushin' his way up through the ground, he's that strong!"

As the old man had proceeded with his story, I had become more and more convinced that he must be telling me the truth, and not merely gibbering in drunkenness. Every detail fitted what Haines had told me. Fear was growing upon me by degrees. With the old wizard now shouting with demoniac laughter, I was tempted to bolt down the narrow stairway and leave that accursed neighborhood. To calm myself, I rose and again looked out of the window. My eyes nearly started from their sockets when I saw that the cross above Vanderhoof's grave had fallen perceptibly since I had last looked at it. It was now tilted to an angle of forty-five degrees!

"Can't we dig up Vanderhoof and restore his soul?" I asked almost breathlessly, feeling that something must be done in a hurry. The old man rose from his chair in terror.

"No, no, no!" he screamed. "He'd kill me! I've fergot th' formula, an' if he gets out he'll be alive, without a soul. He'd kill us both!"

"Where is the bottle that contains his soul?" I asked, advancing threateningly toward him. I felt that some ghastly thing was about to happen, which I must do all in my power to prevent.

"I won't tell ye, ye young whelp!" he snarled. I felt, rather than saw, a queer light in his eyes as he backed into a corner. "An' don't ye touch me, either, or ye'll wish ye hadn't!"

I moved a step forward, noticing that on a low stool behind him there were two black bottles. Foster muttered some peculiar words in a low, singsong voice. Everything began to turn gray before my eyes, and something within me seemed to be dragged upward, trying to get out at my throat. I felt my knees become weak.

Lurching forward, I caught the old sexton by the throat, and with my free arm reached for the bottles on the stool. But the old man fell backward, striking the stool with his foot, and one bottle fell to the floor as I snatched the other. There was a flash of blue flame, and a sulfurous smell filled the room. From the little heap of broken glass a white vapor rose and followed the draft out the window.

"Curse ye, ye rascal!" sounded a voice that seemed faint and far away. Foster, whom I had released when the bottle broke, was crouching against the wall, looking smaller and more shriveled than before. His face was slowly turning greenish-black.

"Curse ye!" said the voice again, hardly sounding as though it came from his lips. "I'm done fer! That one in there was mine! *Dominie Slott took it out two hundred years ago!*"

He slid slowly toward the floor, gazing at me with hatred in eyes that were rapidly dimming. His flesh changed from white to black, and then to yellow. I saw with horror that his body seemed to be crumbling away and his clothing falling into limp folds.

The bottle in my hand was growing warm. I glanced at it, fearfully. It glowed with a faint phosphorescence. Stiff with fright, I set it upon the table, but could not keep my eyes from it. There was an ominous moment of silence as its glow became brighter, and then there came distinctly to my ears the sound of sliding earth. Gasping for breath, I looked out of the window. The moon was now well up in the sky, and by its light I could see that the fresh cross above Vanderhoof's grave had completely fallen. Once again there came the sound of trickling gravel, and no longer able to control myself, I stumbled down the stairs and found my way out of doors. Falling now and then as I raced over the uneven ground, I ran on in abject terror. When I had reached the foot of the knoll, at the entrance to that gloomy tunnel beneath the willows, I heard a horrible roar behind me. Turning, I glanced back toward the church. Its wall reflected the light of the moon, and silhouetted against it was a gigantic, loathsome, black shadow climbing from my uncle's grave and floundering gruesomely toward the church.

I told my story to a group of villagers in Haines's store the next morning. They looked from one to the other with little smiles during my tale, I noticed, but when I suggested that they accompany me to the spot, gave various excuses for not caring to go. Though there seemed to be a limit to their credulity, they cared to run no risks. I informed them that I would go alone, though I must confess that the project did not appeal to me.

As I left the store, one old man with a long, white beard hurried after me and caught my arm.

"I'll go wi' ye, lad," he said. "It do seem that I once heared my gran'pap tell o' su'thin' o' the sort concernin' old Dominie Slott. A queer old man I've heared he were, but Vanderhoof's been worse."

Dominie Vanderhoof's grave was open and deserted when we arrived. Of course it could have been grave-robbers, the two of us agreed, and yet. . . . In the belfry the bottle which I had left upon the table was gone, though the fragments of the broken one were found on the floor. And upon the heap of yellow dust and crumpled clothing that had once been Abel Foster were certain immense footprints.

After glancing at some of the books and papers strewn about the belfry room, we carried them down the stairs and burned them, as something unclean and unholy. With a spade which we found in the church basement we filled in the grave of Johannes Vanderhoof, and, as an afterthought, flung the fallen cross upon the flames.

Old wives say that now, when the moon is full, there walks about the churchyard a gigantic and bewildered figure clutching a bottle and seeking some unremembered goal.

The Last Test

With Adolphe de Castro

I.

Few persons know the inside of the Clarendon story, or even that there is an inside not reached by the newspapers. It was a San Francisco sensation in the days before the fire, both because of the panic and menace that kept it company, and because of its close linkage with the governor of the state. Governor Dalton, it will be recalled, was Clarendon's best friend, and later married his sister. Neither Dalton nor Mrs. Dalton would ever discuss the painful affair, but somehow the facts have leaked out to a limited circle. But for that, and for the years which have given a sort of vagueness and impersonality to the actors, one would still pause before probing into secrets so strictly guarded at the time.

The appointment of Dr. Alfred Clarendon as medical director of San Quentin Penitentiary[1] in 189- was greeted with the keenest enthusiasm throughout California. San Francisco had at last the honour of harbouring one of the greatest biologists and physicians of the period, and solid pathological leaders from all over the world might be expected to flock thither to study his methods, profit by his advice and researches, and learn how to cope with their own local problems. California, almost over night, would become a centre of medical scholarship with earthwide influence and reputation.

Governor Dalton, anxious to spread the news in its fullest significance, saw to it that the press carried ample and dignified accounts of his new appointee. Pictures of Dr. Clarendon and his new home near old Goat Hill,[2] sketches of his career and manifold honours, and popular accounts of his salient scientific discoveries were all presented in the principal California dailies, till the public soon felt a sort of reflected pride in the man whose studies of pyemia[3] in India, of the pest[4] in China, and of every sort of kindred disorder elsewhere would soon enrich the world of medicine with an antitoxin of revolutionary importance—a basic antitoxin combating the whole febrile principle at its very source, and ensuring the ultimate conquest and extirpation of fever in all its diverse forms.

Back of the appointment stretched an extended and not wholly unromantic history of early friendship, long separation, and dramatically renewed acquaintance. James Dalton and the Clarendon family had been friends in New York ten years before—friends and more than friends, since the doctor's only sister, Georgina, was the sweetheart of Dalton's youth, while the doctor himself had been his closest associate and almost his protégé in the days of school and college. The father of Alfred and Georgina, a Wall Street pirate of the ruthless elder breed, had known Dalton's father well; so well, indeed, that he had finally stripped him of all he possessed in a memorable afternoon's fight on the stock exchange. Dalton Senior, hopeless of recuperation and wishing to give his one adored child the benefit of his insurance, had promptly blown out his brains; but James had not sought to retaliate. It was, as he viewed it, all in the game; and he wished no harm to the father of the girl he meant to marry and of the budding young scientist whose admirer and protector he had been throughout their years of fellowship and study. Instead, he turned to the law, established himself in a small way, and in due course of time asked "Old Clarendon" for Georgina's hand.

Old Clarendon had refused very firmly and loudly, vowing that no pauper and upstart lawyer was fit to be his son-in-law; and a scene of considerable violence had occurred. James, telling the wrinkled freebooter at last what he ought to have been told long before, had left the house and the city in a high temper; and was embarked within a month upon the California life which was to lead him to the governorship through many a fight with ring and politician. His farewells to Alfred and Georgina had been brief, and he had never known the aftermath of that scene in the Clarendon library. Only by a day did he miss the news of Old Clarendon's death from apoplexy, and by so missing it, changed the course of his whole career. He had not written Georgina in the decade that followed; knowing her loyalty to her father, and waiting till his own fortune and position might remove all obstacles to the match. Nor had he sent any word to Alfred, whose calm indifference in the face of affection and hero-worship had always savoured of conscious destiny and the self-sufficiency of genius. Secure in the ties of a constancy rare even then, he had worked and risen with thoughts only of the future; still a bachelor, and with a perfect intuitive faith that Georgina also was waiting.

In this faith Dalton was not deceived. Wondering perhaps why no message ever came, Georgina found no romance save in her dreams and expectations; and in the course of time became busy with the new responsibilities brought by her brother's rise to greatness. Alfred's growth had not belied the promise of his youth, and the slim boy had darted quietly up the steps of science with a speed and permanence almost dizzying to contemplate. Lean and ascetic, with steel-rimmed pince-nez and pointed brown beard, Dr. Alfred Clarendon was an authority at twenty-five and an international figure at thirty. Careless of worldly affairs with the negligence of genius, he depended vastly on the care and management of his sister, and was secretly thankful that her memories of James had kept her from other and more tangible alliances.

Georgina conducted the business and household of the great bacteriologist, and was proud of his strides toward the conquest of fever. She bore patiently with his eccentricities, calmed his occasional bursts of fanaticism, and healed those breaches with his friends which now and then resulted from his unconcealed scorn of anything less than a single-minded devotion to pure truth and its progress. Clarendon was undeniably irritating at times to ordinary folk; for he never tired of depreciating the service of the individual as contrasted with the service of mankind as a whole, and in censuring men of learning who mingled domestic life or outside interests with their pursuit of abstract science. His enemies called him a bore; but his admirers, pausing before the white heat of ecstasy into which he would work himself, became almost ashamed of ever having any standards or aspirations outside the one divine sphere of unalloyed knowledge.

The doctor's travels were extensive and Georgina generally accompanied him on the shorter ones. Three times, however, he had taken long, lone jaunts to strange and distant places in his studies of exotic fevers and half-fabulous plagues; for he knew that it is out of the unknown lands of cryptic and immemorial Asia that most of the earth's diseases spring. On each of these occasions he had brought back curious mementoes which added to the eccentricity of his home, not least among which was the needlessly large staff of Thibetan servants picked up somewhere in U-tsang[5] during an epidemic of which the world never heard, but amidst which Clarendon had discovered and isolated the germ of black fever.[6] These men, taller than most Thibetans and clearly belonging to a stock but little investigated in the outside world, were of a skeletonic leanness which made one wonder whether the doctor had sought to symbolise in them the anatomical models of his college years. Their aspect, in the loose black silk robes of Bonpa[7] priests which he chose to give them, was grotesque in the highest degree; and there was an unsmiling silence and stiffness in their motions which enhanced their air of fantasy and gave Georgina a queer, awed feeling of having stumbled into the pages of *Vathek* or the *Arabian Nights*.[8]

But queerest of all was the general factotum or clinic-man, whom Clarendon addressed as Surama, and whom he had brought back with him after a long stay in Northern Africa, during which he had studied certain odd intermittent fevers among the mysterious Saharan Tuaregs, whose descent from the primal race of lost Atlantis is an old archaeological rumour.[9] Surama, a man of great intelligence and seemingly inexhaustible erudition, was as morbidly lean as the Thibetan servants; with swarthy, parchment-like skin drawn so tightly over his bald pate and hairless face that every line of the skull stood out in ghastly prominence—this death's-head effect being heightened by lustrelessly burning black eyes set with a depth which left to common visibility only a pair of dark, vacant sockets. Unlike the ideal subordinate, he seemed despite his impassive features to spend no effort in concealing such emotions as he possessed. Instead, he carried about an insidious atmosphere of irony or amusement, accompanied at certain moments by a deep, guttural chuckle like that of a giant turtle which has just torn to pieces some furry animal and is ambling away toward the sea. His race appeared to be Caucasian, but could not be classified more closely than that. Some of Clarendon's friends thought he looked like a high-caste Hindoo notwithstanding his accentless speech, while many agreed with Georgina—who disliked him—when she gave her opinion that a Pharaoh's mummy, if miraculously brought to life, would form a very apt twin for this sardonic skeleton.

Dalton, absorbed in his uphill political battles and isolated from Eastern interests through the peculiar self-sufficiency of the old West, had not followed the meteoric rise of his former comrade; Clarendon had actually heard nothing of one so far outside his chosen world of science as the governor. Being of independent and even of abundant means, the Clarendons had for many years stuck to their old Manhattan mansion in East Nineteenth Street, whose ghosts must have looked sorely askance at the bizarrerie of Surama and the Thibetans. Then, through the doctor's wish to transfer his base of medical observation, the great change had suddenly come, and they had crossed the continent to take up a secluded life in San Francisco; buying the gloomy old Bannister place near Goat Hill, overlooking the bay, and establishing their strange household in a rambling, French-roofed relic of mid-Victorian design and gold-rush parvenu display, set amidst high-walled grounds in a region still half suburban.

Dr. Clarendon, though better satisfied than in New York, still felt cramped for lack of opportunities to apply and test his pathological theories. Unworldly as he was, he had never thought of using his reputation as an influence to gain public appointment; though more and more he realised that only the medical directorship of a government or a charitable institution—a prison, almshouse, or hospital—would give him a field of sufficient width to complete his researches and make his discoveries of the greatest use to humanity and science at large.

Then he had run into James Dalton by sheer accident one afternoon in Market Street as the governor was swinging out of the Royal Hotel.[10] Georgina had been with him, and an almost instant recognition had heightened the drama of the reunion. Mutual ignorance of one another's progress had bred long explanation and histories, and Clarendon was pleased to find that he had so important an official for a friend. Dalton and Georgina, exchanging many a glance, felt more than a trace of their youthful tenderness; and a friendship was then and there revived which led to frequent calls and a fuller and fuller exchange of confidences.

James Dalton learned of his old protégé's need for political appointment, and sought, true to his protective role of school and college days, to devise some means of giving "Little Alf" the needed position and scope. He had, it is true, wide appointive powers; but the legislature's constant attacks and encroachments forced him to exercise these with the utmost discretion. At length, however, scarcely three months after the sudden reunion, the foremost institutional medical office in the state fell vacant. Weighing all the elements with care, and conscious that his friend's achievements and reputation would justify the most substantial rewards, the governor felt at last able to act. Formalities were few, and on the eighth of November, 189-, Dr. Alfred Schuyler Clarendon became medical director of the California State Penitentiary at San Quentin.

II.

In scarcely more than a month the hopes of Dr. Clarendon's admirers were amply fulfilled. Sweeping changes in methods brought to the prison's medical routine an efficiency never before dreamed of; and though the subordinates were naturally not without jealousy, they were obliged to admit the magical results of a really great man's superintendence. Then came a time where mere appreciation might well have grown to devout thankfulness at a providential conjunction of time, place, and man; for one morning Dr. Jones came to his new chief with a grave face to announce his discovery of a case which he could not but identify as that selfsame black fever whose germ Clarendon had found and classified.

Dr. Clarendon shewed no surprise, but kept on at the writing before him.

"I know," he said evenly; "I came across that case yesterday. I'm glad you recognised it. Put the man in a separate ward, though I don't believe this fever is contagious."

Dr. Jones, with his own opinion of the malady's contagiousness, was glad of this deference to caution; and hastened to execute the order. Upon his return Clarendon rose to leave, declaring that he would himself take charge of the case alone. Disappointed in his wish to study the great man's methods and technique, the junior physician watched his chief stride away toward the lone ward where he had placed the patient, more critical of the new regime than at any time since admiration had displaced his first jealous pangs.

Reaching the ward, Clarendon entered hastily, glancing at the bed and stepping back to see how far Dr. Jones's obvious curiosity might have led him. Then, finding the corridor still vacant, he shut the door and turned to examine the sufferer. The man was a convict of a peculiarly repulsive type, and seemed to be racked by the keenest throes of agony. His features were frightfully contracted, and his knees drawn sharply up in the mute desperation of the stricken. Clarendon studied him closely, raising his tightly shut eyelids, took his pulse and temperature, and finally dissolving a tablet in water, forced the solution between the sufferer's lips. Before long the height of the attack abated, as shewn by the relaxing body and returning normality of expression, and the patient began to breathe more easily. Then, by a soft rubbing of the ears, the doctor caused the man to open his eyes. There was life in them, for they moved from side to side, though they lacked the fine fire which we are wont to deem the image of the soul. Clarendon smiled as he surveyed the peace his help had brought, feeling behind him the power of an all-capable science. He had long known of this case, and had snatched the victim from death with the work of a moment. Another hour and this man would have gone—yet Jones had seen the symptoms for days before discovering them, and having discovered them, did not know what to do.

Man's conquest of disease, however, cannot be perfect. Clarendon, assuring the dubious trusty-nurses[11] that the fever was not contagious, had had the patient bathed, sponged in alcohol, and put to bed; but was told the next morning that the case was lost. The man had died after

117

midnight in the most intense agony, and with such cries and distortions of face that the nurses were driven almost to panic. The doctor took this news with his usual calm, whatever his scientific feelings may have been, and ordered the burial of the patient in quicklime. Then, with a philosophic shrug of the shoulders, he made the usual rounds of the penitentiary.

Two days later the prison was hit again. Three men came down at once this time, and there was no concealing the fact that a black fever epidemic was under way. Clarendon, having adhered so firmly to his theory of noncontagiousness, suffered a distinct loss of prestige, and was handicapped by the refusal of the trusty-nurses to attend the patients. Theirs was not the soul-free devotion of those who sacrifice themselves to science and humanity. They were convicts, serving only because of the privileges they could not otherwise buy, and when the price became too great they preferred to resign the privileges.

But the doctor was still master of the situation. Consulting with the warden and sending urgent messages to his friend the governor, he saw to it that special rewards in cash and in reduced terms were offered to the convicts for the dangerous nursing service; and by this method succeeded in getting a very fair quota of volunteers. He was steeled for action now, and nothing could shake his poise and determination. Additional cases brought only a curt nod, and he seemed a stranger to fatigue as he hastened from bedside to bedside all over the vast stone home of sadness and evil. More than forty cases developed within another week, and nurses had to be brought from the city. Clarendon went home very seldom at this stage, often sleeping on a cot in the warden's quarters, and always giving himself up with typical abandon to the service of medicine and of mankind.

Then came the first mutterings of that storm which was soon to convulse San Francisco. News will out, and the menace of black fever spread over the town like a fog from the bay. Reporters trained in the doctrine of "sensation first" used their imagination without restraint, and gloried when at last they were able to produce a case in the Mexican quarter which a local physician—fonder perhaps of money than of truth or civic welfare—pronounced black fever.

That was the last straw. Frantic at the thought of the crawling death so close upon them, the people of San Francisco went mad en masse, and embarked upon that historic exodus of which all the country was soon to hear over busy wires. Ferries and rowboats, excursion steamers and launches, railways and cable cars, bicycles and carriages, moving-vans and work carts, all were pressed into instant and frenzied service. Sausalito and Tamalpais, as lying in the direction of San Quentin, shared in the flight; while housing space in Oakland, Berkeley, and Alameda rose to fabulous prices. Tent colonies sprang up, and improvised villages lined the crowded southward highways from Millbrae to San Jose. Many sought refuge with friends in Sacramento, while the fright-shaken residue forced by various causes to stay behind could do little more than maintain the basic necessities of a nearly dead city.

Business, save for quack doctors with "sure cures" and "preventives" for use against the fever, fell rapidly to the vanishing-point. At first the saloons offered "medicated drinks", but soon found that the populace preferred to be duped by charlatans of more professional aspect. In strangely noiseless streets persons peered into one another's faces to glimpse possible plague symptoms, and shopkeepers began more and more to refuse admission to their clientele, each customer seeming to them a fresh fever menace. Legal and judicial machinery began to disintegrate as attorneys and county clerks succumbed one by one to the urge for flight. Even the doctors deserted in large numbers, many of them pleading the need of vacations among the mountains and the lakes in the northern part of the state. Schools and colleges, theatres and cafés, restaurants and saloons, all gradually closed their doors; and in a single week San Francisco lay prostrate and inert with only its light, power, and water service even half normal, with newspapers in skeletonic form, and with a crippled parody on transportation maintained by the horse and cable cars.

This was the lowest ebb. It could not last long, for courage and observation are not altogether dead in mankind; and sooner or later the non-existence of any widespread black fever epidemic outside San Quentin became too obvious a fact to deny, notwithstanding several actual cases and the undeniable spread of typhoid in the unsanitary suburban tent colonies. The leaders and editors of the community conferred and took action, enlisting in their service the very reporters whose energies had done so much to bring on the trouble, but now turning their "sensation first" avidity into more constructive channels. Editorials and fictitious interviews appeared, telling of Dr. Clarendon's complete control of the disease, and of the absolute impossibility of its diffusion beyond the prison walls. Reiteration and circulation slowly did their work, and gradually a slim backward trickle of urbanites swelled into a vigorous refluent stream. One of the first healthy symptoms was the start of a newspaper controversy of the approved acrimonious kind, attempting to fix blame for the panic wherever the various participants thought it belonged. The returning doctors, jealously strengthened by their timely vacations, began striking at Clarendon, assuring the public that they as well as he would keep the fever in leash, and censuring him for not doing even more to check its spread within San Quentin.

Clarendon had, they averred, permitted far more deaths than were necessary. The veriest tyro in medicine knew how to check fever contagion; and if this renowned savant did not do it, it was clearly because he chose for scientific reasons to study the final effects of the disease, rather than to prescribe properly and save the victims. This policy, they insinuated, might be proper enough among convicted murderers in a penal institution, but it would not do in San Francisco, where life was still a precious and sacred thing. Thus they went on, and the papers were glad to publish all they wrote, since the sharpness of the campaign, in which Dr. Clarendon would doubtless join, would help to obliterate confusion and restore confidence among the people.

But Clarendon did not reply. He only smiled, while his singular clinic-man Surama indulged in many a deep, testudinous chuckle. He was at home more nowadays, so that reporters began besieging the gate of the great wall the doctor had built around his house, instead of pestering the warden's office at San Quentin. Results, though, were equally meagre; for Surama formed an impassable barrier between the doctor and the outer world—even after the reporters had got into the grounds. The newspaper men getting access to the front hall had glimpses of Clarendon's singular entourage and made the best they could in a "write-up" of Surama and the queer skeletonic Thibetans. Exaggeration, of course, occurred in every fresh article, and the net effect of the publicity was distinctly adverse to the great physician. Most persons hate the unusual, and hundreds who could have excused heartlessness or incompetence stood ready to condemn the grotesque taste manifested in the chuckling attendant and the eight black-robed Orientals.

Early in January an especially persistent young man from the *Observer* climbed the moated eight-foot brick wall in the rear of the Clarendon grounds and began a survey of the varied outdoor appearances which trees concealed from the front walk. With quick, alert brain he took in everything—the rose-arbour, the aviaries, the animal cages where all sorts of mammalia from monkeys to guinea-pigs might be seen and heard, the stout wooden clinic building with barred windows in the northwest corner of the yard—and bent searching glances throughout the thousand square feet of intramural privacy. A great article was brewing, and he would have escaped unscathed but for the barking of Dick, Georgina Clarendon's gigantic and beloved St. Bernard. Surama, instant in his response, had the youth by the collar before a protest could be uttered, and was presently shaking him as a terrier shakes a rat, and dragging him through the trees to the front yard and the gate.

Breathless explanations and quavering demands to see Dr. Clarendon were useless. Surama only chuckled and dragged his victim on. Suddenly a positive fright crept over the dapper scribe, and he began to wish desperately that this unearthly creature would speak, if only to prove that he really was a being of honest flesh and blood belonging to this planet. He became deathly sick, and strove not to glimpse the eyes which he knew must lie at the base of those gaping black sockets. Soon he heard the gate open and felt himself propelled violently through; in another moment waking rudely to the things of earth as he landed wetly and muddily in the ditch which Clarendon had had dug around the entire length of the wall. Fright gave a place to rage as he heard the massive gate slam shut, and he rose dripping to shake his fist at the forbidding portal. Then, as he turned to go, a soft sound grated behind him, and through a small wicket in the gate he felt the sunken eyes of Surama and heard the echoes of a deep-voiced, blood-freezing chuckle.

This young man, feeling perhaps justly that his handling had been rougher than he deserved, resolved to revenge himself upon the household responsible for his treatment. Accordingly he prepared a fictitious interview with Dr. Clarendon, supposed to be held in the clinic building, during which he was careful to describe the agonies of a dozen black fever patients whom his imagination ranged on orderly rows of couches. His master-stroke was the picture of one especially pathetic sufferer gasping for water, while the doctor held a glass of the sparkling fluid just out of his reach, in a scientific attempt to determine the effect of a tantalising emotion on the course of the disease. This invention was followed by paragraphs of insinuating comment so outwardly respectful that it bore a double venom. Dr. Clarendon was, the article ran, undoubtedly the greatest and most single-minded scientist in the world; but science is no friend to individual welfare, and one would not like to have one's gravest ills drawn out and aggravated merely to satisfy an investigator on some point of abstract truth. Life is too short for that.

Altogether, the article was diabolically skilful, and succeeded in horrifying nine readers out of ten against Dr. Clarendon and his supposed methods. Other papers were quick to copy and enlarge upon its substance, taking the cue it offered, and commencing a series of "faked" interviews which fairly ran the gamut of derogatory fantasy. In no case, however, did the doctor condescend to offer a contradiction. He had no time to waste on fools and liars, and cared little for the esteem of a thoughtless rabble he despised. When James Dalton telegraphed his regrets and offered aid, Clarendon replied with an almost boorish curtness. He did not heed the barking of dogs, and could not bother to muzzle them. Nor would he thank anyone for messing with a matter wholly beneath notice. Silent and contemptuous, he continued his duties with tranquil evenness.

But the young reporter's spark had done its work. San Francisco was insane again, and this time as much with rage as with fear. Sober judgment became a lost art; and though no second exodus occurred, there ensued a reign of vice and recklessness born of desperation, and suggesting parallel phenomena in mediaeval times of pestilence. Hatred ran riot against the man who had found the disease and was struggling to restrain it, and a light-headed public forgot his great services to knowledge in their efforts to fan the flames of resentment. They seemed, in their blindness, to hate him in person, rather than the plague which had come to their breeze-cleaned and usually healthy city.

Then the young reporter, playing in the Neronic fire he had kindled, added a crowning personal touch of his own. Remembering the indignities he had suffered at the hands of the cadaverous clinic-man, he prepared a masterly article on the home and environment of Dr. Clarendon, giving especial prominence to Surama, whose very aspect he declared sufficient to scare the healthiest person into any sort of fever. He tried to make the gaunt chuckler appear equally ridiculous and terrible, succeeding best, perhaps, in the latter half of his intention, since a tide of horror always welled up whenever he thought of his brief proximity to the creature. He collected all the rumours current about the man, elaborated on the unholy depth of his reputed scholarship, and hinted darkly that it could have been no godly realm of secret and aeon-weighted Africa wherein Dr. Clarendon had found him.

Georgina, who followed the papers closely, felt crushed and hurt by these attacks upon her brother, but James Dalton, who called often at the house, did his best to comfort her. In this he was warm and sincere; for he wished not only to console the woman he loved, but to utter some measure of the reverence he had always felt for the starward-bound genius who had been his youth's closest comrade. He told Georgina how greatness can never be exempted from the shafts of envy, and cited the long, sad list of splendid brains crushed beneath vulgar heels. The attacks, he pointed out, formed the truest of all proofs of Alfred's solid eminence.

"But they hurt just the same," she rejoined, "and all the more because I know that Alf really suffers from them, no matter how indifferent he tries to be."

Dalton kissed her hand in a manner not then obsolete among well-born persons.

"And it hurts me a thousand times more, knowing that it hurts you and Alf. But never mind, Georgie, we'll stand together and pull through it!"

Thus it came about that Georgina came more and more to rely on the strength of the steel-firm, square-jawed governor who had been her youthful swain, and more and more to confide in him the things she feared. The press attacks and the epidemic were not quite all. There were aspects of the household which she did not like. Surama, cruel in equal measure to man and beast, filled her with the most unnamable repulsion; and she could not but feel that he meant some vague, indefinable harm to Alfred. She did not like the Thibetans, either, and thought it very peculiar that Surama was able to talk with them. Alfred would not tell her who or what Surama was, but had once explained rather haltingly that he was a much older man than would be commonly thought credible, and that he had mastered secrets and been through experiences calculated to make him a colleague of phenomenal value for any scientist seeking Nature's hidden mysteries.

Urged by her uneasiness, Dalton became a still more frequent visitor at the Clarendon home, though he saw that his presence was deeply resented by Surama. The bony clinic-man formed the habit of glaring peculiarly from those spectral sockets when admitting him, and would often, after closing the gate when he left, chuckle monotonously in a manner that made his flesh creep. Meanwhile Dr. Clarendon seemed oblivious of everything save his work at San Quentin, whither he went each day in his launch—alone save for Surama, who managed the wheel while the doctor read or collated his notes. Dalton welcomed these regular absences, for they gave him constant opportunities to renew his suit for Georgina's hand. When he would overstay and meet Alfred, however, the latter's greeting was always friendly despite his habitual reserve. In time the engagement of James and Georgina grew to be a definite thing, and the two awaited only a favourable chance to speak to Alfred.

The governor, whole-souled in everything and firm in his protective loyalty, spared no pains in spreading propaganda on his old friend's behalf. Press and officialdom both felt his influence, and he even succeeded in interesting scientists in the East, many of whom came to California to study the plague and investigate the anti-fever bacillus which Clarendon was so rapidly isolating and perfecting. These doctors and biologists, however, did not obtain the information they wished; so that several of them left with a very unfortunate impression. Not a few prepared articles hostile to Clarendon, accusing him of an unscientific and fame-seeking attitude, and intimating that he concealed his methods through a highly unprofessional desire for ultimate personal profit.

Others, fortunately, were more liberal in their judgments, and wrote enthusiastically of Clarendon and his work. They had seen the patients, and could appreciate how marvellously he held the dread disease in leash. His secrecy regarding the antitoxin they deemed quite justifiable, since its public diffusion in unperfected form could not but do more harm than good. Clarendon himself, whom many of their number had met before, impressed them more profoundly than ever, and they did not hesitate to compare him with Jenner, Lister, Koch, Pasteur, Metchnikoff,[12] and the rest of those whose whole lives have served pathology and humanity. Dalton was careful to save for Alfred all the magazines that spoke well of him, bringing them in person as an excuse to see Georgina. They did not, however, produce much effect save a contemptuous smile; and Clarendon would generally throw them to Surama, whose deep, disturbing chuckle upon reading formed a close parallel to the doctor's own ironic amusement.

One Monday evening early in February Dalton called with the definite intention of asking Clarendon for his sister's hand. Georgina herself admitted him to the grounds, and as they walked toward the house he stopped to pat the great dog which rushed up and laid friendly fore paws on his breast. It was Dick, Georgina's cherished St. Bernard, and Dalton was glad to feel that he had the affection of a creature which meant so much to her.

Dick was excited and glad, and turned the governor nearly half about with his vigorous pressure as he gave a soft quick bark and sprang off through the trees toward the clinic. He did not vanish, though, but presently stopped and looked back, softly barking again as if he wished Dalton to follow. Georgina, fond of obeying her huge pet's playful whims, motioned to James to see what he wanted; and they both walked slowly after him as he trotted relievedly to the rear of the yard where the top of the clinic building stood silhouetted against the stars above the great brick wall.

The outline of lights within shewed around the edges of the dark window-curtains, so they knew that Alfred and Surama were at work. Suddenly from the interior came a thin, subdued sound like a cry of a child—a plaintive call of "Mamma! Mamma!" at which Dick barked, while James and Georgina started perceptibly. Then Georgina smiled, remembering the parrots that Clarendon always kept for experimental uses, and patted Dick on the head either to forgive him for having fooled her and Dalton, or to console him for having been fooled himself.

As they turned slowly toward the house Dalton mentioned his resolve to speak to Alfred that evening about their engagement, and Georgina supplied no objection. She knew that her brother would not relish the loss of a faithful manager and companion, but believed his affection would place no barrier in the way of her happiness.

Later that evening Clarendon came into the house with a springy step and aspect less grim than usual. Dalton, seeing a good omen in this easy buoyancy, took heart as the doctor wrung his hand with a jovial "Ah, Jimmy, how's politics this year?" He glanced at Georgina, and she quietly excused herself, while the two men settled down to a chat on general subjects. Little by little, amidst many reminders of their old youthful days, Dalton worked toward his point; till at last he came out plainly with the crucial query.

"Alf, I want to marry Georgina. Have we your blessing?"

Keenly watching his old friend, Dalton saw a shadow steal over his face. The dark eyes flashed for a moment, then veiled themselves as wonted placidity returned. So science or selfishness was at work after all!

"You're asking an impossibility, James. Georgina isn't the aimless butterfly she was years ago. She has a place in the service of truth and mankind now, and that place is here. She's decided to devote her life to my work—to the household that makes my work possible—and there's no room for desertion or personal caprice."

Dalton waited to see if he had finished. The same old fanaticism—humanity versus the individual—and the doctor was going to let it spoil his sister's life! Then he tried to answer.

"But look here, Alf, do you mean to say that Georgina, in particular, is so necessary to your work that you must make a slave and martyr of her? Use your sense of proportion, man! If it were a question of Surama or somebody in the utter thick of your experiments it might be different; but after all, Georgina is only a housekeeper to you in the last analysis. She has promised to be my wife and says that she loves me. Have you the right to cut her off from the life that belongs to her? Have you the right—"

"That'll do, James!" Clarendon's face was set and white. "Whether or not I have the right to govern my own family is no business of an outsider."

"Outsider—you can say that to a man who—" Dalton almost choked as the steely voice of the doctor interrupted him again.

"An outsider to my family, and from now on an outsider to my home. Dalton, your presumption goes just a little too far! Good evening, Governor!"

And Clarendon strode from the room without extending his hand.

Dalton hesitated for a moment, almost at a loss what to do, when presently Georgina entered. Her face shewed that she had spoken with her brother, and Dalton took both her hands impetuously.

"Well, Georgie, what do you say? I'm afraid it's a choice between Alf and me. You know how I feel—you know how I felt before, when it was your father I was up against. What's your answer this time?"

He paused as she responded slowly.

"James, dear, do you believe that I love you?"

He nodded and pressed her hands expectantly.

"Then, if you love me, you'll wait a while. Don't think of Al's rudeness. He's to be pitied. I can't tell you the whole thing now, but you know how worried I am—what with the strain of his work, the criticisms, and the staring and cackling of that horrible creature Surama! I'm afraid he'll break down—he shews the strain more than anyone outside the family could tell. I can see it, for I've watched him all my life. He's changing—slowly bending under his burdens—and he puts on his extra brusqueness to hide it. You can see what I mean, can't you, dear?"

She paused, and Dalton nodded again, pressing one of her hands to his breast. Then she concluded.

"So promise me, dear, to be patient. I must stand by him; I must! I must!"

Dalton did not speak for a while, but his head inclined in what was almost a bow of reverence. There was more of Christ in this devoted woman than he had thought any human being possessed; and in the face of such love and loyalty he could do no urging.

Words of sadness and parting were brief; and James, whose blue eyes were misty, scarcely saw the gaunt clinic-man as the gate to the street was at last opened to him. But when it slammed to behind him he heard that blood-curdling chuckle he had come to recognise so well, and knew that Surama was there—Surama, whom Georgina had called her brother's evil genius. Walking away with a firm step, Dalton resolved to be watchful, and to act at the first sign of trouble.

III.

Meanwhile San Francisco, the epidemic still on the lips of all, seethed with anti-Clarendon feeling. Actually the cases outside the penitentiary were very few, and confined almost wholly to the lower Mexican element whose lack of sanitation was a standing invitation to disease of every kind; but politicians and the people needed no more than this to confirm the attacks made by the doctor's enemies. Seeing that Dalton was immovable in his championship of Clarendon, the malcontents, medical dogmatists, and ward-heelers turned their attention to the state legislature; lining up the anti-Clarendonists and the governor's old enemies with great shrewdness, and preparing to launch a law—with a veto-proof majority—transferring the authority for minor institutional appointments from the chief executive to the various boards or commissions concerned.

In the furtherance of this measure no lobbyist was more active than Clarendon's chief assistant, Dr. Jones. Jealous of his superior from the first, he now saw an opportunity for turning matters to his liking; and he thanked fate for the circumstance—responsible indeed for his present position—of his relationship to the chairman of the prison board. The new law, if passed, would certainly mean the removal of Clarendon and the appointment of himself in his stead; so, mindful of his own interest, he worked hard for it. Jones was all that Clarendon was not—a natural politician and sycophantic opportunist who served his own advancement first and science only incidentally. He was poor, and avid for salaried position, quite in contrast to the wealthy and independent savant he sought to displace. So with a rat-like cunning and persistence he laboured to undermine the great biologist above him, and was one day rewarded by the news that the new law was passed. Thenceforward the governor was powerless to make appointments to the state institutions, and the medical directorship of San Quentin lay at the disposal of the prison board.

Of all this legislative turmoil Clarendon was singularly oblivious. Wrapped wholly in matters of administration and research, he was blind to the treason of "that ass Jones" who worked by his side, and deaf to all the gossip of the warden's office. He had never in his life read the newspapers, and the banishment of Dalton from his house cut off his last real link with the world of outside events. With the naïveté of a recluse, he at no time thought of his position as insecure. In view of Dalton's loyalty, and of his forgiveness of even the greatest wrongs, as shewn in his dealings with the elder Clarendon who had crushed his father to death on the stock exchange, the possibility of a gubernatorial dismissal was, of course, out of the question; nor could the doctor's political ignorance envisage a sudden shift of power which might place the matter of retention or dismissal in very different hands. Thereupon he merely smiled with satisfaction when Dalton left for Sacramento; convinced that his place in San Quentin and his sister's place in his household were alike secure from disturbance. He was accustomed to having what he wanted, and fancied his luck was still holding out.

The first week in March, a day or so after the enactment of the new law, the chairman of the prison board called at San Quentin. Clarendon was out, but Dr. Jones was glad to shew the august visitor—his own uncle, incidentally—through the great infirmary, including the fever ward made so famous by press and panic. By this time converted against his will to Clarendon's belief in the fever's non-contagiousness, Jones smilingly assured his uncle that nothing was to be feared, and encouraged him to inspect the patients in detail—especially a ghastly skeleton, once a very giant of bulk and vigour, who was, he insinuated, slowly and painfully dying because Clarendon would not administer the proper medicine.

"Do you mean to say," cried the chairman, "that Dr. Clarendon refuses to let the man have what he needs, knowing his life could be saved?"

"Just that," snapped Dr. Jones, pausing as the door opened to admit none other than Clarendon himself. Clarendon nodded coldly to Jones and surveyed the visitor, whom he did not know, with disapproval.

"Dr. Jones, I thought you knew this case was not to be disturbed at all. And haven't I said that visitors aren't to be admitted except by special permission?"

But the chairman interrupted before his nephew could introduce him.

"Pardon me, Dr. Clarendon, but am I to understand that you refuse to give this man the medicine that would save him?"

Clarendon glared coldly, and rejoined with steel in his voice.

"That's an impertinent question, sir. I am in authority here, and visitors are not allowed. Please leave the room at once."

The chairman, his sense of drama secretly tickled, answered with greater pomp and hauteur than were necessary.

"You mistake me, sir! I, not you, am master here. You are addressing the chairman of the prison board. I must say, moreover, that I deem your activity a menace to the welfare of the prisoners, and must request your resignation. Henceforth Dr. Jones will be in charge, and if you wish to remain until your formal dismissal you will take your orders from him."

It was Wilfred Jones's great moment. Life never gave him another such climax, and we need not grudge him this one. After all, he was a small rather than a bad man, and he had only obeyed a small man's code of looking to himself at all costs. Clarendon stood still, gazing at the speaker as if he thought him mad, till in another second the look of triumph on Dr. Jones's face convinced him that something important was indeed afoot. He was icily courteous as he replied.

"No doubt you are what you claim to be, sir. But fortunately my appointment came from the governor of the state, and can therefore be revoked only by him."

The chairman and his nephew both stared perplexedly, for they had not realised to what lengths unworldly ignorance can go. Then the older man, grasping the situation, explained at some length.

"Had I found that the current reports did you an injustice," he concluded, "I would have deferred action; but the case of this poor man and your own arrogant manner left me no choice. As it is—"

But Dr. Clarendon interrupted with a new razor-sharpness in his voice.

"As it is, I am the director in charge at present, and I ask you to leave this room at once."

The chairman reddened and exploded.

"Look here, sir, who do you think you're talking to? I'll have you chucked out of here—damn your impertinence!"

But he had time only to finish the sentence. Transformed by the insult to a sudden dynamo of hate, the slender scientist launched out with both fists in a burst of preternatural strength of which no one would have thought him capable. And if his strength was preternatural, his accuracy of aim was no less so; for not even a champion of the ring could have wrought a neater result. Both men—the chairman and Dr. Jones—were squarely hit; the one full in the face and the other on the point of the chin. Going down like felled trees, they lay motionless and unconscious on the floor; while Clarendon, now clear and completely master of himself, took his hat and cane and went out to join Surama in the launch. Only when seated in the moving boat did he at last give audible vent to the frightful rage that consumed him. Then, with face convulsed, he called down imprecations from the stars and the gulfs beyond the stars; so that even Surama shuddered, made an elder sign that no book of history records, and forgot to chuckle.

IV.

Georgina soothed her brother's hurt as best she could. He had come home mentally and physically exhausted and thrown himself on the library lounge; and in that gloomy room, little by little, the faithful sister had taken in the almost incredible news. Her consolations were instantaneous and tender, and she made him realise how vast, though unconscious, a tribute to his greatness the attacks, persecution, and dismissal all were. He had tried to cultivate the indifference she preached, and could have done so had personal dignity alone been involved. But the loss of scientific opportunity was more than he could calmly bear, and he sighed again and again as he repeated how three months more of study in the prison might have given him at last the long-sought bacillus which would make all fever a thing of the past.

Then Georgina tried another mode of cheering, and told him that surely the prison board would send for him again if the fever did not abate, or if it broke out with increased force. But even this was ineffective, and Clarendon answered only in a string of bitter, ironic, and half-meaningless little sentences whose tone shewed all too clearly how deeply despair and resentment had bitten.

"Abate? Break out again? Oh, it'll abate all right! At least, they'll think it has abated. They'd think anything, no matter what happens! Ignorant eyes see nothing, and bunglers are never discoverers. Science never shews her face to that sort. And they call themselves doctors! Best of all, fancy that ass Jones in charge!"

Ceasing with a quick sneer, he laughed so daemonically that Georgina shivered.

The days that followed were dismal ones indeed at the Clarendon mansion. Depression, stark and unrelieved, had taken hold of the doctor's usually tireless mind; and he would even have refused food had not Georgina forced it upon him. His great notebook of observations lay unopened on the library table, and his little gold syringe of anti-fever serum—a clever device of his own, with a self-contained reservoir, attached to a broad gold finger ring, and single-pressure action peculiar to itself—rested idly in a small leather case beside it. Vigour, ambition, and the desire for study and observation seemed to have died within him; and he made no inquiries about his clinic, where hundreds of germ cultures stood in their orderly phials await-ing his attention.

The countless animals held for experiments played, lively and well fed, in the early spring sunshine; and as Geor-gina strolled out through the rose-arbour to the cages she felt a strangely incongruous sense of happiness about her. She knew, though, how tragically transient that happiness must be; since the start of new work would soon make all these small creatures unwilling martyrs to science. Know-ing this, she glimpsed a sort of compensating element in her brother's inaction, and encouraged him to keep on in a rest he needed so badly. The eight Thibetan servants moved noiselessly about, each as impeccably effective as usual; and Georgina saw to it that the order of the household did not suffer because of the master's relaxation.

Study and starward ambition laid aside in slippered and dressing-gowned indifference, Clarendon was content to let Georgina treat him as an infant. He met her mater-nal fussiness with a slow, sad smile, and always obeyed her multitude of orders and precepts. A kind of faint, wistful felicity came over the languid household, amidst which the only dissenting note was supplied by Surama. He indeed was miserable, and looked often with sullen and resentful eyes at the sunny serenity in Georgina's face. His only joy had been the turmoil of experiment, and he missed the rou-tine of seizing the fated animals, bearing them to the clinic in clutching talons, and watching them with hot brooding gaze and evil chuckles as they gradually fell into the final coma with wide-opened, red-rimmed eyes, and swollen tongue lolling from froth-covered mouth.

Now he was seemingly driven to desperation by the sight of the carefree creatures in their cages, and frequently came to ask Clarendon if there were any orders. Finding the doctor apathetic and unwilling to begin work, he would go away muttering under his breath and glaring curses upon everything; stealing with cat-like tread to his own quarters in the basement, where his voice would sometimes ascend in deep, muffled rhythms of blasphemous strangeness and uncomfortably ritualistic suggestion.

All this wore on Georgina's nerves, but not by any means so gravely as her brother's continued lassitude itself. The duration of the state alarmed her, and little by little she lost the air of cheerfulness which had so provoked the clinic-man. Herself skilled in medicine, she found the doctor's condition highly unsatisfactory from an alienist's[13] point of view; and she now feared as much from his absence of interest and activity as she had formerly feared from his fanatical zeal and overstudy. Was lingering melancholy about to turn the once brilliant man of intellect into an innocuous imbecile?

Then, toward the end of May, came the sudden change. Georgina always recalled the smallest details connected with it; details as trivial as the box delivered to Surama the day before, postmarked Algiers, and emitting a most unpleasant odour; and the sharp, sudden thunderstorm, rare in the extreme for California, which sprang up that night as Surama chanted his rituals behind his locked basement door in a droning chest-voice louder and more intense than usual.[14]

It was a sunny day, and she had been in the garden gathering flowers for the dining-room. Re-entering the house, she glimpsed her brother in the library, fully dressed and seated at the table, alternately consulting the notes in his thick observation book, and making fresh entries with brisk assured strokes of the pen. He was alert and vital, and there was a satisfying resilience about his movements as he now and then turned a page, or reached for a book from the rear of the great table. Delighted and relieved, Georgina hastened to deposit her flowers in the dining-room and return; but when she reached the library again she found that her brother was gone.

She knew, of course, that he must be in the clinic at work, and rejoiced to think that his old mind and purpose had snapped back into place. Realising it would be of no use to delay the luncheon for him, she ate alone and set aside a bite to be kept warm in case of his return at an odd moment. But he did not come. He was making up for lost time, and was still in the great stout-planked clinic when she went for a stroll through the rose-arbour.

As she walked among the fragrant blossoms she saw Surama fetching animals for the test. She wished she could notice him less, for he always made her shudder; but her very dread had sharpened her eyes and ears where he was concerned. He always went hatless around the yard, and the total hairlessness of his head enhanced his skeleton-like aspect horribly. Now she heard a faint chuckle as he took a small monkey from its cage against the wall and carried it to the clinic, his long, bony fingers pressing so cruelly into its furry sides that it cried out in frightened anguish. The sight sickened her, and brought her walk to an end. Her inmost soul rebelled at the ascendancy this creature had gained over her brother, and she reflected bitterly that the two had almost changed places as master and servant.

Night came without Clarendon's return to the house, and Georgina concluded that he was absorbed in one of his very longest sessions, which meant total disregard of time. She hated to retire without a talk with him about his sudden recovery; but finally, feeling it would be futile to wait up, she wrote a cheerful note and propped it before his chair on the library table; then started resolutely for bed.

She was not quite asleep when she heard the outer door open and shut. So it had not been an all-night session after all! Determined to see that her brother had a meal before retiring she rose, slipped on a robe, and descended to the library, halting only when she heard voices from behind the half-opened door. Clarendon and Surama were talking, and she waited till the clinic-man might go.

Surama, however, shewed no inclination to depart; and indeed, the whole heated tenor of the discourse seemed to bespeak absorption and promise length. Georgina, though she had not meant to listen, could not help catching a phrase now and then, and presently became aware of a sinister undercurrent which frightened her very much without being wholly clear to her. Her brother's voice, nervous, incisive, held her notice with disquieting persistence.

"But anyway," he was saying, "we haven't enough animals for another day, and you know how hard it is to get a decent supply at short notice. It seems silly to waste so much effort on comparative trash when human specimens could be had with just a little extra care."

Georgina sickened at the possible implication, and caught at the hall rack to steady herself. Surama was replying in that deep, hollow tone which seemed to echo with the evil of a thousand ages and a thousand planets.

"Steady, steady—what a child you are with your haste and impatience! You crowd things so! When you've lived as I have, so that a whole life will seem only an hour, you won't be so fretful about a day or week or month! You work too fast. You've plenty of specimens in the cages for a full week if you'll only go at a sensible rate. You might even begin on the older material if you'd be sure not to overdo it."

"Never mind my haste!" the reply was snapped out

sharply; "I have my own methods. I don't want to use our material if I can help it, for I prefer them as they are. And you'd better be careful of them anyway—you know the knives those sly dogs carry."

Surama's deep chuckle came.

"Don't worry about that. The brutes eat, don't they? Well, I can get you one any time you need it. But go slow—with the boy gone, there are only eight, and now that you've lost San Quentin it'll be hard to get new ones by the wholesale. I'd advise you to start in on Tsanpo—he's the least use to you as he is, and—"

But that was all Georgina heard. Transfixed by a hideous dread from the thoughts this talk excited, she nearly sank to the floor where she stood, and was scarcely able to drag herself up the stairs and into her room. What was the evil monster Surama planning? Into what was he guiding her brother? What monstrous circumstances lay behind these cryptic sentences? A thousand phantoms of darkness and menace danced before her eyes, and she flung herself upon the bed without hope of sleep. One thought above the rest stood out with fiendish prominence, and she almost screamed aloud as it beat itself into her brain with renewed force. Then Nature, kinder than she expected, intervened at last. Closing her eyes in a dead faint, she did not awake till morning, nor did any fresh nightmare come to join the lasting one which the overheard words had brought.

With the morning sunshine came a lessening of the tension. What happens in the night when one is tired often reaches the consciousness in distorted forms, and Georgina could see that her brain must have given strange colour to scraps of common medical conversation. To suppose her brother—only son of the gentle Frances Schuyler Clarendon—guilty of savage sacrifices in the name of science would be to do an injustice to their blood, and she decided to omit all mention of her trip downstairs, lest Alfred ridicule her fantastic notions.

When she reached the breakfast table she found that Clarendon was already gone, and regretted that not even this second morning had given her a chance to congratulate him on his revived activity. Quietly taking the breakfast served by stone-deaf old Margarita, the Mexican cook, she read the morning paper and seated herself with some needlework by the sitting-room window overlooking the great yard. All was silent out there, and she could see that the last of the animal cages had been emptied. Science was served, and the lime-pit held all that was left of the once pretty and lively little creatures. This slaughter had always grieved her, but she had never complained, since she knew it was all for humanity. Being a scientist's sister, she used to say to herself, was like being the sister of a soldier who kills to save his countrymen from their foes.

After luncheon Georgina resumed her post by the window, and had been busily sewing for some time when the sound of a pistol shot from the yard caused her to look out in alarm. There, not far from the clinic, she saw the ghastly form of Surama, a revolver in his hand, and his skull-face twisted into a strange expression as he chuckled at a cowering figure robed in black silk and carrying a long Thibetan knife. It was the servant Tsanpo, and as she recognised the shrivelled face Georgina remembered horribly what she had overheard the night before. The sun flashed on the polished blade, and suddenly Surama's revolver spat once more. This time the knife flew from the Mongol's hand, and Surama glanced greedily at his shaking and bewildered prey.

Then Tsanpo, glancing quickly at his unhurt hand and

at the fallen knife, sprang nimbly away from the stealthily approaching clinic-man and made a dash for the house. Surama, however, was too swift for him, and caught him in a single leap, seizing his shoulder and almost crushing him. For a moment the Thibetan tried to struggle, but Surama lifted him like an animal by the scruff of the neck and bore him off toward the clinic. Georgina heard him chuckling and taunting the man in his own tongue, and saw the yellow face of the victim twist and quiver with fright. Suddenly realising against her own will what was taking place, a great horror mastered her and she fainted for the second time within twenty-four hours.

When consciousness returned, the golden light of late afternoon was flooding the room. Georgina, picking up her fallen work-basket and scattered materials, was lost in a daze of doubt; but finally felt convinced that the scene which had overcome her must have been all too tragically real. Her worst fears, then, were horrible truths. What to do about it, nothing in her experience could tell her; and she was vaguely thankful that her brother did not appear. She must talk to him, but not now. She could not talk to anybody now. And, thinking shudderingly of the monstrous happening behind those barred clinic windows, she crept into bed for a long night of anguished sleeplessness.

Rising haggardly on the following day, Georgina saw the doctor for the first time since his recovery. He was bustling about preoccupiedly, circulating between the house and the clinic, and paying little attention to anything besides his work. There was no chance for the dreaded interview, and Clarendon did not even notice his sister's worn-out aspect and hesitant manner.

In the evening she heard him in the library, talking to himself in a fashion most unusual for him, and she felt that he was under a great strain which might culminate in the return of his apathy. Entering the room, she tried to calm him without referring to any trying subject, and forced a steadying cup of bouillon upon him. Finally she asked gently what was distressing him, and waited anxiously for his reply, hoping to hear that Surama's treatment of the poor Thibetan had horrified and outraged him.

There was a note of fretfulness in his voice as he responded.

"What's distressing me? Good God, Georgina, what *isn't?* Look at the cages and see if you have to ask again! Cleaned out—milked dry—not a cursed specimen left; and a line of the most important bacterial cultures incubating in their tubes without a chance to do an ounce of good! Days' work wasted—whole programme set back—it's enough to drive a man mad! How shall I ever get anywhere if I can't scrape up some decent subjects?"

Georgina stroked his forehead.

"I think you ought to rest a while, Al dear."

He moved away.

"Rest? That's good! That's damn good! What else have I been doing but resting and vegetating and staring blankly into space for the last fifty or a hundred or a thousand years? Just as I manage to shake off the clouds, I have to run short of material—and then I'm told to lapse back again into drooling stupefaction! God! And all the while some sneaking thief is probably working with my data and getting ready to come out ahead of me with the credit for my own work. I'll lose by a neck—some fool with the proper specimens will get the prize, when one week more with even half-adequate facilities would see me through with flying colours!"

His voice rose querulously, and there was an overtone

of mental strain which Georgina did not like. She answered softly, yet not so softly as to hint at the soothing of a psychopathic case.

"But you're killing yourself with this worry and tension, and if you're dead, how can you do your work?"

He gave a smile that was almost a sneer.

"I guess a week or a month—all the time I need—wouldn't quite finish me, and it doesn't much matter what becomes of me or any other individual in the end. Science is what must be served—science—the austere cause of human knowledge. I'm like the monkeys and birds and guinea-pigs I use—just a cog in the machine, to be used to the advantage of the whole. They had to be killed—I may have to be killed—what of it? Isn't the cause we serve worth that and more?"

Georgina sighed. For a moment she wondered whether, after all, this ceaseless round of slaughter really was worth while.

"But are you absolutely sure your discovery will be enough of a boon to humanity to warrant these sacrifices?"

Clarendon's eyes flashed dangerously.

"Humanity! What the deuce is humanity? Science! Dolts! Just individuals over and over again! Humanity is made for preachers to whom it means the blindly credulous. Humanity is made for the predatory rich to whom it speaks in terms of dollars and cents. Humanity is made for the politician to whom it signifies collective power to be used to his advantage. What is humanity? Nothing! Thank God that crude illusion doesn't last! What a grown man worships is truth—knowledge—science—light—the rending of the veil and the pushing back of the shadow. Knowledge, the juggernaut! There is death in our own ritual. We must kill—dissect—destroy—and all for the sake of discovery—the worship of the ineffable light. The goddess Science demands it. We test a doubtful poison by killing. How else? No thought for self—just knowledge—the effect must be known."

His voice trailed off in a kind of temporary exhaustion, and Georgina shuddered slightly.

"But this is horrible, Al! You shouldn't think of it that way!"

Clarendon cackled sardonically, in a manner which stirred odd and repugnant associations in his sister's mind.

"Horrible? You think what *I* say is horrible? You ought to hear Surama! I tell you, things were known to the priests of Atlantis that would have you drop dead of fright if you heard a hint of them. Knowledge was knowledge a hundred thousand years ago, when our especial forbears were shambling about Asia as speechless semi-apes! They know something of it in the Hoggar region[15]—there are rumours in the farther uplands of Thibet—and once I heard an old man in China calling on Yog-Sothoth—"[16]

He turned pale, and made a curious sign in the air with his extended forefinger. Georgina felt genuinely alarmed, but became somewhat calmer as his speech took a less fantastic form.

"Yes, it may be horrible, but it's glorious too. The pursuit of knowledge, I mean. Certainly, there's no slovenly sentiment connected with it. Doesn't Nature kill—constantly and remorselessly—and are any but fools horrified at the struggle? Killings are necessary. They are the glory of science. We learn something from them, and we can't sacrifice learning to sentiment. Hear the sentimentalists howl against vaccination! They fear it will kill the child. Well, what if it does? How else can we discover the laws of disease concerned? As a scientist's sister you ought to know better than to prate sentiment. You ought to help my work instead of hindering it!"

"But, Al," protested Georgina, "I haven't the slightest intention of hindering your work. Haven't I always tried to help as much as I could? I am ignorant, I suppose, and can't help very actively; but at least I'm proud of you—proud for my own sake and for the family's sake—and I've always tried to smooth the way. You've given me credit for that many a time."

Clarendon looked at her keenly.

"Yes," he said jerkily as he rose and strode from the room, "you're right. You've always tried to help as best you knew. You may yet have a chance to help still more."

Georgina, seeing him disappear through the front door, followed him into the yard. Some distance away a lantern was shining through the trees, and as they approached it they saw Surama bending over a large object stretched on the ground. Clarendon, advancing, gave a short grunt; but when Georgina saw what it was she rushed up with a shriek. It was Dick, the great St. Bernard, and he was lying still with reddened eyes and protruding tongue.

"He's sick, Al!" she cried. "Do something for him, quick!"

The doctor looked at Surama, who had uttered something in a tongue unknown to Georgina.

"Take him to the clinic," he ordered; "I'm afraid Dick's caught the fever."

Surama took up the dog as he had taken poor Tsanpo the day before, and carried him silently to the building near the wall. He did not chuckle this time, but glanced at Clarendon with what appeared to be real anxiety. It almost seemed to Georgina that Surama was asking the doctor to save her pet.

Clarendon, however, made no move to follow, but stood still for a moment and then sauntered slowly toward the house. Georgina, astonished at such callousness, kept up a running fire of entreaties on Dick's behalf, but it was of no use. Without paying the slightest attention to her pleas he made directly for the library and began to read in a large old book which had lain face down on the table. She put her hand on his shoulder as he sat there, but he did not speak or turn his head. He only kept on reading, and Georgina, glancing curiously over his shoulder, wondered in what strange alphabet this brass-bound tome was written.

In the cavernous parlour across the hall, sitting alone in the dark a quarter of an hour later, Georgina came to her decision. Something was gravely wrong—just what, and to what extent, she scarcely dared formulate to herself—and it was time that she called in some stronger force to help her. Of course it must be James. He was powerful and capable, and his sympathy and affection would shew him the right thing to do. He had known Al always, and would understand.

It was by this time rather late, but Georgina had resolved on action. Across the hall the light still shone from the library, and she looked wistfully at the doorway as she quietly donned a hat and left the house. Outside the gloomy mansion and forbidding grounds, it was only a short walk to Jackson Street, where by good luck she found a carriage to take her to the Western Union telegraph office. There she carefully wrote out a message to James Dalton in Sacramento, asking him to come at once to San Francisco on a matter of the greatest importance to them all.

V.

Dalton was frankly perplexed by Georgina's sudden

148

message. He had had no word from the Clarendons since that stormy February evening when Alfred had declared him an outsider to his home; and he in turn had studiously refrained from communicating, even when he had longed to express sympathy after the doctor's summary ousting from office. He had fought hard to frustrate the politicians and keep the appointive power, and was bitterly sorry to watch the unseating of a man who, despite recent estrangements, still represented to him the ultimate ideal of scientific competence.

Now, with this clearly frightened summons before him, he could not imagine what had happened. He knew, though, that Georgina was not one to lose her head or send forth a needless alarm; hence he wasted no time, but took the Overland which left Sacramento within the hour, going at once to his club and sending word to Georgina by a messenger that he was in town and wholly at her service.

Meanwhile things had been quiescent at the Clarendon home, notwithstanding the doctor's continued taciturnity and his absolute refusal to report on the dog's condition. Shadows of evil seemed omnipresent and thickening, but for the moment there was a lull. Georgina was relieved to get Dalton's message and learn that he was close at hand, and sent back word that she would call him when necessity arose. Amidst all the gathering tension some faint compensating element seemed manifest, and Georgina finally decided that it was the absence of the lean Thibetans, whose stealthy, sinuous ways and disturbing exotic aspect had always annoyed her. They had vanished all at once; and old Margarita, the sole visible servant left in the house, told her they were helping their master and Surama at the clinic.

The following morning—the twenty-eighth of May—long to be remembered—was dark and lowering, and Georgina felt the precarious calm wearing thin. She did not see her brother at all, but knew he was in the clinic hard at work at something despite the lack of specimens he had bewailed. She wondered how poor Tsanpo was getting along, and whether he had really been subjected to any serious inoculation, but it must be confessed that she wondered more about Dick. She longed to know whether Surama had done anything for the faithful dog amidst his master's oddly callous indifference. Surama's apparent solicitude on the night of Dick's seizure had impressed her greatly, giving her perhaps the kindliest feeling she had ever had for the detested clinic-man. Now, as the day advanced, she found herself thinking more and more of Dick; till at last her harassed nerves, finding in this one detail a sort of symbolic summation of the whole horror that lay upon the household, could stand the suspense no longer.

Up to that time she had always respected Alfred's imperious wish that he be never approached or disturbed at the clinic; but as this fateful afternoon advanced, her resolution to break through the barrier grew stronger and stronger. Finally she set out with determined face, crossing the yard and entering the unlocked vestibule of the forbidden structure with the fixed intention of discovering how the dog was or of knowing the reason for her brother's secrecy.

The inner door, as usual, was locked; and behind it she heard voices in heated conversation. When her knocking brought no response she rattled the knob as loudly as possible, but still the voices argued on unheeding. They belonged, of course, to Surama and her brother; and as she stood there trying to attract attention she could not help catch something of their drift. Fate had made her for the second time an eavesdropper, and once more the matter she overheard seemed likely to tax her mental poise and nervous endurance to their ultimate bounds. Alfred and Surama were plainly quarrelling with increasing violence, and the purport of their speech was enough to arouse the wildest fears and confirm the gravest apprehensions. Georgina shivered as her brother's voice mounted shrilly to dangerous heights of fanatical tension.

"You, damn you—you're a fine one to talk defeat and moderation to me! Who started all this, anyway? Did *I* have any idea of your cursed devil-gods and elder world? Did *I* ever in my life think of your damned spaces beyond the stars and your crawling chaos Nyarlathotep?[17] I was a normal scientific man, confound you, till I was fool enough to drag you out of the vaults with your devilish Atlantean secrets. You egged me on, and now you want to cut me off! You loaf around doing nothing and telling me to go slow when you might just as well as not be going out and getting material. You know damn well that I don't know how to go about such things, whereas you must have been an old hand at it before the earth was made. It's like you, you damned walking corpse, to start something you won't or can't finish!"

Surama's evil chuckle came.

"You're insane, Clarendon. That's the only reason I let you rave on when I could send you to hell in three minutes. Enough is enough, and you've certainly had enough material for any novice at your stage. You've had all I'm going to get you, anyhow! You're only a maniac on the subject now—what a cheap, crazy thing to sacrifice even your poor sister's pet dog, when you could have spared him as well as not! You can't look at any living thing now without wanting to jab that gold syringe into it. No—Dick had to go where the Mexican boy went—where Tsanpo and the other seven went—where all the animals went! What a pupil! You're no fun any more—you've lost your nerve. You set out to control things, and they're controlling you. I'm about done with you, Clarendon. I thought you had the stuff in you, but you haven't. It's about time I tried somebody else. I'm afraid you'll have to go!"

In the doctor's shouted reply there was both fear and frenzy.

"Be careful, you—! There are powers against your powers—I didn't go to China for nothing, and there are things in Alhazred's *Azif*[18] which weren't known in Atlantis! We've both meddled in dangerous things, but you needn't think you know all my resources. How about the Nemesis of Flame?[19] I talked in Yemen with an old man who had come back alive from the Crimson Desert—he had seen Irem, the City of Pillars, and had worshipped at the underground shrines of Nug and Yeb—Iä! Shub-Niggurath!"[20]

Through Clarendon's shrieking falsetto cut the deep chuckle of the clinic-man.

"Shut up, you fool! Do you suppose your grotesque nonsense has any weight with me? Words and formulae— words and formulae—what do they all mean to one who has the substance behind them? We're in a material sphere now, and subject to material laws. You have your fever; I have my revolver. You'll get no specimens, and I'll get no fever so long as I have you in front of me with this gun between!"

That was all Georgina could hear. She felt her senses reeling, and staggered out of the vestibule for a saving breath of the lowering outside air. She saw that the crisis had come at last, and that help must now arrive quickly if her brother was to be saved from the unknown gulfs of madness and mystery. Summoning up all her reserve energy, she managed to reach the house and get to the library, where she scrawled a hasty note for Margarita to take to James Dalton.

When the old woman had gone, Georgina had just strength enough to cross to the lounge and sink weakly down into a sort of semi-stupor. There she lay for what seemed like years, conscious only of the fantastic creeping up of the twilight from the lower corners of the great, dismal room, and plagued by a thousand shadowy shapes of terror which filed with phantasmal, half-limned pageantry through her tortured and stifled brain. Dusk deepened into darkness, and still the spell held. Then a firm tread sounded in the hall, and she heard someone enter the room and fumble at the match-safe. Her heart almost stopped beating as the gas-jets of the chandelier flared up one by one, but then she saw that the arrival was her brother. Relieved to the bottom of her heart that he was still alive, she gave vent to an involuntary sigh, profound, long-drawn, and tremulous, and lapsed at last into kindly oblivion.

At the sound of that sigh Clarendon turned in alarm toward the lounge, and was inexpressibly shocked to see the pale and unconscious form of his sister there. Her face had a death-like quality that frightened his inmost spirit, and he flung himself on his knees by her side, awake to a realisation of what her passing away would mean to him. Long unused to private practice amidst his ceaseless quest for truth, he had lost the physician's instinct of first aid, and could only call out her name and chafe her wrists mechanically as fear and grief possessed him. Then he thought of water, and ran to the dining-room for a carafe. Stumbling about in a darkness which seemed to harbour vague terrors, he was some time in finding what he sought; but at last he clutched it in shaking hand and hastened back to dash the cold fluid in Georgina's face. The method was crude but effective. She stirred, sighed a second time, and finally opened her eyes.

"You are alive!" he cried, and put his cheek to hers as she stroked his head maternally. She was almost glad she fainted, for the circumstance seemed to have dispelled the strange Alfred and brought her own brother back to her. She sat up slowly and tried to reassure him.

"I'm all right, Al. Just give me a glass of water. It's a sin to waste it this way—to say nothing of spoiling my waist! Is that the way to behave every time your sister drops off for a nap? You needn't think I'm going to be sick, for I haven't time for such nonsense!"

Alfred's eyes shewed that her cool, common-sense speech had had its effect. His brotherly panic dissolved in an instant, and instead there came into his face a vague, calculating expression, as if some marvellous possibility had just dawned upon him. As she watched the subtle waves of cunning and appraisal pass fleetingly over his countenance she became less and less certain that her mode of reassurance had been a wise one, and before he spoke she found herself shivering at something she could not define. A keen medical instinct almost told her that his moment of sanity had passed, and that he was now once more the unrestrained fanatic for scientific research. There was something morbid in the quick narrowing of his eyes at her casual mention of good health. What was he thinking? To what unnatural extreme was his passion for experiment about to be pushed? Wherein lay the special significance of her pure blood and absolutely flawless organic state? None of these misgivings, however, troubled Georgina for more than a second, and she was quite natural and unsuspicious as she felt her brother's steady fingers at her pulse.

"You're a bit feverish, Georgie," he said in a precise, elaborately restrained voice as he looked professionally into her eyes.

"Why, nonsense, I'm all right," she replied. "One would think you were on the watch for fever patients just for the sake of shewing off your discovery! It *would* be poetic, though, if you could make your final proof and demonstration by curing your own sister!"

Clarendon started violently and guiltily. Had she suspected his wish? Had he muttered anything aloud? He looked at her closely, and saw that she had no inkling of the truth. She smiled up sweetly into his face and patted his hand as he stood by the side of the lounge. Then he took a small oblong leather case from his vest pocket, and taking out a little gold syringe, he began fingering it thoughtfully, pushing the piston speculatively in and out of the empty cylinder.

"I wonder," he began with suave sententiousness, "whether you would really be willing to help science in—something like that way—if the need arose? Whether you would have the devotion to offer yourself to the cause of medicine as a sort of Jephthah's daughter[21] if you knew it meant the absolute perfection and completion of my work?"

Georgina, catching the odd and unmistakable glitter in her brother's eyes, knew at last that her worst fears were true. There was nothing to do now but keep him quiet at all hazards and to pray that Margarita had found James Dalton at his club.

"You look tired, Al dear," she said gently. "Why not take a little morphia and get some of the sleep you need so badly?"

He replied with a kind of crafty deliberation.

"Yes, you're right. I'm worn out, and so are you. Each of us needs a good sleep. Morphine is just the thing—wait till I go and fill the syringe and we'll both take a proper dose."

Still fingering the empty syringe, he walked softly out of the room. Georgina looked about her with the aimlessness of desperation, ears alert for any sign of possible help. She thought she heard Margarita again in the basement kitchen, and rose to ring the bell, in an effort to learn of the fate of her message. The old servant answered her summons at once, and declared she had given the message at the club hours ago. Governor Dalton had been out, but the clerk had promised to deliver the note at the very moment of his arrival.

Margarita waddled below stairs again, but still Clarendon did not reappear. What was he doing? What was he planning? She had heard the outer door slam, so knew he must be at the clinic. Had he forgotten his original intention with the vacillating mind of madness? The suspense grew almost unbearable, and Georgina had to keep her teeth clenched tightly to avoid screaming.

It was the gate bell, which rang simultaneously in house and clinic, that broke the tension at last. She heard the cat-like tread of Surama on the walk as he left the clinic to answer it; and then, with an almost hysterical sigh of relief, she caught the firm, familiar accents of Dalton in conversation with the sinister attendant. Rising, she almost tottered to meet him as he loomed up in the library doorway; and for a moment no word was spoken while he kissed her hand in his courtly, old-school fashion. Then Georgina burst forth into a torrent of hurried explanation, telling all that had happened, all she had glimpsed and overheard, and all she feared and suspected.

Dalton listened gravely and comprehendingly, his first bewilderment gradually giving place to astonishment, sympathy, and resolution. The message, held by a careless clerk, had been slightly delayed, and had found him appropriately enough in the midst of a warm lounging-room discussion about Clarendon. A fellow-member, Dr. MacNeil, had brought in a medical journal with an article well calculated to disturb the devoted scientist, and Dalton had just asked to keep the paper for future reference when the message was handed him at last. Abandoning his half-formed plan to take Dr. MacNeil into his confidence regarding Alfred, he called at once for his hat and stick, and lost not a moment in getting a cab for the Clarendon home.

Surama, he thought, appeared alarmed at recognising him; though he had chuckled as usual when striding off again toward the clinic. Dalton always recalled Surama's stride and chuckle on this ominous night, for he was never to see the unearthly creature again. As the chuckler entered the clinic vestibule his deep, guttural gurgles seemed to blend with some low mutterings of thunder which troubled the far horizon.

When Dalton had heard all Georgina had to say, and learned that Alfred was expected back at any moment with an hypodermic dose of morphine, he decided he had better talk with the doctor alone. Advising Georgina to retire to her room and await developments, he walked about the gloomy library, scanning the shelves and listening for Clarendon's nervous footstep on the clinic path outside. The vast room's corners were dismal despite the chandelier, and the closer Dalton looked at his friend's choice of books the less he liked them. It was not the balanced collection of a normal physician, biologist, or man of general culture. There were too many volumes on doubtful borderland themes; dark speculations and forbidden rituals of the Middle Ages, and strange exotic mysteries in alien alphabets both known and unknown.

The great notebook of observations on the table was unwholesome, too. The handwriting had a neurotic cast, and the spirit of the entries was far from reassuring. Long passages were inscribed in crabbed Greek characters, and as Dalton marshalled his linguistic memory for their translation he gave a sudden start, and wished his college struggles with Xenophon and Homer had been more conscientious.[22] There was something wrong—something hideously wrong—here, and the governor sank limply into the chair by the table as he pored more and more closely over the doctor's barbarous Greek. Then a sound came, startlingly near, and he jumped nervously at a hand laid sharply on his shoulder.

"What, may I ask, is the cause of this intrusion? You might have stated your business to Surama."

Clarendon was standing icily by the chair, the little gold syringe in one hand. He seemed very calm and rational, and Dalton fancied for a moment that Georgina must have exaggerated his condition. How, too, could a rusty scholar be absolutely sure about these Greek entries? The governor decided to be very cautious in his interview, and thanked the lucky chance which had placed a specious pretext in his coat pocket. He was very cool and assured as he rose to reply.

"I didn't think you'd care to have things dragged before a subordinate, but I thought you ought to see this article at once."

He drew forth the magazine given him by Dr. Mac-Neil and handed it to Clarendon.

"On page 542—you see the heading, 'Black Fever

Conquered by New Serum.' It's by Dr. Miller of Philadelphia—and he thinks he's got ahead of you with your cure. They were discussing it at the club, and MacNeil thought the exposition very convincing. I, as a layman, couldn't pretend to judge; but at all events I thought you oughtn't to miss a chance to digest the thing while it's fresh. If you're busy, of course, I won't disturb you—"

Clarendon cut in sharply.

"I'm going to give my sister an hypodermic—she's not quite well—but I'll look at what that quack has to say when I get back. I know Miller—a damn sneak and incompetent—and I don't believe he has the brains to steal my methods from the little he's seen of them."

Dalton suddenly felt a wave of intuition warning him that Georgina must not receive that intended dose. There was something sinister about it. From what she had said, Alfred must have been inordinately long preparing it, far longer than was needed for the dissolving of a morphine tablet. He decided to hold his host as long as possible, meanwhile testing his attitude in a more or less subtle way.

"I'm sorry Georgina isn't well. Are you sure that the injection will do her good? That it won't do her any harm?"

Clarendon's spasmodic start shewed that something had been struck home.

"Do her harm?" he cried. "Don't be absurd! You know Georgina must be in the best of health—the very best, I say—in order to serve science as a Clarendon should serve it. She, at least, appreciates the fact that she is my sister. She deems no sacrifice too great in my service. She is a priestess of truth and discovery, as I am a priest."

He paused in his shrill tirade, wild-eyed, and somewhat out of breath. Dalton could see that his attention had been momentarily shifted.

"But let me see what this cursed quack has to say," he continued. "If he thinks his pseudo-medical rhetoric can take a real doctor in, he is even simpler than I thought!"

Clarendon nervously found the right page and began reading as he stood there clutching his syringe. Dalton wondered what the real facts were. MacNeil had assured him that the author was a pathologist of the highest standing, and that whatever errors the article might have, the mind behind it was powerful, erudite, and absolutely honourable and sincere.

Watching the doctor as he read, Dalton saw the thin, bearded face grow pale. The great eyes blazed, and the pages crackled in the tenser grip of the long, lean fingers. A perspiration broke out on the high, ivory-white forehead where the hair was already thinning, and the reader sank gaspingly into the chair his visitor had vacated as he kept on with his devouring of the text. Then came a wild scream as from a haunted beast, and Clarendon lurched forward on the table, his outflung arms sweeping books and paper before them as consciousness went dark like a wind-quenched candle-flame.

Dalton, springing to help his stricken friend, raised the slim form and tilted it back in the chair. Seeing the carafe on the floor near the lounge, he dashed some water into the twisted face, and was rewarded by seeing the large eyes slowly open. They were sane eyes now—deep and sad and unmistakably sane—and Dalton felt awed in the presence of a tragedy whose ultimate depth he could never hope or dare to plumb.

The golden hypodermic was still clutched in the lean left hand, and as Clarendon drew a deep, shuddering breath he unclosed his fingers and studied the glittering thing that rolled about on his palm. Then he spoke—slowly, and with the ineffable sadness of utter, absolute despair.

"Thanks, Jimmy, I'm quite all right. But there's much to be done. You asked me a while back if this shot of morphia would do Georgie any harm. I'm in a position now to tell you that it won't."

He turned a small screw in the syringe and laid a finger on the piston, at the same time pulling with his left hand at the skin of his own neck. Dalton cried out in alarm as a lightning motion of his right hand injected the contents of the cylinder into the ridge of distended flesh.

"Good Lord, Al, what have you done?"

Clarendon smiled gently—a smile almost of peace and resignation, different indeed from the sardonic sneer of the past few weeks.

"You ought to know, Jimmy, if you've still the judgment that made you a governor. You must have pieced together enough from my notes to realise that there's nothing else to do. With your marks in Greek back at Columbia I guess you couldn't have missed much. All I can say is that it's true.

"James, I don't like to pass blame along, but it's only right to tell you that Surama got me into this. I can't tell you who or what he is, for I don't fully know myself, and what I do know is stuff that no sane person ought to know; but I will say that I don't consider him a human being in the fullest sense, and that I'm not sure whether or not he's alive as we know life.

"You think I'm talking nonsense. I wish I were, but the whole hideous mess is damnably real. I started out in life with a clean mind and purpose. I wanted to rid the world of fever. I tried and failed—and I wish to God I had been honest enough to say that I'd failed. Don't let my old talk of science deceive you, James—*I found no antitoxin and was never even half on the track of one!*

"Don't look so shaken up, old fellow! A veteran politician-fighter like you must have seen plenty of unmaskings before. I tell you, I never had even the start of a fever cure. But my studies had taken me into some queer places, and it was just my damned luck to listen to the stories of some still queerer people. James, if you ever wish any man well, tell him to keep clear of the ancient, hidden places of the earth. Old backwaters are dangerous—things are handed down there that don't do healthy people any good. I talked too much with old priests and mystics, and got to hoping I might achieve things in dark ways that I couldn't achieve in lawful ways.

"I shan't tell you just what I mean, for if I did I'd be as bad as the old priests that were the ruin of me. All I need say is that after what I've learned I shudder at the thought of the world and what it's been through. The world is cursed old, James, and there have been whole chapters lived and closed before the dawn of our organic life and the geologic eras connected with it. It's an awful thought—whole forgotten cycles of evolution with beings and races and wisdom and diseases—all lived through and gone before the first amoeba ever stirred in the tropic seas geology tells us about.

"I said gone, but I didn't quite mean that. It would have been better that way, but it wasn't quite so. In places traditions have kept on—I can't tell you how—and certain archaic life-forms have managed to struggle thinly down the aeons in hidden spots. There were cults, you know—bands of evil priests in lands now buried under the sea. Atlantis was the hotbed. That was a terrible place. If heaven is merciful, no one will ever drag up that horror from the deep.

"It had a colony, though, that didn't sink; and when

you get too confidential with one of the Tuareg priests in Africa, he's likely to tell you wild tales about it—tales that connect up with whispers you'll hear among the mad lamas and flighty yak-drivers on the secret table-lands of Asia. I'd heard all the common tales and whispers when I came on the big one. What that was, you'll never know—but it pertained to somebody or something that had come down from a blasphemously long time ago, and could be made to live again—or seem alive again—through certain processes that weren't very clear to the man who told me.

"Now, James, in spite of my confession about the fever, you know I'm not bad as a doctor. I plugged hard at medicine, and soaked up about as much as the next man—maybe a little more, because down there in the Hoggar country I did something no priest had ever been able to do. They led me blindfolded to a place that had been sealed up for generations—and I came back with Surama.

"Easy, James! I know what you want to say. How does he know all he knows?—why does he speak English—or any other language, for that matter—without an accent?—why did he come away with me?—and all that. I can't tell you altogether, but I can say that he takes in ideas and images and impressions with something besides his brain and senses. He had a use for me and my science. He told me things, and opened up vistas. He taught me to worship ancient, primordial, and unholy gods, and mapped out a road to a terrible goal which I can't even hint to you. Don't press me, James—it's for the sake of your sanity and the world's sanity!

"The creature is beyond all bounds. He's in league with the stars and all the forces of Nature. Don't think I'm still crazy, James—I swear to you I'm not! I've had too many glimpses to doubt. He gave me new pleasures that were forms of his palaeogean worship, and the greatest of those was the black fever.

"God, James! Haven't you seen through the business by this time? Do you still believe the black fever came out of Thibet, and that I learned about it there? Use your brains, man! Look at Miller's article here! He's found a basic antitoxin that will end all fever within half a century, when other men learn how to modify it for the different forms. He's cut the ground of my youth from under me—done what I'd have given my life to do—taken the wind out of all the honest sails I ever flung to the breeze of science! Do you wonder his article gave me a turn? Do you wonder it shocks me out of my madness back to the old dreams of my youth? Too late! Too late! But not too late to save others!

"I guess I'm rambling a bit now, old man. You know— the hypodermic. I asked you why you didn't tumble to the facts about black fever. How could you, though? Doesn't Miller say he's cured seven cases with his serum? A matter of diagnosis, James. He only thinks it is black fever. I can read between his lines. Here, old chap, on page 551, is the key to the whole thing. Read it again.

"You see, don't you? The fever cases *from the Pacific Coast* didn't respond to his serum. They puzzled him. They didn't even seem like any true fever he knew. Well, those were *my* cases! Those were the *real* black fever cases! And there can't ever be an antitoxin on earth that'll cure black fever!

"How do I know? *Because black fever isn't of this earth!* It's from *somewhere else,* James—and Surama alone knows where, because he brought it here. He *brought it and I spread it!* That's the secret, James! That's all I wanted the appointment for—*that's all I ever did—just spread the fever that I carried in this gold syringe and in the deadlier finger-ring-*

pump-syringe you see on my index finger! Science? A blind!
I wanted to kill, and kill, and kill! A single pressure on my
finger, and the black fever was inoculated. I wanted to see
living things writhe and squirm, scream and froth at the
mouth. A single pressure of the pump-syringe and I could
watch them as they died, and I couldn't live or think unless
I had plenty to watch. That's why I jabbed everything in
sight with the accursed hollow needle. Animals, criminals,
children, servants—and the next would have been—"

Clarendon's voice broke, and he crumpled up perceptibly in his chair.

"That—that, James—was—my life. Surama made it
so—he taught me, and kept me at it till I couldn't stop.
Then—then it got too much *even for him.* He tried to check
me. Fancy—*he* trying to check anybody in that line! But
now I've got my last specimen. That is my last test. Good
subject, James—I'm healthy—devilish healthy. Deuced
ironic, though—the madness has gone now, so there won't
be any fun watching the agony! Can't be—can't—"

A violent shiver of fever racked the doctor, and Dalton mourned amidst his horror-stupefaction that he could
give no grief. How much of Alfred's story was sheer nonsense, and how much nightmare truth he could not say; but
in any case he felt that the man was a victim rather than
a criminal, and above all, he was a boyhood comrade and
Georgina's brother. Thoughts of the old days came back ka-
leidoscopically. "Little Alf"—the yard at Phillips Exeter—
the quadrangle at Columbia—the fight with Tom Cort-
land when he saved Alf from a pommeling. . . .

He helped Clarendon to the lounge and asked gently
what he could do. There was nothing. Alfred could only
whisper now, but he asked forgiveness for all his offences,
and commended his sister to the care of his friend.

"You—you'll—make her happy," he gasped. "She deserves it. Martyr—to—a myth! Make it up to her, James. Don't—let—her— know—more—than she has to!"

His voice trailed off in a mumble, and he fell into a stupor. Dalton rang the bell, but Margarita had gone to bed, so he called up the stairs for Georgina. She was firm of step, but very pale. Alfred's scream had tried her sorely, but she had trusted James. She trusted him still as he shewed her the unconscious form on the lounge and asked her to go back to her room and rest, no matter what sounds she might hear. He did not wish her to witness the awful spectacle of delirium certain to come, but bade her kiss her brother a final farewell as he lay there calm and still, very like the delicate boy he had once been. So she left him—the strange, moonstruck, star-reading genius she had mothered so long—and the picture she carried away was a very merciful one.

Dalton must bear to his grave a sterner picture. His fears of delirium were not vain, and all through the black midnight hours his giant strength restrained the frenzied contortions of the mad sufferer. What he heard from those swollen, blackening lips he will never repeat. He has never been quite the same man since, and he knows that no one who hears such things can ever be wholly as he was before. So, for the world's good, he dares not speak, and he thanks God that his layman's ignorance of certain subjects makes many of the revelations cryptic and meaningless to him.

Toward morning Clarendon suddenly woke to a sane consciousness and began to speak in a firm voice.

"James, I didn't tell you what must be done—about everything. Blot out these entries in Greek and send my notebook to Dr. Miller. All my other notes, too, that you'll find in the files. He's the big authority today—his article

166

proves it. Your friend at the club was right.

"But everything in the clinic must go. *Everything without exception, dead or alive or—otherwise.* All the plagues of hell are in those bottles on the shelves. Burn them—burn it all—if one thing escapes, Surama will spread black death throughout the world. *And above all burn Surama!*[23] That—that *thing*—must not breathe the wholesome air of heaven. You know now—what I told you— you know why such an entity can't be allowed on earth. It won't be murder—Surama isn't human—if you're as pious as you used to be, James, I shan't have to urge you. Remember the old text—'Thou shalt not suffer a witch to live'[24]—or something of the sort.

"*Burn him, James!* Don't let him chuckle again over the torture of mortal flesh! I say, *burn him*—the Nemesis of Flame—that's all that can reach him, James, unless you can catch him asleep and drive a stake through his heart. . . . *Kill him—extirpate him—cleanse the decent universe of its primal taint—the taint I recalled from its age-long sleep. . . .*"

The doctor had risen on his elbow, and his voice was a piercing shriek toward the last. The effort was too much, however, and he lapsed very suddenly into a deep, tranquil coma. Dalton, himself fearless of fever, since he knew the dread germ to be non-contagious, composed Alfred's arms and legs on the lounge and threw a light afghan over the fragile form. After all, mightn't much of this horror be exaggeration and delirium? Mightn't old Doc MacNeil pull him through on a long chance? The governor strove to keep awake, and walked briskly up and down the room, but his energies had been taxed too deeply for such measures. A second's rest in the chair by the table took matters out of his hands, and he was presently sleeping soundly despite his best intentions.

Dalton started up as a fierce light shone in his eyes, and for a moment he thought the dawn had come. But it was not the dawn, and as he rubbed his heavy lids he saw that it was the glare of the burning clinic in the yard, whose stout planks flamed and roared and crackled heavenward in the most stupendous holocaust he had ever seen. It was indeed the "Nemesis of Flame" that Clarendon had wished, and Dalton felt that some strange combustibles must be involved in a blaze so much wilder than anything normal pine or redwood could afford. He glanced alarmedly at the lounge, but Alfred was not there. Starting up, he went to call Georgina, but met her in the hall, roused as he was by the mountain of living fire.

"The clinic's burning down!" she cried. "How is Al now?"

"He's disappeared—disappeared while I dropped asleep!" replied Dalton, reaching out a steadying arm to the form which faintness had begun to sway.

Gently leading her upstairs toward her room, he promised to search at once for Alfred, but Georgina slowly shook her head as the flames from outside cast a weird glow through the window on the landing.

"He must be dead, James—he could never live, sane and knowing what he did. I heard him quarrelling with Surama, and know that awful things were going on. He is my brother, but—it is best as it is."

Her voice had sunk to a whisper.

Suddenly through the open window came the sound of a deep, hideous chuckle, and the flames of the burning clinic took fresh contours till they half resembled some nameless, Cyclopean creatures of nightmare. James and Georgina paused hesitant, and peered out breathlessly through the landing window. Then from the sky came a thunderous peal, as a forked bolt of lightning shot down with terrible directness into the very midst of the blazing ruin. The deep chuckle ceased, and in its place came a frantic, ululant yelp as of a thousand ghouls and werewolves in torment. It died away with long, reverberant echoes, and slowly the flames resumed their normal shape.

The watchers did not move, but waited till the pillar of fire had shrunk to a smouldering glow. They were glad of a half-rusticity which had kept the firemen from trooping out, and of the wall that excluded the curious. What had happened was not for vulgar eyes—it involved too much of the universe's inner secrets for that.

In the pale dawn, James spoke softly to Georgina, who could do no more than put her head on his breast and sob.

"Sweetheart, I think he has atoned. He must have set the fire, you know, while I was asleep. He told me it ought to be burned—the clinic, and everything in it, Surama, too. It was the only way to save the world from the unknown horrors he had loosed upon it. He knew, and he did what was best.

"He was a great man, Georgie. Let's never forget that. We must always be proud of him, for he started out to help mankind, and was titanic even in his sins. I'll tell you more sometime. What he did, be it good or evil, was what no man ever did before. He was the first and last to break through certain veils, and even Apollonius of Tyana[25] takes second place beside him. But we mustn't talk about that. We must remember him only as the Little Alf we knew—as the boy who wanted to master medicine and conquer fever."

In the afternoon the leisurely firemen overhauled the ruins and found two skeletons with bits of blackened flesh adhering—only two, thanks to the undisturbed lime-pits. One was of a man; the other is still a subject of debate among the biologists of the coast. It was not exactly an ape's or a saurian's skeleton, but it had disturbing suggestions of lines of evolution of which palaeontology has revealed no trace. The charred skull, oddly enough, was very human, and reminded people of Surama; but the rest of the bones were beyond conjecture. Only well-cut clothing could have made such a body look like a man.[26]

But the human bones were Clarendon's. No one disputed this, and the world at large still mourns the untimely death of the greatest doctor of his age; the bacteriologist whose universal fever serum would have far eclipsed Dr. Miller's kindred antitoxin had he lived to bring it to perfection. Much of Miller's late success, indeed, is credited to the notes bequeathed him by the hapless victim of the flames. Of the old rivalry and hatred almost none survived, and even Dr. Wilfred Jones has been known to boast of his association with the vanished leader.

James Dalton and his wife Georgina have always preserved a reticence which modesty and family grief might well account for. They published certain notes as a tribute to the great man's memory, but have never confirmed or contradicted either the popular estimate or the rare hints of marvels that a very few keen thinkers have been known to whisper. It was very subtly and slowly that the facts filtered out. Dalton probably gave Dr. MacNeil an inkling of the truth, and that good soul had not many secrets from his son.

The Daltons have led, on the whole, a very happy life; for their cloud of terror lies far in the background, and a strong mutual love has kept the world fresh for them. But there are things which disturb them oddly—little things, of which one would scarcely ever think of complaining. They cannot bear persons who are lean or deep-voiced beyond certain limits, and Georgina turns pale at the sound of any guttural chuckling. Senator Dalton has a mixed horror of occultism, travel, hypodermics, and strange alphabets which most find hard to unify, and there are still those who blame him for the vast proportion of the doctor's library that he destroyed with such painstaking completeness.

MacNeil, though, seemed to realise. He was a simple man, and he said a prayer as the last of Alfred Clarendon's strange books crumbled to ashes. Nor would anyone who had peered understandingly within those books wish a word of that prayer unsaid.

The Curse of Yig

With Zealia Bishop

n 1925 I went into Oklahoma looking for snake lore, and I came out with a fear of snakes that will last me the rest of my life. I admit it is foolish, since there are natural explanations for everything I saw and heard, but it masters me none the less. If the old story had been all there was to it, I would not have been so badly shaken. My work as an American Indian ethnologist has hardened me to all kinds of extravagant legendry, and I know that simple white people can beat the redskins at their own game when it comes to fanciful inventions. But I can't forget what I saw with my own eyes at the insane asylum in Guthrie.[1]

I called at that asylum because a few of the oldest settlers told me I would find something important there. Neither Indians nor white men would discuss the snake-god legends I had come to trace. The oil-boom newcomers, of course, knew nothing of such matters, and the red men and old pioneers were plainly frightened when I spoke of them. Not more than six or seven people mentioned the asylum, and those who did were careful to talk in whispers. But the whisperers said that Dr. McNeill could shew me a very terrible relic and tell me all I wanted to know. He could explain why Yig, the half-human father of serpents, is a shunned and feared object in central Oklahoma, and why old settlers shiver at the secret Indian orgies which make the autumn days and nights hideous with the ceaseless beating of tom-toms in lonely places.

It was with the scent of a hound on the trail that I went to Guthrie, for I had spent many years collecting data on the evolution of serpent-worship among the Indians. I had always felt, from well-defined undertones of legend and archaeology, that great Quetzalcoatl—benign snake-god of the Mexicans[2]—had had an older and darker prototype; and during recent months I had well-nigh proved it in a series of researches stretching from Guatemala to the Oklahoma plains. But everything was tantalising and incomplete, for above the border the cult of the snake was hedged about by fear and furtiveness.

Now it appeared that a new and copious source of data was about to dawn, and I sought the head of the asylum with an eagerness I did not try to cloak. Dr. McNeill was a small, clean-shaven man of somewhat advanced years, and I saw at once from his speech and manner that he was a scholar of no mean attainments in many branches outside his profession. Grave and doubtful when I first made known my errand, his face grew thoughtful as he carefully scanned my credentials and the letter of introduction which a kindly old ex-Indian agent had given me.

"So you've been studying the Yig legend, eh?" he reflected sententiously. "I know that many of our Oklahoma ethnologists have tried to connect it with Quetzalcoatl, but I don't think any of them have traced the intermediate steps so well. You've done remarkable work for a man as young as you seem to be, and you certainly deserve all the data we can give.

"I don't suppose old Major Moore or any of the others told you what it is I have here. They don't like to talk about it, and neither do I. It is very tragic and very horrible, but that is all. I refuse to consider it anything supernatural. There's a story about it that I'll tell you after you see it—a devilish sad story, but one that I won't call magic. It merely shews the potency that belief has over some people. I'll admit there are times when I feel a shiver that's more than physical, but in daylight I set all that down to nerves. I'm not a young fellow any more, alas!

"To come to the point, the thing I have is what you might call a victim of Yig's curse—a physically living victim. We don't let the bulk of the nurses see it, although most of them know it's here. There are just two steady old chaps whom I let feed it and clean out its quarters—used to be three, but good old Stevens passed on a few years ago. I suppose I'll have to break in a new group pretty soon; for the thing doesn't seem to age or change much, and we old boys can't last forever. Maybe the ethics of the near future will let us give it a merciful release, but it's hard to tell.

"Did you see that single ground-glass basement window over in the east wing when you came up the drive? That's where it is. I'll take you there myself now. You needn't make any comment. Just look through the moveable panel in the door and thank God the light isn't any stronger. Then I'll tell you the story—or as much as I've been able to piece together."

We walked downstairs very quietly, and did not talk as we threaded the corridors of the seemingly deserted basement. Dr. McNeill unlocked a grey-painted steel door, but it was only a bulkhead leading to a further stretch of hallway. At length he paused before a door marked B 116, opened a small observation panel which he could use only by standing on tiptoe, and pounded several times upon the painted metal, as if to arouse the occupant, whatever it might be.

A faint stench came from the aperture as the doctor unclosed it, and I fancied his pounding elicited a kind of low, hissing response. Finally he motioned me to replace him at the peep-hole, and I did so with a causeless and increasing tremor. The barred, ground-glass window, close to the earth outside, admitted only a feeble and uncertain pallor; and I had to look into the malodorous den for several seconds before I could see what was crawling and wriggling about on the straw-covered floor, emitting every now and then a weak and vacuous hiss. Then the shadowed outlines began to take shape, and I perceived that the squirming entity bore some remote resemblance to a human form laid flat on its belly. I clutched at the door-handle for support as I tried to keep from fainting.

The moving object was almost of human size, and entirely devoid of clothing. It was absolutely hairless, and its tawny-looking back seemed subtly squamous in the dim, ghoulish light. Around the shoulders it was rather speckled and brownish, and the head was very curiously flat. As it looked up to hiss at me I saw that the beady little black eyes were damnably anthropoid, but I could not bear to study them long. They fastened themselves on me with a horrible persistence, so that I closed the panel gaspingly and left the creature to wriggle about unseen in its matted straw and spectral twilight. I must have reeled a bit, for I saw that the doctor was gently holding my arm as he guided me away. I was stuttering over and over again: "B-but for God's sake, *what is it?*"

Dr. McNeill told me the story in his private office as I sprawled opposite him in an easy-chair. The gold and crimson of late afternoon changed to the violet of early dusk, but still I sat awed and motionless. I resented every ring of the telephone and every whir of the buzzer, and I could have cursed the nurses and internes whose knocks now and then summoned the doctor briefly to the outer office. Night came, and I was glad my host switched on all the lights. Scientist though I was, my zeal for research was half forgotten amidst such breathless ecstasies of fright as a small boy might feel when whispered witch-tales go the rounds of the chimney-corner.

It seems that Yig, the snake-god of the central plains tribes—presumably the primal source of the more southerly Quetzalcoatl or Kukulcan—was an odd, half-anthropomorphic devil of highly arbitrary and capricious nature. He was not wholly evil, and was usually quite well-disposed toward those who gave proper respect to him and his children, the serpents; but in the autumn he became abnormally ravenous, and had to be driven away by means of suitable rites. That was why the tom-toms in the Pawnee, Wichita, and Caddo country[3] pounded ceaselessly week in and week out in August, September, and October; and why the medicine-men made strange noises with rattles and whistles curiously like those of the Aztecs and Mayas.

Yig's chief trait was a relentless devotion to his children—a devotion so great that the redskins almost feared to protect themselves from the venomous rattlesnakes which thronged the region. Frightful clandestine tales hinted of his vengeance upon mortals who flouted him or wreaked harm upon his wriggling progeny; his chosen method being to turn his victim, after suitable tortures, to a spotted snake.

In the old days of the Indian Territory,[4] the doctor went on, there was not quite so much secrecy about Yig. The plains tribes, less cautious than the desert nomads and Pueblos, talked quite freely of their legends and autumn ceremonies with the first Indian agents, and let considerable of the lore spread out through the neighbouring regions of white settlement. The great fear came in the land-rush days of '89,[5] when some extraordinary incidents had been rumoured, and the rumours sustained, by what seemed to be hideously tangible proofs. Indians said that the new white men did not know how to get on with Yig, and afterward the settlers came to take that theory at face value. Now no old-timer in middle Oklahoma, white or red, could be induced to breathe a word about the snake-god except in vague hints. Yet after all, the doctor added with almost needless emphasis, the only truly authenticated horror had been a thing of pitiful tragedy rather than of bewitchment. It was all very material and cruel—even that last phase which had caused so much dispute.

Dr. McNeill paused and cleared his throat before getting down to his special story, and I felt a tingling sensation as when a theatre curtain rises. The thing had begun when Walker Davis and his wife Audrey left Arkansas to settle in the newly opened public lands in the spring of 1889, and the end had come in the country of the Wichitas—north of the Wichita River, in what is at present Caddo County. There is a small village called Binger there now, and the railway goes through; but otherwise the place is less changed than other parts of Oklahoma.[6] It is still a section of farms and ranches—quite productive in these days—since the great oil-fields do not come very close.

Walker and Audrey had come from Franklin County in the Ozarks[7] with a canvas-topped wagon, two mules, an ancient and useless dog called "Wolf", and all their household goods. They were typical hill-folk, youngish and perhaps a little more ambitious than most, and looked forward to a life of better returns for their hard work than they had had in Arkansas. Both were lean, raw-boned specimens; the man tall, sandy, and grey-eyed, and the woman short and rather dark, with a black straightness of hair suggesting a slight Indian admixture.

In general, there was very little of distinction about them, and but for one thing their annals might not have differed from those of thousands of other pioneers who flocked into the new country at that time. That thing was Walker's almost epileptic fear of snakes, which some laid to prenatal causes, and some said came from a dark prophecy about his end with which an old Indian squaw had tried to scare him when he was small. Whatever the cause, the effect was marked indeed; for despite his strong general courage the very mention of a snake would cause him to grow faint and pale, while the sight of even a tiny specimen would produce a shock sometimes bordering on a convulsion seizure.

The Davises started out early in the year, in the hope of being on their new land for the spring ploughing. Travel was slow; for the roads were bad in Arkansas, while in the Territory there were great stretches of rolling hills and red, sandy barrens without any roads whatever. As the terrain grew flatter, the change from their native mountains depressed them more, perhaps, than they realised; but they found the people at the Indian agencies very affable, while most of the settled Indians seemed friendly and civil. Now and then they encountered a fellow-pioneer, with whom crude pleasantries and expressions of amiable rivalry were generally exchanged.

Owing to the season, there were not many snakes in evidence, so Walker did not suffer from his special temperamental weakness. In the earlier stages of the journey, too, there were no Indian snake-legends to trouble him; for the transplanted tribes from the southeast do not share the wilder beliefs of their western neighbours. As fate would have it, it was a white man at Okmulgee[8] in the Creek country who gave the Davises the first hint of Yig beliefs; a hint which had a curiously fascinating effect on Walker, and caused him to ask questions very freely after that.

Before long Walker's fascination had developed into a bad case of fright. He took the most extraordinary precautions at each of the nightly camps, always clearing away whatever vegetation he found, and avoiding stony places whenever he could. Every clump of stunted bushes and every cleft in the great, slab-like rocks seemed to him now to hide malevolent serpents, while every human figure not obviously part of a settlement or emigrant train seemed to him a potential snake-god till nearness had proved the contrary. Fortunately no troublesome encounters came at this stage to shake his nerves still further.

As they approached the Kickapoo country[9] they found it harder and harder to avoid camping near rocks. Finally it was no longer possible, and poor Walker was reduced to the puerile expedient of droning some of the rustic anti-snake charms he had learned in his boyhood. Two or three times a snake was really glimpsed, and these sights did not help the sufferer in his efforts to preserve composure.

On the twenty-second evening of the journey a savage wind made it imperative, for the sake of the mules, to camp in as sheltered a spot as possible; and Audrey persuaded her husband to take advantage of a cliff which rose uncommonly high above the dried bed of a former tributary of the Canadian River.[10] He did not like the rocky cast of the place, but allowed himself to be overruled this once; leading the animals sullenly toward the protecting slope, which the nature of the ground would not allow the wagon to approach.

Audrey, examining the rocks near the wagon, meanwhile noticed a singular sniffing on the part of the feeble old dog. Seizing a rifle, she followed his lead, and presently thanked her stars that she had forestalled Walker in her discovery. For there, snugly nested in the gap between two boulders, was a sight it would have done him no good to see. Visible only as one convoluted expanse, but perhaps comprising as many as three or four separate units, was a mass of lazy wriggling which could not be other than a brood of new-born rattlesnakes.

Anxious to save Walker from a trying shock, Audrey did not hesitate to act, but took the gun firmly by the barrel and brought the butt down again and again upon the writhing objects. Her own sense of loathing was great, but it did not amount to a real fear. Finally she saw that her task was done, and turned to cleanse the improvised bludgeon in the red sand and dry, dead grass near by. She must, she reflected, cover the nest up before Walker got back from tethering the mules. Old Wolf, tottering relic of mixed shepherd and coyote ancestry that he was, had vanished, and she feared he had gone to fetch his master.

Footsteps at that instant proved her fear well founded. A second more, and Walker had seen everything. Audrey made a move to catch him if he should faint, but he did no more than sway. Then the look of pure fright on his bloodless face turned slowly to something like mingled awe and anger, and he began to upbraid his wife in trembling tones.

"Gawd's sake, Aud, but why'd ye go for to do that? Hain't ye heerd all the things they've been tellin' about this snake-devil Yig? Ye'd ought to a told me, and we'd a moved on. Don't ye know they's a devil-god what gets even if ye hurts his children? What for d'ye think the Injuns all dances and beats their drums in the fall about? This land's under a curse, I tell ye—nigh every soul we've a-talked to sence we come in's said the same. Yig rules here, an' he comes out every fall for to git his victims and turn 'em into snakes. Why, Aud, they won't none of them Injuns across the Canayjin kill a snake for love nor money!

"Gawd knows what ye done to yourself, gal, a-stompin' out a hull brood o' Yig's chillen. He'll git ye, sure, sooner or later, unlessen I kin buy a charm offen some o' the Injun medicine-men. He'll git ye, Aud, as sure's they's a Gawd in heaven—he'll come outa the night and turn ye into a crawlin' spotted snake!"

All the rest of the journey Walker kept up the frightened reproofs and prophecies. They crossed the Canadian near Newcastle,[11] and soon afterward met with the first of the real plains Indians they had seen—a party of blanketed Wichitas, whose leader talked freely under the spell of the whiskey offered him, and taught poor Walker a long-winded protective charm against Yig in exchange for a quart bottle of the same inspiring fluid. By the end of the week the chosen site in the Wichita country was reached, and the Davises made haste to trace their boundaries and perform the spring ploughing before even beginning the construction of a cabin.

The region was flat, drearily windy, and sparse of natural vegetation, but promised great fertility under cultivation. Occasional outcroppings of granite diversified a soil of decomposed red sandstone, and here and there a great flat rock would stretch along the surface of the ground like a man-made floor. There seemed to be a very few snakes, or possible dens for them; so Audrey at last persuaded Walker to build the one-room cabin over a vast, smooth slab of exposed stone. With such a flooring and with a good-sized fireplace the wettest weather might be defied—though it soon became evident that dampness was no salient quality of the district. Logs were hauled in the wagon from the nearest belt of woods, many miles toward the Wichita Mountains.[12]

Walker built his wide-chimneyed cabin and crude barn with the aid of some of the other settlers, though the nearest one was over a mile away. In turn, he helped his helpers at similar house-raisings, so that many ties of friendship sprang up between the new neighbours. There was no town worthy the name nearer than El Reno,[13] on the railway thirty miles or more to the northeast; and before many weeks had passed, the people of the section had become very cohesive despite the wideness of their scattering. The Indians, a few of whom had begun to settle down on ranches, were for the most part harmless, though somewhat quarrelsome when fired by the liquid stimulation which found its way to them despite all government bans.

Of all the neighbours the Davises found Joe and Sally Compton, who likewise hailed from Arkansas, the most helpful and congenial. Sally is still alive, known now as Grandma Compton; and her son Clyde, then an infant in arms, has become one of the leading men of the state. Sally and Audrey used to visit each other often, for their cabins were only two miles apart; and in the long spring and summer afternoons they exchanged many a tale of old Arkansas and many a rumour about the new country.

Sally was very sympathetic about Walker's weakness regarding snakes, but perhaps did more to aggravate than cure the parallel nervousness which Audrey was acquiring through his incessant praying and prophesying about the curse of Yig. She was uncommonly full of gruesome snake stories, and produced a direfully strong impression with her acknowledged masterpiece—the tale of a man in Scott County[14] who had been bitten by a whole horde of rattlers at once, and had swelled so monstrously from poison that his body had finally burst with a pop. Needless to say, Audrey did not repeat this anecdote to her husband, and she implored the Comptons to beware of starting it on the rounds of the countryside. It is to Joe's and Sally's credit that they heeded this plea with the utmost fidelity.

Walker did his corn-planting early, and in midsummer improved his time by harvesting a fair crop of the native grass of the region. With the help of Joe Compton he dug a well which gave a moderate supply of very good water, though he planned to sink an artesian later on. He did not run into many serious snake scares, and made his land as inhospitable as possible for wriggling visitors. Every now and then he rode over to the cluster of thatched, conical huts which formed the main village of the Wichitas, and talked long with the old men and shamans about the snake-god and how to nullify his wrath. Charms were always ready in exchange for whiskey, but much of the information he got was far from reassuring.

Yig was a great god. He was bad medicine. He did not forget things. In the autumn his children were hungry and wild, and Yig was hungry and wild, too. All the tribes made medicine against Yig when the corn harvest came. They gave him some corn, and danced in proper regalia to the sound of whistle, rattle, and drum. They kept the drums pounding to drive Yig away, and called down the aid of Tiráwa,[15] whose children men are, even as the snakes are Yig's children. It was bad that the squaw of Davis killed the children of Yig. Let Davis say the charms many times when the corn harvest comes. Yig is Yig. Yig is a great god.

By the time the corn harvest did come, Walker had succeeded in getting his wife into a deplorably jumpy state. His prayers and borrowed incantations came to be a nuisance; and when the autumn rites of the Indians began, there was always a distant wind-borne pounding of tom-toms to lend an added background of the sinister. It was maddening to have the muffled clatter always stealing over the wide red plains. Why would it never stop? Day and night, week on week, it was always going in exhaustless relays, as persistently as the red dusty winds that carried it. Audrey loathed it more than her husband did, for he saw in it a compensating element of protection. It was with this sense of a mighty, intangible bulwark against evil that he got in his corn crop and prepared cabin and stable for the coming winter.

The autumn was abnormally warm, and except for their primitive cookery the Davises found scant use for the stone fireplace Walker had built with such care. Something in the unnaturalness of the hot dust-clouds preyed on the nerves of all the settlers, but most of all on Audrey's and Walker's. The notions of a hovering snake-curse and the weird, endless rhythm of the distant Indian drums formed a bad combination which any added element of the bizarre went far to render utterly unendurable.

Notwithstanding this strain, several festive gatherings were held at one or another of the cabins after the crops were reaped; keeping naively alive in modernity those curious rites of the harvest-home which are as old as human agriculture itself. Lafayette Smith, who came from southern Missouri and had a cabin about three miles east of Walker's, was a very passable fiddler; and his tunes did much to make the celebrants forget the monotonous beating of the distant tom-toms. Then Hallowe'en drew near, and the settlers planned another frolic—this time, had they but known it, of a lineage older than even agriculture; the dread Witch-Sabbath of the primal pre-Aryans, kept alive through ages in the midnight blackness of secret woods, and still hinting at vague terrors under its latter-day mask of comedy and lightness. Hallowe'en was to fall on a Thursday, and the neighbours agreed to gather for their first revel at the Davis cabin.

It was on that thirty-first of October that the warm spell broke. The morning was grey and leaden, and by noon the incessant winds had changed from searingness to rawness. People shivered all the more because they were not prepared for the chill, and Walker Davis' old dog Wolf dragged himself wearily indoors to a place beside the hearth. But the distant drums still thumped on, nor were the white citizenry less inclined to pursue their chosen rites. As early as four in the afternoon the wagons began to arrive at Walker's cabin; and in the evening, after a memorable barbecue, Lafayette Smith's fiddle inspired a very fair-sized company to great feats of saltatory grotesqueness in the one good-sized but crowded room. The younger folk indulged in the amiable inanities proper to the season, and now and then old Wolf would howl with doleful and spine-tickling ominousness at some especially spectral strain from Lafayette's squeaky violin—a device he had never heard before. Mostly, though, this battered veteran slept through the merriment; for he was past the age of active interests and lived largely in his dreams. Tom and Jennie Rigby had brought their collie Zeke along, but the canines did not fraternise. Zeke seemed strangely uneasy over something, and nosed around curiously all the evening.

Audrey and Walker made a fine couple on the floor, and Grandma Compton still likes to recall her impression of their dancing that night. Their worries seemed forgotten for the nonce, and Walker was shaved and trimmed into a surprising degree of spruceness. By ten o'clock all hands were healthily tired, and the guests began to depart family by family with many handshakings and bluff assurances of what a fine time everybody had had. Tom and Jennie thought Zeke's eerie howls as he followed them to their wagon were marks of regret at having to go home; though Audrey said it must be the far-away tom-toms which annoyed him, for the distant thumping was surely ghastly enough after the merriment within.

The night was bitterly cold, and for the first time Walker put a great log in the fireplace and banked it with ashes to keep it smouldering till morning. Old Wolf dragged himself within the ruddy glow and lapsed into his customary coma. Audrey and Walker, too tired to think of charms or curses, tumbled into the rough pine bed and were asleep before the cheap alarm-clock on the mantel had ticked out three minutes. And from far away, the rhythmic pounding of those hellish tom-toms still pulsed on the chill nightwind.

Dr. McNeill paused here and removed his glasses, as if a blurring of the objective world might make the reminiscent vision clearer.

"You'll soon appreciate," he said, "that I had a great deal of difficulty in piecing out all that happened after the guests left. There were times, though—at first—when I was able to make a try at it." After a moment of silence he went on with the tale.

Audrey had terrible dreams of Yig, who appeared to her in the guise of Satan as depicted in cheap engravings she had seen. It was, indeed, from an absolute ecstasy of nightmare that she started suddenly awake to find Walker already conscious and sitting up in bed. He seemed to be listening intently to something, and silenced her with a whisper when she began to ask what had roused him.

"Hark, Aud!" he breathed. "Don't ye hear somethin' a-singin' and buzzin' and rustlin'? D'ye reckon it's the fall crickets?"

Certainly, there was distinctly audible within the cabin such a sound as he had described. Audrey tried to analyse it, and was impressed with some element at once horrible and familiar, which hovered just outside the rim of her memory. And beyond it all, waking a hideous thought, the monotonous beating of the distant tom-toms came incessantly across the black plains on which a cloudy half-moon had set.

"Walker—s'pose it's—the—the—curse o' Yig?"

She could feel him tremble.

"No, gal, I don't reckon he comes that away. He's shapen like a man, except ye look at him clost. That's what Chief Grey Eagle says. This here's some varmints come in outen the cold—not crickets, I calc'late, but summat like 'em. I'd orter git up and stomp 'em out afore they make much headway or git at the cupboard."

He rose, felt for the lantern that hung within easy reach, and rattled the tin match-box nailed to the wall beside it. Audrey sat up in bed and watched the flare of the match grow into the steady glow of the lantern. Then, as their eyes began to take in the whole of the room, the crude rafters shook with the frenzy of their simultaneous shriek.

For the flat, rocky floor, revealed in the new-born illumination, was one seething, brown-speckled mass of wriggling rattlesnakes, slithering toward the fire, and even now turning their loathsome heads to menace the fright-blasted lantern-bearer.

It was only for an instant that Audrey saw the things. The reptiles were of every size, of uncountable numbers, and apparently of several varieties; and even as she looked, two or three of them reared their heads as if to strike at Walker. She did not faint—it was Walker's crash to the floor that extinguished the lantern and plunged her into blackness. He had not screamed a second time—fright had paralysed him, and he fell as if shot by a silent arrow from no mortal's bow. To Audrey the entire world seemed to whirl about fantastically, mingling with the nightmare from which she had started.

Voluntary motion of any sort was impossible, for will and the sense of reality had left her. She fell back inertly on her pillow, hoping that she would wake soon. No actual sense of what had happened penetrated her mind for some time. Then, little by little, the suspicion that she was really awake began to dawn on her; and she was convulsed with a mounting blend of panic and grief which made her long to shriek out despite the inhibiting spell which kept her mute.

Walker was gone, and she had not been able to help him. He had died of snakes, just as the old witch-woman had predicted when he was a little boy. Poor Wolf had not been able to help, either—probably he had not even awaked from his senile stupor. And now the crawling things must be coming for her, writhing closer and closer every moment in the dark, perhaps even now twining slipperily about the bedposts and oozing up over the coarse woollen blankets. Unconsciously she crept under the clothes and trembled.

It must be the curse of Yig. He had sent his monstrous children on All-Hallows' Night, and they had taken Walker first. Why was that—wasn't he innocent enough? Why not come straight for her—hadn't she killed those little rattlers alone? Then she thought of the curse's form as told by the Indians. She wouldn't be killed—just turned to a spotted snake. Ugh! So she would be like those things she had glimpsed on the floor—those things which Yig had sent to get her and enroll her among their number! She tried to mumble a charm that Walker had taught her, but found she could not utter a single sound.

The noisy ticking of the alarm-clock sounded above the maddening beat of the distant tom-toms. The snakes were taking a long time—did they mean to delay on purpose to play on her nerves? Every now and then she thought she felt a steady, insidious pressure on the bedclothes, but each time it turned out to be only the automatic twitchings of her overwrought nerves. The clock ticked on in the dark, and a change came slowly over her thoughts.

Those snakes *couldn't* have taken so long! They couldn't be Yig's messengers after all, but just natural rattlers that were nested below the rock and had been drawn there by the fire. They weren't coming for her, perhaps—perhaps they had sated themselves on poor Walker. Where were they now? Gone? Coiled by the fire? Still crawling over the prone corpse of their victim? The clock ticked, and the distant drums throbbed on.

At the thought of her husband's body lying there in the pitch blackness a thrill of purely physical horror passed over Audrey. That story of Sally Compton's about the man back in Scott County! He, too, had been bitten by a whole bunch of rattlesnakes, and what had happened to him? The poison had rotted the flesh and swelled the whole corpse, and in the end the bloated thing had *burst* horribly—burst horribly with a detestable *popping* noise. Was that what was happening to Walker down there on the rock floor? Instinctively she felt she had begun to *listen* for something too terrible even to name to herself.

The clock ticked on, keeping a kind of mocking, sardonic time with the far-off drumming that the night-wind brought. She wished it were a striking clock, so that she could know how long this eldritch vigil must last. She cursed the toughness of fibre that kept her from fainting, and wondered what sort of relief the dawn could bring, after all. Probably neighbours would pass—no doubt somebody would call—would they find her still sane? Was she still sane now?

Morbidly listening, Audrey all at once became aware of something which she had to verify with every effort of her will before she could believe it; and which, once verified, she did not know whether to welcome or dread. *The distant beating of the Indian tom-toms had ceased.* They had always maddened her—but had not Walker regarded them as a bulwark against nameless evil from outside the universe? What were some of those things he had repeated to her in whispers after talking with Grey Eagle and the Wichita medicine-men?

She did not relish this new and sudden silence, after all! There was something sinister about it. The loud-ticking clock seemed abnormal in its new loneliness. Capable at last of conscious motion, she shook the covers from her face and looked into the darkness toward the window. It must have cleared after the moon set, for she saw the square aperture distinctly against the background of stars.

Then without warning came that shocking, unutterable sound—ugh!—that dull, putrid *pop* of cleft skin and escaping poison in the dark. God!—Sally's story—that obscene stench, and this gnawing, clawing silence! It was too much. The bonds of muteness snapped, and the black night waxed reverberant with Audrey's screams of stark, unbridled frenzy.

Consciousness did not pass away with the shock. How merciful if only it had! Amidst the echoes of her shrieking Audrey still saw the star-sprinkled square of window ahead, and heard the doom-boding ticking of that frightful clock. Did she hear another sound? Was that square window still a perfect square? She was in no condition to weigh the evidence of her senses or distinguish between fact and hallucination.

No—that window was *not* a perfect square. *Something had encroached on the lower edge.* Nor was the ticking of the clock the only sound in the room. There was, beyond dispute, a heavy breathing neither her own nor poor Wolf's. Wolf slept very silently, and his wakeful wheezing was unmistakable. Then Audrey saw against the stars the black, daemoniac silhouette of something anthropoid—the undulant bulk of a gigantic head and shoulders fumbling slowly toward her.

"Y'aaaah! Y'aaaah! Go away! Go away! Go away, snake-devil! Go 'way, Yig! I didn't mean to kill 'em—I was feared he'd be scairt of 'em. Don't, Yig, don't! I didn't go for to hurt yore chillen—don't come nigh me—don't change me into no spotted snake!"

But the half-formless head and shoulders only lurched onward toward the bed, very silently.

Everything snapped at once inside Audrey's head, and in a second she had turned from a cowering child to a raging madwoman. She knew where the axe was—hung against the wall on those pegs near the lantern. It was within easy reach, and she could find it in the dark. Before she was conscious of anything further it was in her hands, and she was creeping toward the foot of the bed—toward the monstrous head and shoulders that every moment groped their way nearer. Had there been any light, the look on her face would not have been pleasant to see.

"Take *that,* you! And *that,* and *that,* and *that!*"

She was laughing shrilly now, and her cackles mounted higher as she saw that the starlight beyond the window was yielding to the dim prophetic pallor of coming dawn.

Dr. McNeill wiped the perspiration from his forehead and put on his glasses again. I waited for him to resume, and as he kept silent I spoke softly.

"She lived? She was found? Was it ever explained?"

The doctor cleared his throat.

"Yes—she lived, in a way. And it was explained. I told you there was no bewitchment—only cruel, pitiful, material horror."

It was Sally Compton who had made the discovery. She had ridden over to the Davis cabin the next afternoon to talk over the party with Audrey, and had seen no smoke from the chimney. That was queer. It had turned very warm again, yet Audrey was usually cooking something at that hour. The mules were making hungry-sounding noises in the barn, and there was no sign of old Wolf sunning himself in the accustomed spot by the door.

Altogether, Sally did not like the look of the place, so was very timid and hesitant as she dismounted and knocked. She got no answer but waited some time before trying the crude door of split logs. The lock, it appeared, was unfastened; and she slowly pushed her way in. Then, perceiving what was there, she reeled back, gasped, and clung to the jamb to preserve her balance.

A terrible odour had welled out as she opened the door, but that was not what had stunned her. It was what she had seen. For within that shadowy cabin monstrous things had happened and three shocking objects remained on the floor to awe and baffle the beholder.

Near the burned-out fireplace was the great dog—purple decay on the skin left bare by mange and old age, and the whole carcass burst by the puffing effect of rattlesnake poison. It must have been bitten by a veritable legion of the reptiles.

To the right of the door was the axe-hacked remnant of what had been a man—clad in a nightshirt, and with the shattered bulk of a lantern clenched in one hand. *He was totally free from any sign of snake-bite.* Near him lay the ensanguined axe, carelessly discarded.

And wriggling flat on the floor was a loathsome, vacant-eyed thing that had been a woman, but was now only a mute mad caricature. All that this thing could do was to hiss, and hiss, and hiss.

Both the doctor and I were brushing cold drops from our foreheads by this time. He poured something from a flask on his desk, took a nip, and handed another glass to me. I could only suggest tremulously and stupidly:

"So Walker had only fainted that first time—the screams roused him, and the axe did the rest?"

"Yes." Dr. McNeill's voice was low. "But he met his death from snakes just the same. It was his fear working in two ways—it made him faint, and it made him fill his wife with the wild stories that caused her to strike out when she thought she saw the snake-devil."

I thought for a moment.

"And Audrey—wasn't it queer how the curse of Yig seemed to work itself out on her? I suppose the impression of hissing snakes had been fairly ground into her."

"Yes. There were lucid spells at first, but they got to be fewer and fewer. Her hair came white at the roots as it grew, and later began to fall out. The skin grew blotchy, and when she died—"

I interrupted with a start.

"*Died?* Then what was that—that thing downstairs?"

McNeill spoke gravely.

"*That* is what was born to her three-quarters of a year afterward. There were three more of them—two were even worse—but this is the only one that lived."

The Electric Executioner

With Adolphe de Castro

or one who has never faced the danger of legal execution, I have a rather queer horror of the electric chair as a subject. Indeed, I think the topic gives me more of a shudder than it gives many a man who has been on trial for his life. The reason is that I associate the thing with an incident of forty years ago—a very strange incident which brought me close to the edge of the unknown's black abyss.

In 1889 I was an auditor and investigator connected with the Tlaxcala Mining Company of San Francisco, which operated several small silver and copper properties in the San Mateo Mountains in Mexico.[1] There had been some trouble at Mine No. 3, which had a surly, furtive assistant superintendent named Arthur Feldon; and on August 6th the firm received a telegram saying that Feldon had decamped, taking with him all the stock records, securities, and private papers, and leaving the whole clerical and financial situation in dire confusion.

This development was a severe blow to the company, and late in the afternoon President McComb called me into his office to give orders for the recovery of the papers at any cost. There were, he knew, grave drawbacks. I had never seen Feldon, and there were only very indifferent photographs to go by. Moreover, my own wedding was set for Thursday of the following week—only nine days ahead—so that I was naturally not eager to be hurried off to Mexico on a man-hunt of indefinite length. The need, however, was so great that McComb felt justified in asking me to go at once; and I for my part decided that the effect on my status with the company would make ready acquiescence eminently worth while.

I was to start that night, using the president's private car as far as Mexico City, after which I would have to take a narrow-gauge railway to the mines. Jackson, the superintendent of No. 3, would give me all details and any possible clues upon my arrival; and then the search would begin in earnest—through the mountains, down to the coast, or among the byways of Mexico City, as the case might be. I set out with a grim determination to get the matter done—and successfully done—as swiftly as possible; and tempered my discontent with pictures of an early return with papers and culprit, and of a wedding which would be almost a triumphal ceremony.

Having notified my family, fiancée, and principal friends, and made hasty preparations for the trip, I met President McComb at eight p.m. at the Southern Pacific depot, received from him some written instructions and a check-book, and left in his car attached to the 8:15 eastbound transcontinental train. The journey that followed seemed destined for uneventfulness, and after a good night's sleep I revelled in the ease of the private car so thoughtfully assigned me; reading my instructions with care, and formulating plans for the capture of Feldon and the recovery of the documents. I knew the Tlaxcala country[2] quite well—probably much better than the missing man—hence had a certain amount of advantage in my search unless he had already used the railway.

According to the instructions, Feldon had been a subject of worry to Superintendent Jackson for some time; acting secretively, and working unaccountably in the company's laboratory at odd hours. That he was implicated with a Mexican boss and several peons in some thefts of ore was strongly suspected; but though the natives had been discharged, there was not enough evidence to warrant any positive step regarding the subtle official. Indeed, despite his furtiveness, there seemed to be more of defiance than of guilt in the man's bearing. He wore a chip on his shoulder, and talked as if the company were cheating him instead of his cheating the company. The obvious surveillance of his colleagues, Jackson wrote, appeared to irritate him increasingly; and now he had gone with everything of importance in the office. Of his possible whereabouts no guess could be made; though Jackson's final telegram suggested the wild slopes of the Sierra de Malinche,[3] that tall, myth-surrounded peak with the corpse-shaped silhouette, from whose neighbourhood the thieving natives were said to have come.

At El Paso, which we reached at two a.m. of the night following our start, my private car was detached from the transcontinental train and joined to an engine specially ordered by telegraph to take it southward to Mexico City. I continued to drowse till dawn, and all the next day grew bored on the flat, desert Chihuahua landscape. The crew had told me we were due in Mexico City at noon Friday, but I soon saw that countless delays were wasting precious hours. There were waits on sidings all along the single-tracked route, and now and then a hot-box[4] or other difficulty would further complicate the schedule.

At Torreón[5] we were six hours late, and it was almost eight o'clock on Friday evening—fully twelve hours behind schedule—when the conductor consented to do some speeding in an effort to make up time. My nerves were on edge, and I could do nothing but pace the car in desperation. In the end I found that the speeding had been purchased at a high cost indeed, for within a half-hour the symptoms of a hot-box had developed in my car itself; so that after a maddening wait the crew decided that all the bearings would have to be overhauled after a quarter-speed limp ahead to the next station with shops—the factory town of Querétaro.[6] This was the last straw, and I almost stamped like a child. Actually I sometimes caught myself pushing at my chair-arm as if trying to urge the train forward at a less snail-like pace.

It was almost ten in the evening when we drew into Querétaro, and I spent a fretful hour on the station platform while my car was sidetracked and tinkered at by a dozen native mechanics. At last they told me the job was too much for them, since the forward truck needed new parts which could not be obtained nearer than Mexico City. Everything indeed seemed against me, and I gritted my teeth when I thought of Feldon getting farther and farther away—perhaps to the easy cover of Vera Cruz[7] with its shipping or Mexico City with its varied rail facilities—while fresh delays kept me tied and helpless. Of course Jackson had notified the police in all the cities around, but I knew with sorrow what their efficiency amounted to.

The best I could do, I soon found out, was to take

the regular night express for Mexico City, which ran from Aguas Calientes[8] and made a five-minute stop at Queré-taro. It would be along at one a.m. if on time, and was due in Mexico City at five o'clock Saturday morning. When I purchased my ticket I found that the train would be made up of European compartment carriages instead of long American cars with rows of two-seat chairs. These had been much used in the early days of Mexican railroading, ow-ing to the European construction interests back of the first lines; and in 1889 the Mexican Central was still running a fair number of them on its shorter trips. Ordinarily I pre-fer the American coaches, since I hate to have people fac-ing me; but for this once I was glad of the foreign carriage. At such a time of night I stood a good chance of having a whole compartment to myself, and in my tired, nervously hypersensitive state I welcomed the solitude—as well as the comfortably upholstered seat with soft arm-rests and head-cushion, running the whole width of the vehicle. I bought a first-class ticket, obtained my valise from the side-tracked private car, telegraphed both President McComb and Jackson of what had happened, and settled down in the station to wait for the night express as patiently as my strained nerves would let me.

For a wonder, the train was only half an hour late; though even so, the solitary station vigil had about finished my endurance. The conductor, shewing me into a com-partment, told me he expected to make up the delay and reach the capital on time; and I stretched myself comfort-ably on the forward-facing seat in the expectation of a quiet three-and-a-half-hour run. The light from the overhead oil lamp was soothingly dim, and I wondered whether I could snatch some much-needed sleep in spite of my anxiety and nerve-tension. It seemed, as the train jolted into motion, that I was alone; and I was heartily glad of it. My thoughts leaped ahead to my quest, and I nodded with the accelerating rhythm of the speeding string of carriages.

Then suddenly I perceived that I was not alone after all. In the corner diagonally opposite me, slumped down so that his face was invisible, sat a roughly clad man of unusual size, whom the feeble light had failed to reveal before. Beside him on the seat was a huge valise, battered and bulging, and tightly gripped even in his sleep by one of his incongruously slender hands. As the engine whistled sharply at some curve or crossing, the sleeper started nervously into a kind of watchful half-awakening; raising his head and disclosing a handsome face, bearded and clearly Anglo-Saxon, with dark, lustrous eyes. At sight of me his wakefulness became complete, and I wondered at the rather hostile wildness of his glance. No doubt, I thought, he resented my presence when he had hoped to have the compartment alone all the way; just as I was myself disappointed to find strange company in the half-lighted carriage. The best we could do, however, was to accept the situation gracefully; so I began apologising to the man for my intrusion. He seemed to be a fellow-American, and we could both feel more at ease after a few civilities. Then we could leave each other in peace for the balance of the journey.

To my surprise, the stranger did not respond to my courtesies with so much as a word. Instead, he kept staring at me fiercely and almost appraisingly, and brushed aside my embarrassed proffer of a cigar with a nervous lateral movement of his disengaged hand. His other hand still tensely clutched the great, worn valise, and his whole person seemed to radiate some obscure malignity. After a time he abruptly turned his face toward the window, though there was nothing to see in the dense blackness outside.

Oddly, he appeared to be looking at something as intently as if there really were something to look at. I decided to leave him to his own curious devices and meditations without further annoyance; so settled back in my seat, drew the brim of my soft hat over my face, and closed my eyes in an effort to snatch the sleep I had half counted on.

I could not have dozed very long or very fully when my eyes fell open as if in response to some external force. Closing them again with some determination, I renewed my quest of a nap, yet wholly without avail. An intangible influence seemed bent on keeping me awake; so raising my head, I looked about the dimly lighted compartment to see if anything were amiss. All appeared normal, but I noticed that the stranger in the opposite corner was looking at me very intently—intently, though without any of the geniality or friendliness which would have implied a change from his former surly attitude. I did not attempt conversation this time, but leaned back in my previous sleepy posture; half closing my eyes as if I had dozed off once more, yet continuing to watch him curiously from beneath my down-turned hat brim.

As the train rattled onward through the night I saw a subtle and gradual metamorphosis come over the expression of the staring man. Evidently satisfied that I was asleep, he allowed his face to reflect a curious jumble of emotions, the nature of which seemed anything but reassuring. Hatred, fear, triumph, and fanaticism flickered compositely over the lines of his lips and the angles of his eyes, while his gaze became a glare of really alarming greed and ferocity. Suddenly it dawned upon me that this man was mad, and dangerously so.

I will not pretend that I was anything but deeply and thoroughly frightened when I saw how things stood. Perspiration started out all over me, and I had hard work to maintain my attitude of relaxation and slumber. Life had many attractions for me just then, and the thought of dealing with a homicidal maniac—possibly armed and certainly powerful to a marvellous degree—was a dismaying and terrifying one. My disadvantage in any sort of struggle was enormous; for the man was a virtual giant, evidently in the best of athletic trim, while I have always been rather frail, and was then almost worn out with anxiety, sleeplessness, and nervous tension. It was undeniably a bad moment for me, and I felt pretty close to a horrible death as I recognised the fury of madness in the stranger's eyes. Events from the past came up into my consciousness as if for a farewell— just as a drowning man's whole life is said to resurrect itself before him at the last moment.

Of course I had my revolver in my coat pocket, but any motion of mine to reach and draw it would be instantly obvious. Moreover, if I did secure it, there was no telling what effect it would have on the maniac. Even if I shot him once or twice he might have enough remaining strength to get the gun from me and deal with me in his own way; or if he were armed himself he might shoot or stab without trying to disarm me. One can cow a sane man by covering him with a pistol, but an insane man's complete indifference to consequences gives him a strength and menace quite superhuman for the time being. Even in those pre-Freudian days[9] I had a common-sense realisation of the dangerous power of a person without normal inhibitions. That the stranger in the corner was indeed about to start some murderous action, his burning eyes and twitching facial muscles did not permit me to doubt for a moment.

Suddenly I heard his breath begin to come in excited gasps, and saw his chest heaving with mounting excitement.

The time for a showdown was close, and I tried desperately to think of the best thing to do. Without interrupting my pretence of sleep, I began to slide my right hand gradually and inconspicuously toward the pocket containing my pistol; watching the madman closely as I did so, to see if he would detect any move. Unfortunately he did—almost before he had time to register the fact in his expression. With a bound so agile and abrupt as to be almost incredible in a man of his size, he was upon me before I knew what had happened; looming up and swaying forward like a giant ogre of legend, and pinioning me with one powerful hand while with the other he forestalled me in reaching the revolver. Taking it from my pocket and placing it in his own, he released me contemptuously, well knowing how fully his physique placed me at his mercy. Then he stood up at his full height—his head almost touching the roof of the carriage—and stared down at me with eyes whose fury had quickly turned to a look of pitying scorn and ghoulish calculation.

I did not move, and after a moment the man resumed his seat opposite me; smiling a ghastly smile as he opened his great bulging valise and extracted an article of peculiar appearance—a rather large cage of semi-flexible wire, woven somewhat like a baseball catcher's mask, but shaped more like the helmet of a diving-suit. Its top was connected with a cord whose other end remained in the valise. This device he fondled with obvious affection, cradling it in his lap as he looked at me afresh and licked his bearded lips with an almost feline motion of the tongue. Then, for the first time, he spoke—in a deep, mellow voice of softness and cultivation startlingly at variance with his rough corduroy clothes and unkempt aspect.

"You are fortunate, sir. I shall use you first of all. You

shall go into history as the first fruits of a remarkable invention. Vast sociological consequences—I shall let my light shine, as it were. I'm radiating all the time, but nobody knows it.[10] Now you shall know. Intelligent guinea-pig. Cats and burros—it worked even with a burro...."

He paused, while his bearded features underwent a convulsive motion closely synchronised with a vigorous gyratory shaking of the whole head. It was as though he were shaking clear of some nebulous obstructing medium, for the gesture was followed by a clarification or subtilisation of expression which hid the more obvious madness in a look of suave composure through which the craftiness gleamed only dimly. I glimpsed the difference at once, and put in a word to see if I could lead his mind into harmless channels.

"You seem to have a marvellously fine instrument, if I'm any judge. Won't you tell me how you came to invent it?"

He nodded.

"Mere logical reflection, dear sir. I consulted the needs of the age and acted upon them. Others might have done the same had their minds been as powerful—that is, as capable of sustained concentration—as mine. I had the sense of conviction—the available will power—that is all. I realised, as no one else has yet realised, how imperative it is to remove everybody from the earth before Quetzalcoatl[11] comes back, and realised also that it must be done elegantly. I hate butchery of any kind, and hanging is barbarously crude. You know last year the New York legislature voted to adopt electric execution for condemned men—but all the apparatus they have in mind is as primitive as Stephenson's 'Rocket' or Davenport's first electric engine.[12] I knew of a better way, and told them so, but they paid no attention to me. God, the fools! As if I didn't know all there is to know about men and death and electricity—student, man, and boy—technologist and engineer—soldier of fortune. . . ."

He leaned back and narrowed his eyes.

"I was in Maximilian's army twenty years and more ago.[13] They were going to make me a nobleman. Then those damned greasers killed him and I had to go home. But I came back—back and forth, back and forth. I live in Rochester, N.Y. . . ."

His eyes grew deeply crafty, and he leaned forward, touching me on the knee with the fingers of a paradoxically delicate hand.

"I came back, I say, and I went deeper than any of them. I hate greasers, but I like Mexicans! A puzzle? Listen to me, young fellow—you don't think Mexico is really Spanish, do you? God, if you knew the tribes I know! In the mountains—in the mountains—Anahuac—Tenochtitlan[14]—the old ones. . . ."

His voice changed to a chanting and not unmelodious howl.

"Iä! Huitzilopotchli! . . . Nahuatlacatl![15] Seven, seven, seven . . . Xochimilca, Chalca, Tepaneca, Acolhua, Tlahuica, Tlascalteca, Azteca![16] . . . Iä! Iä! I have been to the Seven Caves of Chicomoztoc,[17] but no one shall ever know! I tell you *because you will never repeat it.* . . ."

He subsided, and resumed a conversational tone.

"It would surprise you to know what things are told in the mountains. Huitzilopotchli is coming back . . . of that there can be no doubt. Any peon south of Mexico City can tell you that. But I meant to do nothing about it. I went home, as I tell you, again and again, and was going to benefit society with my electric executioner when that cursed Albany legislature adopted the other way. A joke, sir, a joke!

Grandfather's chair—sit by the fireside—Hawthorne—"[18]

The man was chuckling with a morbid parody of good nature.

"Why, sir, I'd like to be the first man to sit in their damned chair and feel their little two-bit battery current! It wouldn't make a frog's legs dance! And they expect to kill murderers with it—reward of merit—everything! But then, young man, I saw the uselessness—the pointless illogicality, as it were—of killing just a few. Everybody is a murderer—they murder ideas—steal inventions—stole mine by watching, and watching, and watching—"

The man choked and paused, and I spoke soothingly.

"I'm sure your invention was much the better, and probably they'll come to use it in the end."

Evidently my tact was not great enough, for his response shewed fresh irritation.

"'Sure,' are you? Nice, mild, conservative assurance! Cursed lot you care—*but you'll soon know!* Why, damn you, all the good there ever will be in that electric chair will have been stolen from me. The ghost of Nezahualpilli[19] told me that on the sacred mountain. They watched, and watched, and watched—"

He choked again, then gave another of those gestures in which he seemed to shake both his head and his facial expression. That seemed temporarily to steady him.

"What my invention needs is testing. That is it—here. The wire hood or head-net is flexible, and slips on easily. Neckpiece binds but doesn't choke. Electrodes touch forehead and base of cerebellum—all that's necessary. Stop the head, and what else can go? The fools up at Albany, with their carved oak easy-chair, think they've got to make it a head-to-foot affair. Idiots!—don't they know that you don't need to shoot a man through the body after you've

206

plugged him through the brain? I've seen men die in battle—I know better. And then their silly high-power circuit—dynamos—all that. Why didn't they see what I've done with the storage-battery? Not a hearing—nobody knows—I alone have the secret—that's why I and Quetzalcoatl and Huitzilopotchli will rule the world alone—I and they, if I choose to let them. . . . But I must have experimental subjects—subjects—*do you know whom I've chosen for the first?*"

I tried jocoseness, quickly merging into friendly seriousness, as a sedative. Quick thought and apt words might save me yet.

"Well, there are lots of fine subjects among the politicians of San Francisco, where I come from! They need your treatment, and I'd like to help you introduce it! But really, I think I can help you in all truth. I have some influence in Sacramento, and if you'll go back to the States with me after I'm through with my business in Mexico, I'll see that you get a hearing."

He answered soberly and civilly.

"No—I can't go back. I swore not to when those criminals at Albany turned down my invention and set spies to watch me and steal from me. But I must have American subjects. Those greasers are under a curse, and would be too easy; and the full-blood Indians—the real children of the feathered serpent—are sacred and inviolate except for proper sacrificial victims . . . and even those must be slain according to ceremony. I must have Americans without going back—and the first man I choose will be signally honoured. Do you know who he is?"

I temporised desperately.

"Oh, if that's all the trouble, I'll find you a dozen first-rate Yankee specimens as soon as we get to Mexico City!

I know where there are lots of small mining men who wouldn't be missed for days—"

But he cut me short with a new and sudden air of authority which had a touch of real dignity in it.

"That'll do—we've trifled long enough. Get up and stand erect like a man. You're the subject I've chosen, and you'll thank me for the honour in the other world, just as the sacrificial victim thanks the priest for transferring him to eternal glory. A new principle—no other man alive has dreamed of such a battery, and it might never again be hit on if the world experimented a thousand years. Do you know that atoms aren't what they seem? Fools! A century after this some dolt would be guessing if I were to let the world live!"

As I arose at his command, he drew additional feet of cord from the valise and stood erect beside me; the wire helmet outstretched toward me in both hands, and a look of real exaltation on his tanned and bearded face. For an instant he seemed like a radiant Hellenic mystagogue or hierophant.

"Here, O Youth—a libation! Wine of the cosmos— nectar of the starry spaces—Linos—Iacchus—Ialmenos—Zagreus—Dionysos—Atys—Hylas[20]—sprung from Apollo and slain by the hounds of Argos—seed of Psamathë[21]—child of the sun—Evoë! Evoë!"[22]

He was chanting again, and this time his mind seemed far back amongst the classic memories of his college days. In my erect posture I noticed the nearness of the signal cord overhead, and wondered whether I could reach it through some gesture of ostensible response to his ceremonial mood. It was worth trying, so with an antiphonal cry of "Evoë!" I put my arms forward and upward toward him in a ritualistic fashion, hoping to give the cord a tug before he could notice the act. But it was useless. He saw my purpose, and moved one hand toward the right-hand coat pocket where my revolver lay. No words were needed, and we stood for a moment like carven figures. Then he quietly said, "Make haste!"

Again my mind rushed frantically about seeking avenues of escape. The doors, I knew, were not locked on Mexican trains; but my companion could easily forestall me if I tried to unlatch one and jump out. Besides, our speed was so great that success in that direction would probably be as fatal as failure. The only thing to do was to play for time. Of the three-and-a-half-hour trip a good slice was already worn away, and once we got to Mexico City the guards and police in the station would provide instant safety.

There would, I thought, be two distinct times for diplomatic stalling. If I could get him to postpone the slipping on of the hood, that much time would be gained. Of course I had no belief that the thing was really deadly; but I knew enough of madmen to understand what would happen when it failed to work. To his disappointment would be added a mad sense of my responsibility for the failure, and the result would be a red chaos of murderous rage. Therefore the experiment must be postponed as long as possible. Yet the second opportunity did exist, for if I planned cleverly I might devise explanations for the failure which would hold his attention and lead him into more or less extended searches for corrective influences. I wondered just how far his credulity went, and whether I could prepare in advance a prophecy of failure which would make the failure itself stamp me as a seer or initiate, or perhaps a god. I had enough of a smattering of Mexican mythology to make it worth trying; though I would try other delaying influences first and let the prophecy come as a sudden revelation. Would he spare me in the end if I could make him think me a prophet or divinity? Could I "get by" as Quetzalcoatl or Huitzilopotchli? Anything to drag matters out till five o'clock, when we were due in Mexico City.

But my opening "stall" was the veteran will-making ruse. As the maniac repeated his command for haste, I told him of my family and intended marriage, and asked for the privilege of leaving a message and disposing of my money and effects. If, I said, he would lend me some paper and agree to mail what I should write, I could die more peacefully and willingly. After some cogitation he gave a favourable verdict and fished in his valise for a pad, which he handed me solemnly as I resumed my seat. I produced a pencil, artfully breaking the point at the outset and causing some delay while he searched for one of his own. When he gave me this, he took my broken pencil and proceeded to sharpen it with a large, horn-handled knife which had been in his belt under his coat. Evidently a second pencil-breaking would not profit me greatly.

What I wrote, I can hardly recall at this date. It was largely gibberish, and composed of random scraps of memorised literature when I could think of nothing else to set down. I made my handwriting as illegible as I could without destroying its nature as writing; for I knew he would be likely to look at the result before commencing his experiment, and realised how he would react to the sight of obvious nonsense. The ordeal was a terrible one, and I chafed each second at the slowness of the train. In the past I had often whistled a brisk gallop to the sprightly "tac" of wheels on rails, but now the tempo seemed slowed down to that of a funeral march—my funeral march, I grimly reflected.

My ruse worked till I had covered over four pages, six by nine; when at last the madman drew out his watch and told me I could have but five minutes more. What should I do next? I was hastily going through the form of concluding the will when a new idea struck me. Ending with a flourish and handing him the finished sheets, which he thrust carelessly into his left-hand coat pocket, I reminded him of my influential Sacramento friends who would be so much interested in his invention.

"Oughtn't I to give you a letter of introduction to them?" I said. "Oughtn't I to make a signed sketch and description of your executioner so that they'll grant you a cordial hearing? They can make you famous, you know—and there's no question at all but that they'll adopt your method for the state of California if they hear of it through someone like me, whom they know and trust."

I was taking this tack on the chance that his thoughts as a disappointed inventor would let him forget the Aztec-religious side of his mania for a while. When he veered to the latter again, I reflected, I would spring the "revelation" and "prophecy". The scheme worked, for his eyes glowed an eager assent, though he brusquely told me to be quick. He further emptied the valise, lifting out a queer-looking congeries of glass cells and coils to which the wire from the helmet was attached, and delivering a fire of running comment too technical for me to follow yet apparently quite plausible and straightforward. I pretended to note down all he said, wondering as I did so whether the queer apparatus was really a battery after all. Would I get a slight shock when he applied the device? The man surely talked as if he were a genuine electrician. Description of his own invention was clearly a congenial task for him, and I saw he was not as impatient as before. The hopeful grey of dawn glimmered red through the windows before he wound up, and I felt at last that my chance of escape had really become tangible.

But he, too, saw the dawn, and began glaring wildly again. He knew the train was due in Mexico City at five, and would certainly force quick action unless I could override all his judgment with engrossing ideas. As he rose with a determined air, setting the battery on the seat beside the open valise, I reminded him that I had not made the needed sketch; and asked him to hold the headpiece so that I could draw it near the battery. He complied and resumed his seat, with many admonitions to me to hurry. After another moment I paused for some information, asking him how the victim was placed for execution, and how his presumable struggles were overcome.

"Why," he replied, "the criminal is securely strapped to a post. It does not matter how much he tosses his head, for the helmet fits tightly and draws even closer when the current comes on. We turn the switch gradually—you see it here, a carefully arranged affair with a rheostat."

A new idea for delay occurred to me as the tilled fields and increasingly frequent houses in the dawnlight outside told of our approach to the capital at last.

"But," I said, "I must draw the helmet in place on a human head as well as beside the battery. Can't you slip it on yourself a moment so that I can sketch you with it? The papers as well as the officials will want all this, and they are strong on completeness."

I had, by chance, made a better shot than I had planned; for at my mention of the press the madman's eyes lit up afresh.

"The papers? Yes—damn them, you can make even the papers give me a hearing! They all laughed at me and wouldn't print a word. Here, you, hurry up! We've not a second to lose!"

He had slipped the headpiece on and was watching

my flying pencil avidly. The wire mesh gave him a grotesque, comic look as he sat there with nervously twitching hands.

"Now, curse 'em, they'll print pictures! I'll revise your sketch if you make any blunders—must be accurate at any cost. Police will find you afterward—they'll tell how it works. Associated Press item—back up your letter—immortal fame.... Hurry, I say—hurry, confound you!"

The train was lurching over the poorer roadbed near the city, and we swayed disconcertingly now and then. With this excuse I managed to break the pencil again, but of course the maniac at once handed me my own which he had sharpened. My first batch of ruses was about used up, and I felt that I should have to submit to the headpiece in a moment. We were still a good quarter-hour from the terminal, and it was about time for me to divert my companion to his religious side and spring the divine prophecy.

Mustering up my scraps of Nahuan-Aztec mythology, I suddenly threw down pencil and paper and commenced to chant.

"Iä! Iä! Tloquenahuaque,[23] Thou Who Art All In Thyself! Thou too, Ipalnemoan,[24] By Whom We Live! I hear, I hear! I see, I see! Serpent-bearing Eagle, hail! A message! A message! Huitzilopotchli, in my soul echoes thy thunder!"

At my intonations the maniac stared incredulously through his odd mask, his handsome face shewn in a surprise and perplexity which quickly changed to alarm. His mind seemed to go blank a moment, and then to recrystallise in another pattern. Raising his hands aloft, he chanted as if in a dream.

"Mictlanteuctli,[25] Great Lord, a sign! A sign from within thy black cave! Iä! Tonatiuh-Metztli![26] Cthulhutl! Command, and I serve!"

Now in all this responsive gibberish there was one

word which struck an odd chord in my memory. Odd, because it never occurs in any printed account of Mexican mythology, yet had been overheard by me more than once as an awestruck whisper amongst the peons in my own firm's Tlaxcala mines. It seemed to be part of an exceedingly secret and ancient ritual; for there were characteristic whispered responses which I had caught now and then, and which were as unknown as itself to academic scholarship. This maniac must have spent considerable time with the hill peons and Indians, just as he had said; for surely such unrecorded lore could have come from no mere book-learning. Realising the importance he must attach to this doubly esoteric jargon, I determined to strike at his most vulnerable spot and give him the gibberish responses the natives used.

"Ya-R'lyeh! Ya-R'lyeh!" I shouted. "Cthulhutl fhtaghn! Niguratl-Yig! Yog-Sototl—"[27]

But I never had a chance to finish. Galvanised into a religious epilepsy by the exact response which his subconscious mind had probably not really expected, the madman scrambled down to a kneeling posture on the floor, bowing his wire-helmeted head again and again, and turning it to the right and left as he did so. With each turn his obeisances became more profound, and I could hear his foaming lips repeating the syllable "kill, kill, kill," in a rapidly swelling monotone. It occurred to me that I had overreached myself, and that my response had unloosed a mounting mania which would rouse him to the slaying-point before the train reached the station.

As the arc of the madman's turnings gradually increased, the slack in the cord from his headpiece to the battery had naturally been taken up more and more. Now, in an all-forgetting delirium of ecstasy, he began to magnify his turns to complete circles, so that the cord wound round his neck and began to tug at its moorings to the battery on the seat. I wondered what he would do when the inevitable would happen, and the battery would be dragged to presumable destruction on the floor.

Then came the sudden cataclysm. The battery, yanked over the seat's edge by the maniac's last gesture of orgiastic frenzy, did indeed fall; but it did not seem to have wholly broken. Instead, as my eye caught the spectacle in one too-fleeting instant, the actual impact was borne by the rheostat, so that the switch was jerked over instantly to full current. And the marvellous thing is that there *was* a current. The invention was no mere dream of insanity.

I saw a blinding blue auroral coruscation, heard an ululating shriek more hideous than any of the previous cries of that mad, horrible journey, and smelled the nauseous odour of burning flesh. That was all my overwrought consciousness could bear, and I sank instantly into oblivion.

When the train guard at Mexico City revived me, I found a crowd on the station platform around my compartment door. At my involuntary cry the pressing faces became curious and dubious, and I was glad when the guard shut out all but the trim doctor who had pushed his way through to me. My cry was a very natural thing, but it had been prompted by something more than the shocking sight on the carriage floor which I had expected to see. Or should I say, by something *less,* because in truth there was not anything on the floor at all.

Nor, said the guard, had there been when he opened the door and found me unconscious within. My ticket was the only one sold for that compartment, and I was the only person found within it. Just myself and my valise, nothing more. I had been alone all the way from Querétaro. Guard, doctor, and spectators alike tapped their foreheads significantly at my frantic and insistent questions.

Had it all been a dream, or was I indeed mad? I recalled my anxiety and overwrought nerves, and shuddered. Thanking the guard and doctor, and shaking free of the curious crowd, I staggered into a cab and was taken to the Fonda Nacional, where, after telegraphing Jackson at the mine, I slept till afternoon in an effort to get a fresh grip on myself. I had myself called at one o'clock, in time to catch the narrow-gauge for the mining country, but when I got up I found a telegram under the door. It was from Jackson, and said that Feldon had been found dead in the mountains that morning, the news reaching the mine about ten o'clock. The papers were all safe, and the San Francisco office had been duly notified. So the whole trip, with its nervous haste and harrowing mental ordeal, had been for nothing!

Knowing that McComb would expect a personal report despite the course of events, I sent another wire ahead and took the narrow-gauge after all. Four hours later I was rattled and jolted into the station of Mine No. 3, where Jackson was waiting to give a cordial greeting. He was so full of the affair at the mine that he did not notice my still shaken and seedy appearance.

The superintendent's story was brief, and he told me it as he led me toward the shack up the hillside above the *arrastre*,[28] where Feldon's body lay. Feldon, he said, had always been a queer, sullen character, ever since he was hired the year before; working at some secret mechanical device and complaining of constant espionage, and being disgustingly familiar with the native workmen. But he certainly knew the work, the country, and the people. He used to make long trips into the hills where the peons lived, and even to take part in some of their ancient, heathenish ceremonies. He hinted at odd secrets and strange powers as often as he boasted of his mechanical skill. Of late he had disintegrated rapidly; growing morbidly suspicious of his colleagues, and undoubtedly joining his native friends in ore-thieving after his cash got low. He needed unholy amounts of money for something or other—was always having boxes come from laboratories and machine shops in Mexico City or the States.

As for the final absconding with all the papers—it was only a crazy gesture of revenge for what he called "spying". He was certainly stark mad, for he had gone across country to a hidden cave on the wild slope of the haunted Sierra de Malinche, where no white men live, and had done some amazingly queer things. The cave, which would never have been found but for the final tragedy, was full of hideous old Aztec idols and altars; the latter covered with the charred bones of recent burnt-offerings of doubtful nature. The natives would tell nothing—indeed, they swore they knew nothing—but it was easy to see that the cave was an old rendezvous of theirs, and that Feldon had shared their practices to the fullest extent.

The searchers had found the place only because of the chanting and the final cry. It had been close to five that morning, and after an all-night encampment the party had begun to pack up for its empty-handed return to the mines. Then somebody had heard faint rhythms in the distance, and knew that one of the noxious old native rituals was being howled from some lonely spot up the slope of the corpse-shaped mountain. They heard the same old names—Mictlanteuctli, Tonatiuh-Metztli, Cthulhutl, Ya-R'lyeh, and all the rest—but the queer thing was that some English words were mixed with them. Real white man's English, and no greaser patter. Guided by the sound, they had hastened up the weed-entangled mountainside toward it, when after a spell of quiet the shriek had burst upon them. It was a terrible thing—a worse thing than any of them had ever heard before. There seemed to be some smoke, too, and a morbid acrid smell.

Then they stumbled on the cave, its entrance screened by scrub mesquites, but now emitting clouds of foetid smoke. It was lighted within, the horrible altars and grotesque images revealed flickeringly by candles which must have been changed less than a half-hour before; and on the gravelly floor lay the horror that made all the crowd reel backward. It was Feldon, head burned to a crisp by some odd device he had slipped over it—a kind of wire cage connected with a rather shaken-up battery which had evidently fallen to the floor from a nearby altar-pot. When the men saw it they exchanged glances, thinking of the "electric executioner" Feldon had always boasted of inventing—the thing which everyone had rejected, but had tried to steal and copy. The papers were safe in Feldon's open portmanteau which stood close by, and an hour later the column of searchers started back for No. 3 with a grisly burden on an improvised stretcher.

That was all, but it was enough to make me turn pale and falter as Jackson led me up past the *arrastre* to the shed where he said the body lay. For I was not without imagination, and knew only too well into what hellish nightmare this tragedy somehow supernaturally dovetailed. I knew what I should see inside that gaping door around which the curious miners clustered, and did not flinch when my eyes took in the giant form, the rough corduroy clothes, the oddly delicate hands, the wisps of burnt beard, and the hellish machine itself—battery slightly broken, and headpiece blackened by the charring of what was inside. The great, bulging portmanteau did not surprise me, and I quailed only at two things—the folded sheets of paper sticking out of the left-hand pocket, and the queer sagging of the corresponding right-hand pocket. In a moment when no one was looking I reached out and seized the too familiar sheets, crushing them in my hand without daring to look at their penmanship. I ought to be sorry now that a kind of panic fear made me burn them that night with averted eyes. They would have been a positive proof or disproof of something—but for that matter I could still have had proof by asking about the revolver the coroner afterward took from that sagging right-hand coat pocket. I never had the courage to ask about that—because my own revolver was missing after the night on the train. My pocket pencil, too, shewed signs of a crude and hasty sharpening unlike the precise pointing I had given it Friday afternoon on the machine in President McComb's private car.

So in the end I went home still puzzled—mercifully puzzled, perhaps. The private car was repaired when I got back to Querétaro, but my greatest relief was crossing the Rio Grande into El Paso and the States. By the next Friday I was in San Francisco again, and the postponed wedding came off the following week.

As to what really happened that night—as I've said, I simply don't dare to speculate. That chap Feldon was insane to start with, and on top of his insanity he had piled a lot of prehistoric Aztec witch-lore that nobody has any right to know. He was really an inventive genius, and that battery must have been the genuine stuff. I heard later how he had been brushed aside in former years by press, public, and potentates alike. Too much disappointment isn't good for men of a certain kind. Anyhow, some unholy combination of influences was at work. He had really, by the way, been a soldier of Maximilian's.

When I tell my story most people call me a plain liar. Others lay it to abnormal psychology—and heaven knows I *was* overwrought—while still others talk of "astral projection" of some sort. My zeal to catch Feldon certainly sent my thoughts ahead toward him, and with all his Indian magic he'd be about the first one to recognise and meet them. Was he in the railway carriage or was I in the cave on the corpse-shaped haunted mountain? What would have happened to me, had I not delayed him as I did? I'll confess I don't know, and I'm not sure that I want to know. I've never been in Mexico since—and as I said at the start, I don't enjoy hearing about electric executions.

The Mound

With Zealia Bishop

I.

It is only within the last few years that most people have stopped thinking of the West as a *new* land. I suppose the idea gained ground because our own especial civilisation happens to be new there; but nowadays explorers are digging beneath the surface and bringing up whole chapters of life that rose and fell among these plains and mountains before recorded history began. We think nothing of a Pueblo village 2500 years old, and it hardly jolts us when archaeologists put the sub-pedregal culture of Mexico back to 17,000 or 18,000 B. C.[1] We hear rumours of still older things, too—of primitive man contemporaneous with extinct animals and known today only through a few fragmentary bones and artifacts—so that the idea of newness is fading out pretty rapidly. Europeans usually catch the sense of immemorial ancientness and deep deposits from successive life-streams better than we do. Only a couple of years ago a British author spoke of Arizona as a "moon-dim region, very lovely in its way, and stark and old—an ancient, lonely land".[2]

Yet I believe I have a deeper sense of the stupefying—almost horrible—ancientness of the West than any European. It all comes from an incident that happened in 1928; an incident which I'd greatly like to dismiss as three-quarters hallucination, but which has left such a frightfully firm impression on my memory that I can't put it off very easily. It was in Oklahoma, where my work as an American Indian ethnologist constantly takes me and where I had come upon some devilishly strange and disconcerting matters before. Make no mistake—Oklahoma is a lot more than a mere pioneers' and promoters' frontier. There are old, old tribes with old, old memories there; and when the tom-toms beat ceaselessly over brooding plains in the autumn the spirits of men are brought dangerously close to primal, whispered things. I am white and Eastern enough myself, but anybody is welcome to know that the rites of Yig, Father of Snakes, can get a real shudder out of me any day. I have heard and seen too much to be "sophisticated" in such matters. And so it is with this incident of 1928. I'd like to laugh it off—but I can't.

I had gone into Oklahoma to track down and correlate one of the many ghost tales which were current among the white settlers, but which had strong Indian corroboration, and—I felt sure—an ultimate Indian source. They were very curious, these open-air ghost tales; and though they sounded flat and prosaic in the mouths of the white people, they had earmarks of linkage with some of the richest and obscurest phases of native mythology. All of them were woven around the vast, lonely, artificial-looking mounds in the western part of the state, and all of them involved apparitions of exceedingly strange aspect and equipment.

The commonest, and among the oldest, became quite famous in 1892, when a government marshal named John Willis went into the mound region after horse-thieves and came out with a wild yarn of nocturnal cavalry battles in the air between great armies of invisible spectres—battles that involved the rush of hooves and feet, the thud of blows, the clank of metal on metal, the muffled cries of warriors, and the fall of human and equine bodies. These things happened by moonlight, and frightened his horse as well as himself. The sounds persisted an hour at a time; vivid, but subdued as if brought from a distance by a wind, and unaccompanied by any glimpse of the armies themselves. Later on Willis learned that the seat of the sounds was a notoriously haunted spot, shunned by settlers and Indians alike. Many had seen, or half seen, the warring horsemen in the sky, and had furnished dim, ambiguous descriptions. The settlers described the ghostly fighters as Indians, though of no familiar tribe, and having the most singular costumes and weapons. They even went so far as to say that they could not be sure the horses were really horses.

The Indians, on the other hand, did not seem to claim the spectres as kinsfolk. They referred to them as "those people", "the old people", or "they who dwell below", and appeared to hold them in too great a frightened veneration to talk much about them. No ethnologist had been able to pin any tale-teller down to a specific description of the beings, and apparently nobody had ever had a very clear look at them. The Indians had one or two old proverbs about these phenomena, saying that "men very old, make very big spirit; not so old, not so big; older than all time, then spirit he so big he near flesh; those old people and spirits they mix up—get all the same".

Now all of this, of course, is "old stuff" to an ethnologist—of a piece with the persistent legends of rich hidden cities and buried races which abound among the Pueblo and plains Indians, and which lured Coronado centuries ago on his vain search for the fabled Quivira.[3] What took me into western Oklahoma was something far more definite and tangible—a local and distinctive tale which, though really old, was wholly new to the outside world of research, and which involved the first clear descriptions of the ghosts which it treated of. There was an added thrill in the fact that it came from the remote town of Binger, in Caddo County,[4] a place I had long known as the scene of a very terrible and partly inexplicable occurrence connected with the snake-god myth.

The tale, outwardly, was an extremely naive and simple one, and centred in a huge, lone mound or small hill that rose above the plain about a third of a mile west of the village—a mound which some thought a product of Nature, but which others believed to be a burial-place or ceremonial dais constructed by prehistoric tribes. This mound, the villagers said, was constantly haunted by two Indian figures which appeared in alternation; an old man who paced back and forth along the top from dawn till dusk, regardless of the weather and with only brief intervals of disappearance, and a squaw who took his place at night with a blue-flamed torch that glimmered quite continuously till morning. When the moon was bright the squaw's peculiar figure could be seen fairly plainly, and over half the villagers agreed that the apparition was headless.

Local opinion was divided as to the motives and relative ghostliness of the two visions. Some held that the man was not a ghost at all, but a living Indian who had killed and beheaded a squaw for gold and buried her somewhere on the mound. According to these theorists he was pacing the eminence through sheer remorse, bound by the spirit of his victim which took visible shape after dark. But other theorists, more uniform in their spectral beliefs, held that both man and woman were ghosts; the man having killed the squaw and himself as well at some very distant period. These and minor variant versions seemed to have been current ever since the settlement of the Wichita country in 1889, and were, I was told, sustained to an astonishing degree by still-existing phenomena which anyone might observe for himself. Not many ghost tales offer such free and open proof, and I was very eager to see what bizarre wonders might be lurking in this small, obscure village so far from the beaten path of crowds and from the ruthless searchlight of scientific knowledge. So, in the late summer of 1928 I took a train for Binger and brooded on strange mysteries as the cars rattled timidly along their single track through a lonelier and lonelier landscape.

Binger is a modest cluster of frame houses and stores in the midst of a flat windy region full of clouds of red dust. There are about 500 inhabitants[5] besides the Indians on a neighbouring reservation; the principal occupation seeming to be agriculture. The soil is decently fertile, and the oil boom has not reached this part of the state. My train drew in at twilight, and I felt rather lost and uneasy—cut off from wholesome and every-day things—as it puffed away to the southward without me. The station platform was filled with curious loafers, all of whom seemed eager to direct me when I asked for the man to whom I had letters of introduction. I was ushered along a commonplace main street whose rutted surface was red with the sandstone soil of the country, and finally delivered at the door of my prospective host. Those who had arranged things for me had done well; for Mr. Compton was a man of high intelligence and local responsibility, while his mother—who lived with him and was familiarly known as "Grandma Compton"—was one of the first pioneer generation, and a veritable mine of anecdote and folklore.

That evening the Comptons summed up for me all the legends current among the villagers, proving that the phenomenon I had come to study was indeed a baffling and important one. The ghosts, it seems, were accepted almost as a matter of course by everyone in Binger. Two generations had been born and grown up within sight of that queer, lone tumulus and its restless figures. The neighbourhood of the mound was naturally feared and shunned, so that the village and the farms had not spread toward it in all four decades of settlement; yet venturesome individuals had several times visited it. Some had come back to report that they saw no ghosts at all when they neared the dreaded hill; that somehow the lone sentinel had stepped out of sight before they reached the spot, leaving them free to climb the steep slope and explore the flat summit. There was nothing up there, they said—merely a rough expanse of underbrush. Where the Indian watcher could have vanished to, they had no idea. He must, they reflected, have descended the slope and somehow managed to escape unseen along the plain; although there was no convenient cover within sight. At any rate, there did not appear to be any opening into the mound; a conclusion which was reached after considerable exploration of the shrubbery and tall grass on all sides. In a few cases some of the more sensitive searchers declared that they felt a sort of invisible restraining presence; but they could describe nothing more definite than that. It was simply as if the air thickened against them in the direction they wished to move. It is needless to mention that all these daring surveys were conducted by day. Nothing in

the universe could have induced any human being, white
or red, to approach that sinister elevation after dark; and
indeed, no Indian would have thought of going near it even
in the brightest sunlight.

But it was not from the tales of these sane, observant
seekers that the chief terror of the ghost-mound sprang; indeed, had their experience been typical, the phenomenon
would have bulked far less prominently in the local legendry. The most evil thing was the fact that many other seekers
had come back strangely impaired in mind and body, or had
not come back at all. The first of these cases had occurred
in 1891, when a young man named Heaton had gone with
a shovel to see what hidden secrets he could unearth. He
had heard curious tales from the Indians, and had laughed
at the barren report of another youth who had been out to
the mound and had found nothing. Heaton had watched
the mound with a spy glass from the village while the other
youth made his trip; and as the explorer neared the spot,
he saw the sentinel Indian walk deliberately down into the
tumulus as if a trap-door and staircase existed on the top.
The other youth had not noticed how the Indian disappeared, but had merely found him gone upon arriving at
the mound.

When Heaton made his own trip he resolved to get
to the bottom of the mystery, and watchers from the village saw him hacking diligently at the shrubbery atop the
mound. Then they saw his figure melt slowly into invisibility; not to reappear for long hours, till after the dusk
drew on, and the torch of the headless squaw glimmered
ghoulishly on the distant elevation. About two hours after
nightfall he staggered into the village minus his spade and
other belongings, and burst into a shrieking monologue of
disconnected ravings. He howled of shocking abysses and

monsters, of terrible carvings and statues, of inhuman captors and grotesque tortures, and of other fantastic abnormalities too complex and chimerical even to remember. "Old! Old! Old!" he would moan over and over again, "great God, they are older than the earth, and came here from somewhere else—they know what you think, and make you know what they think—they're half-man, half-ghost—crossed the line—melt and take shape again—getting more and more so, yet we're all descended from them in the beginning—children of Tulu[6]—everything made of gold—monstrous animals, half-human—dead slaves—madness—Iä! Shub-Niggurath!—*that white man—oh, my God, what they did to him!...*"

Heaton was the village idiot for about eight years, after which he died in an epileptic fit. Since his ordeal there had been two more cases of mound-madness, and eight of total disappearance. Immediately after Heaton's mad return, three desperate and determined men had gone out to the lone hill together; heavily armed, and with spades and pickaxes. Watching villagers saw the Indian ghost melt away as the explorers drew near, and afterward saw the men climb the mound and begin scouting around through the underbrush. All at once they faded into nothingness, and were never seen again. One watcher, with an especially powerful telescope, thought he saw other forms dimly materialise beside the hapless men and drag them down into the mound; but this account remained uncorroborated. It is needless to say that no searching-party went out after the lost ones, and that for many years the mound was wholly unvisited. Only when the incidents of 1891 were largely forgotten did anybody dare to think of further explorations. Then, about 1910, a fellow too young to recall the old horrors made a trip to the shunned spot and found nothing at all.

By 1915 the acute dread and wild legendry of '91 had largely faded into the commonplace and unimaginative ghost-tales at present surviving—that is, had so faded among the white people. On the nearby reservation were old Indians who thought much and kept their own counsel. About this time a second wave of active curiosity and adventuring developed, and several bold searchers made the trip to the mound and returned. Then came a trip of two Eastern visitors with spades and other apparatus—a pair of amateur archaeologists connected with a small college, who had been making studies among the Indians. No one watched this trip from the village, but they never came back. The searching-party that went out after them—among whom was my host Clyde Compton—found nothing whatsoever amiss at the mound.

The next trip was the solitary venture of old Capt. Lawton, a grizzled pioneer who had helped to open up the region in 1889, but who had never been there since. He had recalled the mound and its fascination all through the years; and being now in comfortable retirement, resolved to have a try at solving the ancient riddle. Long familiarity with Indian myth had given him ideas rather stranger than those of the simple villagers, and he had made preparations for some extensive delving. He ascended the mound on the morning of Thursday, May 11, 1916, watched through spy glasses by more than twenty people in the village and on the adjacent plain. His disappearance was very sudden, and occurred as he was hacking at the shrubbery with a brush-cutter. No one could say more than that he was there one moment and absent the next. For over a week no tidings of him reached Binger, and then—in the middle of the night—there dragged itself into the village the object about which dispute still rages.

It said it was—or had been—Capt. Lawton, but it was definitely *younger* by as much as forty years than the old man who had climbed the mound. Its hair was jet black, and its face—now distorted with nameless fright—free from wrinkles. But it did remind Grandma Compton most uncannily of the captain as he had looked back in '89. Its feet were cut off neatly at the ankles, and the stumps were smoothly healed to an extent almost incredible if the being really were the man who had walked upright a week before. It babbled of incomprehensible things, and kept repeating the name "George Lawton, George E. Lawton" as if trying to reassure itself of its own identity. The things it babbled of, Grandma Compton thought, were curiously like the hallucinations of poor young Heaton in '91; though there were minor differences. "The blue light!—the blue light! . . ." muttered the object, "always down there, before there were any living things—older than the dinosaurs—always the same, only weaker—never death—brooding and brooding and brooding—*the same people, half-man and half-gas*—the dead that walk and work—oh, those beasts, those half-human unicorns—houses and cities of gold—old, old, old, older than time—came down from the stars—Great Tulu—Azathoth—Nyarlathotep[7]—waiting, waiting. . . ." The object died before dawn.

Of course there was an investigation, and the Indians at the reservation were grilled unmercifully. But they knew nothing, and had nothing to say. At least, none of them had anything to say except old Grey Eagle, a Wichita chieftain whose more than a century of age put him above common fears. He alone deigned to grunt some advice.

"You let um 'lone, white man. No good—those people. All under here, all under there, them old ones. Yig, big father of snakes, he there. Yig is Yig. Tiráwa,[8] big father of men, he there. Tiráwa is Tiráwa. No die. No get old. Just same like air. Just live and wait. One time they come out here, live and fight. Build um dirt tepee. Bring up gold— they got plenty. Go off and make new lodges. Me them. You them. Then big waters come. All change. Nobody come out, let nobody in. Get in, no get out. You let um 'lone, you have no bad medicine. Red man know, he no get catch. White man meddle, he no come back. Keep 'way little hills. No good. Grey Eagle say this."

If Joe Norton and Rance Wheelock had taken the old chief's advice, they would probably be here today; but they didn't. They were great readers and materialists, and feared nothing in heaven or earth; and they thought that some Indian fiends had a secret headquarters inside the mound. They had been to the mound before, and now they went again to avenge old Capt. Lawton—boasting that they'd do it if they had to tear the mound down altogether. Clyde Compton watched them with a pair of prism binoculars and saw them round the base of the sinister hill. Evidently they meant to survey their territory very gradually and minutely. Minutes passed, and they did not reappear. Nor were they ever seen again.

Once more the mound was a thing of panic fright, and only the excitement of the Great War served to restore it to the farther background of Binger folklore. It was unvisited from 1916 to 1919, and would have remained so but for the daredeviltry of some of the youths back from service in France. From 1919 to 1920, however, there was a veritable epidemic of mound-visiting among the prematurely hardened young veterans—an epidemic that waxed as one youth after another returned unhurt and contemptuous. By 1920—so short is human memory—the mound was almost a joke; and the tame story of the murdered squaw began to displace darker whispers on everybody's tongues. Then two reckless young brothers—the especially unimaginative and hard-boiled Clay boys—decided to go and dig up the buried squaw and the gold for which the old Indian had murdered her.

They went out on a September afternoon—about the time the Indian tom-toms begin their incessant annual beating over the flat, red-dusty plains. Nobody watched them, and their parents did not become worried at their non-return for several hours. Then came an alarm and a searching-party, and another resignation to the mystery of silence and doubt.

But one of them came back after all. It was Ed, the elder, and his straw-coloured hair and beard had turned an albino white for two inches from the roots. On his forehead was a queer scar like a branded hieroglyph. Three months after he and his brother Walker had vanished he skulked into his house at night, wearing nothing but a queerly patterned blanket which he thrust into the fire as soon as he had got into a suit of his own clothes. He told his parents that he and Walker had been captured by some strange Indians—not Wichitas or Caddos—and held prisoners somewhere toward the west. Walker had died under torture, but he himself had managed to escape at a high cost. The experience had been particularly terrible, and he could not talk about it just then. He must rest—and anyway, it would do no good to give an alarm and try to find and punish the Indians. They were not of a sort that could be caught or punished, and it was especially important for the good of Binger—for the good of the world—that they be not pursued into their secret lair. As a matter of fact, they were not altogether what one could call real Indians—he would explain about that later. Meanwhile he must rest. Better not to rouse the village with the news of his return—he would go upstairs and sleep. Before he climbed the rickety flight to his room he took a pad and pencil from the living-room table, and an automatic pistol from his father's desk drawer.

Three hours later the shot rang out. Ed Clay had put a bullet neatly through his temples with a pistol clutched in his left hand, leaving a sparsely written sheet of paper on the rickety table near his bed. He had, it later appeared from the whittled pencil-stub and stove full of charred paper, originally written much more; but had finally decided not to tell what he knew beyond vague hints. The surviving fragment was only a mad warning scrawled in a curiously backhanded script—the ravings of a mind obviously deranged by hardships—and it read thus; rather surprisingly for the utterance of one who had always been stolid and matter-of-fact:

For gods sake never go nere that mound it is part of some kind of a world so devilish and old it cannot be spoke about me and Walker went and was took into the thing just melted at times and made up agen and the whole world outside is helpless alongside of what they can do—they what live forever young as they like and you cant tell if they are really men or just gostes—and what they do cant be spoke about and this is only 1 entrance—you cant tell how big the whole thing is—after what we seen I dont want to live aney more France was nothing besides this—and see that people always keep away o god they wood if they see poor walker like he was in the end.

Yrs truely
Ed Clay

At the autopsy it was found that all of young Clay's organs were transposed from right to left within his body, as if he had been turned inside out. Whether they had always been so, no one could say at the time, but it was later learned from army records that Ed had been perfectly normal when mustered out of the service in May, 1919. Whether there was a mistake somewhere, or whether some unprecedented metamorphosis had indeed occurred, is still an unsettled question, as is also the origin of the hieroglyph-like scar on the forehead.

That was the end of the explorations of the mound. In the eight intervening years no one had been near the place, and few indeed had even cared to level a spy glass at it. From time to time people continued to glance nervously at the lone hill as it rose starkly from the plain against the western sky, and to shudder at the small dark speck that paraded by day and the glimmering will-o'-the-wisp that danced by night. The thing was accepted at face value as a mystery not to be probed, and by common consent the village shunned the subject. It was, after all, quite easy to avoid the hill; for space was unlimited in every direction, and community life always follows beaten trails. The mound side of the village was simply kept trailless, as if it had been water or swampland or desert. And it is a curious commentary on the stolidity and imaginative sterility of the human animal that the whispers with which children and strangers were warned away from the mound quickly sank once more into the flat tale of a murderous Indian ghost and his squaw victim. Only the tribesmen on the reservation, and thoughtful old-timers like Grandma Compton, remembered the overtones of unholy vistas and deep cosmic menace which clustered around the ravings of those who had come back changed and shattered.

It was very late, and Grandma Compton had long since gone upstairs to bed, when Clyde finished telling me this. I hardly knew what to think of the frightful puzzle, yet rebelled at any notion to conflict with sane materialism. What influence had brought madness, or the impulse of flight and wandering, to so many who had visited the mound? Though vastly impressed, I was spurred on rather than deterred. Surely I must get to the bottom of this matter, as well I might if I kept a cool head and an unbroken determination. Compton saw my mood and shook his head worriedly. Then he motioned me to follow him outdoors.

We stepped from the frame house to the quiet side street or lane, and walked a few paces in the light of a waning August moon to where the houses were thinner. The half-moon was still low, and had not blotted many stars from the sky; so that I could see not only the westering gleams of Altair and Vega,[9] but the mystic shimmering of the Milky Way, as I looked out over the vast expanse of earth and sky in the direction that Compton pointed. Then all at once I saw a spark that was not a star—a bluish spark that moved and glimmered against the Milky Way near the horizon, and that seemed in a vague way more evil and malevolent than anything in the vault above. In another moment it was clear that this spark came from the top of a long distant rise in the outspread and faintly litten plain; and I turned to Compton with a question.

"Yes," he answered, "it's the blue ghost-light—and that is the mound. There's not a night in history that we haven't seen it—and not a living soul in Binger that would walk out over that plain toward it. It's a bad business, young man, and if you're wise you'll let it rest where it is. Better call your search off, son, and tackle some of the other Injun legends around here. We've plenty to keep you busy, heaven knows!"

II.

But I was in no mood for advice; and though Compton gave me a pleasant room, I could not sleep a wink through eagerness for the next morning with its chances to see the daytime ghost and to question the Indians at the reservation. I meant to go about the whole thing slowly and thoroughly, equipping myself with all available data both white and red before I commenced any actual archaeological investigations. I rose and dressed at dawn, and when I heard others stirring I went downstairs. Compton was building the kitchen fire while his mother was busy in the pantry. When he saw me he nodded, and after a moment invited me out into the glamorous young sunlight. I knew where we were going, and as we walked along the lane I strained my eyes westward over the plains.

There was the mound—far away and very curious in its aspect of artificial regularity. It must have been from thirty to forty feet high, and all of a hundred yards from north to south as I looked at it. It was not as wide as that from east to west, Compton said, but had the contour of a rather thinnish ellipse. He, I knew, had been safely out to it and back several times. As I looked at the rim silhouetted against the deep blue of the west I tried to follow its minor irregularities, and became impressed with a sense of something moving upon it. My pulse mounted a bit feverishly, and I seized quickly on the high-powered binoculars which Compton had quietly offered me. Focussing them hastily, I saw at first only a tangle of underbrush on the distant mound's rim—and then something stalked into the field.

It was unmistakably a human shape, and I knew at once that I was seeing the daytime "Indian ghost". I did not wonder at the description, for surely the tall, lean, darkly robed being with the filleted black hair and seamed, coppery, expressionless, aquiline face looked more like an Indian than anything else in my previous experience. And yet my trained ethnologist's eye told me at once that this was no redskin of any sort hitherto known to history, but a creature of vast racial variation and of a wholly different culture-stream. Modern Indians are brachycephalic—round-headed—and you can't find any dolichocephalic or long-headed skulls[10] except in ancient Pueblo deposits dating back 2500 years or more; yet this man's long-headedness was so pronounced that I recognised it at once, even at his vast distance and in the uncertain field of the binoculars. I saw, too, that the pattern of his robe represented a decorative tradition utterly remote from anything we recognise in southwestern native art. There were shining metal trappings, likewise, and a short sword or kindred weapon at his side, all wrought in a fashion wholly alien to anything I had ever heard of.

As he paced back and forth along the top of the mound I followed him for several minutes with the glass, noting the kinaesthetic quality of his stride and the poised way he carried his head; and there was borne in upon me the strong, persistent conviction that this man, whoever or whatever he might be, was certainly *not a savage.* He was the product of a *civilisation,* I felt instinctively, though of what civilisation I could not guess. At length he disappeared beyond the farther edge of the mound, as if descending the opposite and unseen slope; and I lowered the glass with a curious mixture of puzzled feelings. Compton was looking quizzically at me, and I nodded non-committally. "What do you make of that?" he ventured. "This is what we've seen here in Binger every day of our lives."

That noon found me at the Indian reservation talking with old Grey Eagle—who, through some miracle, was still alive; though he must have been close to a hundred and fifty years old. He was a strange, impressive figure—this stern, fearless leader of his kind who had talked with outlaws and traders in fringed buckskin and French officials in knee-breeches and three-cornered hats—and I was glad to see that, because of my air of deference toward him, he appeared to like me. His liking, however, took an unfortunately obstructive form as soon as he learned what I wanted; for all he would do was to warn me against the search I was about to make.

"You good boy—you no bother that hill. Bad medicine. Plenty devil under there—catchum when you dig. No dig, no hurt. Go and dig, no come back. Just same when me boy, just same when my father and he father boy. All time buck he walk in day, squaw with no head she walk in night. All time since white men with tin coats they come from sunset and below big river—long way back—three, four times more back than Grey Eagle—two times more back than Frenchmen—all same after then. More back than that, nobody go near little hills nor deep valleys with stone caves. Still more back, those old ones no hide, come out and make villages. Bring plenty gold. Me them. You them. Then big waters come. All change. Nobody come out, let nobody in. Get in, no get out. They no die—no get old like Grey Eagle with valleys in face and snow on head. Just same like air—some man, some spirit. Bad medicine. Sometimes at night spirit come out on half-man-half-horse-with-horn and fight where men once fight. Keep 'way them place. No good. You good boy—go 'way and let them old ones 'lone."

That was all I could get out of the ancient chief, and the rest of the Indians would say nothing at all. But if I was troubled, Grey Eagle was clearly more so; for he obviously felt a real regret at the thought of my invading the region he feared so abjectly. As I turned to leave the reservation he stopped me for a final ceremonial farewell, and once more tried to get my promise to abandon my search. When he saw that he could not, he produced something half-timidly from a buckskin pouch he wore, and extended it toward me very solemnly. It was a worn but finely minted metal disc about two inches in diameter, oddly figured and perforated, and suspended from a leathern cord.

"You no promise, then Grey Eagle no can tell what get you. But if anything help um, this good medicine. Come from my father—he get from he father—he get from he father—all way back, close to Tiráwa, all men's father. My father say, 'You keep 'way from those old ones, keep 'way from little hills and valleys with stone caves. But if old ones they come out to get you, then you shew um this medicine. They know. They make him long way back. They look, then they no do such bad medicine maybe. But no can tell. You keep 'way, just same. Them no good. No tell what they do.'"

As he spoke, Grey Eagle was hanging the thing around my neck, and I saw it was a very curious object indeed. The more I looked at it, the more I marvelled; for not only was its heavy, darkish, lustrous, and richly mottled substance an absolutely strange metal to me, but what was left of its design seemed to be of a marvellously artistic and utterly unknown workmanship. One side, so far as I could see, had borne an exquisitely modelled serpent design; whilst the other side had depicted a kind of octopus or other tentacled monster. There were some half-effaced hieroglyphs, too, of a kind which no archaeologist could identify or even place conjecturally. With Grey Eagle's permission I later had expert historians, anthropologists, geologists, and chemists pass carefully upon the disc, but from them I obtained only a chorus of bafflement. It defied either classification or analysis. The chemists called it an amalgam of unknown metallic elements of heavy atomic weight, and one geologist suggested that the substance must be of meteoric origin, shot from unknown gulfs of interstellar space.[11] Whether it really saved my life or sanity or existence as a human being I cannot attempt to say, but Grey Eagle is sure of it. He has it again, now, and I wonder if it has any connexion with his inordinate age. All his fathers who had it lived far beyond the century mark, perishing only in battle. Is it possible that Grey Eagle, if kept from accidents, will *never die?* But I am ahead of my story.

When I returned to the village I tried to secure more mound-lore, but found only excited gossip and opposition. It was really flattering to see how solicitous the people were about my safety, but I had to set their almost frantic remonstrances aside. I shewed them Grey Eagle's charm, but none of them had ever heard of it before, or seen anything even remotely like it. They agreed that it could not be an Indian relic, and imagined that the old chief's ancestors must have obtained it from some trader.

When they saw they could not deter me from my trip, the Binger citizens sadly did what they could to aid my outfitting. Having known before my arrival the sort of work to be done, I had most of my supplies already with me—machete and trench-knife for shrub-clearing and excavating, electric torches for any underground phase which might develop, rope, field-glasses, tape-measure, microscope, and incidentals for emergencies—as much, in fact, as might be comfortably stowed in a convenient handbag. To this equipment I added only the heavy revolver which the sheriff forced upon me, and the pick and shovel which

I thought might expedite my work.

I decided to carry these latter things slung over my shoulder with a stout cord—for I soon saw that I could not hope for any helpers or fellow-explorers. The village would watch me, no doubt, with all its available telescopes and field-glasses; but it would not send any citizen so much as a yard over the flat plain toward the lone hillock. My start was timed for early the next morning, and all the rest of that day I was treated with the awed and uneasy respect which people give to a man about to set out for certain doom.

When morning came—a cloudy though not a threatening morning—the whole village turned out to see me start across the dust-blown plain. Binoculars shewed the lone man at his usual pacing on the mound, and I resolved to keep him in sight as steadily as possible during my approach. At the last moment a vague sense of dread oppressed me, and I was just weak and whimsical enough to let Grey Eagle's talisman swing on my chest in full view of any beings or ghosts who might be inclined to heed it. Bidding au revoir to Compton and his mother, I started off at a brisk stride despite the bag in my left hand and the clanking pick and shovel strapped to my back; holding my field-glass in my right hand and taking a glance at the silent pacer from time to time. As I neared the mound I saw the man very clearly, and fancied I could trace an expression of infinite evil and decadence on his seamed, hairless features. I was startled, too, to see that his goldenly gleaming weapon-case bore hieroglyphs very similar to those on the unknown talisman I wore. All the creature's costume and trappings bespoke exquisite workmanship and cultivation. Then, all too abruptly, I saw him start down the farther side of the mound and out of sight. When I reached the place, about ten minutes after I set out, there was no one there.

THE CRAWLING CHAOS

There is no need of relating how I spent the early part of my search in surveying and circumnavigating the mound, taking measurements, and stepping back to view the thing from different angles. It had impressed me tremendously as I approached it, and there seemed to be a kind of latent menace in its too regular outlines. It was the only elevation of any sort on the wide, level plain; and I could not doubt for a moment that it was an artificial tumulus. The steep sides seemed wholly unbroken, and without marks of human tenancy or passage. There were no signs of a path toward the top; and, burdened as I was, I managed to scramble up only with considerable difficulty. When I reached the summit I found a roughly level elliptical plateau about 300 by 50 feet in dimensions; uniformly covered with rank grass and dense underbrush, and utterly incompatible with the constant presence of a pacing sentinel. This condition gave me a real shock, for it shewed beyond question that the "Old Indian", vivid though he seemed, could not be other than a collective hallucination.

I looked about with considerable perplexity and alarm, glancing wistfully back at the village and the mass of black dots which I knew was the watching crowd. Training my glass upon them, I saw that they were studying me avidly with their glasses; so to reassure them I waved my cap in the air with a show of jauntiness which I was far from feeling. Then, settling to my work I flung down pick, shovel, and bag; taking my machete from the latter and commencing to clear away underbrush. It was a weary task, and now and then I felt a curious shiver as some perverse gust of wind arose to hamper my motion with a skill approaching deliberateness. At times it seemed as if a half-tangible force were pushing me back as I worked—almost as if the air thickened in front of me, or as if formless hands tugged at my wrists. My energy seemed used up without producing adequate results, yet for all that I made some progress.

By afternoon I had clearly perceived that, toward the northern end of the mound, there was a slight bowl-like depression in the root-tangled earth. While this might mean nothing, it would be a good place to begin when I reached the digging stage, and I made a mental note of it. At the same time I noticed another and very peculiar thing—namely, that the Indian talisman swinging from my neck seemed to behave oddly at a point about seventeen feet southeast of the suggested bowl. Its gyrations were altered whenever I happened to stoop around that point, and it tugged downward as if attracted by some magnetism in the soil. The more I noticed this, the more it struck me, till at length I decided to do a little preliminary digging there without further delay.

As I turned up the soil with my trench-knife I could not help wondering at the relative thinness of the reddish regional layer. The country as a whole was all red sandstone earth, but here I found a strange black loam less than a foot down. It was such soil as one finds in the strange, deep valleys farther west and south, and must surely have been brought from a considerable distance in the prehistoric age when the mound was reared. Kneeling and digging, I felt the leathern cord around my neck tugged harder and harder, as something in the soil seemed to draw the heavy metal talisman more and more. Then I felt my implements strike a hard surface, and wondered if a rock layer rested beneath. Prying about with the trench-knife, I found that such was not the case. Instead, to my intense surprise and feverish interest, I brought up a mould-clogged, heavy object of cylindrical shape—about a foot long and four inches in diameter—to which my hanging talisman clove with glue-like tenacity. As I cleared off the black loam my wonder and tension increased at the bas-reliefs revealed by that process. The whole cylinder, ends and all, was covered with figures and hieroglyphs; and I saw with growing excitement that these things were in the same unknown tradition as those on Grey Eagle's charm and on the yellow metal trappings of the ghost I had seen through my binoculars.

Sitting down, I further cleaned the magnetic cylinder against the rough corduroy of my knickerbockers, and observed that it was made of the same heavy, lustrous unknown metal as the charm—hence, no doubt, the singular attraction. The carvings and chasings were very strange and very horrible—nameless monsters and designs fraught with insidious evil—and all were of the highest finish and craftsmanship. I could not at first make head or tail of the thing, and handled it aimlessly until I spied a cleavage near one end. Then I sought eagerly for some mode of opening, discovering at last that the end simply unscrewed.

The cap yielded with difficulty, but at last it came off, liberating a curious aromatic odour. The sole contents was a bulky roll of a yellowish, paper-like substance inscribed in greenish characters, and for a second I had the supreme thrill of fancying that I held a written key to unknown elder worlds and abysses beyond time. Almost immediately, however, the unrolling of one end shewed that the manuscript was in Spanish—albeit the formal, pompous Spanish of a long-departed day. In the golden sunset light I looked at the heading and the opening paragraph, trying to decipher the wretched and ill-punctuated script of the vanished writer. What manner of relic was this? Upon what sort of a discovery had I stumbled? The first words set me in a new fury of excitement and curiosity, for instead of diverting me from my original quest they startlingly confirmed me in that very effort.

The yellow scroll with the green script began with a bold, identifying caption and a ceremoniously desperate appeal for belief in incredible revelations to follow:

RELACIÓN DE PÁNFILO[12] DE ZAMACONA Y NUÑEZ, HIDALGO DE LUARCA EN ASTURIAS, TOCANTE AL MUNDO SOTERRÁNEO DE XINAIÁN, A. D. MDXLV

En el nombre de la santísima Trinidad, Padre, Hijo, y Espíritu-Santo, tres personas distintas y un solo. Dios verdadero, y de la santísima Virgen nuestra Señora, YO, PÁNFILO DE ZAMACONA, HIJO DE PE-DRO GUZMAN Y ZAMACONA, HIDALGO, Y DE LA DOÑA YNÉS ALVARADO Y NUÑEZ, DE LUARCA EN ASTURIAS, juro para que todo que deco está verdadero como sacramento....[13]

I paused to reflect on the portentous significance of what I was reading. "The Narrative of Pánfilo de Zamacona y Nuñez, gentleman, of Luarca in Asturias,[14] *Concerning the Subterranean World of Xinaián, A. D. 1545*"... Here, surely, was too much for any mind to absorb all at once. A subterranean world—again that persistent idea which filtered through all the Indian tales and through all the utterances of those who had come back from the mound. And the date—1545—what could this mean? In 1540 Coronado and his men had gone north from Mexico into the wilderness, but had they not turned back in 1542? My eye ran questingly down the opened part of the scroll, and almost at once seized on the name *Francisco Vásquez de Corona-do*. The writer of this thing, clearly, was one of Coronado's men—but what had he been doing in this remote realm three years after his party had gone back? I must read further, for another glance told me that what was now unrolled was merely a summary of Coronado's northward march, differing in no essential way from the account known to history.

It was only the waning light which checked me before I could unroll and read more, and in my impatient bafflement I almost forgot to be frightened at the onrush of night in this sinister place. Others, however, had not forgotten the lurking terror, for I heard a loud distant hallooing from a knot of men who had gathered at the edge of the town. Answering the anxious hail, I restored the manuscript to its strange cylinder—to which the disc around my neck still clung until I pried it off and packed it and my smaller implements for departure. Leaving the pick and shovel for the next day's work, I took up my handbag, scrambled down the steep side of the mound, and in another quarter-hour was back in the village explaining and exhibiting my curious find. As darkness drew on, I glanced back at the mound I had so lately left, and saw with a shudder that the faint bluish torch of the nocturnal squaw-ghost had begun to glimmer.

It was hard work waiting to get at the bygone Spaniard's narrative; but I knew I must have quiet and leisure for a good translation, so reluctantly saved the task for the later hours of night. Promising the townsfolk a clear account of my findings in the morning, and giving them an ample opportunity to examine the bizarre and provocative cylinder, I accompanied Clyde Compton home and ascended to my room for the translating process as soon as I possibly could. My host and his mother were intensely eager to hear the tale, but I thought they had better wait till I could thoroughly absorb the text myself and give them the gist concisely and unerringly.

Opening my handbag in the light of a single electric bulb, I again took out the cylinder and noted the instant magnetism which pulled the Indian talisman to its carven surface. The designs glimmered evilly on the richly lustrous and unknown metal, and I could not help shivering as I studied the abnormal and blasphemous forms that leered at me with such exquisite workmanship. I wish now that I had carefully photographed all these designs—though perhaps it is just as well that I did not. Of one thing I am really glad, and that is that I could not then identify the squatting octopus-headed thing which dominated most of the ornate cartouches, and which the manuscript called "Tulu". Recently I have associated it, and the legends in the manuscript connected with it, with some new-found folklore of monstrous and unmentioned Cthulhu, a horror which seeped down from the stars while the young earth was still half-formed; and had I known of the connexion then, I could not have stayed in the same room with the thing. The secondary motif, a semi-anthropomorphic serpent, I did quite readily place as a prototype of the Yig, Quetzalcoatl, and Kukulcan conceptions. Before opening the cylinder I tested its magnetic powers on metals other than that of Grey Eagle's disc, but found that no attraction existed. It was no common magnetism which pervaded this morbid fragment of unknown worlds and linked it to its kind.

At last I took out the manuscript and began translating—jotting down a synoptic outline in English as I went, and now and then regretting the absence of a Spanish dictionary when I came upon some especially obscure or archaic word or construction. There was a sense of ineffable strangeness in thus being thrown back nearly four centuries in the midst of my continuous quest—thrown back to a year when my own forbears were settled, homekeeping gentlemen of Somerset and Devon under Henry the Eighth,[15] with never a thought of the adventure that was to take their blood to Virginia and the New World; yet when that new world possessed, even as now, the same brooding mystery of the mound which formed my present sphere and horizon. The sense of a throwback was all the stronger because I felt instinctively that the common problem of the Spaniard and myself was one of such abysmal timelessness—of such unholy and unearthly eternity—that the scant four hundred years between us bulked as nothing in comparison. It took no more than a single look at that monstrous and insidious cylinder to make me realise the dizzying gulfs that yawned between all men of the known earth and the primal mysteries it represented. Before that gulf Pánfilo de Zamacona and I stood side by side; just as Aristotle and I, or Cheops and I, might have stood.[16]

III.

Of his youth in Luarca, a small, placid port on the Bay of Biscay, Zamacona told little. He had been wild, and a younger son, and had come to New Spain[17] in 1532, when only twenty years old. Sensitively imaginative, he had listened spellbound to the floating rumours of rich cities and unknown worlds to the north—and especially to the tale of the Franciscan friar Marcos de Niza, who came back from a trip in 1539 with glowing accounts of fabulous Cíbola and its great walled towns with terraced stone houses. Hearing of Coronado's contemplated expedition in search of these wonders—and of the greater wonders whispered to lie beyond them in the land of buffaloes—young Zamacona managed to join the picked party of 300, and started north with the rest in 1540.

History knows the story of that expedition—how Cíbola was found to be merely the squalid Pueblo village of Zuñi, and how de Niza was sent back to Mexico in disgrace for his florid exaggerations; how Coronado first saw the Grand Canyon, and how at Cicuyé, on the Pecos,[18] he heard from the Indian called El Turco of the rich and mysterious land of Quivira, far to the northeast, where gold, silver, and buffaloes abounded, and where there flowed a river two leagues wide. Zamacona told briefly of the winter camp at Tiguex on the Pecos,[19] and of the northward start in April, when the native guide proved false and led the party astray amidst a land of prairie-dogs, salt pools, and roving, bison-hunting tribes.

When Coronado dismissed his larger force and made his final forty-two-day march with a very small and select detachment, Zamacona managed to be included in the advancing party. He spoke of the fertile country and of the great ravines with trees visible only from the edge of their steep banks; and of how all the men lived solely on buffalo-meat. And then came mention of the expedition's farthest limit—of the presumable but disappointing land of Quivira with its villages of grass houses, its brooks and rivers, its good black soil, its plums, nuts, grapes, and mulberries, and its maize-growing and copper-using Indians. The execution of El Turco, the false native guide, was casually touched upon, and there was a mention of the cross which Coronado raised on the bank of a great river in the autumn of 1541—a cross bearing the inscription, "Thus far came the great general, Francisco Vásquez de Coronado".

This supposed Quivira lay at about the fortieth parallel of north latitude, and I see that quite lately the New York archaeologist Dr. Hodge has identified it with the course of the Arkansas River through Barton and Rice Counties, Kansas.[20] It is the old home of the Wichitas, before the Sioux drove them south into what is now Oklahoma, and some of the grass-house village sites have been found and excavated for artifacts. Coronado did considerable exploring hereabouts, led hither and thither by the persistent rumours of rich cities and hidden worlds which floated fearfully around on the Indians' tongues. These northerly natives seemed more afraid and reluctant to talk about the rumoured cities and worlds than the Mexican Indians had been; yet at the same time seemed as if they could reveal a good deal more than the Mexicans had they been willing or dared to do so. Their vagueness exasperated the Spanish leader, and after many disappointing searches he began to be very severe toward those who brought him stories. Zamacona, more patient than Coronado, found the tales especially interesting; and learned enough of the local speech to hold long conversations with a young buck named Charging Buffalo, whose curiosity had led him into much stranger places than any of his fellow-tribesmen had dared to penetrate.

It was Charging Buffalo who told Zamacona of the queer stone doorways, gates, or cave-mouths at the bottom of some of those deep, steep, wooded ravines which the party had noticed on the northward march. These openings, he said, were mostly concealed by shrubbery; and few had entered them for untold aeons. Those who went to where they led, never returned—or in a few cases returned mad or curiously maimed. But all this was legend, for nobody was known to have gone more than a limited distance inside any of them within the memory of the grandfathers of the oldest living men. Charging Buffalo himself had probably been farther than anyone else, and he had seen enough to curb both his curiosity and his greed for the rumoured gold below.

Beyond the aperture he had entered there was a long passage running crazily up and down and round about, and covered with frightful carvings of monsters and horrors that no man had ever seen. At last, after untold miles of windings and descents, there was a glow of terrible blue light; and the passage opened upon a shocking nether world. About this the Indian would say no more, for he had seen something that had sent him back in haste. But the golden cities must be somewhere down there, he added, and perhaps a white man with the magic of the thunderstick might succeed in getting to them. He would not tell the big chief Coronado what he knew, for Coronado would not listen to Indian talk any more. Yes—he could shew Zamacona the way if the white man would leave the party and accept his guidance. But he would not go inside the opening with the white man. It was bad in there.

The place was about a five days' march to the south, near the region of great mounds. These mounds had something to do with the evil world down there—they were probably ancient closed-up passages to it, for once the Old Ones[21] below had had colonies on the surface and had traded with men everywhere, even in the lands that had sunk under the big waters. It was when those lands had sunk that the Old Ones closed themselves up below and refused to deal with surface people. The refugees from the sinking places had told them that the gods of outer earth were against men, and that no men could survive on the outer earth unless they were daemons in league with the evil gods. That is why they shut out all surface folk, and did fearful things to any who ventured down where they dwelt. There had been sentries once at the various openings, but after ages they were no longer needed. Not many people cared to talk about the hidden Old Ones, and the legends about them would probably have died out but for certain ghostly reminders of their presence now and then. It seemed that the infinite ancientness of these creatures had brought them strangely near to the borderline of spirit, so that their ghostly emanations were more commonly frequent and vivid. Accordingly the region of the great mounds was often convulsed with spectral nocturnal battles reflecting those which had been fought in the days before the openings were closed.

The Old Ones themselves were half-ghost—indeed, it was said that they no longer grew old or reproduced their kind, but flickered eternally in a state between flesh and spirit. The change was not complete, though, for they had to breathe. It was because the underground world needed air that the openings in the deep valleys were not blocked up as the mound-openings on the plains had been. These openings, Charging Buffalo added, were probably based on natural fissures in the earth. It was whispered that the Old Ones had come down from the stars to the world when it was very young, and had gone inside to build their cities of solid gold because the surface was not then fit to live on. They were the ancestors of all men, yet none could guess from what star—or what place beyond the stars—they came. Their hidden cities were still full of gold and silver, but men had better let them alone unless protected by very strong magic.

They had frightful beasts with a faint strain of human blood, on which they rode, and which they employed for other purposes. The things, so people hinted, were carnivorous, and like their masters, preferred human flesh; so that although the Old Ones themselves did not breed, they had a sort of half-human slave-class which also served to nourish the human and animal population. This had been very oddly recruited, and was supplemented by a second slave-class of reanimated corpses. The Old Ones knew how to make a corpse into an automaton which would last almost indefinitely and perform any sort of work when directed by streams of thought. Charging Buffalo said that the people had all come to talk by means of thought only; speech having been found crude and needless, except for religious devotions and emotional expression, as aeons of discovery and study rolled by. They worshipped Yig, the great father of serpents, and Tulu, the octopus-headed entity that had brought them down from the stars; appeasing both of these hideous monstrosities by means of human sacrifices offered up in a very curious manner which Charging Buffalo did not care to describe.

Zamacona was held spellbound by the Indian's tale, and at once resolved to accept his guidance to the cryptic doorway in the ravine. He did not believe the accounts of strange ways attributed by legend to the hidden people, for the experiences of the party had been such as to disillusion one regarding native myths of unknown lands; but he did feel that some sufficiently marvellous field of riches and adventure must indeed lie beyond the weirdly carved passages in the earth. At first he thought of persuading Charging Buffalo to tell his story to Coronado—offering to shield him against any effects of the leader's testy scepticism—but later he decided that a lone adventure would be better. If he had no aid, he would not have to share anything he found; but might perhaps become a great discoverer and owner of fabulous riches. Success would make him a greater figure than Coronado himself—perhaps a greater figure than any-

one else in New Spain, including even the mighty viceroy
Don Antonio de Mendoza.[22]

On October 7, 1541, at an hour close to midnight,
Zamacona stole out of the Spanish camp near the grass-
house village and met Charging Buffalo for the long southward journey. He travelled as lightly as possible, and did
not wear his heavy helmet and breastplate. Of the details
of the trip the manuscript told very little, but Zamacona
records his arrival at the great ravine on October 13th. The
descent of the thickly wooded slope took no great time;
and though the Indian had trouble in locating the shrub-
bery-hidden stone door again amidst the twilight of that
deep gorge, the place was finally found. It was a very small
aperture as doorways go, formed of monolithic sandstone
jambs and lintel, and bearing signs of nearly effaced and
now undecipherable carvings. Its height was perhaps seven
feet, and its width not more than four. There were drilled
places in the jambs which argued the bygone presence of a
hinged door or gate, but all other traces of such a thing had
long since vanished.

At sight of this black gulf Charging Buffalo displayed
considerable fear, and threw down his pack of supplies with
signs of haste. He had provided Zamacona with a good
stock of resinous torches and provisions, and had guided
him honestly and well; but refused to share in the venture
that lay ahead. Zamacona gave him the trinkets he had kept
for such an occasion, and obtained his promise to return to
the region in a month; afterward shewing the way southward to the Pecos Pueblo villages. A prominent rock on the
plain above them was chosen as a meeting-place; the one
arriving first to pitch camp until the other should arrive.

In the manuscript Zamacona expressed a wistful
wonder as to the Indian's length of waiting at the rendez-

vous—for he himself could never keep that tryst. At the last moment Charging Buffalo tried to dissuade him from his plunge into the darkness, but soon saw it was futile, and gestured a stoical farewell. Before lighting his first torch and entering the opening with his ponderous pack, the Spaniard watched the lean form of the Indian scrambling hastily and rather relievedly upward among the trees. It was the cutting of his last link with the world; though he did not know that he was never to see a human being—in the accepted sense of that term—again.

Zamacona felt no immediate premonition of evil upon entering that ominous doorway, though from the first he was surrounded by a bizarre and unwholesome atmosphere. The passage, slightly taller and wider than the aperture, was for many yards a level tunnel of Cyclopean masonry, with heavily worn flagstones under foot, and grotesquely carved granite and sandstone blocks in sides and ceiling. The carvings must have been loathsome and terrible indeed, to judge from Zamacona's description; according to which most of them revolved around the monstrous beings Yig and Tulu. They were unlike anything the adventurer had ever seen before, though he added that the native architecture of Mexico came closest to them of all things in the outer world. After some distance the tunnel began to dip abruptly, and irregular natural rock appeared on all sides. The passage seemed only partly artificial, and decorations were limited to occasional cartouches with shocking bas-reliefs.

Following an enormous descent, whose steepness at times produced an acute danger of slipping and tobogganing, the passage became exceedingly uncertain in its direction and variable in its contour. At times it narrowed almost to a slit or grew so low that stooping and even crawling were necessary, while at other times it broadened out into sizeable caves or chains of caves. Very little human construction, it was plain, had gone into this part of the tunnel; though occasionally a sinister cartouche or hieroglyphic on the wall, or a blocked-up lateral passageway, would remind Zamacona that this was in truth the aeon-forgotten highroad to a primal and unbelievable world of living things.

For three days, as best he could reckon, Pánfilo de Zamacona scrambled down, up, along, and around, but always predominately downward, through this dark region of palaeogean night. Once in a while he heard some secret being of darkness patter or flap out of his way, and on just one occasion he half glimpsed a great, bleached thing that set him trembling. The quality of the air was mostly very tolerable; though foetid zones were now and then met with, while one great cavern of stalactites and stalagmites afforded a depressing dampness. This latter, when Charging Buffalo had come upon it, had quite seriously barred the way; since the limestone deposits of ages had built fresh pillars in the path of the primordial abyss-denizens. The Indian, however, had broken through these; so that Zamacona did not find his course impeded. It was an unconscious comfort to him to reflect that someone else from the outside world had been there before—and the Indian's careful descriptions had removed the element of surprise and unexpectedness. More—Charging Buffalo's knowledge of the tunnel had led him to provide so good a torch supply for the journey in and out, that there would be no danger of becoming stranded in darkness. Zamacona camped twice, building a fire whose smoke seemed well taken care of by the natural ventilation.

At what he considered the end of the third day— though his cocksure guesswork chronology is not at any time to be given the easy faith that he gave it—Zamacona encountered the prodigious descent and subsequent prodigious climb which Charging Buffalo had described as the tunnel's last phase. As at certain earlier points, marks of artificial improvement were here discernible; and several times the steep gradient was eased by a flight of rough-hewn steps. The torch shewed more and more of the monstrous carvings on the walls, and finally the resinous flare seemed mixed with a fainter and more diffusive light as Zamacona climbed up and up after the last downward stairway. At length the ascent ceased, and a level passage of artificial masonry with dark, basaltic blocks led straight ahead. There was no need for a torch now, for all the air was glowing with a bluish, quasi-electric radiance that flickered like an aurora. It was the strange light of the inner world that the Indian had described—and in another moment Zamacona emerged from the tunnel upon a bleak, rocky hillside which climbed above him to a seething, impenetrable sky of bluish coruscations, and descended dizzily below him to an apparently illimitable plain shrouded in bluish mist.

He had come to the unknown world at last, and from his manuscript it is clear that he viewed the formless landscape as proudly and exaltedly as ever his fellow-countryman Balboa viewed the new-found Pacific from that unforgettable peak in Darien.[23] Charging Buffalo had turned back at this point, driven by fear of something which he would only describe vaguely and evasively as a herd of bad cattle, neither horse nor buffalo, but like the things the mound-spirits rode at night—but Zamacona could not be deterred by any such trifle. Instead of fear, a strange sense of glory filled him; for he had imagination enough to know what it meant to stand alone in an inexplicable nether world whose existence no other white man suspected.

The soil of the great hill that surged upward behind him and spread steeply downward below him was dark grey, rock-strown, without vegetation, and probably basaltic in origin; with an unearthly cast which made him feel like an intruder on an alien planet. The vast distant plain, thousands of feet below, had no features he could distinguish; especially since it appeared to be largely veiled in a curling, bluish vapour. But more than hill or plain or cloud, the bluely luminous, coruscating sky impressed the adventurer with a sense of supreme wonder and mystery. What created this sky within a world he could not tell; though he knew of the northern lights, and had even seen them once or twice. He concluded that this subterraneous light was something vaguely akin to the aurora; a view which moderns may well endorse, though it seems likely that certain phenomena of radio-activity may also enter in.

At Zamacona's back the mouth of the tunnel he had traversed yawned darkly; defined by a stone doorway very like the one he had entered in the world above, save that it was of greyish-black basalt instead of red sandstone. There were hideous sculptures, still in good preservation and perhaps corresponding to those on the outer portal which time had largely weathered away. The absence of weathering here argued a dry, temperate climate; indeed, the Spaniard already began to note the delightfully spring-like stability of temperature which marks the air of the north's interior. On the stone jambs were works proclaiming the bygone presence of hinges, but of any actual door or gate no trace remained. Seating himself for rest and thought, Zamacona lightened his pack by removing an amount of food and torches sufficient to take him back through the tunnel. These he proceeded to cache at the opening, under a cairn hastily formed of the rock fragments which everywhere lay around. Then, readjusting his lightened pack, he commenced his descent toward the distant plain; preparing to invade a region which no living thing of outer earth had penetrated in a century or more, which no white man had ever penetrated, and from which, if legend were to be believed, no organic creature had ever returned sane.

Zamacona strode briskly along down the steep, interminable slope; his progress checked at times by the bad walking that came from loose rock fragments, or by the excessive precipitousness of the grade. The distance of the mist-shrouded plain must have been enormous, for many hours' walking brought him apparently no closer to it than he had been before. Behind him was always the great hill stretching upward into a bright aërial sea of bluish coruscations. Silence was universal; so that his own footsteps, and the fall of stones that he dislodged, struck on his ears with startling distinctness. It was at what he regarded as about noon that he first saw the abnormal footprints which set him to thinking of Charging Buffalo's terrible hints, precipitate flight, and strangely abiding terror.

The rock-strown nature of the soil gave few opportunities for tracks of any kind, but at one point a rather level interval had caused the loose detritus to accumulate in a ridge, leaving a considerable area of dark-grey loam absolutely bare. Here, in a rambling confusion indicating a large herd aimlessly wandering, Zamacona found the abnormal prints. It is to be regretted that he could not describe them more exactly, but the manuscript displayed far more vague fear than accurate observation. Just what it was that so frightened the Spaniard can only be inferred from his later hints regarding the beasts. He referred to the prints as 'not hooves, nor hands, nor feet, nor precisely paws—nor so large as to cause alarm on that account'. Just why or how long ago the things had been there, was not easy to guess. There was no vegetation visible, hence grazing was out of the question; but of course if the beasts were carnivorous they might well have been hunting smaller animals, whose tracks their own would tend to obliterate.

Glancing backward from this plateau to the heights above, Zamacona thought he detected traces of a great winding road which had once led from the tunnel downward to the plain. One could get the impression of this former highway only from a broad panoramic view, since a trickle of loose rock fragments had long ago obscured it; but the adventurer felt none the less certain that it had existed. It had not, probably, been an elaborately paved trunk route; for the small tunnel it reached seemed scarcely like a main avenue to the outer world. In choosing a straight path of descent Zamacona had not followed its curving course, though he must have crossed it once or twice. With his attention now called to it, he looked ahead to see if he could trace it downward toward the plain; and this he finally thought he could do. He resolved to investigate its surface when next he crossed it, and perhaps to pursue its line for the rest of the way if he could distinguish it.

Having resumed his journey, Zamacona came some time later upon what he thought was a bend of the ancient road. There were signs of grading and of some primal attempt at rock-surfacing, but not enough was left to make the route worth following. While rummaging about in the soil with his sword, the Spaniard turned up something that glittered in the eternal blue daylight, and was thrilled at beholding a kind of coin or medal of a dark, unknown, lustrous metal, with hideous designs on each side. It was utterly and bafflingly alien to him, and from his description I have no doubt but that it was a duplicate of the talisman given me by Grey Eagle almost four centuries afterward. Pocketing it after a long and curious examination, he strode onward; finally pitching camp at an hour which he guessed to be the evening of the outer world.

The next day Zamacona rose early and resumed his descent through this blue-litten world of mist and desolation and preternatural silence. As he advanced, he at last became able to distinguish a few objects on the distant plain below—trees, bushes, rocks, and a small river that came into view from the right and curved forward at a point to the left of his contemplated course. This river seemed to be spanned by a bridge connected with the descending roadway, and with care the explorer could trace the route of the road beyond it in a straight line over the plain. Finally he even thought he could detect towns scattered along the rectilinear ribbon; towns whose left-hand edges reached the river and sometimes crossed it. Where such crossings occurred, he saw as he descended, there were always signs of bridges either ruined or surviving. He was now in the midst of a sparse grassy vegetation, and saw that below him the growth became thicker and thicker. The road was easier to define now, since its surface discouraged the grass which the looser soil supported. Rock fragments were less frequent, and the barren upward vista behind him looked bleak and forbidding in contrast to his present milieu.

It was on this day that he saw the blurred mass moving over the distant plain. Since his first sight of the sinister footprints he had met with no more of these, but something about that slowly and deliberately moving mass peculiarly sickened him. Nothing but a herd of grazing animals could move just like that, and after seeing the footprints he did not wish to meet the things which had made them. Still, the moving mass was not near the road—and his curiosity and greed for fabled gold were great. Besides, who could really judge things from vague, jumbled footprints or from the panic-twisted hints of an ignorant Indian?

In straining his eyes to view the moving mass Zamacona became aware of several other interesting things. One was that certain parts of the now unmistakable towns glittered oddly in the misty blue light. Another was that, besides the towns, several similarly glittering structures of a more isolated sort were scattered here and there along the road and over the plain. They seemed to be embowered in clumps of vegetation, and those off the road had small avenues leading to the highway. No smoke or other signs of life could be discerned about any of the towns or buildings. Finally Zamacona saw that the plain was not infinite in extent, though the half-concealing blue mists had hitherto made it seem so. It was bounded in the remote distance by a range of low hills, toward a gap in which the river and roadway seemed to lead. All this—especially the glittering of certain pinnacles in the towns—had become very vivid when Zamacona pitched his second camp amidst the endless blue day. He likewise noticed the flocks of high-soaring birds, whose nature he could not clearly make out.

The next afternoon—to use the language of the outer world as the manuscript did at all times—Zamacona reached the silent plain and crossed the soundless, slow-running river on a curiously carved and fairly well-preserved bridge of black basalt. The water was clear, and contained large fishes of a wholly strange aspect. The roadway was now paved and somewhat overgrown with weeds and creeping vines, and its course was occasionally outlined by small pillars bearing obscure symbols. On every side the grassy level extended, with here and there a clump of trees or shrubbery, and with unidentifiable bluish flowers growing irregularly over the whole area. Now and then some spasmodic motion of the grass indicated the presence of serpents. In the course of several hours the traveller reached a grove of old and alien-looking evergreen-trees which he knew, from distant viewing, protected one of the glittering-roofed isolated structures. Amidst the encroaching vegetation he saw the hideously sculptured pylons of a stone gateway leading off the road, and was presently forcing his way through briers above a moss-crusted tessellated walk lined with huge trees and low monolithic pillars.

At last, in this hushed green twilight, he saw the crumbling and ineffably ancient facade of the building—a temple, he had no doubt. It was a mass of nauseous bas-reliefs; depicting scenes and beings, objects and ceremonies, which could certainly have no place on this or any sane planet. In hinting of these things Zamacona displays for the first time that shocked and pious hesitancy which impairs the informative value of the rest of his manuscript. We cannot help regretting that the Catholic ardour of Renaissance Spain had so thoroughly permeated his thought and feeling. The door of the place stood wide open, and absolute darkness filled the windowless interior. Conquering the repulsion which the mural sculptures had excited, Zamacona took out flint and steel, lighted a resinous torch, pushed aside curtaining vines, and sallied boldly across the ominous threshold.

For a moment he was quite stupefied by what he saw. It was not the all-covering dust and cobwebs of immemorial aeons, the fluttering winged things, the shriekingly loathsome sculptures on the walls, the bizarre form of the many basins and braziers, the sinister pyramidal altar with the hollow top, or the monstrous, octopus-headed abnormality in some strange, dark metal leering and squatting broodingly on its hieroglyphed pedestal, which robbed him of even the power to give a startled cry. It was nothing so unearthly as this—but merely the fact that, with the exception of the dust, the cobwebs, the winged things, and the gigantic emerald-eyed idol, every particle of substance in sight was composed of pure and evidently solid gold.

Even the manuscript, written in retrospect after Zamacona knew that gold is the most common structural metal of a nether world containing limitless lodes and veins of it, reflects the frenzied excitement which the traveller felt upon suddenly finding the real source of all the Indian legends of golden cities. For a time the power of detailed observation left him, but in the end his faculties were recalled by a peculiar tugging sensation in the pocket of his doublet. Tracing the feeling, he realised that the disc of strange metal he had found in the abandoned road was being attracted strongly by the vast octopus-headed, emerald-eyed idol on the pedestal, which he now saw to be composed of the same unknown exotic metal. He was later to learn that this strange magnetic substance—as alien to the inner world as to the outer world of men—is the one precious metal of the blue-lighted abyss. None knows what it is or where it occurs in Nature, and the amount of it on this planet came down from the stars with the people when great Tulu, the octopus-headed god, brought them for the first time to this earth. Certainly, its only known source was a stock of preexisting artifacts, including multitudes of Cyclopean idols. It could never be placed or analysed, and even its magnetism was exerted only on its own kind. It was the supreme ceremonial metal of the hidden people, its use being regulated by custom in such a way that its magnetic properties might cause no inconvenience. A very weakly magnetic alloy of it with such base metals as iron, gold, silver, copper, or zinc, had formed the sole monetary standard of the hidden people at one period of their history.

Zamacona's reflections on the strange idol and its magnetism were disturbed by a tremendous wave of fear as, for the first time in this silent world, he heard a rumble of very definite and obviously approaching sound. There was no mistaking its nature. It was a thunderously charging herd of large animals; and, remembering the Indian's panic, the footprints, and the moving mass distantly seen, the Spaniard shuddered in terrified anticipation. He did not analyse his position, or the significance of this onrush of great lumbering beings, but merely responded to an elemental urge toward self-protection. Charging herds do not stop to find victims in obscure places, and on the outer earth Zamacona would have felt little or no alarm in such a massive, grove-girt edifice. Some instinct, however, now bred a deep and peculiar terror in his soul; and he looked about frantically for any means of safety.

There being no available refuge in the great, gold-patined interior, he felt that he must close the long-disused door; which still hung on its ancient hinges, doubled back against the inner wall. Soil, vines, and moss had entered the opening from outside, so that he had to dig a path for the great gold portal with his sword; but he managed to perform this work very swiftly under the frightful stimulus of the approaching noise. The hoofbeats had grown still louder and more menacing by the time he began tugging at the heavy door itself; and for a while his fears reached a frantic height, as hope of starting the age-clogged metal grew faint. Then, with a creak, the thing responded to his youthful strength, and a frenzied siege of pulling and pushing ensued. Amidst the roar of unseen stampeding feet success came at last, and the ponderous golden door clanged shut, leaving Zamacona in darkness but for the single lighted torch he had wedged between the pillars of a basin-tripod. There was a latch, and the frightened man blessed his patron saint that it was still effective.

Sound alone told the fugitive the sequel. When the roar grew very near it resolved itself into separate footfalls, as if the evergreen grove had made it necessary for the herd to slacken speed and disperse. But feet continued to approach, and it became evident that the beasts were advancing among the trees and circling the hideously carven temple walls. In the curious deliberation of their tread Zamacona found something very alarming and repulsive, nor did he like the scuffling sounds which were audible even through the thick stone walls and heavy golden door. Once the door rattled ominously on its archaic hinges, as if under a heavy impact, but fortunately it still held. Then, after a seemingly endless interval, he heard retreating steps and realised that his unknown visitors were leaving. Since the herds did not seem to be very numerous, it would have perhaps been safe to venture out within a half-hour or less; but Zamacona took no chances. Opening his pack, he prepared his camp on the golden tiles of the temple's floor, with the great door still securely latched against all comers; drifting eventually into a sounder sleep than he could have known in the blue-litten spaces outside. He did not even mind the hellish, octopus-headed bulk of great Tulu, fashioned of unknown metal and leering with fishy, sea-green eyes, which squatted in the blackness above him on its monstrously hieroglyphed pedestal.

Surrounded by darkness for the first time since leaving the tunnel, Zamacona slept profoundly and long. He must have more than made up the sleep he had lost at his two previous camps, when the ceaseless glare of the sky had kept him awake despite his fatigue, for much distance was covered by other living feet while he lay in his healthily dreamless rest. It is well that he rested deeply, for there were many strange things to be encountered in his next period of consciousness.

IV.

What finally roused Zamacona was a thunderous rapping at the door. It beat through his dreams and dissolved all the lingering mists of drowsiness as soon as he knew what it was. There could be no mistake about it—it was a definite, human, and peremptory rapping; performed apparently with some metallic object, and with all the measured quality of conscious thought or will behind it. As the awakening man rose clumsily to his feet, a sharp vocal note was added to the summons—someone calling out, in a not unmusical voice, a formula which the manuscript tries to represent as *"oxi, oxi, giathcán ycá relex"*. Feeling sure that his visitors were men and not daemons, and arguing that they could have no reason for considering him an enemy, Zamacona decided to face them openly and at once; and accordingly fumbled with the ancient latch till the golden door creaked open from the pressure of those outside.

As the great portal swung back, Zamacona stood facing a group of about twenty individuals of an aspect not calculated to give him alarm. They seemed to be Indians; though their tasteful robes and trappings and swords were not such as he had seen among any of the tribes of the outer world, while their faces had many subtle differences from the Indian type. That they did not mean to be irresponsibly hostile, was very clear; for instead of menacing him in any way they merely probed him attentively and significantly with their eyes, as if they expected their gaze to open up some sort of communication. The longer they gazed, the more he seemed to know about them and their mission; for although no one had spoken since the vocal summons before the opening of the door, he found himself slowly realising that they had come from the great city beyond the low hills, mounted on animals, and that they had been summoned by animals who had reported his presence; that they were not sure what kind of person he was or just where he had come from, but that they knew he must be associated with that dimly remembered outer world which they sometimes visited in curious dreams. How he read all this in the gaze of the two or three leaders he could not possibly explain; though he learned why a moment later.

As it was, he attempted to address his visitors in the Wichita dialect he had picked up from Charging Buffalo; and after this failed to draw a vocal reply he successively tried the Aztec, Spanish, French, and Latin tongues—adding as many scraps of lame Greek, Galician, and Portuguese, and of the Bable peasant patois of his native Asturias,[24] as his memory could recall. But not even this polyglot array—his entire linguistic stock—could bring a reply in kind. When, however, he paused in perplexity, one of the visitors began speaking in an utterly strange and rather fascinating language whose sounds the Spaniard later had much difficulty in representing on paper. Upon his failure to understand this, the speaker pointed first to his own eyes, then to his forehead, and then to his eyes again, as if commanding the other to gaze at him in order to absorb what he wanted to transmit.

Zamacona, obeying, found himself rapidly in possession of certain information. The people, he learned, conversed nowadays by means of unvocal radiations of thought; although they had formerly used a spoken language which still survived as the written tongue, and into which they still dropped orally for tradition's sake, or when strong feeling demanded a spontaneous outlet. He could understand them merely by concentrating his attention upon their eyes; and could reply by summoning up a mental image of what he wished to say, and throwing the substance of this into his glance. When the thought-speaker paused, apparently inviting a response, Zamacona tried his best to follow the prescribed pattern, but did not appear to succeed very well. So he nodded, and tried to describe himself and his journey by signs. He pointed upward, as if to the outer world, then closed his eyes and made signs as of a mole burrowing. Then he opened his eyes again and pointed downward, in order to indicate his descent of the great slope. Experimentally he blended a spoken word or two with his gestures—for example, pointing successively to himself and to all of his visitors and saying *"un hombre"*, and then pointing to himself alone and very carefully pronouncing his individual name, *Pánfilo de Zamacona*.

Before the strange conversation was over, a good deal of data had passed in both directions. Zamacona had begun to learn how to throw his thoughts, and had likewise picked up several words of the region's archaic spoken language. His visitors, moreover, had absorbed many beginnings of an elementary Spanish vocabulary. Their own old language was utterly unlike anything the Spaniard had ever heard, though there were times later on when he was to fancy an infinitely remote linkage with the Aztec, as if the latter represented some far stage of corruption, or some very thin infiltration of loan-words. The underground world, Zamacona learned, bore an ancient name which the manuscript records as *"Xinaián"*, but which, from the writer's supplementary explanations and diacritical marks, could probably be best represented to Anglo-Saxon ears by the phonetic arrangement *K'n-yan*.

It is not surprising that this preliminary discourse did not go beyond the merest essentials, but those essentials were highly important. Zamacona learned that the people of K'n-yan were almost infinitely ancient, and that they had come from a distant part of space where physical conditions are much like those of the earth. All this, of course, was legend now; and one could not say how much truth was in it, or how much worship was really due to the octopus-headed being Tulu who had traditionally brought them hither and whom they still reverenced for aesthetic reasons. But they knew of the outer world, and were indeed the original stock who had peopled it as soon as its crust was fit to live on. Between glacial ages they had had some remarkable surface civilisations, especially one at the South Pole near the mountain Kadath.[25]

At some time infinitely in the past most of the outer world had sunk beneath the ocean, so that only a few refugees remained to bear the news to K'n-yan. This was undoubtedly due to the wrath of space-devils hostile alike to men and to men's gods—for it bore out rumours of a primordially earlier sinking which had submerged the gods themselves, including great Tulu, who still lay prisoned and dreaming in the watery vaults of the half-cosmic city Relex.[26] No man not a slave of the space-devils, it was argued, could live long on the outer earth; and it was decided that all beings who remained there must be evilly connected. Accordingly traffic with the lands of sun and starlight abruptly ceased. The subterraneous approaches to K'n-yan, or such as could be remembered, were either blocked up or carefully guarded; and all encroachers were treated as dangerous spies and enemies.

But this was long ago. With the passing of ages fewer and fewer visitors came to K'n-yan, and eventually sentries ceased to be maintained at the unblocked approaches. The mass of the people forgot, except through distorted memories and myths and some very singular dreams, that an outer world existed; though educated folk never ceased to recall the essential facts. The last visitors ever recorded—centuries in the past—had not even been treated as devil-spies; faith in the old legendry having long before died out. They had been questioned eagerly about the fabulous outer regions; for scientific curiosity in K'n-yan was keen, and the myths, memories, dreams, and historical fragments relating to the earth's surface had often tempted scholars to the brink of an external expedition which they had not quite dared to attempt. The only thing demanded of such visitors was that they refrain from going back and informing the outer world of K'n-yan's positive existence; for after all, one could not be sure about these outer lands. They coveted gold and silver, and might prove highly troublesome intruders. Those who had obeyed the injunction had lived happily, though regrettably briefly, and had told all they could about their world—little enough, however, since their accounts were all so fragmentary and conflicting that one could hardly tell what to believe and what to doubt. One wished that more of them would come. As for those who disobeyed and tried to escape—it was very unfortunate about them. Zamacona himself was very welcome, for he appeared to be a higher-grade man, and to know much more about the outer world, than anyone else who had come down within memory. He could tell them much—and they hoped he would be reconciled to his lifelong stay.

Many things which Zamacona learned about K'n-yan in that first colloquy left him quite breathless. He learned, for instance, that during the past few thousand years the phenomena of old age and death had been conquered; so that men no longer grew feeble or died except through violence or will. By regulating the system, one might be as physiologically young and immortal as he wished; and the only reason why any allowed themselves to age, was that they enjoyed the sensation in a world where stagnation and commonplaceness reigned. They could easily become young again when they felt like it. Births had ceased, except for experimental purposes, since a large population had been found needless by a master-race which controlled Nature and organic rivals alike. Many, however, chose to die after a while; since despite the cleverest efforts to invent new pleasures, the ordeal of consciousness became too dull for sensitive souls—especially those in whom time and satiation had blinded the primal instincts and emotions of self-preservation. All the members of the group before Zamacona were from 500 to 1500 years old; and several had seen surface visitors before, though time had blurred the recollection. These visitors, by the way, had often tried to duplicate the longevity of the underground race; but had been able to do so only fractionally, owing to evolutionary differences developing during the million or two years of cleavage.

These evolutionary differences were even more strikingly shewn in another particular—one far stranger than the wonder of immortality itself. This was the ability of the people of K'n-yan to regulate the balance between matter and abstract energy, even where the bodies of living organic beings were concerned, by the sheer force of the technically trained will. In other words, with suitable effort a learned man of K'n-yan could dematerialise and rematerialise himself—or, with somewhat greater effort and subtler technique, any other object he chose; reducing solid matter to free external particles and recombining the particles again without damage. Had not Zamacona answered his visitors' knock when he did, he would have discovered this accomplishment in a highly puzzling way; for only the strain and bother of the process prevented the twenty men from passing bodily through the golden door without pausing for a summons. This art was much older than the art of perpetual life; and it could be taught to some extent, though never perfectly, to any intelligent person. Rumours of it had reached the outer world in past aeons; surviving in secret traditions and ghostly legendry. The men of K'n-yan had been amused by the primitive and imperfect spirit tales brought down by outer-world stragglers. In practical life this principle had certain industrial applications, but was generally suffered to remain neglected through lack of any particular incentive to its use. Its chief surviving form was in connexion with sleep, when for excitement's sake many dream-connoisseurs resorted to it to enhance the vividness of their visionary wanderings. By the aid of this method certain dreamers even paid half-material visits to a strange, nebulous realm of mounds and valleys and varying light which some believed to be the forgotten outer world. They would go thither on their beasts, and in an age of peace live over the old, glorious battles of their forefathers. Some philosophers thought that in such cases they actually coalesced with immaterial forces left behind by these warlike ancestors themselves.

The people of K'n-yan all dwelt in the great, tall city of Tsath beyond the mountains. Formerly several races of them had inhabited the entire underground world, which stretched down to unfathomable abysses and which included besides the blue-litten region a red-litten region called Yoth,[27] where relics of a still older and non-human race were found by archaeologists. In the course of time, however, the men of Tsath had conquered and enslaved the rest; interbreeding them with certain horned and four-footed animals of the red-litten region, whose semi-human leanings were very peculiar, and which, though containing a certain artificially created element, may have been in part the degenerate descendants of those peculiar entities who had left the relics. As aeons passed, and mechanical discoveries made the business of life extremely easy, a concentration of the people of Tsath took place; so that all the rest of K'n-yan became relatively deserted.

It was easier to live in one place, and there was no object in maintaining a population of overflowing proportions. Many of the old mechanical devices were still in use, though others had been abandoned when it was seen that they failed to give pleasure, or that they were not necessary for a race of reduced numbers whose mental force could govern an extensive array of inferior and semi-human industrial organisms. This extensive slave-class was highly composite, being bred from ancient conquered enemies, from outer-world stragglers, from dead bodies curiously galvanised into effectiveness, and from the naturally inferior members of the ruling race of Tsath. The ruling type itself had become highly superior through selective breeding and social evolution—the nation having passed through a period of idealistic industrial democracy which gave equal opportunities to all, and thus, by raising the naturally intelligent to power, drained the masses of all their brains and stamina. Industry, being found fundamentally futile except for the supplying of basic needs and the gratification of inescapable yearnings, had become very simple. Physical comfort was ensured by an urban mechanisation of standardised and easily maintained pattern, and other elemental needs were supplied by scientific agriculture and stock-raising. Long travel was abandoned, and people went back to using the horned, half-human beasts instead of maintaining the profusion of gold, silver, and steel transportation machines which had once threaded land, water, and air. Zamacona could scarcely believe that such things had ever existed outside dreams, but was told he could see specimens of them in museums. He could also see the ruins of other vast magical devices by travelling a day's journey to the valley of Do-Hna, to which the race had spread during its period of greatest numbers. The cities and temples of this present plain were of a far more archaic period, and had never been other than religious and antiquarian shrines during the supremacy of the men of Tsath.

In government, Tsath was a kind of communistic or semi-anarchical state; habit rather than law determining the daily order of things. This was made possible by the age-old experience and paralysing ennui of the race, whose wants and needs were limited to physical fundamentals and to new sensations. An aeon-long tolerance not yet undermined by growing reaction had abolished all illusions of values and principles, and nothing but an approximation to custom was ever sought or expected. To see that the mutual encroachments of pleasure-seeking never crippled the mass life of the community—this was all that was desired. Family organisation had long ago perished, and the civil and social distinction of the sexes had disappeared. Daily life was organised in ceremonial patterns; with games, intoxication, torture of slaves, day-dreaming, gastronomic and emotional orgies, religious exercises, exotic experiments, artistic and philosophical discussions, and the like, as the principal occupations. Property—chiefly land, slaves, animals, shares in the common city enterprise of Tsath, and ingots of magnetic Tulu-metal, the former universal money standard—was allocated on a very complex basis which included a certain amount equally divided among all the freemen. Poverty was unknown, and labour consisted only of certain administrative duties imposed by an intricate system of testing and selection. Zamacona found difficulty in describing conditions so unlike anything he had previously known; and the text of his manuscript proved unusually puzzling at this point.

Art and intellect, it appeared, had reached very high levels in Tsath; but had become listless and decadent. The dominance of machinery had at one time broken up the growth of normal aesthetics, introducing a lifelessly geometrical tradition fatal to sound expression. This had soon been outgrown, but had left its mark upon all pictorial and decorative attempts; so that except for conventionalised religious designs, there was little depth or feeling in any later work. Archaistic reproductions of earlier work had been found much preferable for general enjoyment. Literature was all highly individual and analytical, so much so as to be wholly incomprehensible to Zamacona. Science had been profound and accurate, and all-embracing save in the one direction of astronomy. Of late, however, it was falling into decay, as people found it increasingly useless to tax their minds by recalling its maddening infinitude of details and ramifications. It was thought more sensible to abandon the deepest speculations and to confine philosophy to conventional forms. Technology, of course, could be carried on by rule of thumb. History was more and more neglected, but exact and copious chronicles of the past existed in the libraries. It was still an interesting subject, and there would be a vast number to rejoice at the fresh outer-world knowledge brought in by Zamacona. In general, though, the modern tendency was to feel rather than to think; so that men were now more highly esteemed for inventing new diversions than for preserving old facts or pushing back the frontier of cosmic mystery.

Religion was a leading interest in Tsath, though very few actually believed in the supernatural. What was desired was the aesthetic and emotional exaltation bred by the mystical moods and sensuous rites which attended the colourful ancestral faith. Temples to Great Tulu, a spirit of universal harmony anciently symbolised as the octopus-headed god who had brought all men down from the stars, were the most richly constructed objects in all K'n-yan; while the cryptic shrines of Yig, the principle of life symbolised as the Father of all Serpents, were almost as lavish and remarkable. In time Zamacona learned much of the orgies and sacrifices connected with this religion, but seemed piously reluctant to describe them in his manuscript. He himself never participated in any of the rites save those which he mistook for perversions of his own faith; nor did he ever lose an opportunity to try to convert the people to that faith of the Cross which the Spaniards hoped to make universal.

Prominent in the contemporary religion of Tsath was a revived and almost genuine veneration for the rare, sacred metal of Tulu—that dark, lustrous, magnetic stuff which was nowhere found in Nature, but which had always been with men in the form of idols and hieratic implements. From the earliest times any sight of it in its unalloyed form had impelled respect, while all the sacred archives and litanies were kept in cylinders wrought of its purest substance. Now, as the neglect of science and intellect was dulling the critically analytical spirit, people were beginning to weave around the metal once more that same fabric of awestruck superstition which had existed in primitive times.

Another function of religion was the regulation of the calendar, born of a period when time and speed were regarded as prime fetiches in man's emotional life. Periods of alternate waking and sleeping, prolonged, abridged, and inverted as mood and convenience dictated, and timed by the tail-beats of Great Yig, the Serpent, corresponded very roughly to terrestrial days and nights; though Zamacona's sensations told him they must actually be almost twice as long. The year-unit, measured by Yig's annual shedding of his skin, was equal to about a year and a half of the outer world. Zamacona thought he had mastered this calendar very well when he wrote his manuscript, whence the confidently given date of 1545; but the document failed to suggest that his assurance in this matter was fully justified.

As the spokesman of the Tsath party proceeded with his information, Zamacona felt a growing repulsion and alarm. It was not only what was told, but the strange, telepathic manner of telling, and the plain inference that return to the outer world would be impossible, that made the Spaniard wish he had never descended to this region of magic, abnormality, and decadence. But he knew that nothing but friendly acquiescence would do as a policy, hence decided to coöperate in all his visitors' plans and furnish all the information they might desire. They, on their part, were fascinated by the outer-world data which he managed haltingly to convey.

It was really the first draught of reliable surface information they had had since the refugees straggled back from Atlantis and Lemuria[28] aeons before, for all their subsequent emissaries from outside had been members of narrow and local groups without any knowledge of the world at large—Mayas, Toltecs, and Aztecs at best, and mostly ignorant tribes of the plains. Zamacona was the first European they had ever seen, and the fact that he was a youth of education and brilliancy made him of still more emphatic value as a source of knowledge. The visiting party shewed their breathless interest in all he contrived to convey, and it was plain that his coming would do much to relieve the flagging interest of weary Tsath in matters of geography and history.

The only thing which seemed to displease the men of Tsath was the fact that curious and adventurous strangers were beginning to pour into those parts of the upper world where the passages to K'n-yan lay. Zamacona told them of the founding of Florida[29] and New Spain, and made it clear that a great part of the world was stirring with the zest of adventure—Spanish, Portuguese, French, and English. Sooner or later Mexico and Florida must meet in one great colonial empire—and then it would be hard to keep outsiders from the rumoured gold and silver of the abyss. Charging Buffalo knew of Zamacona's journey into the earth. Would he tell Coronado, or somehow let a report get to the great viceroy, when he failed to find the traveller at the promised meeting-place? Alarm for the continued secrecy and safety of K'n-yan shewed in the faces of the visitors, and Zamacona absorbed from their minds the fact that from now on sentries would undoubtedly be posted once more at all the unblocked passages to the outside world which the men of Tsath could remember.

V.

The long conversation of Zamacona and his visitors took place in the green-blue twilight of the grove just outside the temple door. Some of the men reclined on the weeds and moss beside the half-vanished walk, while others, including the Spaniard and the chief spokesman of the Tsath party, sat on the occasional low monolithic pillars that lined the temple approach. Almost a whole terrestrial day must have been consumed in the colloquy, for Zamacona felt the need of food several times, and ate from his well-stocked pack while some of the Tsath party went back for provisions to the roadway, where they had left the animals on which they had ridden. At length the prime leader of the party brought the discourse to a close, and indicated that the time had come to proceed to the city.

There were, he affirmed, several extra beasts in the cavalcade, upon one of which Zamacona could ride. The prospect of mounting one of those ominous hybrid entities whose fabled nourishment was so alarming, and a single sight of which had set Charging Buffalo into such a frenzy of flight, was by no means reassuring to the traveller. There was, moreover, another point about the things which disturbed him greatly—the apparently preternatural intelligence with which some members of the previous day's roving pack had reported his presence to the men of Tsath and brought out the present expedition. But Zamacona was not a coward, hence followed the men boldly down the weed-grown walk toward the road where the things were stationed.

And yet he could not refrain from crying out in terror at what he saw when he passed through the great vine-draped pylons and emerged upon the ancient road. He did not wonder that the curious Wichita had fled in panic, and had to close his eyes a moment to retain his sanity. It is unfortunate that some sense of pious reticence prevented him from describing fully in his manuscript the nameless sight he saw. As it is, he merely hinted at the shocking morbidity of these great floundering white things, with black fur on their backs, a rudimentary horn in the centre of their foreheads, and an unmistakable trace of human or anthropoid blood in their flat-nosed, bulging-lipped faces. They were, he declared later in his manuscript, the most terrible objective entities he ever saw in his life, either in K'n-yan or in the outer world. And the specific quality of their supreme terror was something apart from any easily recognisable or describable feature. The main trouble was that they were not wholly products of Nature.

The party observed Zamacona's fright, and hastened to reassure him as much as possible. The beasts or *gyaa-yothn*, they explained, surely were curious things; but were really very harmless. The flesh they ate was not that of intelligent people of the master-race, but merely that of a special slave-class which had for the most part ceased to be thoroughly human, and which indeed was the principal meat stock of K'n-yan. They—or their principal ancestral element—had first been found in a wild state amidst the Cyclopean ruins of the deserted red-litten world of Yoth which lay below the blue-litten world of K'n-yan. That part of them was human, seemed quite clear; but men of science could never decide whether they were actually the descendants of the bygone entities who had lived and reigned in the strange ruins. The chief ground for such a supposition was the well-known fact that the vanished inhabitants of Yoth had been quadrupedal. This much was known from the very few manuscripts and carvings found in the vaults of Zin,[30] beneath the largest ruined city of Yoth. But it was also known from these manuscripts that the beings of Yoth had possessed the art of synthetically creating life,[31] and had made and destroyed several efficiently designed races of industrial and transportational animals in the course of their history—to say nothing of concocting all manner of fantastic living shapes for the sake of amusement and new sensations during the long period of decadence. The beings of Yoth had undoubtedly been reptilian in affiliations, and most physiologists of Tsath agreed that the present beasts had been very much inclined toward reptilianism before they had been crossed with the mammal slave-class of K'n-yan.

It argues well for the intrepid fire of those Renaissance Spaniards who conquered half the unknown world, that Pánfilo de Zamacona y Nuñez actually mounted one of the morbid beasts of Tsath and fell into place beside the leader of the cavalcade—the man named Gll'-Hthaa-Ynn, who had been most active in the previous exchange of information. It was a repulsive business; but after all, the seat was very easy, and the gait of the clumsy *gyaa-yoth* surprisingly even and regular. No saddle was necessary, and the animal appeared to require no guidance whatever. The procession moved forward at a brisk gait, stopping only at certain abandoned cities and temples about which Zamacona was curious, and which Gll'-Hthaa-Ynn was obligingly ready to display and explain. The largest of these towns, B'graa, was a marvel of finely wrought gold, and Zamacona studied the curiously ornate architecture with avid interest. Buildings tended toward height and slenderness, with roofs bursting into a multitude of pinnacles. The streets were narrow, curving, and occasionally picturesquely hilly, but Gll'-Hthaa-Ynn said that the later cities of K'n-yan were far more spacious and regular in design. All these old cities of the plain shewed traces of levelled walls—reminders of the archaic days when they had been successively conquered by the now dispersed armies of Tsath.

There was one object along the route which Gll'-Hthaa-Ynn exhibited on his own initiative, even though it involved a detour of about a mile along a vine-tangled side path. This was a squat, plain temple of black basalt blocks without a single carving, and containing only a vacant onyx pedestal. The remarkable thing about it was its story, for it was a link with a fabled elder world compared to which even cryptic Yoth was a thing of yesterday. It had been built in imitation of certain temples depicted in the vaults of Zin, to house a very terrible black toad-idol found in the red-litten world and called Tsathoggua in the Yothic manuscripts.[32] It had been a potent and widely worshipped god, and after its adoption by the people of K'n-yan had lent its name to the city which was later to become dominant in that region. Yothic legend said that it had come from a mysterious inner realm beneath the red-litten world—a black realm of peculiar-sensed beings which had no light at all, but which had had great civilisations and mighty gods before ever the reptilian quadrupeds of Yoth had come into being. Many images of Tsathoggua existed in Yoth, all of which were alleged to have come from the black inner realm, and which were supposed by Yothic archaeologists to represent the aeon-extinct race of that realm. The black realm called N'kai in the Yothic manuscripts had been explored as thoroughly as possible by these archaeologists, and singular stone troughs or burrows had excited infinite speculation.

When the men of K'n-yan discovered the red-litten world and deciphered its strange manuscripts, they took over the Tsathoggua cult and brought all the frightful toad images up to the land of blue light—housing them in shrines of Yoth-quarried basalt like the one Zamacona now saw. The cult flourished until it almost rivalled the ancient cults of Yig and Tulu, and one branch of the race even took it to the outer world, where the smallest of the images eventually found a shrine at Olathoë, in the land of Lomar near the earth's north pole.[33] It was rumoured that this outer-world cult survived even after the great ice-sheet and the hairy Gnophkehs[34] destroyed Lomar, but of such matters not much was definitely known in K'n-yan. In that world of blue light the cult came to an abrupt end, even though the name of Tsath was suffered to remain.

What ended the cult was the partial exploration of the black realm of N'kai beneath the red-litten world of Yoth. According to the Yothic manuscripts, there was no surviving life in N'kai, but something must have happened in the aeons between the days of Yoth and the coming of men to the earth; something perhaps not unconnected with the end of Yoth. Probably it had been an earthquake, opening up lower chambers of the lightless world which had been closed against the Yothic archaeologists; or perhaps some more frightful juxtaposition of energy and electrons, wholly inconceivable to any sort of vertebrate minds, had taken place. At any rate, when the men of K'n-yan went down into N'kai's black abyss with their great atom-power search-lights they found living things—living things that oozed along stone channels and worshipped onyx and basalt images of Tsathoggua. But they were not toads like Tsathoggua himself. Far worse—they were amorphous lumps of viscous black slime that took temporary shapes for various purposes.[35] The explorers of K'n-yan did not pause for detailed observations, and those who escaped alive sealed the passage leading from red-litten Yoth down into the gulfs of nether horror. Then all the images of Tsathoggua in the land of K'n-yan were dissolved into the ether by disintegrating rays, and the cult was abolished forever.

Aeons later, when naive fears were outgrown and supplanted by scientific curiosity, the old legends of Tsathoggua and N'kai were recalled, and a suitably armed and equipped exploring party went down to Yoth to find the closed gate of the black abyss and see what might still lie beneath. But they could not find the gate, nor could any man ever do so in all the ages that followed. Nowadays there were those who doubted that any abyss had ever existed, but the few scholars who could still decipher the Yothic manuscripts believed that the evidence for such a thing was adequate, even though the middle records of K'n-yan, with accounts of the one frightful expedition into N'kai, were more open to question. Some of the later religious cults tried to suppress remembrance of N'kai's existence, and attached severe penalties to its mention; but these had not begun to be taken seriously at the time of Zamacona's advent to K'n-yan.

As the cavalcade returned to the old highway and approached the low range of mountains, Zamacona saw that the river was very close on the left. Somewhat later, as the terrain rose, the stream entered a gorge and passed through the hills, while the road traversed the gap at a rather higher level close to the brink. It was about this time that light rainfall came. Zamacona noticed the occasional drops and drizzle, and looked up at the coruscating blue air, but there was no diminution of the strange radiance. Gll'-Hthaa-Ynn then told him that such condensations and precipitations of water-vapour were not uncommon, and that they never dimmed the glare of the vault above. A kind of mist, indeed, always hung about the lowlands of K'n-yan, and compensated for the complete absence of true clouds.

The slight rise of the mountain pass enabled Zamacona, by looking behind, to see the ancient and deserted plain in panorama as he had seen it from the other side. He seems to have appreciated its strange beauty, and to have vaguely regretted leaving it; for he speaks of being urged by Gll'-Hthaa-Ynn to drive his beast more rapidly. When he faced frontward again he saw that the crest of the road was very near; the weed-grown way leading starkly up and ending against a blank void of blue light. The scene was undoubtedly highly impressive—a steep green mountain wall on the right, a deep river-chasm on the left with another green mountain wall beyond it, and ahead, the churning sea of bluish coruscations into which the upward path dissolved. Then came the crest itself, and with it the world of Tsath outspread in a stupendous forward vista.

Zamacona caught his breath at the great sweep of peopled landscape, for it was a hive of settlement and activity beyond anything he had ever seen or dreamed of. The downward slope of the hill itself was relatively thinly strown with small farms and occasional temples; but beyond it lay an enormous plain covered like a chessboard with planted trees, irrigated by narrow canals cut from the river, and threaded by wide, geometrically precise roads of gold or basalt blocks. Great silver cables borne aloft on golden pillars linked the low, spreading buildings and clusters of buildings which rose here and there, and in some places one could see lines of partly ruinous pillars without cables. Moving objects shewed the fields to be under tillage, and in some cases Zamacona saw that men were ploughing with the aid of the repulsive, half-human quadrupeds.

But most impressive of all was the bewildering vision of clustered spires and pinnacles which rose afar off across the plain and shimmered flower-like and spectral in the coruscating blue light. At first Zamacona thought it was a mountain covered with houses and temples, like some of the picturesque hill cities of his own Spain, but a second glance shewed him that it was not indeed such. It was a city of the plain, but fashioned of such heaven-reaching towers that its outline was truly that of a mountain. Above it hung a curious greyish haze, through which the blue light glistened and took added overtones of radiance from the million golden minarets. Glancing at Gll'-Hthaa-Ynn, Zamacona knew that this was the monstrous, gigantic, and omnipotent city of Tsath.

As the road turned downward toward the plain, Zamacona felt a kind of uneasiness and sense of evil. He did not like the beast he rode, or the world that could provide such a beast, and he did not like the atmosphere that brooded over the distant city of Tsath. When the cavalcade began to pass occasional farms, the Spaniard noticed the forms that worked in the fields; and did not like their motions and proportions, or the mutilations he saw on most of them. Moreover, he did not like the way that some of these forms were herded in corrals, or the way they grazed on the heavy verdure. Gll'-Hthaa-Ynn indicated that these beings were members of the slave-class, and that their acts were controlled by the master of the farm, who gave them hypnotic impressions in the morning of all they were to do during the day. As semi-conscious machines, their industrial efficiency was nearly perfect. Those in the corrals were inferior specimens, classified merely as livestock.

Upon reaching the plain, Zamacona saw the larger farms and noted the almost human work performed by the repulsive horned *gyaa-yothn*. He likewise observed the more manlike shapes that toiled along the furrows, and felt a curious fright and disgust toward certain of them whose motions were more mechanical than those of the rest. These, Gll'-Hthaa-Ynn explained, were what men called the *y'm-*

bhi—organisms which had died, but which had been mechanically reanimated for industrial purposes by means of
atomic energy and thought-power. The slave-class did not
share the immortality of the freemen of Tsath, so that with
time the number of *y'm-bhi* had become very large. They
were dog-like and faithful, but not so readily amenable
to thought-commands as were living slaves. Those which
most repelled Zamacona were those whose mutilations
were greatest; for some were wholly headless, while others
had suffered singular and seemingly capricious subtrac-
tions, distortions, transpositions, and graftings in various
places. The Spaniard could not account for this condition,
but Gll'-Hthaa-Ynn made it clear that these were slaves who
had been used for the amusement of the people in some of
the vast arenas; for the men of Tsath were connoisseurs of
delicate sensation, and required a constant supply of fresh
and novel stimuli for their jaded impulses.[36] Zamacona,
though by no means squeamish, was not favourably impressed by what he saw and heard.

Approached more closely, the vast metropolis became
dimly horrible in its monstrous extent and inhuman height.
Gll'-Hthaa-Ynn explained that the upper parts of the great
towers were no longer used, and that many had been tak-
en down to avoid the bother of maintenance. The plain
around the original urban area was covered with newer and
smaller dwellings, which in many cases were preferred to
the ancient towers. From the whole mass of gold and stone
a monotonous roar of activity droned outward over the
plain, while cavalcades and streams of wagons were constantly entering and leaving over the great gold- or stone-
paved roads.

Several times Gll'-Hthaa-Ynn paused to shew Zamacona some particular object of interest, especially the tem-

ples of Yig, Tulu, Nug, Yeb, and the Not-to-Be-Named
One[37] which lined the road at infrequent intervals, each
in its embowering grove according to the custom of K'n-
yan. These temples, unlike those of the deserted plain beyond the mountains, were still in active use; large parties
of mounted worshippers coming and going in constant
streams. Gll'-Hthaa-Ynn took Zamacona into each of
them, and the Spaniard watched the subtle orgiastic rites
with fascination and repulsion. The ceremonies of Nug
and Yeb[38] sickened him especially—so much, indeed, that
he refrained from describing them in his manuscript. One
squat, black temple of Tsathoggua was encountered, but it
had been turned into a shrine of Shub-Niggurath, the All-
Mother and wife of the Not-to-Be-Named One. This deity was a kind of sophisticated Astarte,[39] and her worship
struck the pious Catholic as supremely obnoxious. What
he liked least of all were the emotional sounds emitted by
the celebrants—jarring sounds in a race that had ceased to
use vocal speech for ordinary purposes.

Close to the compact outskirts of Tsath, and well
within the shadow of its terrifying towers, Gll'-Hthaa-Ynn
pointed out a monstrous circular building before which
enormous crowds were lined up. This, he indicated, was
one of the many amphitheatres where curious sports and
sensations were provided for the weary people of K'n-yan.
He was about to pause and usher Zamacona inside the vast
curved facade, when the Spaniard, recalling the mutilated
forms he had seen in the fields, violently demurred. This
was the first of those friendly clashes of taste which were
to convince the people of Tsath that their guest followed
strange and narrow standards.

Tsath itself was a network of strange and ancient
streets; and despite a growing sense of horror and alien-

age, Zamacona was enthralled by its intimations of mystery and cosmic wonder. The dizzy giganticism of its overawing towers, the monstrous surge of teeming life through its ornate avenues, the curious carvings on its doorways and windows, the odd vistas glimpsed from balustraded plazas and tiers of titan terraces, and the enveloping grey haze which seemed to press down on the gorge-like streets in low ceiling-fashion, all combined to produce such a sense of adventurous expectancy[40] as he had never known before. He was taken at once to a council of executives which held forth in a gold-and-copper palace behind a gardened and fountained park, and was for some time subjected to close, friendly questioning in a vaulted hall frescoed with vertiginous arabesques. Much was expected of him, he could see, in the way of historical information about the outside earth; but in return all the mysteries of K'n-yan would be unveiled to him. The one great drawback was the inexorable ruling that he might never return to the world of sun and stars and Spain which was his.

A daily programme was laid down for the visitor, with time apportioned judiciously among several kinds of activities. There were to be conversations with persons of learning in various places, and lessons in many branches of Tsathic lore. Liberal periods of research were allowed for, and all the libraries of K'n-yan both secular and sacred were to be thrown open to him as soon as he might master the written languages. Rites and spectacles were to be attended—except when he might especially object—and much time would be left for the enlightened pleasure-seeking and emotional titillation which formed the goal and nucleus of daily life. A house in the suburbs or an apartment in the city would be assigned him, and he would be initiated into one of the large affection-groups, including many noblewomen of the most extreme and art-enhanced beauty, which in latter-day K'n-yan took the place of family units. Several horned *gyaa-yothn* would be provided for his transportation and errand-running, and ten living slaves of intact body would serve to conduct his establishment and protect him from thieves and sadists and religious orgiasts on the public highways. There were many mechanical devices which he must learn to use, but Gll'-Hthaa-Ynn would instruct him immediately regarding the principal ones.

Upon his choosing an apartment in preference to a suburban villa, Zamacona was dismissed by the executives with great courtesy and ceremony, and was led through several gorgeous streets to a cliff-like carven structure of some seventy or eighty floors. Preparations for his arrival had already been instituted, and in a spacious ground-floor suite of vaulted rooms slaves were busy adjusting hangings and furniture. There were lacquered and inlaid tabourets, velvet and silk reclining-corners and squatting-cushions, and infinite rows of teakwood and ebony pigeon-holes with metal cylinders containing some of the manuscripts he was soon to read—standard classics which all urban apartments possessed. Desks with great stacks of membrane-paper and pots of the prevailing green pigment were in every room—each with graded sets of pigment brushes and other odd bits of stationery. Mechanical writing devices stood on ornate golden tripods, while over all was shed a brilliant blue light from energy-globes set in the ceiling. There were windows, but at this shadowy ground-level they were of scant illuminating value. In some of the rooms were elaborate baths, while the kitchen was a maze of technical contrivances. Supplies were brought, Zamacona was told, through the network of underground passages which lay beneath Tsath, and which had once accommodated curious mechanical transports. There was a stable on that underground level for the beasts, and Zamacona would presently be shewn how to find the nearest runway to the street. Before his inspection was finished, the permanent staff of slaves arrived and were introduced; and shortly afterward there came some half-dozen freemen and noblewomen of his future affection-group, who were to be his companions for several days, contributing what they could to his instruction and amusement. Upon their departure, another party would take their place, and so onward in rotation through a group of about fifty members.

VI.

Thus was Pánfilo de Zamacona y Nuñez absorbed for four years into the life of the sinister city of Tsath in the blue-litten nether world of K'n-yan. All that he learned and saw and did is clearly not told in his manuscript; for a pious reticence overcame him when he began to write in his native Spanish tongue, and he dared not set down everything. Much he consistently viewed with repulsion, and many things he steadfastly refrained from seeing or doing or eating. For other things he atoned by frequent countings of the beads of his rosary. He explored the entire world of K'n-yan, including the deserted machine-cities of the middle period on the gorse-grown plain of Nith,[41] and made one descent into the red-litten world of Yoth to see the Cyclopean ruins. He witnessed prodigies of craft and machinery which left him breathless, and beheld human metamorphoses, dematerialisations, rematerialisations, and reanimations which made him cross himself again and again. His very capacity for astonishment was blunted by the plethora of new marvels which every day brought him.

But the longer he stayed, the more he wished to leave, for the inner life of K'n-yan was based on impulses very plainly outside his radius. As he progressed in historical knowledge, he understood more; but understanding only heightened his distaste. He felt that the people of Tsath were a lost and dangerous race—more dangerous to themselves than they knew—and that their growing frenzy of monotony-warfare and novelty-quest was leading them rapidly toward a precipice of disintegration and utter horror. His own visit, he could see, had accelerated their unrest; not only by introducing fears of outside invasion, but by exciting in many a wish to sally forth and taste the diverse external world he described. As time progressed, he noticed an increasing tendency of the people to resort to dematerialisation as an amusement; so that the apartments and amphitheatres of Tsath became a veritable Witches' Sabbath of transmutations, age-adjustments, death-experiments, and projections. With the growth of boredom and restlessness, he saw, cruelty and subtlety and revolt were growing apace. There was more and more cosmic abnormality, more and more curious sadism, more and more ignorance and superstition, and more and more desire to escape out of physical life into a half-spectral state of electronic dispersion.

All his efforts to leave, however, came to nothing. Persuasion was useless, as repeated trials proved; though the mature disillusion of the upper classes at first prevented them from resenting their guest's open wish for departure. In a year which he reckoned as 1543 Zamacona made an actual attempt to escape through the tunnel by which he had entered K'n-yan, but after a weary journey across the deserted plain he encountered forces in the dark passage which discouraged him from future attempts in that direction. As a means of sustaining hope and keeping the image of home in mind, he began about this time to make rough draughts of the manuscript relating his adventures; delighting in the loved, old Spanish words and the familiar letters of the Roman alphabet. Somehow he fancied he might get the manuscript to the outer world; and to make it convincing to his fellows he resolved to enclose it in one of the Tulu-metal cylinders used for sacred archives. That alien, magnetic substance could not but support the incredible story he had to tell.

But even as he planned, he had little real hope of ever establishing contact with the earth's surface. Every known gate, he knew, was guarded by persons or forces that it were better not to oppose. His attempt at escape had not helped matters, for he could now see a growing hostility to the outer world he represented. He hoped that no other European would find his way in; for it was possible that later comers might not fare as well as he. He himself had been a cherished fountain of data, and as such had enjoyed a privileged status. Others, deemed less necessary, might receive rather different treatment. He even wondered what would happen to him when the sages of Tsath considered him drained dry of fresh facts; and in self-defence began to be more gradual in his talks on earth-lore, conveying whenever he could the impression of vast knowledge held in reserve.

One other thing which endangered Zamacona's status in Tsath was his persistent curiosity regarding the ultimate abyss of N'kai, beneath red-litten Yoth, whose existence the dominant religious cults of K'n-yan were more and more inclined to deny. When exploring Yoth he had vainly tried to find the blocked-up entrance; and later on he experimented in the arts of dematerialisation and projection, hoping that he might thereby be able to throw his consciousness downward into the gulfs which his physical eyes could not discover. Though never becoming truly proficient in these processes, he did manage to achieve a series of monstrous and portentous dreams which he believed included some elements of actual projection into N'kai; dreams which greatly shocked and perturbed the leaders of Yig and Tulu-worship when he related them, and which he was advised by friends to conceal rather than exploit. In time those dreams became very frequent and maddening; containing things which he dared not record in his main manuscript, but of which he prepared a special record for the benefit of certain learned men in Tsath.

It may have been unfortunate—or it may have been mercifully fortunate—that Zamacona practiced so many reticences and reserved so many themes and descriptions for subsidiary manuscripts. The main document leaves one to guess much about the detailed manners, customs, thoughts, language, and history of K'n-yan, as well as to form any adequate picture of the visual aspect and daily life of Tsath. One is left puzzled, too, about the real motivations of the people; their strange passivity and craven unwarlikeness, and their almost cringing fear of the outer world despite their possession of atomic and dematerialising powers which would have made them unconquerable had they taken the trouble to organise armies as in the old days. It is evident that K'n-yan was far along in its decadence—reacting with mixed apathy and hysteria against the standardised and time-tabled life of stultifying regularity which machinery had brought it during its middle period. Even the grotesque and repulsive customs and modes of thought and feeling can be traced to this source; for in his historical research Zamacona found evidence of bygone eras in which K'n-yan had held ideas much like those of the classic and renaissance outer world, and had possessed a national character and art full of what Europeans regard as dignity, kindness, and nobility.

The more Zamacona studied these things, the more apprehensive about the future he became; because he saw that the omnipresent moral and intellectual disintegration was a tremendously deep-seated and ominously accelerating movement. Even during his stay the signs of decay multiplied. Rationalism degenerated more and more into fanatical and orgiastic superstition, centring in a lavish adoration of the magnetic Tulu-metal, and tolerance steadily dissolved into a series of frenzied hatreds, especially toward the outer world of which the scholars were learning so much from him. At times he almost feared that the people might some day lose their age-long apathy and brokenness and turn like desperate rats against the unknown lands above them, sweeping all before them by virtue of their singular and still-remembered scientific powers. But for the present they fought their boredom and sense of emptiness in other ways; multiplying their hideous emotional outlets and increasing the mad grotesqueness and abnormality of their diversions. The arenas of Tsath must have been accursed and unthinkable places—Zamacona never went near them. And what they would be in another century, or even in another decade, he did not dare to think. The pious Spaniard crossed himself and counted his beads more often than usual in those days.

In the year 1545, as he reckoned it, Zamacona began what may well be accepted as his final series of attempts to leave K'n-yan. His fresh opportunity came from an unexpected source—a female of his affection-group who conceived for him a curious individual infatuation based on some hereditary memory of the days of monogamous wedlock in Tsath. Over this female—a noblewoman of moderate beauty and of at least average intelligence named T'la-yub—Zamacona acquired the most extraordinary influence; finally inducing her to help him in an escape, under the promise that he would let her accompany him. Chance proved a great factor in the course of events, for T'la-yub came of a primordial family of gate-lords who had retained oral traditions of at least one passage to the outer world which the mass of people had forgotten even at the time of the great closing; a passage to a mound on the level plains of earth which had, in consequence, never been sealed up or guarded. She explained that the primordial gate-lords were not guards or sentries, but merely ceremonial and economic proprietors, half-feudal and baronial in status, of an era preceding the severance of surface-relations. Her own family had been so reduced at the time of the closing that their gate had been wholly overlooked; and they had ever afterward preserved the secret of its existence as a sort of hereditary secret—a source of pride, and of a sense of reserve power, to offset the feeling of vanished wealth and influence which so constantly irritated them.

Zamacona, now working feverishly to get his manuscript into final form in case anything should happen to him, decided to take with him on his outward journey only five beast-loads of unalloyed gold in the form of the small ingots used for minor decorations—enough, he calculated, to make him a personage of unlimited power in his own world. He had become somewhat hardened to the sight of the monstrous *gyaa-yothn* during his four years of residence in Tsath, hence did not shrink from using the creatures; yet he resolved to kill and bury them, and cache the gold, as soon as he reached the outer world, since he knew that even a glimpse of one of the things would drive any ordinary Indian mad. Later he could arrange for a suitable expedition to transport the treasure to Mexico. T'la-yub he would perhaps allow to share his fortunes, for she was by no means unattractive; though possibly he would arrange for her sojourn amongst the plains Indians, since he was not overanxious to preserve links with the manner of life in Tsath. For a wife, of course, he would choose a lady of Spain—or at worst, an Indian princess of normal outer-world descent and a regular and approved past. But for the present T'la-yub must be used as a guide. The manuscript he would carry on his own person, encased in a book-cylinder of the sacred and magnetic Tulu-metal.

The expedition itself is described in the addendum to Zamacona's manuscript, written later, and in a hand shewing signs of nervous strain. It set out amidst the most careful precautions, choosing a rest-period and proceeding as far as possible along the faintly lighted passages beneath the city. Zamacona and T'la-yub, disguised in slaves' garments, bearing provision-knapsacks, and leading the five laden beasts on foot, were readily taken for commonplace workers; and they clung as long as possible to the subterranean way—using a long and little-frequented branch which had formerly conducted the mechanical transports to the now ruined suburb of L'thaa.[42] Amidst the ruins of L'thaa they came to the surface, thereafter passing as rapidly as possible over the deserted, blue-litten plain of Nith toward the Grh-yan range of low hills. There, amidst the tangled underbrush, T'la-yub found the long disused and half-fabulous entrance to the forgotten tunnel; a thing she had seen but once before—aeons in the past, when her father had taken her thither to shew her this monument to their family pride. It was hard work getting the laden *gyaa-yothn* to scrape through the obstructing vines and briers, and one of them displayed a rebelliousness destined to bear

dire consequences—bolting away from the party and lop-
ing back toward Tsath on its detestable pads, golden burden and all.

It was nightmare work burrowing by the light of blue-
ray torches upward, downward, forward, and upward again
through a dank, choked tunnel that no foot had trodden
since ages before the sinking of Atlantis; and at one point
T'la-yub had to practice the fearsome art of dematerialisation on herself, Zamacona, and the laden beasts in order to
pass a point wholly clogged by shifting earth-strata. It was
a terrible experience for Zamacona; for although he had
often witnessed dematerialisation in others, and even practiced it himself to the extent of dream-projection, he had
never been fully subjected to it before. But T'la-yub was
skilled in the arts of K'n-yan, and accomplished the double
metamorphosis in perfect safety.

Thereafter they resumed the hideous burrowing
through stalactited crypts of horror where monstrous carvings leered at every turn; alternately camping and advancing for a period which Zamacona reckoned as about three
days, but which was probably less. At last they came to a
very narrow place where the natural or only slightly hewn
cave-walls gave place to walls of wholly artificial masonry,
carved into terrible bas-reliefs. These walls, after about a
mile of steep ascent, ended with a pair of vast niches, one
on each side, in which monstrous, nitre-encrusted images
of Yig and Tulu squatted, glaring at each other across the
passage as they had glared since the earliest youth of the
human world. At this point the passage opened into a prodigious vaulted and circular chamber of human construction; wholly covered with horrible carvings, and revealing
at the farther end an arched passageway with the foot of
a flight of steps. T'la-yub knew from family tales that this

must be very near the earth's surface, but she could not tell just how near. Here the party camped for what they meant to be their last rest-period in the subterraneous world.

It must have been hours later that the clank of metal and the padding of beasts' feet awakened Zamacona and T'la-yub. A bluish glare was spreading from the narrow passage between the images of Yig and Tulu, and in an instant the truth was obvious. An alarm had been given at Tsath—as was later revealed, by the returning *gyaa-yoth* which had rebelled at the brier-choked tunnel-entrance—and a swift party of pursuers had come to arrest the fugitives. Resistance was clearly useless, and none was offered. The party of twelve beast-riders proved studiously polite, and the return commenced almost without a word or thought-message on either side.

It was an ominous and depressing journey, and the ordeal of dematerialisation and rematerialisation at the choked place was all the more terrible because of the lack of that hope and expectancy which had palliated the process on the outward trip. Zamacona heard his captors discussing the imminent clearing of this choked place by intensive radiations, since henceforward sentries must be maintained at the hitherto unknown outer portal. It would not do to let outsiders get within the passage, for then any who might escape without due treatment would have a hint of the vastness of the inner world and would perhaps be curious enough to return in greater strength. As with the other passages since Zamacona's coming, sentries must be stationed all along, as far as the very outermost gate; sentries drawn from amongst all the slaves, the dead-alive *y'mbhi*, or the class of discredited freemen. With the overrunning of the American plains by thousands of Europeans, as the Spaniard had predicted, every passage was a potential source of danger; and must be rigorously guarded until the technologists of Tsath could spare the energy to prepare an ultimate and entrance-hiding obliteration as they had done for many passages in earlier and more vigorous times.

Zamacona and T'la-yub were tried before three *gn'agn* of the supreme tribunal in the gold-and-copper palace behind the gardened and fountained park, and the Spaniard was given his liberty because of the vital outer-world information he still had to impart. He was told to return to his apartment and to his affection-group; taking up his life as before, and continuing to meet deputations of scholars according to the latest schedule he had been following. No restrictions would be imposed upon him so long as he might remain peacefully in K'n-yan—but it was intimated that such leniency would not be repeated after another attempt at escape. Zamacona had felt that there was an element of irony in the parting words of the chief *gn'ag*—an assurance that all of his *gyaa-yothn*, including the one which had rebelled, would be returned to him.

The fate of T'la-yub was less happy. There being no object in retaining her, and her ancient Tsathic lineage giving her act a greater aspect of treason than Zamacona's had possessed, she was ordered to be delivered to the curious diversions of the amphitheatre; and afterward, in a somewhat mutilated and half-dematerialised form, to be given the functions of a *y'm-bhi* or animated corpse-slave and stationed among the sentries guarding the passage whose existence she had betrayed. Zamacona soon heard, not without many pangs of regret he could scarcely have anticipated, that poor T'la-yub had emerged from the arena in a headless and otherwise incomplete state, and had been set as an outermost guard upon the mound in which the passage had been found to terminate. She was, he was told, a night-sentinel, whose automatic duty was to warn off all comers with a torch; sending down reports to a small garrison of twelve dead slave *y'm-bhi* and six living but partly dematerialised freemen in the vaulted, circular chamber if the approachers did not heed her warning. She worked, he was told, in conjunction with a day-sentinel—a living freeman who chose this post in preference to other forms of discipline for other offences against the state. Zamacona, of course, had long known that most of the chief gate-sentries were such discredited freemen.

It was now made plain to him, though indirectly, that his own penalty for another escape-attempt would be service as a gate-sentry—but in the form of a dead-alive *y'm-bhi* slave, and after amphitheatre-treatment even more picturesque than that which T'la-yub was reported to have undergone. It was intimated that he—or parts of him—would be reanimated to guard some inner section of the passage; within sight of others, where his abridged person might serve as a permanent symbol of the rewards of treason. But, his informants always added, it was of course inconceivable that he would ever court such a fate. So long as he remained peaceably in K'n-yan, he would continue to be a free, privileged, and respected personage.

Yet in the end Pánfilo de Zamacona did court the fate so direfully hinted to him. True, he did not really expect to encounter it; but the nervous latter part of his manuscript makes it clear that he was prepared to face its possibility. What gave him a final hope of scatheless escape from K'n-yan was his growing mastery of the art of dematerialisation. Having studied it for years, and having learned still more from the two instances in which he had been subjected to it, he now felt increasingly able to use it independently and effectively. The manuscript records several notable experiments in this art—minor successes accomplished in his apartment—and reflects Zamacona's hope that he might soon be able to assume the spectral form in full, attaining complete invisibility and preserving that condition as long as he wished.

Once he reached this stage, he argued, the outward way lay open to him. Of course he could not bear away any gold, but mere escape was enough. He would, though, dematerialise and carry away with him his manuscript in the Tulu-metal cylinder, even though it cost additional effort; for this record and proof must reach the outer world at all hazards. He now knew the passage to follow; and if he could thread it in an atom-scattered state, he did not see how any person or force could detect or stop him. The only trouble would be if he failed to maintain his spectral condition at all times. That was the one ever-present peril, as he had learned from his experiments. But must one not always risk death and worse in a life of adventure? Zamacona was a gentleman of Old Spain; of the blood that faced the unknown and carved out half the civilisation of the New World.

For many nights after his ultimate resolution Zamacona prayed to St. Pamphilus and other guardian saints, and counted the beads of his rosary. The last entry in the manuscript, which toward the end took the form of a diary more and more, was merely a single sentence—*"Es más tarde de lo que pensaba—tengo que marcharme"*. . . . "It is later than I thought; I must go." After that, only silence and conjecture—and such evidence as the presence of the manuscript itself, and what that manuscript could lead to, might provide.

VII.

When I looked up from my half-stupefied reading and note-taking the morning sun was high in the heavens. The electric bulb was still burning, but such things of the real world—the modern outer world—were far from my whirling brain. I knew I was in my room at Clyde Compton's at Binger—but upon what monstrous vista had I stumbled? Was this thing a hoax or a chronicle of madness? If a hoax, was it a jest of the sixteenth century or of today? The manuscript's age looked appallingly genuine to my not wholly unpracticed eyes, and the problem presented by the strange metal cylinder I dared not even think about.

Moreover, what a monstrously exact explanation it gave of all the baffling phenomena of the mound—of the seemingly meaningless and paradoxical actions of diurnal and nocturnal ghosts, and of the queer cases of madness and disappearance! It was even an accursedly *plausible* explanation—evilly *consistent*—if one could adopt the incredible. It must be a shocking hoax devised by someone who knew all the lore of the mound. There was even a hint of social satire in the account of that unbelievable nether world of horror and decay. Surely this was the clever forgery of some learned cynic—something like the leaden crosses in New Mexico, which a jester once planted and pretended to discover as a relique of some forgotten Dark Age colony from Europe.[43]

Upon going down to breakfast I hardly knew what to tell Compton and his mother, as well as the curious callers who had already begun to arrive. Still in a daze, I cut the Gordian Knot by giving a few points from the notes I had made, and mumbling my belief that the thing was a subtle and ingenious fraud left there by some previous explorer of the mound—a belief in which everybody seemed to concur when told of the substance of the manuscript. It is curious how all that breakfast group—and all the others in Binger to whom the discussion was repeated—seemed to find a great clearing of the atmosphere in the notion that somebody was playing a joke on somebody. For the time we all forgot that the known, recent history of the mound presented mysteries as strange as any in the manuscript, and as far from acceptable solution as ever.

The fears and doubts began to return when I asked for volunteers to visit the mound with me. I wanted a larger excavating party—but the idea of going to that uncomfortable place seemed no more attractive to the people of Binger than it had seemed on the previous day. I myself felt a mounting horror upon looking toward the mound and glimpsing the moving speck which I knew was the daylight sentinel; for in spite of all my scepticism the morbidities of that manuscript stuck by me and gave everything connected with the place a new and monstrous significance. I absolutely lacked the resolution to look at the moving speck with my binoculars. Instead, I set out with the kind of bravado we display in nightmares—when, knowing we are dreaming, we plunge desperately into still thicker horrors, for the sake of having the whole thing over the sooner. My pick and shovel were already out there, so I had only my handbag of smaller paraphernalia to take. Into this I put the strange cylinder and its contents, feeling vaguely that I might possibly find something worth checking up with some part of the green-lettered Spanish text. Even a clever hoax might be founded on some actual attribute of the mound which a former explorer had discovered—and that magnetic metal was damnably odd! Grey Eagle's cryptic talisman still hung from its leathern cord around my neck.

I did not look very sharply at the mound as I walked toward it, but when I reached it there was nobody in sight. Repeating my upward scramble of the previous day, I was troubled by thoughts of what *might* lie close at hand *if*, by any miracle, any part of the manuscript *were* actually half-true. In such a case, I could not help reflecting, the hypothetical Spaniard Zamacona must have barely reached the outer world when overtaken by some disaster—perhaps an involuntary rematerialisation. He would naturally, in that event, have been seized by whichever sentry happened to be on duty at the time—either the discredited freeman, or, as a matter of supreme irony, the very T'la-yub who had planned and aided his first attempt at escape—and in the ensuing struggle the cylinder with the manuscript might well have been dropped on the mound's summit, to be neglected and gradually buried for nearly four centuries. But, I added, as I climbed over the crest, one must not think of extravagant things like that. Still, if there *were* anything in the tale, it must have been a monstrous fate to which Zamacona had been dragged back . . . the amphitheatre . . . mutilation . . . duty somewhere in the dank, nitrous tunnel as a dead-alive slave . . . a maimed corpse-fragment as an automatic interior sentry. . . .

It was a very real shock which chased this morbid speculation from my head, for upon glancing around the elliptical summit I saw at once that my pick and shovel had been stolen. This was a highly provoking and disconcerting development; baffling, too, in view of the seeming reluctance of all the Binger folk to visit the mound. Was this reluctance a pretended thing, and had the jokers of the village been chuckling over my coming discomfiture as they solemnly saw me off ten minutes before? I took out my binoculars and scanned the gaping crowd at the edge of the village. No—they did not seem to be looking for any comic climax; yet was not the whole affair at bottom a colossal joke in which all the villagers and reservation people were concerned—legends, manuscript, cylinder, and all? I thought of how I had seen the sentry from a distance, and then found him unaccountably vanished; thought also of the conduct of old Grey Eagle, of the speech and expressions of Compton and his mother, and of the unmistakable fright of most of the Binger people. On the whole, it could not very well be a village-wide joke. The fear and the problem were surely real, though obviously there were one or two jesting daredevils in Binger who had stolen out to the mound and made off with the tools I had left.

Everything else on the mound was as I had left it— brush cut by my machete, slight, bowl-like depression toward the north end, and the hole I had made with my trench-knife in digging up the magnetism-revealed cylinder. Deeming it too great a concession to the unknown jokers to return to Binger for another pick and shovel, I resolved to carry out my programme as best I could with the machete and trench-knife in my handbag; so extracting these, I set to work excavating the bowl-like depression which my eye had picked as the possible site of a former entrance to the mound. As I proceeded, I felt again the suggestion of a sudden wind blowing against me which I had noticed the day before—a suggestion which seemed stronger, and still more reminiscent of unseen, formless, opposing hands laid on my wrists, as I cut deeper and deeper through the root-tangled red soil and reached the exotic black loam beneath. The talisman around my neck appeared to twitch oddly in the breeze—not in any one direction, as when attracted by the buried cylinder, but vaguely and diffusely, in a manner wholly unaccountable.

Then, quite without warning, the black, root-woven earth beneath my feet began to sink cracklingly, while I heard a faint sound of sifting, falling matter far below me. The obstructing wind, or forces, or hands now seemed to be operating from the very seat of the sinking, and I felt that they aided me by pushing as I leaped back out of the hole to avoid being involved in any cave-in. Bending down over the brink and hacking at the mould-caked root-tangle with my machete, I felt that they were against me again— but at no time were they strong enough to stop my work. The more roots I severed, the more falling matter I heard below. Finally the hole began to deepen of itself toward the centre, and I saw that the earth was sifting down into some large cavity beneath, so as to leave a good-sized aperture when the roots that had bound it were gone. A few more hacks of the machete did the trick, and with a parting cave-in and uprush of curiously chill and alien air the last barrier gave way. Under the morning sun yawned a huge opening at least three feet square, and shewing the top of a flight of stone steps down which the loose earth of the collapse was still sliding. My quest had come to something at last! With an elation of accomplishment almost overbalancing fear for the nonce, I replaced the trench-knife and machete in my handbag, took out my powerful electric torch, and prepared for a triumphant, lone, and utterly rash invasion of the fabulous nether world I had uncovered.

It was rather hard getting down the first few steps, both because of the fallen earth which had choked them and because of a sinister up-pushing of a cold wind from below. The talisman around my neck swayed curiously, and I began to regret the disappearing square of daylight above me. The electric torch shewed dank, water-stained, and salt-encrusted walls fashioned of huge basalt blocks, and now and then I thought I descried some trace of carving beneath the nitrous deposits. I gripped my handbag more tightly, and was glad of the comforting weight of the sheriff's heavy revolver in my right-hand coat pocket. After a time the passage began to wind this way and that, and the staircase became free from obstructions. Carvings on the walls were now definitely traceable, and I shuddered when I saw how clearly the grotesque figures resembled the monstrous bas-reliefs on the cylinder I had found. Winds and forces continued to blow malevolently against me, and at one or two bends I half fancied the torch gave glimpses of thin, transparent shapes not unlike the sentinel on the mound as my binoculars had shewed him. When I reached this stage of visual chaos I stopped for a moment to get a grip on myself. It would not do to let my nerves get the better of me at the very outset of what would surely be a trying experience, and the most important archaeological feat of my career.

But I wished I had not stopped at just that place, for the act fixed my attention on something profoundly disturbing. It was only a small object lying close to the wall on one of the steps below me, but that object was such as to put my reason to a severe test, and bring up a line of the most alarming speculations. That the opening above me had been closed against all material forms for generations was utterly obvious from the growth of shrub-roots and accumulation of drifting soil; yet the object before me was most distinctly *not* many generations old. For it was an electric torch much like the one I now carried—warped and encrusted in the tomb-like dampness, but none the less perfectly unmistakable. I descended a few steps and picked it up, wiping off the evil deposits on my rough coat. One of the nickel bands bore an engraved name and address, and I

309

recognised it with a start the moment I made it out. It read "Jas. C. Williams, 17 Trowbridge St., Cambridge, Mass."— and I knew that it had belonged to one of the two daring college instructors who had disappeared on June 28, 1915. Only thirteen years ago, and yet I had just broken through the sod of centuries! How had the thing got there? Another entrance—or was there something after all in this mad idea of dematerialisation and rematerialisation?

Doubt and horror grew upon me as I wound still farther down the seemingly endless staircase. Would the thing never stop? The carvings grew more and more distinct, and assumed a narrative pictorial quality which brought me close to panic as I recognised many unmistakable correspondences with the history of K'n-yan as sketched in the manuscript now resting in my handbag. For the first time I began seriously to question the wisdom of my descent, and to wonder whether I had not better return to the upper air before I came upon something which would never let me return as a sane man. But I did not hesitate long, for as a Virginian I felt the blood of ancestral fighters and gentlemen-adventurers pounding a protest against retreat from any peril known or unknown.

My descent became swifter rather than slower, and I avoided studying the terrible bas-reliefs and intaglios that had unnerved me. All at once I saw an arched opening ahead, and realised that the prodigious staircase had ended at last. But with that realisation came horror in mounting magnitude, for before me there yawned a vast vaulted crypt of all-too-familiar outline—a great circular space answering in every least particular to the carving-lined chamber described in the Zamacona manuscript.

It was indeed the place. There could be no mistake. And if any room for doubt yet remained, that room was abolished by what I saw directly across the great vault. It was a second arched opening, commencing a long, narrow passage and having at its mouth two huge opposite niches bearing loathsome and titanic images of shockingly familiar pattern. There in the dark unclean Yig and hideous Tulu squatted eternally, glaring at each other across the passage as they had glared since the earliest youth of the human world.

From this point onward I ask no credence for what I tell—for what I *think* I saw. It is too utterly unnatural, too utterly monstrous and incredible, to be any part of sane human experience or objective reality. My torch, though casting a powerful beam ahead, naturally could not furnish any general illumination of the Cyclopean crypt; so I now began moving it about to explore the giant walls little by little. As I did so, I saw to my horror that the space was by no means vacant, but was instead littered with odd furniture and utensils and heaps of packages which bespoke a populous recent occupancy—no nitrous reliques of the past, but queerly shaped objects and supplies in modern, every-day use. As my torch rested on each article or group of articles, however, the distinctness of the outlines soon began to grow blurred; until in the end I could scarcely tell whether the things belonged to the realm of matter or to the realm of spirit.

All this while the adverse winds blew against me with increasing fury, and the unseen hands plucked malevolently at me and snatched at the strange magnetic talisman I wore. Wild conceits surged through my mind. I thought of the manuscript and what it said about the garrison stationed in this place—twelve dead slave *y'm-bhi* and six living but partly dematerialised freemen—that was in 1545—three hundred and eighty-three years ago. . . . What since then?

Zamacona had predicted change . . . subtle disintegration . . . more dematerialisation . . . weaker and weaker . . . was it Grey Eagle's talisman that held them at bay—their sacred Tulu-metal—and were they feebly trying to pluck it off so that they might do to me what they had done to those who had come before? . . . It occurred to me with shuddering force that I was building my speculations out of a full belief in the Zamacona manuscript—this must not be—I must get a grip on myself—

But, curse it, every time I tried to get a grip I saw some fresh sight to shatter my poise still further. This time, just as my will power was driving the half-seen paraphernalia into obscurity, my glance and torch-beam had to light on two things of very different nature; two things of the eminently real and sane world; yet they did more to unseat my shaky reason than anything I had seen before—because I knew what they were, and knew how profoundly, in the course of Nature, they ought not to be there. *They were my own missing pick and shovel, side by side, and leaning neatly against the blasphemously carved wall of that hellish crypt.* God in heaven—and I had babbled to myself about daring jokers from Binger!

That was the last straw. After that the cursed hypnotism of the manuscript got at me, and I actually *saw* the half-transparent shapes of the things that were pushing and plucking; pushing and plucking—those leprous palaeogean things with something of humanity still clinging to them—the *complete* forms, and the forms that were morbidly and perversely *incomplete* . . . all these, and hideous *other entities*—the four-footed blasphemies with ape-like face and projecting horn . . . and not a sound so far in all that nitrous hell of inner earth. . . .

Then there *was* a sound—a flopping; a padding; a

312

dull, advancing sound which heralded beyond question a being as structurally material as the pickaxe and the shovel—something wholly unlike the shadow-shapes that ringed me in, yet equally remote from any sort of life as life is understood on the earth's wholesome surface. My shattered brain tried to prepare me for what was coming, but could not frame any adequate image. I could only say over and over again to myself, "It is of the abyss, but it is *not* dematerialised." The padding grew more distinct, and from the mechanical cast of the tread I knew it was a dead thing that stalked in the darkness. Then—oh, God, *I saw it in the full beam of my torch; saw it framed like a sentinel in the narrow passage between the nightmare idols of the serpent Yig and the octopus Tulu.* . . .

Let me collect myself enough to hint at what I saw; to explain why I dropped torch and handbag and fled empty-handed in the utter blackness, wrapped in a merciful unconsciousness which did not wear off until the sun and the distant yelling and the shouting from the village roused me as I lay gasping on the top of the accursed mound. I do not yet know what guided me again to the earth's surface. I only know that the watchers in Binger saw me stagger up into sight three hours after I had vanished; saw me lurch up and fall flat on the ground as if struck by a bullet. None of them dared to come out and help me; but they knew I must be in a bad state, so tried to rouse me as best they could by yelling in chorus and firing off revolvers.

It worked in the end, and when I came to I almost rolled down the side of the mound in my eagerness to get away from that black aperture which still yawned open. My torch and tools, and the handbag with the manuscript, were all down there; but it is easy to see why neither I nor anyone else ever went after them. When I staggered across the plain and into the village I dared not tell what I had seen. I only muttered vague things about carvings and statues and snakes and shaken nerves. And I did not faint again until somebody mentioned that the ghost-sentinel had reappeared about the time I had staggered half way back to town. I left Binger that evening, and have never been there since, though they tell me the ghosts still appear on the mound as usual.

But I have resolved to hint here at last what I dared not hint to the people of Binger on that terrible August afternoon. I don't know yet just how I can go about it—and if in the end you think my reticence strange, just remember that to imagine such a horror is one thing, *but to see it is another thing.* I saw it. I think you'll recall my citing early in this tale the case of a bright young man named Heaton who went out to that mound one day in 1891 and came back at night as the village idiot, babbling for eight years about horrors and then dying in an epileptic fit. What he used to keep moaning was *"That white man—oh, my God, what they did to him. . . ."*

Well, I saw the same thing that poor Heaton saw—and I saw it after reading the manuscript, so I know more of its history than he did. That makes it worse—for I know all that it *implies;* all that must be still brooding and festering and waiting down there. I told you it had padded mechanically toward me out of the narrow passage and had stood sentry-like at the entrance between the frightful eidola of Yig and Tulu. That was very natural and inevitable—because the thing *was* a sentry. It had been made a sentry for punishment, and it was quite dead—besides lacking head, arms, lower legs, and other customary parts of a human being. Yes—it had been a very human being once; and what is more, it had been *white.* Very obviously, if that manuscript

314

was as true as I think it was, this being had been used for the *diversions of the amphitheatre* before its life had become wholly extinct and supplanted by automatic impulses controlled from outside.

On its white and only slightly hairy chest some letters had been gashed or branded—I had not stopped to investigate, but had merely noted that they were in an awkward and fumbling Spanish; an awkward Spanish implying a kind of ironic use of the language by an alien inscriber familiar neither with the idiom nor the Roman letters used to record it. The inscription had read *"Secuestrado a la voluntad de Xinaián en el cuerpo decapitado de Tlayúb"*—*"Seized by the will of K'n-yan in the headless body of T'la-yub."*

Appendix

Four O'Clock

by Sonia H. Greene

About two in the morning I knew it was coming. The great black silences of night's depth told me, and a monstrous cricket, chirping with a persistence too hideous to be unmeaning, made it certain. It is to be at four o'clock—at four in the dusk before dawn, just as he said it would be. I had not fully believed it previously, because the prophecies of vindictive madmen are seldom to be taken with seriousness. Besides, I was not justly to be blamed for what had befallen him at four o'clock on that other morning; that terrible morning whose memory will never leave me. And when, at length, he had died and was buried in the ancient cemetery just across the road from my east windows, I was certain that his curse could not harm me. Had I not seen his lifeless clay securely pinned down by huge shovelfuls of mould? Might I not feel assured that his crumbling bones would be powerless to bring me the doom at a day and an hour so precisely stated? Such, indeed, had been my thoughts until this shocking night itself; this night of incredible chaos, of shattered certainties, and of nameless portents.

I had retired early, hoping fatuously to snatch a few hours of sleep despite the prophecy which haunted me. Now that the time was so close at hand, I found it harder and harder to dismiss the vague fears which had always lain beneath my conscious thoughts. As the cooling sheets soothed my fevered body, I could find nothing to soothe my still more fevered mind; but lay tossing and uneasily awake, trying first one position and then another in a desperate effort to banish with slumber that one damnably insistent notion—*that it is to occur at four o'clock.*

Was this frightful unrest due to my surroundings; to the fateful locality in which I was sojourning after so many years? Why, I now asked myself bitterly, had I permitted circumstance to place me, on this night of all nights, in that well-remembered house and that well-remembered room whose east windows overlook the lonely road and the ancient country cemetery beyond? In my mind's eye every detail of that unpretentious necropolis rose before me—its white fence, its ghost-like granite shafts, and the hovering auras of those on whom the worms fed. Finally the force of the conception led my vision to depths more remote and more forbidden, and I saw under the neglected grass the silent shapes of the things from which the auras came— the calm sleepers, the rotting things, the things which had twisted frantically in their coffins before sleep came, and the peaceful bones in every stage of disintegration from the complete and coherent skeleton to the huddled handful of dust. Most of all I envied the dust. Then new terror came as my fancy encountered *his* grave. Into that sepulchre I dared not let my thought stray, and I should have screamed had not something forestalled the malign power that pulled my mental sight. That something was a sudden gust of wind, sprung from nowhere amidst the calm night, which unfastened the shutter of the nearest window, throwing it back with a shivery slam and uncovering to my actual waking glance the antique cemetery itself, brooding spectrally beneath an early morning moon.

I speak of this gust as something merciful, yet know now that it was only transiently and mockingly so. For no sooner had my eyes compassed the moonlight scene than I became aware of a fresh omen, this time too unmistakable to be classed as an empty phantasm, which arose from among the gleaming tombs across the road. Having glanced with instinctive apprehension toward the spot where *he* lay mouldering—a spot cut off from my gaze by the window-frame—I perceived with trepidation the approach of an indescribable something which flowed menacingly from that very direction; a vague, vaporous, formless mass of greyish-white substance of spirit, dull and tenuous as yet, but every moment increasing in awesome and cataclysmic potentiality. Try as I might to dismiss it as a natural meteorological phenomenon, its fearsomely portentous and *deliberate* character grew upon me amidst new thrills of horror and apprehension; so that I was scarcely unprepared for the definitely purposeful and malevolent culmination which soon occurred. That culmination, bringing with it a hideous symbolic foreshadowing of the end, was equally simple and threatening. The vapor each moment thickened and piled up, assuming at last a half tangible aspect; while the surface toward me gradually became circular in outline, and markedly concave, as it slowly ceased its advance and stood spectrally at the end of the road. And as it stood there, faintly quivering in the damp night air under that unwholesome moon, I saw that its aspect was that of the pallid and gigantic dial of a distorted *clock*.

Hideous events now followed in demoniac succession.[1] There took shape in the lower right-hand part of the vaporous dial a black and formidable creature, shapeless and only half seen, yet having four prominent claws which reached out greedily at me—claws redolent of noxious fatality in their very contour and location; since they formed too plainly the dreaded outlines, and filled too unmistakably the exact position, of the numeral IV on the quivering dial of doom. Presently the monstrosity stepped or wriggled out of the concave surface of the dial, and began to approach me by some unexplained kind of locomotion. The four talons, long, thin, and straight, were now seen to be tipped by disgusting, thread-like tentacles, each with a vile intelligence of its own, which groped about incessantly, slowly at first, but gradually increasing in velocity until I was nearly driven mad by the sheer dizziness of their motion. And as a crowning horror I began to hear all the subtle and cryptical noises that pierced the intensified night silence; a thousandfold magnified, and in one voice reminding me of the abhorred hour of *four*. In vain I tried to pull up the coverlet to shut them out; in vain I tried to drown them with my screams. I was mute and paralyzed, yet agonizingly aware of every unnatural sight and sound in that devastating, moon-cursed stillness. Once I managed to get my head beneath the covers—once when the cricket's shrieking of that hideous phrase, *four-o'clock,* seemed about to shatter my brain—but that only aggravated the terror, making the roars of that detestable creature strike me like the blows of a titanic sledge-hammer.

And now, as I withdrew my tortured head from its fruitless protection, I found augmented diabolism to harass my eyes. Upon the newly painted wall of my apartment, as if called forth by the tentacled monster from the tomb, there danced mockingly before me a myriad company of beings, black, grey, and white, such as only the fancy of the god-stricken might visualize. Some were of infinitesimal smallness; others covered vast areas. In minor details each had a grotesque and horrible individuality; in general outlines they all conformed to the same nightmare pattern despite their vastly varied size. Again I tried to shut out the abnormalities of the night, but vainly as before. The dancing things on the wall waxed and waned in magnitude, approaching and receding as they trod their morbid and menacing measure. And the aspect of each was that of some demon clock-face with one sinister hour always figured thereon—the dreaded, the doom-delivering hour of *four*.

Baffled in every attempt to shake off the circling and relentless delirium, I glanced once more toward the unshuttered window and beheld again the monster which had come from the grave. Horrible it had been before; indescribable it had now become. The creature, formerly of indeterminate substance, was now formed of red and malignant fire; and waved repulsively its four tentacled claws—unspeakable tongues of living flame. It stared and stared at me out of the blackness; sneeringly, mockingly; now advancing, now retiring. Then, in the tenebrous silence, those four writhing talons of fire beckoned invitingly to their demoniacally dancing counterparts on the walls, and seemed to beat time rhythmically to the shocking saraband till the world was one ghoulishly gyrating vortex of leaping, prancing, gliding; leering, taunting, threatening *four o'clocks.*

Somewhere, beginning afar off and advancing over the sphinx-like sea and the febrile marshes, I heard the early morning wind come soughing; faintly at first, then louder and louder until its unceasing burden flowed as a deluge of whirring, buzzing cacophony, bringing always the hideous threat, *"four o'clock, four o'clock,* FOUR O'CLOCK." Monotonously it grew from a whimper to a deafening roar, as of a giant cataract, but finally reached a climax and began to subside. As it receded into the distance it left upon my sensitive ears such a vibration as is left by the passing of a swift and ponderous railway train; this, and a stark dread whose intensity gave it something of the tranquility of resignation.

The end is near. All sound and vision have become one vast chaotic maelstrom of lethal, clamorous menace, wherein are fused all the ghastly and unhallowed four o'clocks which have existed since immemorial time began, and all which will exist in eternities to come. The flaming monster is advancing closely now, its charnel tentacles brushing my face and its talons curving hungrily as they grope toward my throat. At last I can see its face through the churning and phosphorescent vapors of the graveyard air, and with devastating pangs I realize that it is in essence an awful, colossal, gargoyle-like caricature of *his* face—the face of him from whose uneasy grave it has issued. Now I know that my doom is indeed sealed; that the wild threats of the madman were in truth the demon maledictions of a potent fiend, and that my innocence will prove no protection against the malign volition which craves a causeless vengeance. He is determined to pay me with interest for what he suffered at that spectral hour; determined to drag me out of the world into realms which only the mad and the devil-ridden know.

And as amidst the seething of hell's flames and the tumult of the damned those fiery claws point murderously at my throat, I hear upon the mantel the faint whirring sound of a timepiece; the whirring which tells me that it is about to strike the hour whose name now flows incessantly from the death-like and cavernous throat of the rattling, jeering, croaking grave-monster before me—the accursed, the infernal hour of *four o'clock.*

A Sacrifice to Science

by Gustav Adolphe Danziger

I.

There are many people living now, who will recall with a shudder the frightful epidemic which raged in the city of San Francisco a score of years ago. This epidemic was a malignant typhoid fever, which made its appearance first in the hospital of the county jail. More than fifty-eight convicts died in one summer of that mysterious disease, which manifested always the same symptoms and always ended with a fatal result. The people in the city knew at first very little of this dreadful calamity; moreover, they were quite unconcerned whether more or fewer convicts lived or died behind the massive walls of the county's penal institute. However, the newspapers soon spread the matter abroad; people became cognizant of the danger that threatened the community. Thus far, the people of San Francisco had been mercifully spared; but while some spoke in whispers about the epidemic which was raging among the outcasts of society, others spoke with pride of Dr. Clinton, the penitentiary physician, who had discovered the disease, and was the first to give a minute description of it. He had not been able to cure any of the convicts, but his fame had reached the remotest corners of the civilized world.

Dr. Clinton lived in a gloomy house at the outer end of Broadway, which stood alone in a block of land. He was not very sociable, but that did not prevent the wealthiest people from calling him to their houses.

Dr. Clinton was born in the city of New York, had graduated from the medical college at quite an early age, had gone to Europe, and after years and years of hard study at the great universities, had at last gone with a scientific expedition to study the fever epidemic and other noxious diseases among the natives of the West Indies, finally settling in San Francisco.

Some of the younger physicians were enthusiastic about Dr. Clinton's discovery (the older practitioners were less demonstrative), and adored his fine scholarship. It was a pity, they said, that he was so exclusive, and buried himself in the old house on Broadway, when society was eager to lionize him. The Doctor paid no attention to gossip, either favorable or otherwise. The prison and his gloomy house on Broadway were his world; he was satisfied.

With Dr. Clinton lived his sister, Alvira, who kept house for him, and a dismal-looking servant by the name of Mort, who had accompanied the doctor on his travels.

Alvira Clinton was wealthy in her own right; her parents, at their death, had left her and her brother enough means to live in luxury all their lives, but the Doctor's love of science had made him careless of ease.

Alvira Clinton, without being very beautiful, lacked by no means a certain attractiveness. She had big black eyes, which were expressive of intelligence; about her mouth there was that peculiar expression said to be expressive of an indomitable will. But when Alvira talked she was positively handsome. There was a bubbling over of spirit, a sparkling of wit, that charmed all men. She talked but seldom now; her devotion to her brother, her tireless help in his scientific labors, occupied her time. She did not care for society, its gossip and its parties, but was seen more frequently in the houses of the poor, her neighbors and well-wishers. She went to see them because, curiously enough, the miserable Mexicans in the neighborhood were afraid to enter the gloomy house, which was surrounded by a high fence and tall eucalyptus trees.

At a short distance from the house was a large stable containing the animals on which the Doctor experimented, and which Mort called the "Clinic."

Alvira shuddered when she heard her brother give the details for the dog clinic; the whinings of the tortured animals filled her with unspeakable horror. This annoyed her brother, and he made her enter the gruesome hospital. He desired her to satisfy herself that the animals were not being tortured, and the noise came from the dogs playing in the garden. Alvira was compelled to acknowledge that the animals in the "Clinic" were quite as lively as the dogs in the garden; there was no sign of cruelty, nor even harshness, visible; everything was kept scrupulously clean, making quite a pleasing impression. Of course, there were several of the sick rabbits stretched out in their cages; the light had gone from their eyes, and they seemed to wait for the end which was sure to come. But this had to be; it was in perfect harmony with a hospital.

"Are you satisfied now?" Dr. Clinton asked his sister.

"Yes," said Alvira; "still, I think I had better keep away from your clinic."

"Suit yourself," said he, calmly. It was just as well she staid away; he had no need of her there, and she might be in Mort's way. The latter attended to all the business in that domain.

Mort was Clinton's right-hand man. He was absolutely indispensable. He contrived to keep the "Clinic" supplied with the animals necessary for anatomical purposes and to dispose of them after that. Alvira hated him because he seemed too familiar with her brother. She shuddered when he came near her; he was so repulsive-looking. From the back of his head to his forehead there was not a hair. His head looked like a huge ball of polished ivory. He had neither brows nor eyelashes, and his nose was flattened down to a wide mouth with colorless lips and immense teeth. His body was lank and his clothes too wide. The skin of his face and hands looked like yellow parchment drawn taut. One invariably imagined that his clothes covered a horrible skeleton. And this individual, at the sight of whom dogs drew in their tails and ran away, had the fullest confidence of her brother.

"No one outside of the Doctor and myself shall see what we are about in our hospital," he once said to a presumptuous reporter. And thus they lived, secluded from the world, with nothing to disturb them. The many famous physicians and the lesser lights who had come to study the peculiar disease, and had expected to be treated hospitably by Dr. Clinton, were somewhat disappointed. Not that he did not treat them with the necessary civility, but while he took them to the prison hospital, he coldly refused to admit them to his private study or to Mort's "Clinic." They should neither see his notes nor the means he employed to check the disease.

His persistent refusal to show his private "workshop"

caused the learned doctors to shake their heads suspicious-
ly. Clinton saw it and bit his lips; but when they had gone
his rage was uncontrollable. "The idiots!" he cried, and ran
into the garden, racing up and down. Mort, who knew the
cause of the Doctor's rage, roundly abused the "Eastern
quacks." This invariably had a pacifying effect upon the
Doctor. He smiled, and a defiant look came into his face.
Let them shake their heads. Mort and himself, and not a
living human soul besides, should enter his sanctum until
the work is done.

Any person who ventured into the garden or into the
house was treated most ungraciously by Mort. "What do
you want? We don't receive visitors," was the stereotyped
remark with which he sent away men and women.

However, one man, George Dalton, was an exception.
He alone dared to enter the lonely house without being
sent away.

II.

George Dalton was a lawyer who had known the Clinton family in New York, and had transacted their business
there. He had asked Mr. Alfred Clinton, Sen., for permission to pay his respects to the only daughter, but was met
with such harshness by the old gentleman that he did not
make a second attempt. Of course, George Dalton was an
impecunious young lawyer, but he was young, well educated, of a jovial disposition, and quite hopeful. When the old
Mr. Clinton told Dalton that he could aspire to transact
the legal business of the family, and to nothing else, George
said nothing. But he no sooner left the Clinton mansion
than he proceeded to the nearest barber, had his blonde
locks and beard cut and shaved, went home, packed his

portmanteau, and went West. In less than five years George Dalton had made a reputation and a fortune; but his early timidity never left him. He recalled the words of Clinton, Sen., and he stayed in the city of San Francisco.

Ten years more had gone by and one day George saw Alvira on the street. The hot wave that suffused his face when he saw her clearly told that years and space had no effect upon his affections. Alvira, too, was happy to see him. She told him of the death of her parents, of her brother's great learning and fame, and their intention to locate in the city. They were indeed a handsome pair as they walked up Broadway. Dr. Clinton was favorable to Dalton, as far as he was capable of showing his regard. He spoke a word or two with the friend of his sister, and then left them alone. Dr. Clinton had no interest in anything or anybody that did not betray the symptoms of typhoid fever. But when George Dalton succeeded in getting him the position in the prison hospital, he condescended to express his appreciation, not to Dalton, but to Alvira. She was happy that he thought well of George; for, be it understood, she loved the lawyer, and would have followed him, were it not that she pitied her brother, who would have been helpless without her. Nor could she think of leaving him alone with his "evil genius," as she called Mort.

Dr. Clinton was sure of his sister. He knew that she would not leave him for any man. He did not object to Dalton's visits, which, however, were not so frequent as to cause him any uneasiness. Every Sunday evening the gloomy house, or, to be more precise, the family sitting-room, was enlivened by George Dalton's pleasant conversation; and because Alvira seemed to enjoy the lively chit-chat, her brother rather encouraged the visitor. Without it, the Doctor thought she might tire of the loneliness and

gloom, and—who knows?—might leave him alone—the
very thought caused him to shudder—with his factotum,
Mort. The latter knew that this thought upset the Doctor,
and he never failed to allude to it. These allusions enraged
Clinton, and he would have chastised his servant or dismissed him—if he could. But as he could not do either, he
raved in impotent rage, and then consoled himself with the
thought that Alvira was too sensible to entertain any such
ideas. How could she?

One bright, sunny morning, it was on a Sunday, a
scene was enacted in Dr. Clinton's garden that caused Alvira to weep, the Doctor to rave, and Mort to grin; and when
Mort grinned, the birds in the trees ceased their chirping
and flew away; everything seemed to wither when Mort's
eyes glistened and Mort's mouth grinned. The scene was as
follows: In an altana[1] in the garden sat George Dalton, Alvira, and the Doctor. Dalton seemed depressed,—strange
for a man of his temper; the Doctor was smoking, and Alvira was speaking rather hastily and incoherently. At some
distance, but near enough for him to hear, was Mort with
his dogs. Clinton had just thrown away the stump of a cigar, and Alvira, glad at the pretext, went into the house to
fetch some fresh cigars.

Dalton took advantage of Alvira's absence and said, "I
might as well say it now as at any other time. Dr. Clinton,
I love Alvira; have loved her for years, and have reason to
believe that she is not indifferent to me. In a word, I desire
to marry your sister. She shall never have any cause to regret
it. Give us your consent, Doctor."

Dr. Clinton seemed to think of a proper expression to
couch his refusal. Dalton's speech had evidently displeased
him, but it did not come unexpected. He had grown tired
of the lawyer's visits. He wanted absolute seclusion. If the

lawyer suffered a second rebuff, he was sure to stay away for good. He stroked his beard, and a smile of satisfaction flitted across his pale face.

"You are speaking of an impossibility, Dalton," he said. "My sister has concluded, once for all, to devote her life to such an unworthy old bachelor as I am."

"But you cannot—you dare not—accept such a sacrifice, Dr. Clinton," said Dalton. "Alvira is not the girl to spend her life in the society of that fellow Mort and his dogs. You ought to be more reasonable, Doctor."

Dr. Clinton rose from his seat. He was a shade paler than usual. His dark eyes shot flashes of malignant hatred and contempt. Dalton involuntarily stepped back as the Doctor hissed the answer into his face: "Whether I have the right to accept the sacrifice of my sister,—if to resign the drudgery of a commonplace marriage can be called a sacrifice,—this, I judge, is no business of a stranger."

"But I am—"

"A stranger for us," said the Doctor. "You could have spared yourself this explanation if your feelings had been less youthful than your age would lead one to believe."

George Dalton was astounded, but he gradually gained his balance. "We two are done, Dr. Clinton," he said. "Miss Alvira is of age, and mistress of her own action. I will ask her to decide."

"There she is," said Clinton. "I will leave you two alone, so that you do not accuse me of influencing her decision."

When Alvira returned she was astonished to find her brother and Dalton facing each other in evident excitement. Clinton cut the matter short by saying: "Alvira, Mr. Dalton desires to speak to you. I will, in the mean time, look after Mort's boarders."

Alvira took a seat and motioned Dalton to do likewise. But when Dalton was about to speak, she said, "Do not speak." Her voice was soft and sad. "Whatever changes you desire to bring about, do not count upon my consent. Years ago, yes; but now it is different. I feel it is my sacred duty to care for Alfred, who would be lost without me. Besides, I do not feel at all lonely," she added, with all the feminine tenderness she was capable of, "since you come to the house. Leave matters as they are. We have peace; do not disturb the mutual harmony."

"My dear Alvira, what you have said," replied Dalton, "demonstrates to me one fact, namely, that you appreciate my visits, and because of that I tell you, if you do love me a little, you will not refuse me. You will not cast aside the true devotion of a man tried and found loyal. I say again, Alvira, be my wife."

The girl looked at Dalton with eyes that mirrored the gratitude of her soul. She knew that she loved him, and had he taken her to his breast in youthful passion, she would have followed him. She would have forsaken her brother, if Dalton had kissed the confession from her lips. But as he appeared in a matter of fact manner, speaking friendly and sensibly, it was her duty to be sensible, too, and this demanded that she tell him where her duty lay, namely, with her brother. The reason why she would not leave him was that he was sacrificing his health and his life to science. She said it with a sigh that clearly told of her sufferings.

"Then you stay with him out of sheer pity?" Dalton asked.

Alvira took hold of Dalton's hand, and with every evidence of anxiety she said: "Forgive me, George, but I cannot act otherwise. My brother believes in my faithful love and devotion, and he shall not be disappointed. On the day that he needs my life it shall be fettered by no other bonds.

I must be at his side."

Alvira sank back into her seat and covered her face with her hands. Dalton saw the tears trickle through her fingers. His heart ached to see the woman he loved suffer so much.

"Your brother is ill. He ought to give up his work. Let him travel,—anything that will keep him away from his labors," said he.

"You are right," said Alvira. "His work will be his death; but he cannot live without it. You ought to have seen him when he discovered the first case at the prison hospital. He had evidently been baffled by something in his investigations, and the epidemic at the hospital had come at the most opportune moment. He suffered, nevertheless, because he believed himself responsible for every person that died,—as if he, and not God, had brought on the epidemic. The first evening—when the dread disease made its appearance—was the most horrible. I shall never forget it. He came into the house without saying a word, and ran out into the garden again, running up and down as if possessed, trampling upon flowers and the shrubbery, and laughing loudly. It terrified me, but I did not dare to speak to him. He is quiet now, and with nothing to excite him, we live quite happily. And now I see the dark clouds again. This time, dear friend, you are the disturber. For my sake, George, be friends with Alfred, and when you come again do not broach that other subject."

"My dear Miss Alvira, I am grieved to tell you that after the hard words that have passed between your brother and me it would be quite impossible for me to call at his house again; but granted I did come, it would be equally impossible for me to subdue my feelings, now more than ever, since I know how unhappy you are."

He rose and stretched out his hand, which she grasped, saying: "I know that you will forever remain my dearest, my best, friend, and because of that I ask you to promise me when I call you that you will come to me. Promise me, George!" He knew what she suffered, and without a word he pressed her hand in token of a promise, and left. Dr. Clinton saw Dalton, the only friend of the family, leave the house, but he seemed to be engrossed in some subject which Mort had shown him, and did not turn.

III.

Added to gossip that Dalton's withdrawal occasioned, was the fact that the Doctor's star was on the wane. The people became disappointed in Dr. Clinton. It is true, he had made a great discovery, and the medical journals all over the world were still discussing the subject; but suffering and death are old evils, and the discovery of one more disease was interesting, but not quite agreeable to contemplate, considering that one might become a victim to the new discovery. Dr. Clinton had not found a remedy against the epidemic, and therefore had achieved nothing.

But this was not all. He had managed to make more enemies than any man in his profession. When he had become the fashion in the city, and every one consulted the eminent "fever doctor," he was found deficient in that one quality,—a *sine qua non* to the success of a physician,—to flatter the rich, to humor their ills, especially the female patients, and be interested in the babies of fond mothers. To make matters worse, it so happened that he had some differences with one of the prison directors, who told him that he (Dr. Clinton) was merely an official at the hospital, but not the master. And last, but not least for Dr. Clinton, was the fact that the epidemic had disappeared as suddenly as it had come.

People began to lose their dread of the disease and their respect for the discoverer. Added to this was the opinion of a prominent college professor of New York, who had spent months in the city to investigate the disease. "This disease is not a new discovery," the professor said, "and it is due to the boundless conceit of Dr. Clinton that it was given so much prominence. If Dr. Clinton had discovered a mode by which the organic disease germs can be developed and scientifically explained, if he had found the bacillus and learned to conquer its poisonous and deadly effect, let him proclaim it, and the world would hail him a Messiah. If he had not done this, he had not merited any recognition, outside of the fact that he had opened one more of the many problems which science is working hard to solve. However, the problem was not put by Dr. Clinton, but by his suffering patients. Dr. Clinton," the professor concluded, "has done nothing; he has not even attempted to save the lives of those who fell victims to the fever."

The opinion of this eminent man, being published, had the effect that not one person could be found in the city of San Francisco who would consent to be treated by Dr. Clinton. Even the poorest people were afraid to consult him, and only those who could not get the services of any other physician free of charge called him to their bedsides.

But that peculiarly malignant smile never left Dr. Clinton's lips. In the fever ward of the prison hospital he was still master; there no one interfered with him.

But one day the whole matter came to a sudden end. Dr. Clinton came home and told Alvira that he had been dismissed. Alvira desired to know what cause the Directors had for such an action.

"They at first made all sorts of charges," said Clinton. "I was too independent. I told them I would consult them in the future on all matters. Then they trumped up a charge of infidelity. One of them—the fellow is a deacon in a church—objected to an atheistic physician; and that cur pretends to be an American. I laughed in their faces at first, but ultimately promised that for the sake of peace I would go to church and partake of communion, or that I would embrace any faith they pleased."

"You would not have done that," said Alvira. "I don't believe it! You would never have sacrificed your honor; because to dissemble is dishonorable."

Clinton looked at his sister with a contemptuous smile upon his lips.

"I have laid so many sacrifices upon the altar of science and investigation," said he, grimly, "that a lie more or less could not possibly make much difference. But they would not consider my proposition.

"The next charge was, that I was too extravagant at the cost of the institution, by giving chickens and wine to the prisoners. Poor devils! I should have deprived them of the necessary nutriment, while I am experimenting on their carcasses. To hamper my work on account of such trifles! I mastered myself, and promised to let the sick starve as much as possible. But it came out at last. They told me that I do not prescribe any medicine for the sick. Not prescribe enough medicine! Ha, ha, ha!

"After this I was, of course, forced to leave. The professional honor demanded that I should leave! The professional honor! Ha, ha, ha! Do these fools think I am like those quacks who believe, and make their patients believe, that they can and will cure them? We are not here for the sake of hospitals, but hospitals are here for our sakes,—for the sake of science. But there was no use fighting; they had made up their minds to get rid of me, and I went."

His restless eyes gazed upon the instruments in the cabinet, then upon the big volumes in his library. There, upon long shelves, stood a fine selection of all the classical and standard medical works from Aristotle down to Pasteur. Alvira understood his looks. Among these princes of science, among the greatest of the great, should be Dr. Clinton's work on the origin and cause of fever germs and their conquest. Otherwise he had nothing to live for. Alvira, with the instinct of a tender woman, found the right words to encourage her brother. "You are on the road to fame already; in fact, you are near the goal, and in spite of the petty jealousy of small men, you will yet be glorious, brother. You have made all the observations at the hospital that you needed, and as the epidemic is on the wane, it would be the proper time to bring your work to a close." Clinton seemed absentminded, but at Alvira's last words he shook his head, and said, as if speaking to himself: "But three months more and I would have been done. I could have offered to the world the very greatest work of science,—a collection of deadly and of protecting bacilli."

But Alvira staid by her argument. "Of course, I am not competent to judge," she said; "but from the information which I gleaned from your remarks made at odd moments, I am inclined to think that new cases of the dread disease could hardly make much difference, and should the epidemic break out again at the hospital, I am sure they will have to call you. Who else could fill your place?"

"The epidemic is gone. I was mistaken. It does not make its appearance where bunglers are at work," Clinton said with a hoarse laugh, while his right hand mechanically played with his golden hypodermic injector. He then took up a book and was soon engrossed in his reading. His sister took it as a good omen. "He may yet succeed, and be counted among the foremost men of all times," she said, going to her own room.

But Alvira's hopes were not fulfilled. He grew darker and moodier every day. He lost all interest in his dog clinic, and when Mort approached to make some report regarding one of the animals he drove him away.

"Go to the devil with your dog stories," Alvira heard her brother scream at the top of his voice. "I do not need dogs. I need human beings, and these were taken from me,—stolen. Not even a condemned murderer would they give me."

Alvira could not hear Mort's answer, but she heard his tuneless laughter and a cry of rage from her brother, who threatened to knock him down.

IV.

Not like a young physician anxious for practice, but like a panting deer crying for water, did Dr. Clinton look for a patient. A patient!—only one sick person whom he could study; but he looked in vain. Not a soul came to the house. Alvira went from room to room and sighed. She never left the house now, and Mort, who attended to all affairs on the outside, came and went like a shadow. No one in the vicinity or in any part of the city thought of calling Dr. Clinton.

Unable to bear it any longer, the Doctor left the house, incognito, to find a patient, if possible. He entered the huts of the poorest people and bribed them with food and wine. He gave the parents money and the children candy, until he had gained their confidence. Then he told them that he was a physician, and when any one complained he volunteered his services. His life received a fresh impetus; he was happy. His science had found new material for investigation; Dr. Clinton was himself once more.

The best reason for his good humor was not so much the new and varied practice which he had found as the fact that the fever had made its appearance among the Mexicans in lower Broadway. It was as yet in its mildest form, but it was there, evidently and unmistakably. That no cases were reported from the prison hospital was probably due to the ignorance of the physicians, Dr. Clinton said. Those bunglers would not know the disease if they were laid low with it themselves. There was but one Dr. Clinton!

As the months passed, it was noticed that the epidemic had reached a very dangerous degree. None had died as yet; the Doctor's art had conquered death thus far, but the epidemic raged with frightful violence.

It was in the spring of the year that the poor people whom Dr. Clinton had assisted with food, medicine, and money grew to suspect a compact between Dr. Clinton and the Devil. This suspicion was fostered by the relentless hatred of an old Mexican fisherman whom the Doctor had had the misfortune to displease. As the old Mexican was the oracle among his kind, his words carried weight. "He is in league with the Devil," he was heard to say. "Look out for yourselves; he brings you the sickness." But there were some who laughed at the padre, and told him to consult the Doctor for the affection of the eyes. After much persuasion the old Mexican so far mastered his antagonism as to send for Dr. Clinton. The latter performed an operation with so much skill and success that the populace danced with joy, and told the old padre that he was mistaken about the good Doctor. Nothing could now have shaken their faith in Dr.

Clinton, were it not that the old Mexican caught the fever. In his delirium he uttered frightful imprecations against the Doctor. When Clinton made his visit the next morning, he was met by a mob, who warned him to keep away from their houses, else he would get hurt. He tried to reason with them. He begged; he pleaded,—all in vain. "You are the Devil," they said. "You gave us food and money, and you bought us body and soul; but you shall not come here again. Wherever you go, there is death." And he was forced to retreat.

"The dogs! the curs!" he cried, running up and down in his study. "They are afraid of their miserable lives, as if their lives were worth anything, if they did not serve to enrich science. They want to live. Well, let them live, and starve."

As it was, these wretches had added their mite toward assisting his studies. The raging fever had revealed to him many new points of interest. If he could have brought one of those cases under the microscope, and if he could also have succeeded in curing a most violent case, his ambition would have been satisfied, his work done, and he would have laughed at their ingratitude. He was so excited that he discussed the subjects of his research with his sister and Mort. The latter taunted the Doctor with cowardice, to retreat before a mob of dirty Mexicans. Alvira suffered unspeakably. Why was her learned brother so haughty to everybody and so submissive to the taunts and insults of his servant? Did Mort know the *modus operandi* of the new method? and did her brother fear that his servant might reveal it to one of the many jealous physicians, who would benefit by the labors of her brother? Probably.

A few days later, Alvira and her brother were walking in the garden, arm in arm. Mort was busy tending to some plants, but his sharp ears never lost one word of the conversation between brother and sister.

"Ah! if I could only get to work again,—to work among people, and not among rabbits and dogs in that clinic over there," said Clinton.

"Are you sure, Alfred," said Alvira, "that mankind will be benefited by your discovery?"

A contemptuous smile played about Mort's lips. Alvira caught that smile, and shivered.

"Mankind is but a drop in the ocean of nature," said Dr. Clinton, "and nature refuses to be helped. She laughs and jeers at us when we are presumptuous enough to attempt to conquer her. Nature is without consideration. She is the most powerful murderess in existence, and science, in order to know nature, must be in sympathy with her."

"But where is the benefit to mankind?" said Alvira, sick at heart.

"Our science, my dear Alvira," said Clinton, with a smile, "knows of cases where enthusiastic pupils took poison to assist their perplexed masters in demonstrating its effects. You have heard of the painter's daughter who permitted herself to be crucified, so that her father might catch the proper expression for a picture of the Saviour? Natural science knows of such models who have sacrificed their lives mundane to live eternally in the sacred history of science. We live for science, not for mankind. Mort," the Doctor cried, "what do you say to the idea of advertising for such volunteers for scientific research?"

Clinton's eyes sparkled with a brilliancy and wildness that frightened his poor sister. Mort, however, seemed to have considered the Doctor's proposition. "We might try it," he said. "But I don't believe it would be a success. You cannot rely upon volunteers. One must take his subjects wherever he finds them."

Alvira was horrified to hear Mort speak so to her brother. In the mouth of the latter those words seemed but the exaggeration of an exuberant fancy, but in the mouth of Mort they sounded like the words of a scoundrel. She was so overcome that she could hardly stand. She ran into the house, that her brother might not notice her weakness.

For days after this conversation, Alvira shivered at the recollection, and remained in her room so as to avoid meeting her brother's evil genius.

Dr. Clinton's endeavors to visit the poor were met with determined opposition. When he showed himself, a shower of stones and other missiles met his advance; once he was even shot at. Had he incurred the displeasure of the Americans in the same degree as that of the superstitious Mexicans, he would have been tarred and feathered, if not shot. But when the Americans heard one of those absurd stories about the luckless Dr. Clinton, they merely laughed at the horror that was expressed in the faces of the "Greasers" at the mention of his name. They had wisely or providentially been spared an intimate acquaintance with Dr. Clinton's philanthropy.

But the repeated rebuffs that he suffered from the Mexicans doubled his energy and his desire for investigation. He experimented on the animals, and very soon all the dogs and rabbits in Mort's clinic lay either sick or dead. Mort pleaded in vain against the total extermination of his animals; he refused to bring new specimens, in spite of his master's commands and threats. A gruesome stillness had now fallen upon the lonely house and in the garden. Bruno, the big St. Bernard dog, was the sole animal left; he was Alvira's pet, and sacred. He greeted his master with mighty jumps, and gave a joyous howl whenever his mistress showed herself in the garden.

One bright morning, in the middle of May, as Mort entered the library, he found the dog lying on the floor, with red eyes, and its swollen tongue protruding from its mouth,—the dog had caught the fever. Mort uttered a hoarse laugh as he dragged the splendid animal into his "Clinic." Alvira was very sad when she heard of Bruno's illness, but she did not give up the hope of his recovery. The dog had been her brother's pet, and he would surely cure him.

As often as Dr. Clinton came from the "Clinic," she asked him after the dog's health. On the third day after Bruno's illness, Alvira concluded to see the poor animal herself, and, mastering her dislike for Mort and his establishment, the girl crossed the garden toward the "Clinic." But she halted at the door, because of the angry words which her brother spoke to Mort. The two were evidently engaged in a violent quarrel. The door was partly open, and Alvira could look into the experimental room without being seen. Dr. Clinton walked up and down, gesticulating wildly and uttering curses at his factotum, while the latter busied himself with cleansing the microscope, but kept a vigilant eye on his master.

"Your spite and obstinacy be damned!" cried the Doctor. "You miserable wretch, you would prevent me from completing my work by refusing to bring me the necessary subjects, eh? I have asked you again and again to bring some, but you have not brought me a mouse, even. I would like to experiment day and night, but am hampered by your obstinacy."

"Ha, ha, ha!" laughed Mort. This laugh caused Alvira's heart to stop. How dared the wretch be so insolent to her brother! She listened again.

"You are experimenting! Ha, ha, ha! Well, I don't propose to go to the penitentiary for stealing dogs. If I am to hang, I want to be as great as you are, Doctor. I shall then have done my share of work by the million."

"Shut up!" cried Dr. Clinton, his voice hoarse with passion. "You miserable cur, you know very well why I desire to complete my work just now. It is the last moment. I am maddened by the thought that while I am longing for subjects to finish my work some one else might publish a book on the subject, and spoil the work of a lifetime."

"No one in America or Europe can do that," replied Mort, with a grin. "To do what we have done one must have a steady hand like you, and be without prejudice. I can rely upon you! No one else could possibly accomplish your work. After Bruno's death there is nothing left but to experiment on yourself; who else would—"

"Shut up, or—" Alvira was unable to listen any longer; the knowledge that her brother had sacrificed his pet dog was too much for her. She understood that science could not have benefited by Bruno's death; that her brother must certainly have acted under mental stress. In that case, however, he was not bad; he was only unfortunate; his work and anxiety were too much; they had undermined his health. But what could she do? Her brother, she knew, would sooner die than give up his work. She was miserable beyond expression. There was no one to help her; she was alone in the world, without a friend or relative. But no; she was not without a friend. There was her friend Dalton, of whom she had so often thought with love and longing; she would call him. Alvira was about to return to the house when the noise of falling furniture and a wild cry from her brother attracted her to the spot. Suddenly she saw Mort come from the "Clinic," a long knife in his hand, and, walking backwards, followed by Dr. Clinton, whom he sought to keep at a distance. Alvira being concealed behind the door, held on to it to support herself. The sight had made her faint.

"Keep away from me, Dr. Clinton, or I'll run this knife into you. Not one step, I say. Don't commit any foolishness. You could not kill me quick enough to prevent me from giving you away. I tell you, have a care!"

Alvira could stand it no longer. Satisfied that her brother did not follow his servant, she slipped behind a bush and ran into the house. Quickly she wrote a few lines to George Dalton, asking him to come to her house, either that very evening or the following morning. She was so excited and nervous that she frequently paused in writing. The note being written and sealed, she hastened into the street, and luckily finding a boy, gave him half a dollar to carry the note to George Dalton's office.

But all this had completely exhausted her strength. She barely managed to reach the library, when she fell upon the lounge, shaken by cold and fever. She had not been in there more than half an hour when the door was opened and Dr. Clinton came in. It was already dark, and he did not see his sister. He ran up and down, gesticulating and fighting imaginary foes. He was striking at one of those phantoms, when he was startled by a sigh. He was so scared that he stood as if rooted to the spot.

"Is it you, Alvira?" he asked, quite unnerved. But being answered by another sigh, he lighted a candle and stepped up to the lounge.

"For God's sake! you have the fever," he cried, in terrible excitement. But he soon mastered himself. Covering her with a heavy blanket, he hastened into the kitchen and made her a hot drink. When Alvira's fever had quieted down, he sat by her side, her hand in his. Once in a while his eyes became restless, and his hand moved toward the vest pocket where his "injector" was. Alvira, who felt much better, smiled at her brother gratefully.

"You have the fever," said her brother.

"Whose fever,—yours?" Alvira asked, frightened.

Dr. Clinton made no answer, but he gazed at her absently.

"This would be a fine affair for you and science if you were to find the very case you were after in your own house. You could be proud of your sister, Alfred."

Clinton stared at her with eyes wide open. "Is it possible, Alvira, that your thoughts could take such sublime flights? You, of all people, could comprehend me and my work? Alvira, I am your brother! Do you suppose I would sacrifice my own sister?"

"Keep quiet, dear," said Alvira, "I shall be all right tomorrow morning. Keep quiet, that you don't get sick yourself. I have not your fever, have I?"

Dr. Clinton had the thumb and index of his right hand in his vest pocket, where he toyed with his instrument, as was his habit.

"This would have been one of those tragic conflicts," said Dr. Clinton, still toying with his hypodermic needle, "if a loving brother could reach the highest aim of his life by the death of his own sister. Don't be frightened, Alvira; it is but one of those crazy questions which doctors are apt to ask. But why would it not be reality? Why should a girl not be permitted to sacrifice her life in the same manner as we? We sacrifice our life to science, and with our lives our pleasures, our youth, and all our desires. Every drop of blood, every fiber of our brain, labors for science, and thus our whole life is one chain of denials, abnegations, and sacrifices. Why should not a girl take that one brave step for the sake of science, which alone would place her on a level with the greatest of men?"

"You look quite tired, dear," said Alvira. "Follow my advice, and take a dose of morphine and go to bed. I feel sick. I would like to sleep a little, if possible."

"You are right," said Clinton, gathering his energy. "A morphine injection will do me good, and, come to think of it, you, too, would sleep better if you had one. You would, in fact, not be able to sleep at all without it," and drawing himself up to his full height, he continued, resolutely, "I will fetch the necessary articles from my room."

He left the room with a heavy tread.

V.

"Did you hear the latest?" said a physician to George Dalton as the two were walking towards the latter's office.

"No," said Dalton; "what is it?"

The physician handed Dalton a medical journal, which contained a full description of the peculiar disease discovered by Dr. Clinton. The writer stated that he had succeeded in discovering the germ as entirely independent of the person ill with the fever. He had brought this independent fever germ to its highest strength in virulence, and then weakened it so that it became absolutely harmless. All this he had tested by experiment on animals, and demonstrated publicly, and while Dr. Clinton had certainly given an impetus to investigation, he had achieved nothing new.

"This will bring Dr. Clinton down a peg or two," said the disciple of Esculapius, not without malice.

Dalton's heart was heavy as he stepped into his private office, and he experienced something of a shock when his office-boy handed him Alvira's note. He lost no time, but hastened to the call of the woman he had loved these many years.

"I am so glad you have come," said Alvira, after telling him of all that had transpired within the last few hours.

"And where is your brother now?" Dalton inquired.

"He has just gone down to get me a morphine injection. I think he is right. I shall not be able to sleep without it."

"And did he give you nothing else against the fever? Did he give you any medicine?" asked Dalton.

"No; he don't believe much in medicines," said Alvira. "I will be all right soon. Are you going to leave me now?" she asked, seeing Dalton rise.

"I am going to see your brother," the latter replied, resolutely.

"That is right," said Alvira. "But be patient with him, for my sake, and, above all things, try and excuse your presence in the house."

Dalton left the room. He stepped down hastily, and as he turned to the Doctor's room he noticed the light coming through the open door. Dalton halted and looked into the room. At the table sat Dr. Clinton, staring into the light. Before him lay an open book in which he had evidently been writing; his right hand held a pen, and his left toyed with the golden injector. Dalton entered, and as Dr. Clinton recognized his visitor, he jumped from his chair and said: "My sister has a slight attack of fever. I was afraid she might grow worse, and concluded to give her an injection of morphine, which I had just now chemically tested. Remedies like those require the greatest care."

He had evidently forgotten how he had dismissed his sister's suitor. Clinton's words, at first full of embarrassment, grew rather mocking in tone at the end. Dalton lost all control of himself. His eyes involuntarily fell upon the book, and there, in the Doctor's large, bold handwriting, stood the date of the day, the month, and the year, and beneath it, in red ink, the words *8:30 P.M., last trial.* Clinton turned toward the door, and was about to leave, but Dalton barred his way.

"Can you give me your word of honor, Dr. Clinton, that this injection will do your sister no harm?"

Dalton said this in a hoarse voice. Clinton was stunned at Dalton's words, but he soon regained his composure and his mocking tone: "This remedy is reliable, I assure you."

But suddenly changing his tone, he said: "May I ask the reason of your visit at such a late hour, Mr. Dalton? I had an idea that we had done with each other for life."

Dalton kept an eye on Clinton. Taking the medical journal containing the article against the "Fever" from his pocket, Dalton spoke in measured tones: "In this journal, Dr. Clinton, you will find an article which is of the greatest importance to you, as it affects your lifelong labors. Read it."

Under the pressure of Dalton's gaze, Clinton looked at the journal. He had hardly read the heading of the article when he turned deathly pale. The hand that held the hypodermic syringe trembled, and, totally unnerved, he sank into a chair. Clinton read the article, and after he had finished, he heaved a deep sigh, like one who has received a deathblow. He looked at Dalton as if he desired to read the latter's thoughts. Dalton could barely stand this look, for he felt as if he had spoken Dr. Clinton's death-sentence. Suddenly Clinton rose from his seat, stepped to the other side of the big table, so that the table was between him and Dalton. His eyes shone with radiance that beautified his face.

"You have asked me a while ago whether I would pledge my honor upon the reliability of this remedy. I will pledge my life." Dr. Clinton had taken hold of the loose skin on his neck, and before Dalton could move, injected the contents of the syringe. At first Dalton was paralyzed, but he soon ran up to Dr. Clinton and tore the injector from the latter's hand. It was too late. Clinton tried to make light of the matter, saying that he only meant to scare Dalton; but when he saw the latter's despair, his bravado gave way to a like feeling. With a cry of horror he threw himself on Dalton's breast and said: "For God's sake, George, save Alvira. I am lost, but you will spare me for her sake."

"I will," said Dalton; "and now lie down and rest. I think you will need to. I will look after Alvira."

Slowly Dalton went upstairs again, so as to collect himself, and not to frighten Alvira by his looks. He told the girl not to despair about her brother; that he was all right, and except the interruption caused by some physical disarrangement, will continue his work. However, he thought it advisable that Alvira should look after her brother once in a while, and for that purpose she must try to get well soon. He also said that he had made up with her brother, and that he would now call more frequently, after which he left her in a blissful deception, but himself heartsore and troubled.

Two days passed. Dalton came twice a day, and Alvira's reports were quite encouraging. "Her brother felt tired," she said. "He writes everything in his book of scientific notes,—his pulse, his temperature. To me he is quite tender, and he is full of praise about your manliness and worth"; and the girl smiled as a woman only can smile when proud of the man she loves.

On the third day a frightful fever attacked Dr. Clinton. His sister watched by his side during the day, and at night Dalton changed with Mort. Upon a little table near the bed was the day-journal in which Clinton wrote notes as often as he was clear-headed. During the day, while his sister was by his side, he seldom uttered a word; his power of will seemed strong enough, even in the heat of fever. He would not shock the poor girl. But it was different before the men. Now he seemed to be among the Mexicans, whom he gave snakes. "They are good; they don't bite; eat then, eat them!" he cried. Then, again, he seemed to be in the West Indies, where he and Mort were hunting patients. But he could not find them; and if he did not find them within a specified time, he would be hanged. The library seemed full of laughing and grinning doctors, howling dogs, and gnawing rats. He was looking for his great book upon the "Fever Bacillus," which he could not find. Some one of the grinning doctors had stolen it, trying to rob him of his fame.

When Dalton heard these ravings, he shuddered and disliked to stay. But when Mort came into the room, and Dalton saw that moving skeleton grin and leer at the poor Doctor, he was loath to leave him alone with that abominable wretch.

Five days had gone by. Clinton was still raving. Dalton sat by his side, contemplating the sad end of a brilliant career, when Clinton suddenly sat up in his bed. "George, promise me," he said, and his words came hard and slow. "It will be too late to-morrow. Send this book to the fellow who wrote that article. Let him use it."

"If this book is so valuable, why not publish it for Alvira's benefit?" asked Dalton.

"No, no!" cried Clinton. "I have worked for science only. Everything for science; for humanity, nothing. If you don't send it, destroy it. Another thing, George: in Mort's 'Clinic' over there,—in the glass tubes,—all the diseases in the world are in those tubes. There are the 'Fever Bacilli.' I want rest in the grave. They will come from those tubes and destroy mankind to the last. Swear, Dalton, that you will destroy them—"

"How are the poisons to be destroyed?" Dalton faltered.

"By fire, by fire, by fire!" screamed Clinton. "Otherwise that fellow Mort is sure to come and carry the diseases and death among the people. He was always so hard against my dog Bruno,—I have no time now. I am looking for fresh subjects. I want to make my last injection. Ha, ha, ha! I am the creator of the fever! The fools did not know it,—one more"; and Clinton became again delirious.

About two o'clock in the morning Mort entered and desired to take Dalton's place, but the latter remained until daybreak. When he left he heard Clinton cry, "Burn them, Dalton, and Mort, too."

Dalton was gone about two hours, and was about to lie down to rest for a little while when the fire alarm was sounded. Looking out of the window, he saw the flames rising from the direction of Dr. Clinton's house. He dressed hastily and went thither. Dalton found Alvira wringing her hands in front of Mort's "Clinic," which was being consumed in spite of all efforts of the firemen. The house, being quite a distance from the "Clinic," was not in danger.

"Where is your brother?" cried Dalton.

"I don't know," answered the weeping girl. "I went to his room some time ago and found him and Mort gone."

In the afternoon the firemen found the charred remains of two bodies lying upon the stone floor of the "Clinic."

Dalton examined them and identified his poor friend Dr. Clinton, as well as his evil genius, Mort. In the breast of the latter was found a long Persian dagger.

The Automatic Executioner

by Gustav Adolphe Danziger

M r. Giers, Feldon has gone, and left things down in Mexico in confusion. I have just received a dispatch; he has taken along all the stock, securities, and the private papers. You must go down at once and look the matter up. Get those papers at all hazards. As the scoundrel left but yesterday, he must be within reach. My private car will take you as far as the City of Mexico; there you take the narrow gauge to Orizaba.[1] Your old friend Jackson will meet you at the station and assist you. Get ready. Steam is up; in five minutes you will have to start."

The morrow was to have been my wedding-day. I was sorry to think of the annoyance which this sudden departure would cause my beautiful Beatrice and her family. I had long learned to make the interests of my chief my own; delay was impossible; I could not even bid them good by. Duty before everything.

With feelings in which bitterness was curiously blended with satisfaction—satisfaction with the new evidence of confidence that I was giving—I said that I would be ready.

Returning to my office, I hastily wrote a note to Beatrice, took a box of cigars, and in another two minutes found myself in the chief's private car. He handed me written instructions and a check-book, and wishing me a safe journey, gave the signal to the engineer. A shrill whistle, and away we sped at a tremendous rate.

I read the instructions carefully. Special stress was laid upon the recovery of those private papers which the chief had mentioned. Being acquainted with the country, I was sanguine of success, if I could but get hold of Feldon, although I did not know him personally.

We reached El Paso almost before I knew it. On we sped through Mexico, until we arrived at Queretaro, where an accident happened to the car. Fortunately we were within twenty minutes of the night express from Aguas Calientes to the City of Mexico, which stops in Queretaro.

Having telegraphed the chief regarding the accident, I ordered the car and the engine side-tracked until the next day, and procured a ticket for a first-class compartment to the City of Mexico.

I say "a first-class compartment" because the ticket agent had informed me that the express was made up of English coaches, with doors on both sides. I don't feel myself called upon to discuss the difference between English coaches and American cars, but although there are some disadvantages in English coaches, owing to the fact that the passengers face each other, a first-class compartment, when occupied by one or two passengers, is certainly far more convenient than the American car, with its two-seat chairs. The seats, which run the whole width of the English compartment-coaches, are comfortably upholstered, with soft arm-rests and head-cushions.

I was talking with the engineer, who swore at the Mexicans in choice machine-shop terms, when the express rushed into the station. I was ushered into a compartment by the conductor; the engine gave a shriek, and we sped toward the City of Mexico.

The light in the compartment being rather dim, I did not, on entering, observe the presence of any other person. But I was made aware that I had a fellow-traveler by something like a growl. My companion had evidently been disturbed in his slumber, and did not greatly relish it. As I looked more closely, I saw that he was well dressed, of gigantic size, and evidently an American. I apologized for the intrusion, but he made no answer. I had been traveling alone the whole day, and was inclined to talk to some one, so, nothing daunted, I stepped across to his corner, and offered him a cigar; he refused, and turned his head towards the window.

I said no more, and, drawing my soft felt over my eyes, I tried to sleep. But—how shall I say it?—a mysterious power seemed to keep me awake. Opening my eyes, they met the steady gaze of the stranger. Again I closed them, and feigned sleep by a good imitation of a snore, while I looked at him through half-closed lids.

His gaze was still upon me; turn as I might, my eyes reverted to his, and the annoyance which I felt at first soon changed into horror, for suddenly his eyes took that strange brilliancy peculiar to savage beasts and the insane. The longer I looked at him, the firmer my conviction grew that I was the companion of a madman. It is literally true that this knowledge positively paralyzed me, for as I thought of rising, I could not move. The horror grew so intense that I felt the perspiration oozing from every pore of my body.

Thoughts chased one another through my brain with the rapidity of lightning; my school days, my life as a newsboy, my meeting with the chief, my first step to an honored position, my lovely affianced, my rise to the highest position in the gift of the chief, my race after Feldon,—all flashed before my mind; and there I was, my eyes spellbound by those of the madman.

I tried to recall my energy; I sought to coax my limbs into mobility. I reasoned with my fingers, asking them to move just a little; I knew if they but moved one hundredth of an inch, I should be safe. I tried to persuade them to move in the direction of my overcoat pocket, where I had my revolver. Life is so sweet (I reasoned); I am young, beloved, and well to do, and you know that I am a dead shot; move, oh, move just a little! All in vain; they could not or would not obey my will. In sheer despair I tried to scream, but while I heard the wheels roll upon the rails, heard the breathing of the madman, whose face was livid with mania, and heard the beating of my own heart, I could not utter a sound. My God! Dumb and palsied in the bloom of life, in the chase after fortune, at the gate of domestic paradise! Help! help! But no sound escaped my lips, and those terrible eyes still upon me!

Now he rose and slowly came to my side. What a tremendous fellow he was!—his head touched the ceiling. He stooped and looked into my eyes; his glance went right through me. He put his hand into my overcoat pocket, out of which he took my revolver and slipped it into his own pocket; as he did so he smiled a ghastly smile, more horrifying even than his gaze. Now he tapped me on the forehead, at the same time saying, "Get up, Mister!"

His touch acted on me like a powerful battery; I was up in an instant. Strange to say, and as I stood on my feet, my faculties returned, but with them the recognition that I was absolutely at the disposition of the merciless maniac.

For a moment I thought he had hypnotized me, and wanted some sport, but I soon found out my mistake; he was obviously insane.

"What do you want of me, sir?" I cried.

"I want *you!*" he replied, ferociously.

"You want my money, I suppose. Here it is," and I handed him my pocket-book.

"Keep your money; I am not a robber; I am a philanthropist."

"And what do you want of me?"

"I want to show you an invention of my own; the automatic executioner."

"I shall be pleased to see it," said I.

"Shall you? I am glad of that."

With this he took from his pocket a curiously twisted cord, and continued thus: "I have worked on this for years, and am at last ready to show the world what real genius is like. As sheriff of Montreal, I have executed many criminals in my time, but their last struggle was always a disgusting sight. My invention does away with all this; one end of the electro-automatic executioner is fastened to a hook, the noose is slipped over the criminal's head, and in a fraction of a second he is with the silent majority. Do you see the advantage of my invention?"

I thought it advisable to humor the trend of his mania, and said, "This is truly a great invention. I should like to introduce this among the politicians of San Francisco."

"Introduce it, eh? Why, yes, certainly; it shall be introduced, but I will do that myself!"

"And what do you want me to do in the matter?" I asked, trembling as the thought dawned upon me that he possibly wanted to try his invention on me. His answer confirmed my fears. He said:

"You? Why, you shall be made glorious by verifying the utility of my invention. I have been hunting in every country in the world for the proper person, worthy enough for that grand purpose, but Heaven bade me wait until this evening. I knew you would come, and am prepared to execute Heaven's command."

Imagine my horror! If I could have fainted, I should have experienced relief, and would have been executed without consciousness. But my nerves had grown strong during the last moments. I had perfect control over my faculties and feelings, and thought of means to escape an untimely death.

Involuntarily I looked at the bell-cord line, which, unfortunately for me, was on the other side of the compartment.

Madmen are cunning; he caught my look, and said, "It is useless to look for that rope there; this train does not stop at any of the way-stations; nor would Heaven permit this work to be interrupted. When we reach the City of Mexico, I shall be famous and you in heaven!"

For a moment I thought of jumping at the door, opening it, and saving myself; but the idea was not feasible, because, at the rate the train was moving, I would be dashed to death, were I lucky enough to escape the grasp of the powerful maniac.

"Make haste," said he, drawing his watch; "the execution must be completed before five, and it is now twenty minutes to five."

This intelligence caused me a thrill of joy; since force would only hasten my awful end, I must seek to gain time. The train was due in the City of Mexico at five o'clock; if I could divert him for that length of time, I was saved.

"My dear sir," said I, "I am quite willing that you should try your invention on me, but before I die, I ask you to grant me a favor."

"What is it? Speak! it is granted!"

"I wish to write my will, and a letter to a lady to whom I am betrothed, and would ask you to mail the letters in the City of Mexico. Will you do that?"

"Certainly, with pleasure; only be quick about it."

"I thank you very much. Ah, how provoking!" said I, searching in my pockets. "I have no paper to write the letters. Could you oblige me with a sheet of paper?"

"Certainly, sir; I have plenty of that," said he, extracting from his breast-pocket a tablet of paper and two envelopes.

While he was taking the paper from his pocket, I managed to break the point of my pencil.

"Just see how troublesome I am! The point of my pencil has broken off, and I have no knife to sharpen it."

"Oh, no trouble at all," he replied. "Just hand me the pencil and I will sharpen it for you." With this he took a keen-edged dagger from the belt under his coat and sharpened the pencil. He was evidently as well armed as he was physically powerful. Having sharpened the pencil, he sheathed his dagger, and told me to go on.

I thought of writing a lot of nonsense, but could not, for the life of me,—which really was at stake,—compose a simple sentence. In my despair I copied the alphabet. I drew the characters with care, in order to fill up time and space. Oh, my sorry fate! how slowly the moments passed by! how miserably slow the train moved on! I had often whistled a gallop to the "tac" the wheels were beating as they touched the connecting points of the rail, but now they were so slow that funeral music would have required a quicker *tempo*.

At last the sheet was full, and my executioner asked me if I were ready.

"I am ready with my will, but I have not written the letter to my affianced."

"Well, write quickly," said he, and his look was threatening.

"I should like to describe to her your wonderful invention. Can you show me how it works, so that I may write intelligently on the subject."

"Decidedly, I will. You are a good fellow, entirely unlike those cowards in Montreal."

"Ah, but where will you fasten it?" I asked.

"Nothing easier; I slip the end through that lamp-bracket in the ceiling,—just the place for it."

So said, so done; but while he was thus occupied, I cast a glance at the window, and my heart gave a leap, for I saw the first houses of the great Mexican city. To gain a little more time was all that I needed; but my life depended on my doing so.

"Behold how it is done," said he, holding the cord in one hand.

"Ah, but you would have to engage a living executioner to slip the noose over the criminal's head," I argued.

"There is where you are at fault. You need no one at all to assist in the execution. The criminal himself slips it over his head, the automatic executioner being so charged with electricity that it no sooner touches his neck than it kills him."

He became frightfully excited, and in his rage did not hear the whistle of the locomotive. The sound inspired me with hope and courage. Now, another minute and I am safe!

"This is indeed the greatest invention of the age," said I.

"The only thing that perplexes me is how you prevent the criminal from slipping out of the noose. You would then need a man, after all, to keep the noose in the proper place."

"There is the great point of my invention. The electricity draws the noose together the instant it slips over his head and—"

"Can you draw?" I interrupted him.

"No," he replied. "Why?"

"Because I should like to send my affianced a sketch of this wonderful executioner; she would enjoy it. But as you cannot draw, and as I, who am a first-class sketcher, could not possibly make a sketch after my death, she will have to do without it. She will be doubly sorry, because she edits a newspaper."

"A newspaper, did you say?" he cried, his eyes flashing wildly. "They refused to mention my invention in the papers in Montreal, the curs!"

"My affianced would be only too happy to do it, if—"

"If what?" he cried. "Why don't you finish?"

"I was going to say, if you would consent to slip the noose over your head, so that I might sketch you. She would publish the description only if it is accompanied by a sketch."

"This is a capital idea," said he; "and if you are quick about it, I'll do it."

"I will be quick," I cried. "Get ready."

I had hardly finished when he slipped the cord over his head; but quicker than thought I was at the door, opened it, and jumped. I fell into a crowd of people,—we were at the station of the City of Mexico. As I jumped I heard the gurgling sounds of the strangling maniac. Regaining my feet I hastened to the compartment, anticipating the horrible sight of the madman, strangled by the invention of his disordered mind. But imagine my surprise, when, on reaching the place of my late adventure, I found it—vacant.

Had I been dreaming, or was I mad? Had all that I suffered been an hallucination?

The curious crowd made such a noise that the conductor came forward, eager to know the cause of the tumult. I asked him if he knew my traveling companion,—if he had seen him leave. He looked at me in blank astonishment; he had seen no one leave the compartment except myself,—in the peculiar manner described. He said that I had been the sole occupant of that compartment from Queretaro; and, turning to the crowd, said, in Spanish, "The American is crazy." This caused the crowd to disperse, panic-stricken. Seeing that I could get no satisfactory explanation from the conductor, I took my overcoat and bought a ticket for Orizaba. At the station there I was met by Jackson, who received me very cordially, and informed me that Feldon had been found. I had experienced so many shocks in the last few hours, that this news hardly surprised me. Still, I asked, "Where was he found?"

"In Jalapa,"[2] was Jackson's reply.

"When was that?" I queried.

"Last night," said Jackson.

"What has he got to say?" said I, sternly.

"To say!" cried Jackson; "the poor fellow has nothing to say; he is as crazy as a loon. I pity him. It took six men to manage him last night."

We had just arrived at the quartz-mills, and Jackson conducted me into the room where Feldon was strapped to an iron bedstead, a raving maniac. As I looked into his face, I nearly fell, the shock was so tremendous. Great God! it was my traveling companion of the night before!

When I told Jackson the cause of my agitation, he was perplexed. "The automatic executioner is the very thing he raved about. We found him half dead, with a riata around his neck. This is very strange!" said Jackson.

My story met with many incredulous smiles in San Francisco. My dear wife alone believes it. "It is the projected consciousness, or your *Astral Body,* that experienced all this," she says.

Notes

Abbreviations:

A.Ms.	autograph manuscript
AT	*The Ancient Track* (2001)
CE	*Collected Essays* (2004–06; 5 vols.)
D	*Dagon and Other Macabre Tales* (1986)
DH	*The Dunwich Horror and Others* (1984)
HR	*The Horror in the Museum and Other Revisions* (1970/1989)
IAP	Joshi, *I Am Providence* (2010)
JHL	H. P. Lovecraft Papers, John Hay Library, Brown University (Providence, RI)
MM	*At the Mountains of Madness and Other Novels* (1985)
MW	*Miscellaneous Writings* (1995)
OED	*Oxford English Dictionary* (1933 ed.)
OFF	*O Fortunate Floridian* (2007)
SL	*Selected Letters* (1965–76; 5 vols.)
T.Ms.	typed manuscript

NOTES

Introduction

1. HPL to John T. Dunn, 14 October 1916; *Books at Brown* 38–39 (1991–92 [1995]): 198–99.
2. Because of copyright restrictions, these four stories are omitted from this edition.
3. HPL to Frank Belknap Long, 14 February 1924 (*SL* 1.311–12).
4. HPL to Frank Belknap Long, 3 November 1930 (*SL* 3.204).
5. HPL refers to Eugene B. Kuntz, D.D., an amateur poet. HPL edited and copublished his book of poems, *Thoughts and Pictures* (1932), probably revising the poems contained in it.
6. HPL to R. H. Barlow, 25 September 1934; *OFF* 179.

The Green Meadow

"The Green Meadow" was apparently written in 1918–19. It was written in collaboration with Winifred Virginia Jackson (1876–1959), a woman with whom HPL had many dealings in the amateur journalism community. In speaking of this story and another collaboration with Jackson, "The Crawling Chaos," HPL says in a letter that the dream by Jackson that inspired the latter tale "occurred in the early part of 1919" and that the "Green Meadow" dream was "of earlier date" (*SL* 1.116), so that the dream itself may date to 1918, even if the actual writing of the story took place a little later. Indeed, HPL's confession that he did not complete the story until a few months after his mother "broke down" (i.e., her hospitalization in March 1919) (*Letters to Alfred Galpin* 82) suggests that the full narrative was not finished until May or June 1919. HPL goes on to note that Jackson's dream "was exceptionally singular in that I had one exactly like it myself—save that mine did not extend so far. It was only when I had related my dream that Miss J. related the similar and more fully developed one. The opening paragraph of 'The Green Meadow' was written for my own dream, but after hearing the other, I incorporated it into the tale which I developed therefrom" (*SL* 1.116). Elsewhere HPL says that Jackson supplied "a *map*" of the scene of "The Green Meadow," and that he added the "quasi-realistic . . . introduction from my own imagination" (*SL* 1.136). Ralph E. Vaughan (see Further Reading) conjectures that this introduction was inspired by an actual message-bearing meteorite as reported in the September 1910 issue of the *Scientific American*. The meteorite, found in Mexico, bore hieroglyphs on its exterior, probably made by Mayans after the meteorite had landed.

Most or all of the prose of the story is probably HPL's, since he admitted that "in prose technique she [Jackson] fails, hence can utilise *story* ideas only in collaboration with some technician" (*SL* 1.136). HPL probably exaggerated the degree of similarity between his dream and Jackson's, although we have no account of either dream. The mention in the text of an "Egyptian book" is of interest, as it constitutes one of the earliest instances of HPL's use of the "forbidden book" theme.

Texts: Vagrant [Spring 1927]: 188–95. In *Beyond the Wall of Sleep* (1943); *HR* (1970/1989). The story was also apparently included in the second issue (c. 1921) of HPL's manuscript magazine, *Hesperia* (see *IAP* 281), but this has not been located.

Further Reading: Ralph E. Vaughan, "A Factual Basis for 'The Green Meadow'?" *Crypt of Cthulhu* no. 11 (Candlemas 1983): 37–38. Stefan Dziemianowicz, "'The Green Meadow' and 'The Willows': Lovecraft, Blackwood, and a Peculiar Coincidence," *Lovecraft Studies* nos. 19/20 (Fall 1989): 33–39.

1. The city is fictitious.

2. It may not be possible to ascertain the significance of this date, but HPL may be alluding to the fact that, in 146 B.C.E., Greece was definitively conquered by Rome and became a Roman colony.

3. Democritus of Abdera (460?–370? B.C.E.) was in fact a leading Presocratic philosopher and the co-inventor (with Leucippus) of the atomic theory—a theory that, with considerable modifications, was adopted by European thinkers of the seventeenth century. As a mechanistic materialist, he is one of HPL's own philosophical forbears. HPL is perhaps alluding to Poe's reference to "His [God's] works, *which have a depth in them greater than the well of Democritus*" (epigraph to "A Descent into the Maelström"), quoted in "The Transition of Juan Romero" (1919; *D* 340) and paraphrased in "The Horror at Red Hook" (1925; *D* 265). Poe's epigraph is taken from a work by the theologian Joseph Glanvill.

4. Scythia was a large tract of land north and east of the Caspian Sea, settled since at least the 8th century B.C.E.

5. Meroë is a city in what is now the Sudan. Formerly the capital of the Nubian kingdom of Kush, it was in existence from at least the 8th century B.C.E. until its fall in 350 C.E.

6. Cf. the beginning of "Nyarlathotep" (1920): "Nyarlathotep . . . the crawling chaos . . . I am the last . . . I will tell the audient void" (*MW* 32).

Poetry and the Gods

"Poetry and the Gods" is HPL's only signed collaborative story with a woman, aside from the two Winifred Jackson collaborations. Crofts (1889–1975) was an amateur writer living in North Adams, Massachusetts, in the far northwestern corner of the state; she later married Joseph Bernard McCuen and lived in Williamstown. She spent many years as a teacher. (I am grateful to Kenneth W. Faig, Jr., for this information on Crofts.) For the 1920–21 UAPA official year, she was Eastern Manuscript Manager and HPL was Official Editor, so they may have come into correspondence at this time. No letters by or to her survive; HPL never mentions Crofts or this story in any extant correspondence.

The story was probably written in the summer of 1920. The fact that Crofts's name is placed before HPL's does not mean much, as HPL would have considered it gentlemanly to have taken second billing; much of the language is clearly his, and it is difficult to imagine what Crofts's contribution could have been. The prose seems vaguely imitative of the prose of Lord Dunsany, especially Hermes' long speech to Marcia; but in reality this bit sounds like a conventional translation of the period from Greek or Latin literature. It is facile to say that the idea of using a female protagonist must have come from Crofts, but perhaps not so facile to think that the description of her attire ("in a low-cut evening dress of black") is not likely to have been arrived at by a man so seemingly unworldly as HPL.

The long bit of free verse is an extract from a poem entitled "Sky Lotus," by Elizabeth Jane Coatsworth (1893–1986), first published in *Asia* 19 (August 1919): 741, and reprinted in Coatsworth's poetry collection *Fox Footprints* (1923). Crofts probably found the poem in the magazine.

HPL, as an opponent of free verse, initially makes fun of it in the story, but then goes on to give it qualified praise. The poetic fragment is certainly not meant parodically, and is presumably supposed to be by that "poet of poets" whom Marcia meets later.

Texts: United Amateur 20, no. 1 (September 1920): 1–4. In *The Lovecraft Collectors Library,* ed. George T. Wetzel (1952–55), Vol. 1; in *The Shuttered Room* (1959); in *D* (1965/1986).

1. Arcady is a poetic name for Arcadia, a region in Greece that came to be associated by poets ancient and modern with pastoral beauty and tranquility.

2. For HPL's strong disapproval of *vers libre* (free verse), or verse that eschewed the standard meters of traditional English poetry, see "The Vers Libre Epidemic" (*Conservative,* January 1917), in which certain practitioners of free verse (the Imagists of the Amy Lowell school) are described as "a motley horde of hysterical and half-witted rhapsodists whose basic principle is the recording of their momentary moods and psychopathic phenomena in whatever amorphous and meaningless phrases may come to their tongues or pens at the moment of inspirational (or epileptic) seizure" (*CE* 2.20). HPL generally adhered to formal meter and rhyme in his poetic work, although late in life he found some instances of free verse to be not lacking in merit (see "What Belongs in Verse" [1935], *CE* 2.182–83).

3. Hermes is, in Greek mythology, the messenger of

the gods and the patron of literature and poetry. Apollo, a still more powerful god, is the god of music, poetry, and the arts.

4. In Greek myth, Cyane was a nymph who attempted to prevent Hades from abducting Persephone and taking her to the underworld; she subsequently turned into a pool. No ancient text mentions any sisters of Cyane. The Atlantides were the offspring of Atlas—the Pleiades, the Hyades, and the Hesperides, the first two of which became constellations.

5. Aphrodite is the Greek goddess of love. Pallas is the nickname of Athene, the goddess of wisdom and civilization.

6. The Sibyl of Cumae was a prophetess who presided over the oracle of Apollo at Cumae, a Greek colony located near the modern city of Naples.

7. Mount Maenalus was a mountain in Arcadia sacred to Pan, god of the shepherds. Cf. "The Moon-Bog" (1921): "Yet still there came that monotonous piping from afar; wild, weird airs that made me think of some dance of fauns on distant Maenalus" (*D* 121).

8. *Hesperian* is the adjectival form of Hesperus (the evening star), hence a reference to lands in the west.

9. Paphos is a city on the western coast of Cyprus, sacred to Aphrodite. It is said that she rose out of the foam off the coast of the city.

10. Helicon is a mountain in Greece containing two springs sacred to the Muses.

11. Tartarus, strictly speaking, is one of the five rivers of the Greek underworld; here HPL appears to be using the term metonymically to refer to the underworld as a whole. The Titans were giants who challenged the supremacy of the Olympian gods but were defeated and consigned

to the underworld.

12. Mount Aetna is a mountain in Sicily. Uranus is the son of Gaea (the earth); subsequently, she bore such creatures as the giants Briareus, Gyges, and Cottus, and the Cyclopes.

13. Saturnus is a Roman agricultural god thought to be the offspring of Uranus and Gaea and identified with the Greek god Cronus, who was overthrown by Zeus.

14. Parnassus is a mountain in Greece sacred to Apollo and the home of the Muses.

15. Aiolos (or Aeolus) was the god of the four winds.

16. Dionysus was the god of wine and frequently associated with madness and ecstasy. Bacchae (or maenads) are female followers of Dionysus. (He was named Bacchus in Roman mythology.)

17. The Corycian cave is a cave on the slopes of Mount Parnassus, named after a nymph, Corycia. Late in life, HPL engaged in a round-robin correspondence with a group that called itself The Coryciani; they chiefly discussed poetry.

18. HPL refers to Homer (sometimes called Maeonides because it was thought that he came from Maeonia, an alternate name for the Greek propvince of Lydia); Italian poet Dante Alighieri (1265?–1321) (HPL calls him "Avernian" because his most celebrated work, the *Commedia divina* [*Divine Comedy*], dealt extensively with the underworld, one of the entrances to which was, in Roman legend, a cave near the Lake of Avernus); British poet John Milton (1608–1674); German poet Johann Wolfgang von Goethe (1749–1832); and British poet John Keats (1795–1821).

19. The Thunderer is Zeus, the king of the gods, because he wielded the thunderbolt.

20. Phaeton (more properly Phaëthon) was the son of Helios (the sun). One morning Helios unwisely allowed Phaëthon to ride in the chariot of the sun, but he could not control the horses; on occasion he rode too low, burning the fields, and at other times he rode too high, generating excessive cold. Zeus was forced to kill him with a thunderbolt. HPL wrote an allegorical poem, "Phaeton" (1918; *AT* 435–36), on the subject.

21. The reference is to World War I, and specifically the battles in France (Gaul). HPL's description may have been influenced by Lord Dunsany's pensive sketches of postwar France, *Unhappy Far-Off Things* (1919), which he probably read in December 1919 (see *SL* 1.93).

22. Ares is the god of war.

23. Deimos (fear) and Phobos (terror) were two of the sons of Aphrodite and Ares.

24. Tellus is Mother Earth in Roman mythology. The word means "earth" in Latin.

25. The Erinyes ("the angry ones") are Greek goddesses of vengeance. Some authors declare that they are three in number and are named Alecto, Megaera, and Tisiphone.

26. Astraea was a virgin goddess who dwelt with humans during the Bronze Age but then fled because of man's increasing corruption.

27. Alpheus was the god of a river of that name in Greece; he pursued the nymph Arethusa, who fled to Syracuse, in Sicily, and became a well, whereupon he united his waters with the well.

28. The Hymn to Aphrodite is one of the thirty-three extant Homeric Hymns; but they were probably written over a long period (roughly, the 8th to the 6th centuries B.C.E.). They are among the earliest choral odes in Greek

literature.

29. Shakespeare, *All's Well That Ends Well* 3.4.8–11. "Sweet Swan of Avon" was a title given to Shakespeare by his friend, the playwright Ben Jonson (1572–1637), because Shakespeare was born in Stratford-on-Avon.

30. Milton, "Il Penseroso" (1645), ll. 85–92, 97–100 (in l. 87, "may" for "might").

31. Keats, "Ode on a Grecian Urn" (1820), ll. 11–12, 46–50.

32. Memnon was an Ethiopian king, son of Tithonus and Aurora (the dawn). He brought an army to Troy to battle the Greeks and was killed by Achilles. Zeus later granted him immortality.

33. Phoebus is a nickname of Apollo.

34. Orpheus was the son of Oeagrus, King of Thrace, and the Muse Calliope; he was reputed to have wondrous musical powers, such as the ability to charm wild beasts with the lyre.

The Crawling Chaos

"The Crawling Chaos" must be considered in conjunction with the prose-poem "Nyarlathotep," written in December 1920; the title is clearly derived from the opening of the prose-poem ("Nyarlathotep . . . the crawling chaos . . ." [*MW* 32]), although Nyarlathotep himself makes no appearance in the story. HPL admits in a letter: "I took the title C. C. from my Nyarlathotep sketch . . . because I liked the sound of it" (*OFF* 191). This may or may not help in dating the collaboration; it cannot, at least, have been written before the prose-poem, hence probably does not date any earlier than December 1920. HPL appears to allude to the genesis of the story in a letter of May 1920, in which he notes the previous collaboration with Jackson, "The Green Meadow": "I will enclose—subject to return—an account of a Jacksonian dream which occurred in the early part of 1919, and which I am some time going to weave into a horror story " (*SL* 1.116). It is, of course, not entirely certain whether this dream was the nucleus of "The Crawling Chaos"; but since there are no other story collaborations with Jackson, the conjecture seems likely.

As Robert M. Price (see Further Reading) reports, a copy of the *United Co-operative* that HPL sent to Clark Ashton Smith appears to indicate the extent of HPL's hand in the story. Smith reported in a letter to August Derleth (14 April 1937): "HPL wrote the beginning and the end, as indicated on margins; the main portions being Mrs. Jackson's." HPL was probably being charitable here; even the sections that are purportedly "by" Jackson were probably heavily revised by HPL.

In certain external features of the plot "The Crawling Chaos" is surprisingly reminiscent of "The Green Meadow"; but it is, on the whole, a somewhat more interesting tale than its predecessor, although still quite insubstantial. Toward the end, in imagery very reminiscent of "Nyarlathotep," the narrator appears to witness the destruction of the world. Various points in the account carry the implication that the narrator is not actually dreaming or hallucinating but envisioning the far future of the world—a point made very clumsily by his conceiving of Rudyard Kipling as an "ancient" author. But the final passage is impressive on its own as a set piece, and is the sole connection with the prose-poem that inspired the story's title.

In an amateur review, Alfred Galpin assessed the story favorably: "... I recall the attention of amateurs to the most important story recently published, 'The Crawling Chaos,' pseudonymously written by Winifred Virginia Jackson and H. P. Lovecraft. The narrative power, vivid imagination and poetic merit of this story are such as to elevate it above certain minor but aggravating faults of organisation and composition" ("Department of Public Criticism," *United Amateur* 21, no. 2 [November 1921]: 21). But not everyone was so enthusiastic. HPL, in the "News Notes" for the January 1922 *United Amateur,* takes a certain glee in reporting the hostile reaction of one amateur: "...during a denunciation of Lovecraftian stories [he] remarked, 'We can hardly go them. That Crawling Chaos is the limit. His attempts at Poe-esque tales will hand him—'" (*CE* 1.308). I do not know who this person is; Lovecraft merely identifies him, archly, as a "prominent politician with a distaste for the 'wild, weird tales' of H. P. Lovecraft."

Texts: United Co-operative 1, no. 3 (April 1921): 1–6; *Tesseract* 2, no. 4 (April 1937): 7–8; 2, no. 5 (May 1937): 7–8; *Tesseract Annual* no. 1 (1939): 5–8. In *Beyond the Wall of Sleep* (1943); *HR* (1970/1989).

Further Reading: Robert M. Price, "New Clues to Lovecraft's Role in 'Out of the Eons' and 'The Crawling Chaos,'" *Crypt of Cthulhu* no. 17 (Hallowmas 1983): 29–31.

1. British essayist and critic Thomas De Quincey (1785–1859) created a sensation with the publication of *Confessions of an English Opium-Eater* (*London Magazine,* September–October 1821; book publication 1822), both because of its subject-matter and because of its stately and baroque style. French poet and critic Charles Pierre Baudelaire (1821–1867) wrote *Les Paradis artificiels* (1860; Artificial Paradises), an account of his experiences in taking opium and hashish, inspired in part by De Quincey.

2. From De Quincey's *Confessions of an English Opium-Eater,* under the date May 1818.

3. The Corinthian is one of the three major orders of Graeco-Roman architecture, the others being Doric and Ionic. Corinthian columns are generally fluted and feature elaborate floral decorations at the capitals.

4. The work by Rudyard Kipling (1865–1936) that HPL's protagonist is thinking of is presumably *The Jungle Book* (1894).

5. The names Arinurian and Teloe are HPL's invention; but the latter is reminiscent of Teloth, a city cited frequently in "The Quest of Iranon" (1921). It is not clear whether this story or "The Quest of Iranon" was written first.

6. Imaginary; but cf. the name Cydathria, an imaginary region cited in "The Doom That Came to Sarnath" (*D* 48) and "The Quest of Iranon" (*D* 116). The name may have been inspired by Sardathrion, cited in Lord Dunsany's "Time and the Gods" (in *Time and the Gods,* 1906).

7. Choriambic verse is a metrical form used in Greek and Latin poetry whereby a trochee (a metrical foot consisting of a short syllable paired with a long one) is followed by an iamb (a short syllable). In English poetry, choriambics were written by Algernon Charles Swinburne and Rupert Brooke, among others. HPL may be using the term here more generally to refer to songs.

The Horror at Martin's Beach

This story was the product of a visit to Magnolia, Massachusetts, that HPL and Sonia H. Greene (1883–1972) took in late June and early July 1922. In her memoir, Sonia writes: "... the full moon reflecting its light in the water, a peculiar and unusual noise heard at a distance as of a loud snorting and grunting, the shimmering light forming a moon-path on the water, the round tops of the submerged piles in the water exposed a rope connecting them like a huge spider's guy-line, gave the vivid imagination full play for an interesting weird tale. 'Oh, Howard,' I exclaimed, 'here you have the setting for a real strange and mysterious story.' Said he, 'Go ahead, and write it.' 'Oh, no, I couldn't do it justice,' I answered. 'Try it. Tell me what the scene pictures to your imagination.' And as we walked along we neared the edge of the water. Here I described my interpretation of the scene and the noises. His encouragement was so enthusiastic and sincere that when we parted for the night, I sat up and wrote the general outline which he later revised and edited" (*The Private Life of H. P. Lovecraft* [West Warwick, RI: Necronomicon Press, rev. ed. 1992], 19). When the story appeared in *Weird Tales*, HPL was mortified that it appeared under the crude title "The Invisible Monster." As he remarked to the editor, Edwin Baird: ". . . Mrs. Sonia H. Greene, whose 'Horror at Martin's Beach' you re-named 'The Invisible Monster' after I had very carefully removed Mrs. Greene's original title 'The Nameless Monster'!" (*SL* 1.303).

Texts: *Weird Tales* 2, no. 4 (November 1923): 75–76, 83 (as by "Sonia H. Greene"; as "The Invisible Monster"). In *Something about Cats* (1949); in *HR* (1970/1989).

1. A prominent New England family name. A Granny Orne would later be cited in "The Strange High House in the Mist" (1926; *D* 269); Simon/Jedediah Orne is a colleague of Joseph Curwen in *The Case of Charles Dexter Ward* (1927); and an Orne family lives in Innsmouth in "The Shadow over Innsmouth" (1931; *DH* 362–64).

2. "Cyclopean" (characteristic of the Cyclops, the one-eyed giant from Greek myth) primarily refers to a type of masonry characterized by the use of immense limestone blocks. Here, HPL seems to be using it more broadly as a synonym for "immense" or "monstrous."

Under the Pyramids

"Under the Pyramids" was ghostwritten for the Hungarian-born magician Harry Houdini (born Ehrich Weiss, 1874–1926) in February 1924. HPL recounts at length in letters how he came to be assigned the writing of this tale. *Weird Tales* was struggling financially and the owner, J. C. Henneberger, felt that the celebrated Houdini's affiliation with the magazine might attract readers. Houdini was the reputed author of a column ("Ask Houdini") that ran in the issues of March, April, and May–June–July 1924, as well as two short stories probably ghostwritten by other hands. In mid-February Henneberger commissioned HPL to write "Under the Pyramids." Houdini was claiming that he had actually been bound and gagged by Arabs and dropped down a shaft in the pyramid called Campbell's Tomb; but as HPL began exploring the historical and geographical background of the account, he came to the conclusion that it was complete fiction, and so he received permission from Henneberger to elaborate the account with his own imaginative additions. HPL received a fee of $100 for the tale, paid in advance.

HPL's Egyptian research was probably derived from several volumes in his library, notably *The Tomb of Perneb* (1916), a volume issued by the Metropolitan Museum of Art. He had seen many Egyptian antiquities at first hand at the museum in 1922. Some of the imagery of the story probably also derives from Théophile Gautier's non-supernatural tale of Egyptian horror, "One of Cleopatra's Nights"; HPL owned Lafcadio Hearn's translation of *One of Cleopatra's Nights and Other Fantastic Romances* (1882).

The tale was published in *Weird Tales* and in all subsequent editions until the 1986 revised edition of *D* as "Imprisoned with the Pharaohs." But HPL's original title was "Under the Pyramids," as indicated in a classified ad in the *Providence Journal* (3 March 1924) that HPL took out when he lost the typescript of the story in Union Station, Providence, as he was heading to New York to marry Sonia H. Greene. HPL fortunately had the autograph manuscript with him, and after their wedding he and Sonia spent the evening preparing a new typescript and sent it on to *Weird Tales.* The A.Ms. has recently surfaced and is currently being offered for sale by L. W. Currey.

Texts: Weird Tales 4, no. 2 (May–June-July 1924): 3–12 (as "Imprisoned with the Pharaohs"; as by "Houdini"). *Weird Tales* 34, no. 1 (June–July 1939): 133–50 (as "Imprisoned with the Pharaohs"; as by "Houdini"). *Marginalia* (1944) (as "Imprisoned with the Pharaohs"). In *D* (1965 [as "Imprisoned with the Pharaohs"]/1986).

Further Reading: Leigh Blackmore, "Under the Pyramids: On Lovecraft and Houdini," *EOD Magazine* no. 4 (September 1991): 17–39; no. 5 (December 1991): 54–83.

1. Houdini became a professional magician in 1891, at the age of seventeen; by the turn of the century he was the most celebrated escape artist of his time. His pseudonym derives from Jean-Eugène Robert-Houdin (1805–1871), French magician and author of *Confidences d'un prestidigitateur* (1859).

2. Among Houdini's own accounts of his escapades are the early volume *The Adventurous Life of a Versatile Artist* (1906) and the article "The Thrills in the Life of a Magician" (*Strand Magazine,* 5 January 1919).

3. Houdini began an extensive European tour in the fall of 1908. He spent most of 1909 in England, but by the autumn he had moved on to Germany. In January 1910 he sailed from Marseilles en route to an engagement in Australia. The ship traversed the Suez Canal and Houdini did stop briefly at Port Said, but that was the extent of his Egyptian stay. By the end of January he was in Adelaide, Australia. See Kenneth Silverman, *Houdini!!!* (New York: HarperCollins, 1996), 137–39.

4. Houdini married Wilhelmina Beatrice Rahner (whom he had first met earlier in 1894, when she was eighteen and still in high school) on 22 June 1894.

5. Ferdinand Marie, Viscomte de Lesseps (1804–1895), a French diplomat, was one of the leading promoters of the Suez Canal, which opened in 1869. Lesseps founded the city of Port Said, a major Egyptian seaport at the northern end of the Suez Canal. On 17 November 1899, the thirtieth anniversary of the opening of the canal, a 24-foot bronze statue of Lesseps was erected at the jetty at Port Said.

6. Alexandria had been founded in 331 B.C.E. by Alexander the Great after his conquest of Egypt. It was the most significant Egyptian city in the Graeco-Roman world.

7. HPL's misspelling of Shepheard's, a hotel that was built in 1849 by the Egyptian Samuel Shepheard on the banks of a lake (subsequently filled in to form the al-Azbakiyyah Garden; see n. 10). It was demolished in 1862 and another hotel was built on the same site, becoming one of the great hotels of the world. It was destroyed in anti-Brit-

ish riots in 1952.

8. Harun ar-Rashid (766–809) was the fifth caliph of the Abbasid dynasty (r. 786–809), which ruled the Islamic world, then extending from the western Mediterranean to India. His reign is glorified in the *Arabian Nights*. HPL had in his library an old biography, Edward Henry Palmer's *The Caliph Haroun Alraschid and Saracen Civilization* (1881).

9. The travel guides published by the German firm of Karl Baedeker, beginning in 1829 and subsequently translated into many languages, became world-famous for their comprehensiveness and ease of use.

10. The al-Azbakiyyah Garden in the al-Azbakiyyah district of Cairo is an immense rectangular park on the site of a lake that was filled in during the early nineteenth century. It remained the focal point of the tourist and business trade in Cairo until well into the twentieth century. Al-Muski is a street branching off from the southeast side of the garden.

11. Cf. HPL's initial conception of the god Nyarlathotep, who "was of the old native blood and looked like a Pharaoh" ("Nyarlathotep" [1920], *MW* 32). This conception had come to HPL in a dream (see *SL* 1.160-62).

12. Heliopolis ("the city of the sun"), now in the northeast part of the Cairo metropolitan area, is one of the most ancient Egyptian cities, founded no later than the 5th dynasty (c. 2500 B.C.E.) and being the seat of worship for the sun-god Ré. It became the center of a Roman colony around 16 B.C.E. and is the site of several large Graeco-Roman temples built in the first and second centuries C.E. The Emperor Augustus made Egypt a part of his personal estate. There were probably only two legions stationed in Egypt during his reign, neither of which were at Heliopolis.

13. The Egyptian Museum, on the north side of al-

Tahrir Square, is the oldest and largest of Cairo's museums of Egyptian antiquities. It was built in the neoclassical style (hence HPL's later reference to its "great Roman dome") and opened in 1902 under the name of the Cairo Museum.

14. Saladin (1138–1193), Sultan of Egypt and Syria, built an immense citadel (now on the eastern edge of Cairo) in the 1170s, as well as a fortified wall around what was then the entire territory of the city.

15. More properly, Ré-Horakhty, or Re-Horus of the Horizon.

16. Tut'ankamun, twelfth king of the 18th dynasty (r. 1333–1323 B.C.E.), died at the age of nineteen after a ten-year reign. The rediscovery of his nearly intact tomb by Howard Carter and Lord Carnarvon on 4 November 1922 was one of the most spectacular events in Egyptian archaeology.

17. Khem ("black") is the native ancient name for Egypt (cognate with the Biblical Ham). Cf. "The Haunter of the Dark" (1935): "Is it not an avatar of Nyarlathotep, who in antique and shadowy Khem even took the form of man?" (*DH* 114). Ré is the sun-god of the Egyptians. Amen (more properly Amon) is a god associated with the dynamic force of life; his name means "hidden." Isis and Osiris are the two principal gods of the Egyptian pantheon. Isis is the mother of the gods; Osiris, the husband of Isis, was originally a god of agriculture.

18. The Emperor Napoleon's fleet landed in Alexandria in 1798 and left the next year, leaving a general in charge of the country; but the French were ousted by a combined Egyptian and British force in 1801.

19. Bedouins are desert and steppe dwellers in the Middle East and North Africa, chiefly Arabian Muslims.

20. Khufu (Cheops) was the second king of the 4th

dynasty (r. 2551–2528 B.C.E.). He ordered the building of the Great Pyramid at Giza. It is not clear why HPL is so far off on the date of this and the other pyramids discussed in this passage.

21. Khafre (Khephren) was the fourth king of the 4th dynasty (r. 2520–2494 B.C.E.), the son of Khufu. He ordered the building of the second pyramid.

22. Menkauré (Mycerinus) was the fifth king of the 4th dynasty (r. 2490–2472 B.C.E.), the son of Khafre. His is the third and smallest pyramid at Giza.

23. The Sphinx—a crouching lion with a human head—was, by tradition, built by Khafre. Some Egyptologists now believe that it may be thousands of years older than the conventional dating, but their findings are the subject of debate. There is no suggestion that the present face of the Sphinx (probably representing Khafre himself) was recarved from some previous face.

24. Pery-Neb was lord chamberlain toward the end of the 5th dynasty (c. 2450 B.C.E.). At that time he built a small mastaba (tomb) for himself in the cemetery at Saqqara. In 1913 the tomb was purchased from the Egyptian government by the Metropolitan Museum of Art in New York, dismantled, and reconstructed in the Egyptian Wing of the museum. It is still on display there today. HPL first saw it on his first trip to New York in April 1922. HPL owned a guidebook, *The Tomb of Perneb* (1916), published by the Metropolitan Museum.

25. The Temple of the Sphinx lies directly in front (i.e., to the east) of the Sphinx and is larger in area than the Sphinx. It is built of limestone faced with granite and has two entrances in the front, leading to a colonnaded interior courtyard.

26. The diorite statue of the seated King Khafre in Gallery 42 of the Egyptian Museum is one of its choicest holdings.

27. See "The Horror at Martin's Beach," n. 2.

28. Thutmose IV was the eighth king of the 18th dynasty (r. 1412–1403 B.C.E.). His restoration of the Sphinx is recorded in a "Dream Stela" placed between the two paws of the statue. In it he declares that as a prince he had a dream in which the sun-god (of whom, at that time, the Sphinx was believed to be a representation) came to him and begged him to remove the sand that then covered most of the statue.

29. Now called the Tomb of Pakap, lying between the Sphinx and the Great Pyramid. It was named after Col. Patrick Campbell by Col. Richard Vyse, who discovered it in 1837.

30. The step pyramid of Zozer at Saqqara is the oldest of the pyramids, having been constructed during the reign of Zozer, second king of the 3rd dynasty (r. 2667–2648 B.C.E.).

31. All these names (except the last) refer to individuals whose lives were at least tangentially associated with Egypt. "Rameses" denotes eleven kings of that name during the 19th and 20th dynasties (1307–1070 B.C.E.). Mark Twain (1835–1910) visited Egypt and the Holy Land in 1867 and wrote of his travels in *The Innocents Abroad* (1869). Financier John Pierpont Morgan (1837–1913) traveled to Egypt on several occasions from 1876 to the end of his life. Minnehaha is the American Indian maiden who marries Hiawatha in Henry Wadsworth Longfellow's poem *The Song of Hiawatha* (1855).

32. This anecdote about Queen Nitokris (ruling in the 6th Dynasty, c. 2180 B.C.E.) is found in Herodotus,

Histories 2.100. It was also used as the basis of Lord Dunsany's play *The Queen's Enemies* (1916), which HPL heard Dunsany recite in Boston in 1919 (see *SL* 1.91).

33. From Thomas Moore (1779–1852), *Alciphron* (1839), Letter IV, ll. 28–30.

34. Although many mummified animals have been found in Egyptian tombs, no composite mummies of the sort described by HPL are known to exist.

35. HPL had a distinctly low opinion of the films of his day, even though he enjoyed the films of Charlie Chaplin (and even wrote a poem to him, "To Charlie of the Comics" [1915]) and works such as D. W. Griffith's *The Birth of a Nation* (see *SL* 1.89). See S. T. Joshi, "Lovecraft and the Films of His Day," *Crypt of Cthulhu* No. 77 (Eastertide 1991): 8–10; rpt. in Joshi's *Primal Sources: Essays on H. P. Lovecraft* (New York: Hippocampus Press, 2003), 43–46.

36. A sambuke (more properly sambuca) is a triangular stringed instrument with a shrill tone; a sistrum is a metal tambourine; a tympanum is a drum.

37. *aegipanic:* noun form of *aegipan.* Neither word is found in the *OED;* but the proper noun *Aigipan* ("goat-Pan," or goat-footed Pan) is found in the Greek writers Eratosthenes and Plutarch. Cf. "The Horror at Red Hook" (1925): "… aegipans chased endlessly after misshapen fauns over rocks twisted like swollen toads" (*D* 260), where the reference appears to be to a certain type of fantastic monster. Here the word is perhaps meant to suggest Pan-pipes.

38. The adverb *thaumatropically* is derived from the adjective *thaumatropical,* itself derived from *thaumatrope,* "a disk or cylinder bearing a series of figures which, on being rapidly rotated and viewed through a slit, produce the impression of a moving object" (*OED*). *OED* does not acknowledge the existence of the adverb.

39. The term is meant to signify the immensity of the door by referring to Polyphemus, the Cyclops that threatens Odysseus in the *Odyssey*. Cf. "Dagon": "Vast, Polyphemus-like, and loathsome, it darted like a stupendous monster of nightmares . . ." (*D* 18).

40. Horus is the Greek name for Hor, a solar deity in the form of a falcon. Anubis is the Greek name for Anpu or Anup, the guide of the afterlife, usually depicted in the form of a jackal-headed man.

41. A similar "surprise ending" is found in "The Shunned House" (written later in 1924), where what looks like a "doubled-up human figure" in the basement of an old house in Providence proves to be the "titan *elbow*" (*MM* 239, 261) of an immensely larger creature.

42. In a letter written shortly after the completion of the story, HPL explains the need to conclude the tale in this manner: "To square it with the character of a popular showman, I tacked on the 'it-was-all-a-dream' bromide" (*SL* 1.326).

Two Black Bottles

"Two Black Bottles" was written in the summer of 1926. An initial draft was produced by Wilfred Blanch Talman (1904–1986), a late member of the Kalem Club whom HPL had first met in August 1925. Talman had previously published only a book of poetry, *Cloisonné and Other Verses* (1923). HPL found promise in the tale but felt that changes were in order. By October the tale was finished, more or less to both writers' satisfaction. It was presently accepted by *Weird Tales*.

The tale works up a convincing atmosphere of clutching horror toward the end, largely via the colloquial patois of Foster's account. What is in question is the exact degree of HPL's role in the shaping and writing of the story. Judging from his letters to Talman, it seems clear that HPL has not only written some of the tale—especially the portions in dialect—but also made significant suggestions regarding its structure. Talman had evidently sent HPL both a draft and a synopsis—or, perhaps, a draft of only the beginning and a synopsis of the rest. HPL recommended a simplification of the structure so that all the events are seen through the eyes of the first-person narrator, Hoffman. In terms of the diction, HPL wrote: "As for what I've done to the MS.—I am sure you'll find nothing to interfere with your sense of creation. My changes are in virtually every case merely verbal, and all in the interest of finish and fluency of style" (*SL* 2.61). In his memoir of HPL, Talman reveals some irritation at Lovecraft's revisions: "He did some minor gratuitous editing, particularly of dialog... After re-reading it in print, I wish Lovecraft hadn't changed the dialog, for his use of dialect was stilted" (*The Normal Lovecraft* [Saddle River, NJ: Gerry de la Ree, 1973], 8). This appears to imply that HPL wrote (or revised) only the dialect portions of the tale; it appears, however, that Talman's irritation has led him to downplay HPL's role in the work, for there are many passages beyond the dialect portions that clearly reveal his hand.

Texts: Weird Tales 10, no. 2 (August 1927): 251–58. In *HM* (1970/1989).

1. Daalbergen is imaginary, but the Ramapo Mountains are a chain of mountains in northern New Jersey and southern New York. They are an extension of the Appalachian Mountains.

2. *Dominie* is a Scottish term for a schoolmaster or

(as in this case) a minister.

The Last Test

"The Last Test" is an extensive revision of a previously published story, "A Sacrifice to Science," by Gustav Adolphe Danziger (1859–1959), who later changed his name to Adolphe de Castro. The story was published in Danziger's collection *In the Confessional and the Following* (San Francisco: Western Authors Publishing Co., 1893). (See the Appendix for the original text.) De Castro came in touch with HPL in the fall of 1927, as he was also working on a memoir of Ambrose Bierce that he wished HPL to revise (HPL declined this job, because de Castro would not pay him in advance). HPL finished the revision by November or December 1927 but did not finish typing the tale until April 1928 (see HPL to Adolphe de Castro, 1 April 1928; ms., JHL). He charged de Castro $16.00 for the revision; de Castro received $175.00 when he sold it to *Weird Tales*. In one letter HPL refers to the story as "Clarendon's Last Test" (*SL* 2.207); it is not clear whether the change of title was made at a later stage by HPL himself (or by de Castro) or by Farnsworth Wright, the editor of *Weird Tales*. In light of this uncertainty, it has been decided to retain the title under which the story was published.

It should be noted that de Castro's original tale is not at all supernatural. It is merely a long drawn-out melodrama or adventure story in which a scientist seeks a cure for a new type of fever (never described at all in detail) and, having run out of patients because of the bad reputation he has gained as a man who cares only for science and not for human life, seeks to convince his own sister to be a "sacrifice to science" in the furtherance of his quest. HPL has turned the whole scenario into a supernatural tale while preserving the basic framework—the California setting, the characters (although the names of some have been changed), the search for a cure to a new type of fever, and (although this now becomes only a minor part of the climax) Clarendon's attempt to persuade his sister to sacrifice herself. But—aside from replacing the nebulously depicted assistant of Dr. Clarendon ("Dr. Clinton" in de Castro) named Mort with the much more redoubtable Surama—he has added much better motivation for the characters and the story as a whole. He has made the tale about half again as long as de Castro's original; and although he remarked of the latter that "I nearly exploded over the dragging monotony of [the] silly thing" (*SL* 2.207), HPL's own version is not without monotony and prolixity of its own. To liven things up, if only for himself, HPL has thrown in irrelevant references to his own developing myth-cycle. Oddly enough, in a few cases these constitute the only instances where certain elements in his myth-cycle are cited in a story.

Texts: Weird Tales 12, no. 5 (November 1928): 625–56. In *Something about Cats* (1949); *HM* (1970/1989).

Further Reading: Will Murray, "Mysteries of the Hoggar Region," *Crypt of Cthulhu* no. 17 (Hallowmas 1983): 32, 39. Robert M. Price, "Who Were the Boupa Priests?" *Crypt of Cthulhu* no. 11 (Candlemas 1983): 44.

1. San Quentin State Prison, in Marin County on the north side of San Francisco Bay in central California, was founded in 1852. It is the state's oldest prison.

2. Goat Hill is the original name of the San Francisco hill now called Telegraph Hill. It was renamed in 1849, so that HPL's use of it here is anachronistic.

3. Pyemia is a kind of septicemia caused by microor-

ganisms in the blood.

4. *Pest,* as used here, is an archaic term for the plague.

5. More properly, Ü-Tsang or Tsang-Ü, one of the three traditional provinces of Tibet, in the western and south-central portion of the state, nearest to Nepal, Bhutan, and India. *Thibet* is an archaic spelling of Tibet.

6. Black fever, more properly known as visceral leishmaniasis, is a disease caused by protozoan parasites. It was first identified in 1824 in India, whre the native term, *kala-azar* ("black fever") alludes to the blackening of the skin in the extremities and abdomen that results from the progression of the disease.

7. The Bönpa religion was the indigenous religion of Tibet, focusing on magic and the exorcism of demons. It was supplanted by Tantric Buddhism in the 8th century C.E.

8. *Vathek* was an Arabian fantasy written originally in French by the British dilettante William Beckford (1760–1844). The French version was published in 1787, but an English translation by Beckford's colleague Samuel Henley was printed without Beckford's authorization the previous year. HPL was much taken with *Vathek* when he read it in 1921; it seems to have inspired the novel fragment "Azathoth" (1922), and its construction without chapter divisions may have inspired the similar construction of his dream-fantasy, *The Dream-Quest of Unknown Kadath* (1926–27). The *Arabian Nights* (or *A Thousand and One Nights*) is a collection of Arabian folktales, many of them with a fantastic element, dating to around the 9th century. HPL's early interest in weird fiction was in part triggered by his reading of an abridged English translation in 1895.

9. The Tuaregs are a Berber nomadic people dwelling in the interior of the Sahara. They are probably descended

from the ancient Libyans.

10. The Royal Hotel on Fourth Street, on Telegraph Hill, was destroyed in the earthquake and fire of 1906.

11. The adjective *trusty,* in the sense meant here, refers to a convict who, as a special privilege for good behavior, is allowed to serve as a nurse.

12. Edward Jenner (1749–1823) was a British chemist who was largely responsible for the smallpox vaccine. Joseph Lister (1827–1912) was a British physician who pioneered antiseptic surgery by the use of carbolic acid. Robert Koch (1843–1910) was a German physician who did pioneering work in the study of tuberculosis and cholera. Louis Pasteur (1822–1895) was a French chemist who discovered a cure for rabies and was a pioneer in the preservation of milk and wine, a process that came to be known as pasteurization. Ilya Ilyitch Mechnikov (1845–1916) was a Russian biologist who did pioneering work in the immune system.

13. An *alienist* is a physician brought in to determine whether a patient requires internment for mental or psychological aberration. The term was used frequently in HPL's novel *The Case of Charles Dexter Ward* (1927), especially in regard to the resurrected Joseph Curwen's killing of Charles Dexter Ward and his attempt to adopt his identity.

14. The passage is reminiscent of several passages in *The Case of Charles Dexter Ward* (1927), where Charles Dexter Ward utters chants behind the closed door of his bedroom to raise the ashes of Joseph Curwen: "Late in the afternoon young Ward began repeating a certain formula in a singularly loud voice, at the same time burning some substance so pungent that its fumes escaped over the entire house" (*MM* 170).

15. The Hoggar, or Ahaggar, Mountains are a high-land region in the central Sahara. The region is cited again in "Medusa's Coil" (Vol. 2, p. 146).

16. This is, chronologically, only the second story in which Yog-Sothoth is mentioned, following *The Case of Charles Dexter Ward* (see *MM* 151f.); in neither story can this entity's attributes be ascertained with any precision.

17. See the headnote to "The Crawling Chaos."

18. This is, incredibly, the first and only time that the original Arabic title (*Al Azif*) of the *Necronomicon* is cited in a story written or revised by HPL. This story was proba-bly written very shortly after HPL had drawn up his whim-sical "history" of the book, "History of the *Necronomicon*" (fall 1927; see *SL* 2.201), where he notes that the "original title [was] *Al Azif*—*azif* being the word used by Arabs to designate that nocturnal sound (made by insects) suppos'd to be the howling of daemons" (*MW* 52). (HPL derived this conception from Samuel Henley's notes to Beckford's *Vathek*—see n. 8 above). HPL had coined the name Abdul Alhazred in the story "The Nameless City" (1921), and the term *Necronomicon* in "The Hound" (1922).

19. Possibly derived from Algernon Blackwood's story "The Nemesis of Fire," in *John Silence—Physician Extraordinary* (1908).

20. Cf. "History of the *Necronomicon*": "Alhazred [was] a mad poet of Sanaá, in Yemen . . . He . . . spent ten years alone in the great southern desert of Arabia—the Roba el Khaliyeh or 'Empty Space' of the ancients—and 'Dahna' or 'Crimson' desert of the modern Arabs, which is held to be inhabited by protective evil spirits and monsters of death" (*MW* 52). This description is taken almost verba-tim from the article on "Arabia" (by William Gifford Pal-grave) in the 9th edition of the *Encyclopaedia Britannica,*

which HPL owned. HPL also derived his information on Irem, the City of Pillars (first cited in "The Nameless City") from the same article. Nug and Yeb are first cited here; indeed, they are cited only in this story and the revisions "The Mound" and "Out of the Aeons." In a later letter HPL refers to them (perhaps whimsically) as the twin offspring of Yog-Sothoth and Shub-Niggurath (*SL* 4.183, 5.303). This passage also represents the first citation of Shub-Niggurath and, hence, of the cry "Iä! Shub-Niggurath!" In a late letter HPL declares that "Yog-Sothoth's wife is the hellish cloud-like entity Shub-Niggurath, in whose honour nameless cults hold the rite of the Goat with a Thousand Young" (*SL* 5.303).

21. The story of Jephthah and his daughter is found in the Old Testament (Judges 11:1–40). Jephthah, a member of the Tribe of Manassah, had led the Israelites in their defeat of the Ammonites. He had previously vowed that, if he returned victorious, he would sacrifice the first person he saw coming out of his house. This person proved to be his daughter (not named in the text), and Jephthah in fact sacrificed her.

22. HPL may have been thinking of himself here. Speaking of his school days, he wrote in 1933: "In Greek I had no quarrel—and didn't get beyond the first six books of Xenophon anyhow" (*SL* 4.173). HPL probably refers to Xenophon's *Anabasis* (The March Up-Country), a thrilling account of his leading the Ten Thousand, a band of Greek mercenaries hired by the Persian emperor Cyrus the Great, from Mesopotamia to the Black Sea. It is a text frequently assigned to beginning Greek students. Homer's *Iliad* and *Odyssey,* although among the oldest texts in extant Greek literature and written in Ionic Greek, is also relatively simple and can be read by students with a basic understanding

of Greek grammar.

23. Cf. Charles Dexter Ward's command to Dr. Willett: "Shoot Dr. Allan [i.e., Joseph Curwen] on sight *and dissolve his body in acid.* Don't burn it" (*MM* 182). In this case, the instruction not to burn Curwen's body reflects Ward's fear that his "essential salts" could one day be found and he be resurrected once more.

24. Exodus 18:22.

25. Apollonius of Tyana (1st century C.E.) was a Neopythagorean philosopher and wonder-worker from Tyana, in the Roman province of Cappadocia (now in central Turkey), whose life (which purportedly includes a number of "miracles") has often been compared with that of Jesus. Virtually all our information on him comes from Philostratus' *Life of Apollonius of Tyana,* written almost a century and a half after his death, a work that many scholars regard as fanciful or largely fictitious.

26. Cf. the description of the death of Wilbur Whateley in "The Dunwich Horror" (1928): ". . . only generous clothing could ever have enabled it to walk on earth unchallenged or uneradicated" (*DH* 174).

The Curse of Yig

"The Curse of Yig" was written for Zealia Brown Reed Bishop (1897–1968), who at this time was studying journalism at Columbia and also writing articles and stories to support herself and her young son. It appears that she was divorced. In her memoir, "H. P. Lovecraft: A Pupil's View" (1953), she states that one day while in Cleveland (she dates this to 1928, but this is clearly an error), she wandered into a bookstore managed by Samuel Loveman, who told her about HPL's revisory service. She wrote to him in what must have been late spring of 1927, for this is when the first of HPL's letters to her appears. At some point she returned to her sister's ranch in Oklahoma, where she heard some tales by Grandma Compton, her sister's mother-in-law, about a pioneer couple in Oklahoma not far away. Bishop concludes: "I wrote a tale called 'The Curse of Yig,' in which snakes figured, wove it around some of my Aztec knowledge instilled in me by Lovecraft, and sent it off to him. He was delighted with this trend toward realism and horror, and fairly showered me with letters and instructions" (269).

This would seem to suggest that she wrote a draft of the tale that HPL revised, but HPL's own letters tell a different tale. Consider this passage in a letter to August Derleth (6 October [1929]): "By the way—if you want to see a new story which is practically mine, read 'The Curse of Yig' in the current W.T. Mrs. Reed is a client for whom Long & I have done oceans of work, & this story is about 75% mine. All I had to work on was a synopsis describing a couple of pioneers in a cabin with a nest of rattlesnakes beneath, the killing of the husband by snakes, the bursting of the corpse, & the madness of the wife, who was an eyewitness to the horror. There was no plot or motivation—no prologue or aftermath to the incident—so that one might say the story, as a story, is wholly my own. I invented the snake-god & the curse, the tragic wielding of the axe by the wife, the matter of the snake-victim's identity, & the asylum epilogue. Also, I worked up the geographic & other incidental colour—getting some data from the alleged authoress, who knows Oklahoma, but more from books" (*Essential Solitude* 1.222).

HPL sent the completed tale to Bishop in early March 1928, making it clear in his letter to her that even the title is his. He adds: "I took a great deal of care with this tale, and was especially anxious to get the beginning smoothly adjusted.... For geographical atmosphere and colour I had of course to rely wholly on your answers to my questionnaire, plus such printed descriptions of Oklahoma as I could find." Of Yig he states: "The deity in question is entirely a product of my own imaginative theogony" (*SL* 2.232). Yig becomes a minor deity in the evolving Lovecraft pantheon, although cited only once in an original work of fiction ("The Whisperer in Darkness," and there only in passing) as opposed to revisions, where it appears with some frequency. The fact that HPL had her fill out a questionnaire (presumably about the history and topography of Oklahoma) is of interest, as we do not hear of any such practice in regard to other revisions. HPL charged Bishop $17.50 for the tale. She managed to sell the story to *Weird Tales*, receiving $45.00 for it. It was her only sale to *Weird Tales* in HPL's lifetime, as the two other stories of hers that were revised by HPL only appeared after HPL's death.

Texts: Weird Tales 14, no. 5 (November 1929): 625–36 (as by "Zealia Brown Reed"). In Christine Campbell Thomson, ed., *Switch On the Light.* London: Selwyn & Blount, 1931, 9–31. In Christine Campbell Thomson, ed., *The "Not at Night" Omnibus.* London: Selwyn & Blount, [1937], 13–29. *Weird Tales* 33, no. 4 (April 1939): 140–51. In *Beyond the Wall of Sleep* (1943). In Bishop's *The Curse of Yig* (1953). In *HM* (1970/1989).

Further Reading: Zealia Bishop, "H. P. Lovecraft: A Pupil's View," in Bishop's *The Curse of Yig* (Sauk City, WI: Arkham House, 1953); rpt. in Peter Cannon, ed., *Lovecraft Remembered* (Sauk City, WI: Arkham House, 1998), 264–74. J. J. Koblas, "In Search of Yig," *Nyctalops* 2, no. 2 (July 1974): 11–12. Robert M. Price, "The Allegory of Yig," *Crypt of Cthulhu* no. 11 (Candlemas 1983): 46.

1. Guthrie is the county seat of Logan County in central Oklahoma. It was founded in 1889, when Oklahoma was still a territory; it was the state capital from the time that Oklahoma became a state (1907) until 1913. There has never been an insane asylum there.

2. Quetzalcoatl is a Mesoamerican deity whose name (in Nahuatl) means "feathered serpent." Worship of a feathered serpent in this region can be dated to as early as 400 B.C.E., but the name Quetzalcoatl first appears in the Postclassic period (900–1519 C.E.). In Mayan his name was known as Kukulcan. He is generally believed to have been a symbol of fertility, rain, and agriculture.

3. HPL refers to three of the prominent Native American tribes in the general vicinity of Oklahoma. The Pawnee, living in the area later occupied by Nebraska and Kansas from as early as 1250 C.E., were restricted to a reservation in Oklahoma in 1859. The Wichita, indigenous to Kansas, Oklahoma, and Texas, date to at least 1450 C.E. but by 1719 had migrated to Oklahoma; they later moved north to establish a village on the site of what became Wichita, Kansas. The Caddo is a confederacy of native American tribes that is now restricted largely to the town of Binger, Oklahoma.

4. Indian Territory was the official name of the eastern half of what later became the state of Oklahoma. In 1834 it was set aside for Native Americans following the Indian Removal Act of 1830.

5. HPL refers to the Land Run of 1889, when, after the passage of the Dawes Act in 1887, certain portions of land in the Indian Territory formerly designated for settlement by Native Americans was thrown open to white settlement.

6. Caddo County is in southwestern Oklahoma. Binger is a small town in the northeastern part of the county.

7. Franklin County is in the west-central part of Arkansas.

8. Okmulgee is the county seat of Okmulgee County in east-central Oklahoma. It has been the capital of the Muscogee (Creek) nation since the Civil War.

9. The Kickapoo are a Native American tribe that are now restricted to reservations in Kansas, Oklahoma, and Texas. The Oklahoma contingent is now based in McLoud, in Pottawatomie county in the central part of the state.

10. The Canadian River runs east-west through central Oklahoma.

11. Newcastle is a city in McClain County in central Oklahoma; it is now part of the metropolitan area of Oklahoma City.

12. The Wichita Mountains are a small mountain range in southwestern Oklahoma. There is now a Wichita Mountains Wildlife Refuge in the area.

13. El Reno is the county seat of Canadian County in central Oklahoma, about 25 miles west of Oklahoma City.

14. Scott County is in west-central Arkansas, south of Franklin County.

15. Tirawa is the creator-god of the Pawnee, believed to have taught the tribe the use of fire, hunting, agriculture, and other skills.

The Electric Executioner

"The Electric Executioner" was revised by HPL in July 1929 (see *Essential Solitude* 1.200) from a previously published story by Adolphe de Castro (Gustav Adolphe Danziger) called "The Automatic Executioner" (see Appendix for the text). In the course of rewriting it, HPL transformed it into a *comic* weird tale—not a parody, but a story that actually mingles humor and horror. In de Castro's stilted and lifeless prose, the tale comes off as *unintentionally* funny; HPL makes it consciously so. In so doing, he makes several in-jokes. Part of the characterization of the madman Feldon is drawn from a more harmless person whom HPL met on the train ride from New York to Washington on a recent journey to Virginia (1 May 1929). Later, in the course of uttering the names of various Aztec gods, the narrator spews forth various terms in HPL's pseudomythology; there are various spelling variants (e.g., "Cthulhutl"), as HPL wished to give an Aztec cast to the names so as to suggest they were part of that culture's theology. Otherwise, HPL has followed de Castro's plot far more faithfully than in "The Last Test"—retaining character names, the basic sequence of incidents, and even the final supernatural twist (although sensibly suggesting that it was Feldon's astral body, not the narrator's, that was in the car). He has, of course, fleshed out the plot considerably, adding better motivation and livelier descriptive and narrative touches. De Castro surprisingly paid HPL in advance for the story; the amount given is not known, nor is the amount de Castro himself received for its sale to *Weird Tales*.

Texts: Weird Tales 16, no. 2 (August 1930): 223–36. In *Something about Cats* (1949). In *HM* (1970/1989).

1. HPL appears to be in error. The only San Mateo Mountains are in Socorro county in west-central new Mexico.

2. HPL refers to Tlaxcala, a state in east-central

Mexico, originally settled by the Aztecs.

3. The mountain called Malinche is an extinct volcano on the border between the state of Tlaxcala and the state of Puebla, to the south and east.

4. Hot box is a now antiquated term to refer to an overheated axle on a railroad or subway car. During his New York period (1924–26) HPL occasionally rode subway cars that were subject to hot box, requiring them to stand still for an hour or more before the train could proceed.

5. Torreón is a large city in the state of Coahuila in northern Mexico, about 400 miles northwest of Mexico City.

6. Quarétaro is a state in central Mexico and its capital is officially named Santiago de Quarétaro, but it is customarily referred to merely as Quarétaro. The city is about 160 miles northwest of Mexico City.

7. Vera Cruz (now Veracruz) is a major port city in the state of Veracruz in east-central Mexico, on the shore of the Gulf of Mexico.

8. Aguas Calientes (now Aguascalientes) is the capital of the state of Aguascalientes in central Mexico.

9. HPL had discovered the work of Sigmund Freud (1856–1939) no later than 1921, when he remarked in a letter: "Dr. Sigmund Freud of Vienna, whose system of psycho-analysis I have begun to investigate, will probably prove the end of idealistic thought. In details, I think he has his limitations; and I am inclined to accept the modifications of [Alfred] Adler, who in placing the ego above the eros makes a scientific return to the position which Nietzsche assumed for wholly philosophical reasons" (*SL* 1.134). Cf. also *In Defence of Dagon* (1921): "We may not like to accept Freud, but I fear we shall have to do so" (*CE*

5.52).

10. Cf. "Travels in the Provinces of America" (1929), where HPL describes encountering an eccentric man on a train: "The journey was made amusing by the presence in the seat beside me of a slightly demented German—a well-drest and respectable-looking fellow whom I had observ'd at the tavern reading a German paper before the start of the coach. He shew'd no signs of affliction till we reach'd a sort of stagnant mill-pond near Newark, when suddenly he burst forth with the question, 'Iss diss der Greadt Zalt Lake?' Deeming the inquiry addrest to me, I reply'd that I scarcely thought his identification correct; whereupon he reliev'd me of all responsibility by remarking in a far-off, sententious voice—'I vasn't talkingk to you; I vass shoost leddingk my light shine!' . . . After a time he became vocal again, confiding to the empty air ahead, 'I'm radiatingk all der time, und nopotty knows it!'" (*CE* 4.34).

11. For Quetzalcoatl, see n. 2 to "The Curse of Yig."

12. New York State adopted the electric chair as a method of execution in 1889; the first such execution occurred on 6 August 1890. The British engineer George Stephenson and his son Robert established Robert Stephenson and Company, a locomotive company, in 1823 and designed an innovative steam engine called the Rocket in 1829. The American inventor Thomas Davenport (1802–1851) designed the first battery-powered electric motor in 1834.

13. Maximilian I (1832–1867), a member of the Habsburg line, was commander-in-chief of the Austrian Navy (1854–64). In 1864 Emperor Napoleon III helped to establish him as Emperor of Mexico; but President Benito Juarez refused to acknowledge his rule, and Maximilan's French forces battled constantly with Juarez's. Maximilian

was captured on 15 May 1867 and executed by firing squad on 19 June.

14. Anahuac ("Land Between the Waters") is the Aztec name for the Valley of Mexico, a highlands plateau in central Mexico. Tenochtitlan was a city founded by the Aztecs in 1325. It was located on an island in Lake Texcoco in Anahuac and became the chief city of the Aztec empire until its capture by the Spanish in 1521.

15. The name is HPL's misspelling of Huitzilopochtli, the Aztec god of war and the patron deity of Tenochtitlan. Nahuatlacatl is the name for a speaker of the Aztec language of Nahuatl.

16. The first six names are those of Mesoamerican peoples who established themselves near the Aztecs in the Valley of Mexico.

17. Chicomoztoc is the name of the mythical place of origin of the Aztecs and some of the other peoples mentioned above. The seven caves of Chicomoztoc each produced one of the seven peoples. The word means "at the seven caves."

18. The character is free-associating: the mention of Nathaniel Hawthorne (1804–1864) was inspired by his earlier reference to "Grandfather's chair," an allusion to Hawthorne's *Grandfather's Chair* (1841), a children's book relating stories from New England history.

19. Nezahualpilli (1464–1515) was the ruler of the city-state of Texcoco (1473–1515). The reference to him is ironic, since he abolished capital punishment for many crimes during his reign.

20. A succession of names from Greek mythology. For Linos, see n. 21. Iacchus and Zagreus are names for Dionysus (see n. 16 to "Poetry and the Gods"). Ialmenos is the son of Ares and Astyoche; he participated in the

Trojan War. Atys (or Attis) was the son and lover of the mother-goddess Cybele; he subsequently castrated himself, as related in a vivid poem by Catullus (Poem 63). Cf. "The Rats in the Walls": "The reference to Atys made me shiver, for I had read Catullus and knew something of the hideous rites of the Eastern god, whose worship was so mixed with that of Cybele" (*DH* 37). Hylas was, according to Ovid and other sources, the son of Herakles (Hercules) and the nymph Melite; he accompanied the Argonauts on their quest to capture the golden fleece. Cf. HPL's poem "Hylas and Myrrha: A Tale" (1919; *AT* 125–30), a poem about the young Alfred Galpin's love affairs.

21. The last two phrases refer not to Hylas but to Linos, who was the son of Psamathë (the daughter of Crotopus, king of Argos) and Apollo. He was later torn to pieces by dogs.

22. The cry "Evoë!" (in Greek, $\varepsilon \upsilon o \hat{\imath}$) was a cry associated with the cult of Dionysus.).

23. More properly, Tloque Nahuaque, the creator god of the Aztecs, the original bestower of all life.

24. More properly, Ipalnemohuani, the Aztec sun god.

25. Mictlanteuctli (or Mictlantecuhtli) is the Aztec god of the dead.

26. Tonatiuh-Metztli is the Aztec moon god.

27. HPL has deliberately given the names of his own pseudonymological entities an Aztec cast. Cthulhu was first cited in "The Call of Cthulhu" (1926) as being trapped in his underwater city of R'lyeh. In that story the expression "Cthulhu fhtagn" (not "fhtaghn") is found (*DH* 143). For Shub-Niggurath, see n. 19 to "The Last Test." For Yig, see "The Curse of Yig." For Yog-Sothoth, see n. 15 to "The Last Test."

28. An arrastre is a device for pulverizing ores.

The Mound

"The Mound" is perhaps the best, as it is certainly the longest, of HPL's revisions. That it is entirely the work of HPL can be gauged by Bishop's original plot-germ, as recorded by R. H. Barlow: "There is an Indian mound near here, which is haunted by a headless ghost. Sometimes it is a woman" (ms. note on the typescript of "The Mound," JHL). HPL found this idea "insufferably tame & flat" (*SL* 3.97) and fabricated an entire novelette of underground horror, incorporating many conceptions of his evolving myth-cycle, including Cthulhu (under the variant form Tulu).

The story was, in fact, a far longer work than HPL needed to write for his revision client, and this length bode ill for its publication prospects. *Weird Tales* was on increasingly shaky ground, and Farnsworth Wright had to be careful what he accepted. HPL lamented in early 1930: "The damned fool has just turned down the story I 'ghost-wrote' for my Kansas City client, on the ground that it was too long for single publication, yet structurally unadapted to division. I'm not worrying, because I've got my cash; but it does sicken me to watch the caprices of that editorial jackass!" (*Essential Solitude* 1.251). HPL does not say how much he got from Bishop for the work; there may be a certain wish-fulfillment here, for as late as 1934 she still owed him a fair amount of money.

The lingering belief that Frank Belknap Long had some hand in the writing of the story—derived from Zealia Bishop's declaration that "Long . . . advised and worked with me on that short novel" (271)—has presumably been squelched by Long's own declaration that "I had nothing whatever to do with the writing of *The Mound*. That brooding, somber, and magnificently atmospheric story is Lovecraftian from the first page to the last" (*Howard Phillips Lovecraft: Dreamer on the Nightside* [Sauk City, WI: Arkham House, 1975], xiii–xiv). Long does not explain how or why Bishop attributed the work to him (perhaps because he had already forgotten), but documentary evidence can provide a fairly clear account of the matter. Long was at this time acting as Bishop's agent. He shared HPL's disgust over the tale's rejection: "It was incredibly asinine of him [Wright] to reject The Mound—and on such a flimsy pretext" (Frank Belknap Long to HPL, [c. 19 March 1930]; ms., JHL). Long's involvement up to this point had, so far as I can tell, extended only to the degree of typing HPL's handwritten manuscript of the tale, for the typescript seems to come from Long's typewriter (and there are portions of the text that are garbled or incoherent—the presumable result of his inability to read HPL's handwriting in these places). It was now evidently decided (probably by Bishop) to abridge the text in order to make it more salable. Long did this by reducing the initial typescript's 82 pages to 69—not by retyping, but by merely omitting some sheets and scratching out portions of others with a pen. The carbon was kept intact. Long must have made some attempt to market this shortened version (he in fact said so to me), but HPL later expressed skepticism on the point, writing in 1934: "I assumed that Sonny Belknap . . . *had* done so [i.e., tried to market the story]; & am astonished to find that any stone was left unturned" (*OFF* 143). Whatever the case, the story obviously failed to land anywhere, and it was finally first published posthumously in *Weird Tales*, and then in a severely abridged form. Later, August Derleth abridged and rewrote portions of the text for publication in *Beyond the Wall of Sleep;* he would continue to use this adulterated text in several subsequent Arkham House editions. The text was not restored until it appeared in the 1989 edition of *HM.*

Although perhaps not as carefully written as many of HPL's original works, it is successful in depicting vast gulfs of time and in vivifying with a great abundance of detail the underground world of K'n-yan. It is also evident that "The Mound" is the first, but by no means the last, of HPL's tales to utilize an alien civilization as a transparent metaphor for certain phases of human (and, more specifically, Western) civilization. Initially, K'n-yan seems a Lovecraftian utopia: the people have conquered old age, have no poverty because of their relatively few numbers and their thorough mastery of technology, use religion only as an aesthetic ornament, practice selective breeding to ensure the vigor of the "ruling type," and pass the day largely in aesthetic and intellectual activity. HPL makes no secret of the parallels he is drawing to contemporary Western civilization. But the culture of K'n-yan undergoes a slow decadence. Science begins "falling into decay"; history is "more and more neglected"; and gradually religion becomes less a matter of aesthetic ritual and more a sort of degraded superstition. Many of the reflections on the culture of K'n-yan find precise parallels in HPL's dissection of contemporary Western civilization as found in his letters and essays.

Some interesting literary influences have been suggested. Both Joshi ("Some Sources . . .") and Price suggest that the cylindrical tube (made of "Tulu-metal") in which Zamacona's manuscript is found was inspired by James De Mille's *Strange Manuscript Found in a Copper Cylinder* (1888), a book HPL had in his library. Peter Levi believes that several features of the text—especially Zamacona's discovery of an underground civilization and the creatures inhabiting that civilization—were inspired by A. Merritt's "The Face in the Abyss," first published in the *Argosy* (8 September 1923) and revised as "The Snake Mother" (*Argosy,* 25 October–6 December 1930) and published as a novel under the title *The Face in the Abyss* (1931). HPL admitted that he had purchased the 1923 *Argosy* issue containing the earlier version (*Essential Solitude* 2.545).

Texts: T.Ms. (JHL). *Weird Tales* 35, no. 6 (November 1940): 98–120 (abridged; as by "Zealia Brown Bishop"). In *Beyond the Wall of Sleep* (1943). In Bishop's *The Curse of Yig* (1953). In *HM* (1970/1989).

Further Reading: W. E. Beardson, "The Mound of Yig?" *Etchings and Odysseys* no. 1 (1973): 1013. Marc Beherec, "H. P. Lovecraft and the Archaeology of 'Roman' Arizona," *Lovecraft Annual* 2 (2008): 192–202. Zealia Bishop, "H. P. Lovecraft: A Pupil's View" (see headnote to "The Curse of Yig"). Peter Cannon, "'The Mound': An Appreciation," *Crypt of Cthulhu* no. 11 (Candlemas 1983): 30–32, 51. Michael DiGregorio, "Yig, 'The Mound,' and American Indian Lore," *Crypt of Cthulhu* no. 11 (Candlemas 1983): 25–26, 31. S. T. Joshi, "Who Wrote 'The Mound'?" *Nyctalops* 2, no. 7 (March 1978): 41–42; rev. ed. *Crypt of Cthulhu* no. 11 (Candlemas 1983): 27–29, 38. S. T. Joshi, "Some Sources for 'The Mound' and At the Mountains of Madness," in Joshi's *Primal Sources: Essays on H. P. Lovecraft* (New York: Hippocampus Press, 2003), 185–89. Peter Levi, "'They Have Conquered Dream': A. Merritt's 'The Face in the Abyss' and H. P. Lovecraft's 'The Mound,'" *Lovecraft Annual* 1 (2007): 91–93. Will Murray, "The Trouble with Shoggoths," *Crypt of Cthulhu* no. 32 (St. John's Eve 1985): 35–38, 41. David A. Oakes, "H. P. Lovecraft," in Oakes's *Science and Destabilization in the*

Modern American Gothic: Lovecraft, Matheson, and King
(Westport, CT: Greenwood Press, 2000), 29–62. Robert
M. Price, "Strange Cylinders," *Crypt of Cthulhu* no. 78 (St.
John's Eve 1991): 20–21. Richard L. Tierney, "Cthulhu
in Mesoamerica," in Meade and Penny Frierson, ed., *HPL*
(Birmingham, AL: Meade and Penny Frierson, 1972), 48–
49; rpt. *Crypt of Cthulhu* no. 9 (Hallowmas 1982): 19–21.

    1. By "sub-pedregal" HPL means the ancient ag-
ricultural civilization in the Valley of Mexico, remains of
which were found under the *pedregal,* or volcanic flow in
that area. Remains in this region have now been dated to
21,000 B.C.E.
    2. "'Arizona is a moon-dim region, very lovely in its
way and stark and old, but I had to leave it. You know I was
always a sceptic, rather a wooden one, as I remember; well,
that ancient lonely land set my lung-polluted mind working.'" From H. Russell Wakefield (1888–1964), "'He Cometh and He Passeth By,'" in *They Return at Evening* (1928).
HPL read the book in September 1928 (see HPL to August
Derleth, [27 September 1928]; in *Essential Solitude* 1.159).
    3. Francisco Vásquez de Coronado y Luján (1510–
1554) was a Spanish conquistador who came to Mexico in
1535 and was for a time governor of the Mexican province
of Nueva Galicia. In early 1540 he headed north, having
heard from the Franciscan friar Marcos de Niza of a golden
city named Cíbola; some parts of his expedition reached as
far as the Grand Canyon. Coronado then heard of another
wealthy region called Quivira to the east, in what is now
the Texas panhandle. He came upon Quivira in late 1541;
it was in the area now occupied by Kansas and was probably a settlement of ancestors of the Wichita tribe. Finding
no wealth in the area, he returned to Nueva Galicia.

4. Binger is a town in Caddo County in west-central Oklahoma. See also n. 3 to "The Curse of Yig."

5. The population has not increased much in the interim; the 2000 census records a total of 712 inhabitants in Binger.

6. An obvious dialectical variant of Cthulhu (see n. 27 to "The Electric Executioner"), as the narrator himself remarks later (p 228.).

7. Azathoth was first cited in the novel-fragment "Azathoth" (1922), although the entity is not actually mentioned in the 500 words of surviving text. He is described in *The Dream-Quest of Unknown Kadath* (1926–27) as a "boundless daemon-sultan . . . whose name no lips dare speak aloud, and who gnaws hungrily in inconceivable, unlighted chambers beyond time amidst the muffled, maddening beating of vile drums and the thin, monotonous whine of accursed flutes" (*MM* 308). For Nyarlathotep, see the headnote to "The Crawling Chaos."

8. For Tirawa, see n. 15 to "The Curse of Yig."

9. Altair is the brightest star in the constellation Aquila. Vega is the brightest star in the constellation Lyra.

10. The distinction between brachycephalic and dolichocephalic skulls is a feature of the now discredited theory of craniological measurement, whereby it was believed that different races could be distinguished by the size of their skulls. It was later ascertained that skull size was in fact widely divergent even within a specific race and that purported variations across races were more plausibly explained by environmental and other factors.

11. In HPL's next story, "The Whisperer in Darkness" (1930), the fungi from Yuggoth come from their planet to earth "to get metals from mines that go deep under the hills" (*DH* 218). In "The Dreams in the Witch

House" (1932), Walter Gilman finds himself in possession of a metal object of unusual properties: "Professor Ellery found platinum, iron, and tellurium in the strange alloy; but mixed with these were at least three other apparent elements of high atomic weight which chemistry was absolutely powerless to classify. Not only did they fail to correspond with any known element, but they did not even fit the vacant places reserved for probable elements in the periodic system" (*MM* 284).

12. In the surviving typescript of the story the name is rendered simply "Panfilo"; but this name is customarily rendered in Spanish with an acute accent on the *a,* so this change has been made throughout the text.

13. This paragraph can be translated as follows: "In the name of the most sacred Trinity, Father, Son, and Holy Spirit, three distinct persons and yet one. The true God, and the most sacred Virgin, Our Lady, I, PÁNFILO DE ZAMACONA, SON OF PEDRO GUZMAN Y ZAMACONA, GENTLEMAN, AND OF YNÉS ALVARADO Y NUÑEZ, OF LUARCA IN ASTURIAS, swear that all that I say is as true as a sacrament. . . ."

14. Luarca is a city in the province of Asturias in the northwestern corner of Spain, on the shores of the Bay of Biscay.

15. HPL himself believed that he could trace the Lovecraft line back to a Devon family named Lovecraft or Lovecroft, dating to as far back as the 15th century; but there is now reason to doubt the details of HPL's reconstruction of this phase of his ancestry.

16. Aristotle (384–322 B.C.E.), Greek philosopher; Cheops (now more properly rendered Khufu, r. 2589–2566 B.C.E.), Egyptian pharaoh.

17. New Spain (Nueva España) was the designation

for a viceroyalty established by the Spanish in 1521 and at one point containing the entirety of Mexico and Latin America as well as much of the American West and the Spanish West Indies.

18. Cicuye is a Pueblo village now located in Pecos National Historical Park south of Santa Fe, New Mexico. Coronado visited it in 1540.

19. Tiguex is a Pueblo village whose ruins lie on the north side of the Rio Grande in the area of Bernalillo, in north-central New Mexico. Coronado fought battles with Pueblo tribes there in 1540–41.

20. Frederick Webb Hodge (1864–1956) was a British-born American anthropologist and archaeologist. HPL refers to an unsigned article that he presumably read, "Coronado's Route Traced into Kansas," *New York Times* (29 September 1929): N3, in which it was stated that Hodge had determined that the path that Coronado had taken in quest of Quivira had to be along the Arkansas River through Barton and Rice counties in Kansas. Hodge found archaeological remains in these locales.

21. HPL had already used the term Old Ones to refer to some of his extraterrestrial "gods" or entities (see the passage from the *Necronomicon* in "The Dunwich Horror" [*DH* 170]), and he would subsequently apply the term to the barrel-shaped entities in *At the Mountains of Madness* (1931).

22. Antonio de Mendoza (1495–1552), first viceroy of New Spain (1535–50).

23. Vasco Nuñez de Balboa (1474–1519), Spanish explorer and conquistador, crossed the Isthmus of Panama and reached the Pacific Ocean—and specifically the province of Darién—in 1513. HPL alludes to the celebrated lines of John Keats's sonnet "On First Looking into Chap-

man's Homer" (1816): "Or like stout Cortez [*sic*] when with eagle eyes / He star'd at the Pacific . . . / Silent, upon a peak in Darien" (ll. 11–14).

24. Bable is a term sometimes used to designate the Asturian language, spoken in the province of Asturias. It was formerly thought to be a dialect of Spanish but has now been ascertained to be a separate language descending from vulgar Latin.

25. The mention of Kadath (first cited in "The Other Gods" [*D* 127]) is of interest. In *The Dream-Quest of Unknown Kadath* it is of course a region in the dreamworld, but the mention here appears to anticipate its identification with an inaccessibly high mountain range described in *At the Mountains of Madness:* "For this far violet line could be nothing else than the terrible mountains of the forbidden land . . . beyond doubt the unknown archetype of that dreaded Kadath in the Cold Waste beyond abhorrent Leng, whereof unholy primal legends hint evasively" (*MM* 103).

26. A variant or dialectical spelling of R'lyeh.

27. Invented here, but cited again in "The Whisperer in Darkness" ("'They [the fungi from Yuggoth]'ve been inside the earth, too . . . and great worlds of unknown life [are] down there; blue-litten K'n-yan, red-litten Yoth, and black, lightless N'kai" [*DH* 254]) and in "The Man of Stone" (see Vol. 2, p. 274).

28. HPL had made fictional use of Atlantis as early as "The Temple" (1920), when the German submarine commander, descending to the bottom of the Atlantic Ocean and coming upon an undersea city there, remarks: "Confronted at last with the Atlantis I had formerly deemed largely a myth . . ." (*D* 67). See HPL's late discussion of the Atlantis myth as found in Plato and other writ-

ers (*SL* 5.267–69). Lemuria is a continent once thought to have existed in the Indian Ocean; it was hypothesized by the biologist Ernst Haeckel (1834–1919) to account for the presence of lemurs and other animals and plants in southern Africa and the Malay Peninsula. HPL, although philosophically influenced by Haeckel, learned of Lemuria primarily from W. Scott-Elliot's *The Story of Atlantis and the Lost Lemuria* (1925), which is mentioned in "The Call of Cthulhu" (*DH* 128).

29. The Spanish explorer Juan Ponce de León bestowed the name Florida on the region when he landed there on 2 April 1513.

30. The phrase "the vaults of Zin" was first cited in the poem "To a Dreamer" (1920): "I, too, have known . . . / The vaults of Zin" (*AT* 54; ll. 13, 15). It was then cited frequently in *The Dream-Quest of Unknown Kadath* as a locale in the dreamworld: ". . . the ghasts, those repulsive beings which die in the light, and which live in the vaults of Zin" (*MM* 339).

31. The Old Ones of *At the Mountains of Madness* were also capable of creating synthetic life for "industrial" purposes, in particular the protoplasmic shoggoths.

32. Tsathoggua was a toad-god invented by Clark Ashton Smith in the story "The Tale of Satampra Zeiros" (written 16 November 1929). HPL read the story in early December 1929, just before beginning "The Mound," and was enthusiastic about it: "I must not delay in expressing my well-nigh delirious delight at 'The Tale of Satampra Zeiros'—which has veritably given me the one arch-kick of 1929!" (*SL* 3.87). Smith had set the story in the city of Commoriom, in the imaginary ancient realm of Hyperborea, probably to be identified with Greenland. This mention in "The Mound" is HPL's first citation of Tsath-

oggua. The first mention of the god in print occurred in "The Whisperer in Darkness" (written 1930; *Weird Tales,* August 1931), which preceded "The Tale of Satampra Zeiros" (*Weird Tales,* December 1931) into print, leading many to believe that HPL had invented Tsathoggua. In his tale HPL tries to reconcile the apparent contradiction in the origin of Tsathoggua by writing: "It's from N'kai that frightful Tsathoggua came—you know, the amorphous, toad-like god-creature mentioned in the Pnakotic Manuscripts and the *Necronomicon* and the Commoriom mythcycle preserved by the Atlantean high-priest Klarkash-Ton" (*DH* 254).

33. Olathoë in the land of Lomar was first cited in the story "Polaris" (1918; *D* 21–23), where it was an ancient city in the far north. It was then cited in *The Dream-Quest of Unknown Kadath* as a city in the dreamworld (*MM* 310); it then returned to the real (ancient) world in "The Mound" and *At the Mountains of Madness* (*MM* 47).

34. First cited, in almost this exact language but with a lower-case *g,* in "Polaris" (*D* 22) and *The Dream-Quest of Unknown Kadath* (*MM* 310).

35. The image appears to derive from Smith's "The Tale of Satampra Zeiros": "...the bowl was filled with a sort of viscous and semi-liquescent substance, quite opaque and of a sooty color" (*A Rendezvous in Averoigne* [Sauk City, WI: Arkham House, 1988], 157). The image in turn appears to have been used to describe the shoggoths in *At the Mountains of Madness.*

36. The phrase is reminiscent of HPL's Decadent phase of the early 1920s, as exemplified in "The Hound" (1922): "Wearied with the commonplaces of a prosaic world, where even the joys of romance and adventure soon grew stale, St. John and I had followed enthusiastically ev-

ery aesthetic and intellectual movement which promised respite from our devastating ennui" (*D* 171).

37. The expression appears to be adapted from a similar one in *The Dream-Quest of Unknown Kadath*: "Carter surmised . . . that he was indeed come to that most dreadful and legendary of all places, the remote and pre-historic monastery wherein dwells uncompanioned the high-priest not to be described" (*MM* 370). Note also that, in HPL's great "Roman dream" of late 1927, he dreamed of something called the Magnum Innominandum ("the Great Not-to-Be-Named"), evidently an "unknown, un-nameable deity" (*SL* 2.190) worshipped by the hill tribes of ancient Spain. The mention later in this paragraph that Shub-Niggurath is the wife of the Not-to-Be-Named One suggests that the entity in question is Yog-Sothoth (see n. 19 to "The Last Test"). In "The Whisperer in Darkness," the expression "Him Who is not to be Named" occurs (*DH* 226), possibly also in reference to Yog-Sothoth.

38. See n. 19 to "The Last Test."

39. Astarte is the Greek form of the name of a Se-mitic fertility goddess ('Ashtart in Phoenician, Ashroreth in Hebrew).

40. The phrase is an important component of HPL's personal aesthetic. "What has haunted my dreams for near-ly forty years is *a strange sense of adventurous expectancy con-nected with landscape and architecture and sky-effects*" (*SL* 3.100). The phrase occurs in several of his stories.

41. Nith was first invented in "The Cats of Ulthar" (1920), but there it is the name of a person: "Then the lean Nith remarked that no one had seen the old man or his wife since the night the cats were away" (*D* 57). It is possible that HPL had forgotten his invention of the name when he cited it here.

42. It is possible that this invented locale is a phonetic reversal of *Athol,* a city in central Massachusetts that HPL knew well, especially because it was the home of his colleagues W. Paul Cook and H. Warner Munn.

43. HPL refers to a hoax perpetrated in December 1925, in which it was contended that some relics found in Arizona attested to a settlement founded by Roman Jews. The matter was extensively reported in the *New York Times* for that period. HPL has misremembered the fact that the relicts were found in Arizona, not New Mexico. On the matter see Beherec.

Appendix

Four O'Clock

"Four O'Clock" was apparently written by Sonia H. Greene about the same time as "The Horror at Martin's Beach," in the summer of 1922. In a letter to Winfield Townley Scott (11 December 1948; ms., JHL), Sonia declared that HPL only suggested changes in the prose of the tale, hence I concluded that it does not belong in the Lovecraft corpus and did not include it in the revised version of *HM* (1989). Judging, however, from her later memoir, it does not appear as if Sonia was a very skilled, polished, or even coherent writer, so that HPL probably did contribute something to this story, which is even slighter than its predecessor. It is not clear whether the tale was ever submitted to a magazine for publication; it presumably was, and was rejected.

Texts: In *Something about Cats* (1949). In *HM* (1970 ed. only).

1. The sentence is reminiscent of one found in "The Hound" (1922): "Bizarre manifestations were now too frequent to count" (*D* 176).

A Sacrifice to Science

"A Sacrifice to Science" is Gustav Adolphe Danziger's original version of the story that HPL revised as "The Last Test."

Texts: In Danziger's *In the Confessional and the Following* (San Francisco: Western Authors Publishing Co., 1893), 154–215. *Crypt of Cthulhu* no. 10 (1982): 31–45.

1. An altana is a covered terrace, usually on a roof.

The Automatic Executioner

"The Automatic Executioner" is Gustav Adolphe Danziger's original version of the story that HPL revised as "The Electric Executioner."

Texts: In Danziger's *In the Confessional and the Following* (San Francisco: Western Authors Publishing Co., 1893), 133–53. *Crypt of Cthulhu* no. 10 (1982): 21–25.

1. Orizaba is a city in the state of Veracruz on the east coast of Mexico (see n. 7 to "The Electric Executioner").

2. More properly, Xalapa, the capital city of Veracruz.

Bibliography

Bishop, Zealia. *The Curse of Yig.* Sauk City, WI: ArkhamHouse, 1953.

Joshi, S. T. *I Am Providence: The Life and Times of H. P. Lovecraft.* New York: Hippocampus Press, 2010. 2 vols.

Lovecraft, H. P. *The Ancient Track: Complete Poetical Works.* Edited by S. T. Joshi. San Francisco: Night Shade, 2001.

———. *At the Mountains of Madness and Other Novels.* Selected by August Derleth; Texts Edited by S. T. Joshi. Sauk City, WI: Arkham House, 1985.

———. *Beyond the Wall of Sleep.* Compiled by August Derleth and Donald Wandrei. Sauk City, WI: Arkham House, 1943.

———. *Collected Essays.* Edited by S. T. Joshi. New York: Hippocampus Press, 2004–06. 5 vols.

———. *Dagon and Other Macabre Tales.* Selected by August Derleth; Texts Edited by S. T. Joshi. Sauk City, WI: Arkham House, 1986.

———. *The Dark Brotherhood and Other Pieces.* Compiled by August Derleth. Sauk City, WI: Arkham House, 1966.

———. *The Dunwich Horror and Others.* Selected by August Derleth; Texts Edited by S. T. Joshi. Sauk City, WI: Arkham House, 1984.

——. *Essential Solitude: The Letters of H. P. Lovecraft and August Derleth.* Edited by David E. Schultz and S. T. Joshi. New York: Hippocampus Press, 2008. 2 vols.

——. *The Horror in the Museum and Other Revisions.* Selected by August Derleth. Sauk City, WI: Arkham House, 1970. Rev. ed. (by S. T. Joshi), 1989.

——. *Letters to Alfred Galpin.* Edited by S. T. Joshi and David E. Schultz. New York: Hippocampus Press, 2003.

——. *Marginalia.* Compiled by August Derleth. Sauk City, WI: Arkham House, 1943.

——. *Miscellaneous Writings.* Edited by S. T. Joshi. Sauk City, WI. Arkham House, 1995.

——. *O Fortunate Floridian: H. P. Lovecraft's Letters to R. H. Barlow.* Edited by S. T. Joshi and David E. Schultz. Tampa: University of Tampa Press, 2007.

——. *Selected Letters.* Edited by August Derleth, Donald Wandrei, and James Turner. Sauk City, WI: Arkham House, 1965–76. 5 vols.

——. *Something about Cats and Other Pieces.* Compiled by August Derleth. Sauk City, WI: Arkham House, 1949.

CPSIA information can be obtained
at www.ICGtesting.com
Printed in the USA
LVOW03s1148200717

541972LV00002B/179/P